Essays of Shin, Young-Bok

Journey of the River

Journey of the River
— Essays of Shin, Young-Bok

First published January 15, 2018

Written by Shin, Young-Bok
Translated by Cho, Byung-Eun
Edited & Prefaced by R. C. Richardson

Publisher Han, Chul-hee
Published in Korea by Dolbegae Publishers

Registered August 25, 1979 No. 406-2003-018
Address 532-4 Pajubookcity Munbal-li Gyoha-eup, Paju-si, Gyeonggi-do, Korea 10881
Tel (+82) 31-955-5020
Fax (+82) 31-955-5050
Website www.dolbegae.co.kr
E-mail book@dolbegae.co.kr

Executive Editor Kim, Soo-Han
Editorial Director Lee, Kyoung-A
Book Design Lee, Eun-jeong, Lee, Yon-gyong
Cover Design Min, Jin-ki
Printing & Bookbinding Sangjisa P&B

ISBN 978-89-7199-841-0 (03810)

Essays of
Shin, Young-Bok

Journey
of the
River

Written by Shin, Young-Bok

Translated by Cho, Byung-Eun

Edited & prefaced by R. C. Richardson

Dolbegae Publishers

Preface

Shin, Young-Bok(1941~2016) revered in South Korea as a thinker, a voice of his times, an opponent of mindless, intrusive bureaucracy, of the rigidities of capitalism, and of social inequalities, deserves to be much better known in the West. This timely translation of his prison letters will surely assist in making it possible.

The son of a patriotic provincial schoolmaster, in his early childhood, he grew up under Japanese occupation and lived through the horrors of the Korean War and later after 1968, as a man marked out for his unacceptably radical views, endured more than twenty years in prison—some of them in solitary confinement. These letters and essays document his powers of endurance, resignation to his situation, his stoicism and serenity, and inner strength. They demonstrate also his lack of self-pity, compassion for others, and deep-seated love for his own brutalised and wounded country. His powers of observation and ability to make unexpected connections and associations stand out remarkably, as do his carefully devised strategies for preserving his own sanity in the midst of isolation and unremitting stress. In the vacuum he was forced to occupy for so many years the smallest things—weeds and wild flowers growing in the prison compound, a bird flying in through the bars of an open window, the sound of passing trains—gained special significance and offered precious glimpses of liberty. Released after 1988, his stature as a poet and prose-writer, calligrapher and university teacher grew steadily and he became, unquestionably, one of the jewels in the crown of SungKongHoe University. There, and indeed throughout the whole of South Korea, he will be sadly missed after his death. But his memory will undoubtedly live on as a potent inspiration to others and to his country itself in his fervent hope for re-unification and the achievement of a brave new world. Like Nelson Mandela his was an unstoppable voice of freedom. He challenges us all to listen and to act out our convictions.

R. C. Richardson*

---

* Emeritus Professor of History, University of Winchester, UK.
He is a Fellow of the Royal Historical Society and for several years he has served as co-editor of the international journal *Literature and History*. He is a frequent visitor to South Korea where he has a large network of friends and former students.

Table of Contents

I   Standing as a Clump of Short Field Grass

II   I Want to Walk

차례

- This translation is based on the 2003 edition of Shin, Young-Bok's essays and letters published in *Masterpiece Korean Essays Series, No.01: Shin, Young-Bok*, Dolbegae Publishing Co., Seoul, Korea.
- Among the letters and essays, "Memories of ChungGuHoe" is excluded here since it was already published in Korean-English version on its own by Dolbegae Publishing Co., in 2008, and instead a letter entitled "A Prisoner's Teeth" from *Reflections from the Prison* is added.

I

Standing as a Clump of
Short Field Grass

The Economics of Taps

수도꼭지의 경제학 • 187p

There were eight taps in the washroom on the upper level of the 4th floor in Correctional Institution C, but we were only able to use two of them. The other six taps were useless because the T-shaped handles had been taken off and the remaining bolts had been fastened tightly with a spanner. There was no way we could turn them on with our bare hands. Needless to say, it was to save water, since the prisoners were all, without exception, 'wild geese eagerly looking for water.'

So far as scarcity is concerned, water is equal to rice in prison. It is as rare as rice. This seems quite natural for us who never had much water in prison. Taking a bath was hardly imaginable, not to mention, the daily three-time dish-washing after each meal, as well as washing our faces, hands, and clothes from time to time. Nevertheless, there were days we badly wanted to take a cold rundown with a wet towel. So, whenever we had a chance, we tried to fill up whatever pitcher, water pail, or other container that came our way. And when we had collected sufficient water, we felt as rich as if we had a rice chest filled up in store. Water was invaluable.

In summertime, or even in winter, nobody would say

'no' to a cold bath, or no one would mind washing blankets. For this reason, the tension between prison authority and the inmates could not but remain tense all four seasons.

Leaving only two taps working and deliberately shutting off the remaining six taps was customary practice to control water use in any prison, because it was the surest way to close the fountainhead.

Nevertheless, it did not work that way. In no time, tremendous waste of water occurred in the prison.

The first incident involved the missing of T-shaped handles of the two functioning taps. They were replaced by the authority a couple of times, but they went missing again as soon as they got replaced. As all the handles of the taps were attached by a screw, they could be easily disengaged by loosening the screw. And once we got a handle, we could attach it to any tap and turn it on to get water anywhere.

Since there were a number of cases where the handles had disappeared, now the prison authority ended up detaching them and keeping them in a special drawer. To access them to use water, we had to go through a rather complicated bureaucratic process. The value of the handles we kept hidden increased significantly. What is more, the taps in the washrooms of other buildings began to vanish. Eventually whether it was in the factory, or in the public bathroom, or even in the prison staff's lavatory, there was no place where the tap handles had not disappeared.

We kept a tap handle hidden in our cell as well. Of the

eleven prison cells at the upper level on the fourth floor, there was no cell without a tap handle or two of its own, concealed for the inmates' own use. Depending on the power of inmates, some cells had two tap handles of their own. Some prisoners, like K, a powerful figure among the inmates in our prison, had one, two or three extra taps for each individual's private use just in case some tap handles either went missing or were confiscated.

Soon, the taps became precious presents for close friends or for those we were indebted to. Also they often became saleable goods and were exchanged for other items. The taps were worth more than their mere intrinsic value. They were considered precious items. A tap handle had its own special value independent of its link with water.

Though I was not exactly sure how many taps were kept in the cells of the upper part on the fourth floor, I made a rough estimation by calculating the number of individual taps kept in the eleven cells plus four or five more taps belonging to the prisoners who wielded power. All in all there was a total of about twenty taps. Compared to the eight taps in the washroom of the building, the number of taps was about two to three times more. In spite of this, people still wanted more taps. This was mainly due to the inconvenience involved in getting permission to use a tap from the 'manager' who was in charge of the tap inside the cell. At first, we did not mind borrowing taps from the inmates, but as time went by, it came to be regarded as a source of distress.

I calculated how many taps would be needed for 100 prisoners to use at the upper level on the fourth floor without complaints or inconvenience. One tap for each inmate plus one extra tap per person would make 200 taps in total. Compared to the original eight taps, this new total is twenty to thirty times more. Although we were able to have access to water by using the taps, it was still illegal to do so. In fact, several people got caught, and punished, and had their taps confiscated. They were usually those who annoyed the staff and regarded themselves as victims of discrimination inside the prison. They were perceived as 'unlucky people,' having been caught.

Anyhow, in this way the original plan to control water by closing off the taps came to naught and more water was consumed than if all the eight taps had been kept in full working order. There was no use fastening six taps tightly with a wrench. It was only effective for an inmate who was bare-handed. For those who had handles, water, just like the *kisang*, a professional entertainer in bed services, slackened its body and came flowing.

As such, in spite of the number of taps, water was still highly sought after for most people who felt the inconvenience of borrowing the handle each time they wanted to get water. Lack of water led to an unnecessary desire for a personal tap handle, even at the cost of getting blamed and self-disgraced when caught.

This, of course, is the story of prison life and the greed of 'wild geese looking for water', and of people's greed for water in prison. But now, here and there in Seoul, I am frequently reminded of the bitter memory of the taps in prison. Sitting on a bus stopped in the middle of a congested street where walking is faster than riding a bus, I think of the taps in the past. Among the crowd in the bustling show house for new apartments, I am reminded of the time when I was slavering over in front of the shut-down taps.

There are numerous instances in the world outside prison in which 20 or 30 taps cannot meet the need that 8 taps could easily satisfy. It is applicable to cars, apartments, land, college entrance exams, and numerous merchandising goods in luxurious department stores. Walking on the rather unfamiliar streets in Seoul, I am often reminded of the taps as if by habit. I am reminded of the pain in my thumb and index finger that became pale from the blood being cut off while I was trying in vain to wrench the taps with my bare hands. Each time, I think how tremendous waste is brought about by unjust possession and unrighteous private ownership, and how much poverty is felt among needy people. Then, I think of the thirsty wild geese that fly above the boundless ocean.

— July 8, 1991, from *Economic Justice*

A prisoner's Teeth

to my younger sister-in-law

죄수의 이빨 · 191p

At the dental clinic, they pulled out teeth and put them into a glass bottle filled with formalin. How long had they been collecting teeth? After having my tooth put into the bottle containing numerous teeth, my heart felt heavy.

The other day, I took out a tooth myself, without going to the dentist's. I tied it on a string and pulled it, as it was already quite loose. I kept it in my pocket for some time and threw it over the prison wall of over 4.5 meters high during exercise time. It was a gesture to release a part of myself from prison. Though it is less consoling than the childhood story of milk teeth thrown onto the roof for a bird to pick up and fly away with it, it is far more comforting than having it put into a formalin glass bottle.

More than 10 years ago, I pulled out a tooth of mine with a string in a prison factory with a younger inmate's help. But at that time, I didn't have a chance to approach the wall, so I secretly put it into a factory girl's work overall, a supporter weaver from Poong-Han Textile Ind. Co., and set it free. I have been feeling sorry about this until now. I cannot help but feel sorry, thinking how shocked she might have been at seeing a prisoner's tooth in her pocket, however neatly it was wrapped with paper.

During my imprisonment, I had a number of my decayed teeth pulled out. Some of them were put inside the formalin bottle, some were buried in the prison grounds, while others were set free over the prison wall.

Thinking back, it is not only our teeth that we come to share and bury. During our life, we come to share parts of our body with different people, and bury them here and there. From a casual remark to sweaty efforts of life, each of us has buried parts of ourselves into our friend's heart, into a piece of a field for cultivation, on a depraved alley of a city, or on a large plaza of history.

Looking back, I buried a large portion of myself in the prison, and that made me heavy-hearted just like when my teeth were put into a formalin glass bottle at the dentist's.

On the one hand, it seems quite natural, considering that prison is a closed space, and is likely to be a space of stagnancy like the formalin bottle. But on the other hand, prison is not detached from the world, but is in fact quite closely tied to our society and our age, at the center of society.

It is located at the very apex of an upside-down pyramid of social stratification, the very point where the entire gravity of the pyramid converges, and where the point touches the land. As such, prison is a place linked to the paradoxical structure of society, and thus, is open to the whole of society.

Why then do I feel so destitute at the thought of my 20 years that I buried into the prison? Why does it remind me of the formalin bottle?

Although I did not feel anxious and tense all the time in prison, I was alarmed at the loosening of my consciousness and the emptiness of my heart. It was no less than the hollowness caused by an accumulation of unawakened days — the hollowness of consciousness shown at the point where the whole gravity of the pyramid is hung! I have come to realize the formidable reality of prison life.

The residue of my *petite bourgeoisie*, which, not having been cleared off yet, blinded me from realizing that to ask is to grow and to share is to spread. And such consciousness stabs me with a more intense pain than toothache.

Whenever I write to you, younger sister-in-law, I become hesitant. I wonder what my letters might mean to you. I am worried that my letters, filled with stories of prison life, would break through the windows of your room and let cold wind blow in through them.

Nevertheless, reading your letters, I have been impressed by your thoughtful character and your generous attitude toward others, and I can easily dispel such a worry.

— May 28, 1987, JeonJu Correctional Institute

The Body Temperature of Neighbors

to my younger sister-in-law

이웃의 체온 • 194p

Prisoners are confronted by walls all the time.

As people are met by stops on their way to work, as antelopes are hounded by the hunters, so the prisoners are confronted by walls in every walk of their prison life. Even in their dreams, during rare moments of freedom, they are still bound by walls. In between these mazes of walls, in a narrow squared space which does not leave much room for moving our bodies, we constantly wished to break down the walls of thoughts. We wished to expel the veil of thoughts, so that, as was expressed by a Chinese Phrase, we could finally raise "the voice of the wild field", and "the whimper of the heart as round as the moon."

My father wrote in his letter that we are having the coldest winter in six years, but I do not feel such cold and I was wondering why. Then I realized that it was my fellow prisoners' body temperature that has warmed us in this dreary space in the freezing cold of a deep winter. While warming each other by sharing our body temperature, we came to understand little by little what the cold space and the winter taught us—the meaning of 'friends,' and the importance of our neighbors' warmth.

Now the spring equinox has passed and soon the river will flow and warm spring winds will bring out early flowers. By then, perhaps our neighbors' warmth planted in our bodies during winter will blossom into splendid flowers. For human affection will melt into the smiling petals of flowers.

Thank you for the New Year's letter and the enclosed pocket money. The pleasure of having one more person who cares elates me as if I were a proud boy. They say that the relationship between a brother and his sister-in-law is rather uncomfortable, but I believe it is not true in our generation. I do not deny that our relationship exists with my brother in-between, thus, lacking intimate understanding since we do not share our day to day lives. Nevertheless, considering that in the future we have to share our lives together as members of a family, exchanging our news through letters from now on will ease the difficulty of the 'uncomfortable relationship.' I wish you the very best.

— February 11, 1976, DaeJeon Correctional Institute

Theory of Relationship in Calligraphy
to my father

서도의 관계론 · 196p

My talking of calligraphy might sound preposterous, but I hope you do not mind, since it is merely a fragment of a thought on a postcard.

When my careful brush stroke goes wrong, I try to cover up the mistake by changing the place and shape of the next stroke.

It is, of course, not merely because I cannot erase or correct the stroke I have already made, but rather because I understand that the success of a stroke does not lie in the stroke itself but in the 'relationship' between a stroke and the next stroke. How can a stroke form a letter without meeting another stroke? A stroke, just like humans, cannot exist on its own; it is a 'half,' or a 'tally.' In the same way, I try to compensate a fault made while writing a letter with the next letter or the one after that. I also try to embrace my mistake in making a line by drawing the next line, and stanza, by forming another stanza. Thus, a piece of calligraphy writing is created through an accumulation of faults and errors, studded with failures, compensations, mistakes, apologies and efforts.

The calligraphy work hereby completed is an achievement

in which strokes, letters, lines, and stanzas depend on one another in various forms, be they big or small, strong or weak, rough or detailed, written with a pause or with speed, or thick or thin. They count on one another, yield to others, and cover up faults and flaws. Otherwise even one letter and one stroke would collapse the entire frame, and even the seal contributes to the balance of the whole. In close interconnectedness and unity, and in the contrast and harmony of the black and the white (of the ink and the space) lies calligraphy writing of a high standard. Compared to this, a collection of stereotypical word-processed letters gives us the impression of mass coexistence where cold faces meet as strangers, where we seldom meet the friendly faces of people we want to shake hands with.

The very thought that the fault of breaking a window can be compensated by a new piece of glass window is perceived as drearily as the fact that human labor can simply be paid for with a certain sum of money without showing any human affection. In the same way that I keep my brush balanced between strokes, and between letters, I intend to maintain a warm connection between a human being and another human being.

Now at the peak of April, we can fully enjoy the season, the weather being neither cold nor hot.

— April 15, 1977, DaeJeon Correctional Institute

Two Kinds of Bell-Sounds

to my father

두 개의 종소리 · 198p

Every dawn, I hear two kinds of bell-sounds, one from the bronze bell of a nearby Buddhist temple at 4 O'clock in the morning, and the other from the church bell a little later. To me, the two bell sounds ring in great contrast. The church bell peals high and is of consecutive metallic sounds; whereas the bronze bell sounds like someone's low whispering voice, without the metallic tone. The church bell is an intruder into the tranquillity of the dawn, meanwhile the bronze bell that peals once every 29th pulse deepens the silence just like the buddhist's drum of the high gate. The peal of the church bell trills as if it were scattered from the iron stipple of the forest of buildings, reminding me of an unwelcome person's knock at the door. On the other hand, the bronze bell ringing from the dew-dropped mountain temple to the core of the earth comes as the calling voice of the mountains. In the reverberating church bell sound, one can see the busy gesture of the porter who hits the bell, looking at his watch with a flashlight in his hands; in the reverberation of the bronze bell, one can see a motionless hermit.

When the church bell breaks my meditation and the

quietude I have reached with the sound of the bronze bell, as if it were a pane of window glass, I pick up the fragments of my thoughts and fall back to sleep until the third new sound, the morning bugle rings. Getting lost in deep thought somewhere between these two bell sounds is a pleasure itself for a tired soul of the prison, however small it may be.

I am neither a Buddhist nor a Christian. I find it rather awkward to associate myself with the concept of 'believing.' Of course, I do believe in certain principles and people, but such belief is only a comprehensive expression of understanding and evaluating someone's personality or some objectified experience. It is, I think, totally different from the unilateral acceptance of 'belief without understanding.' After all, my like or dislike of the church bell and the bronze bell has nothing to do with my religious preferences, nor with my feelings or disposition. It may be an expression of my consciousness that forms part of my inner landscape. Lying between these two kinds of bell sounds, I listen to several more bell sounds that have been engraved in my consciousness. I realize the sounds of strange bells that have been deeply-rooted in the consciousness of my generation while growing up in the midst of a dominant foreign culture.

— July 27, 1977, DaeJeon Correctional Institute

'Magic Pen' and Calligraphy Brush

to my father

매직펜과 붓 · 200p

It is autumn equinox today. After the heavy storm last night, the sunlight in the morning is not so hot as it ushers in the autumn season.

Thank you very much for the ink and paper for calligraphy, and your letter. I hope mother is well and so are all the rest of the family.

I mainly write with the calligraphy brush, but from time to time, I have to draw lines and write letters with the so-called 'magic pen.' This magic pen is a kind of stationery made up of a small bottle of ink, which I hold while I am writing. It is very convenient in that we do not need a special skill to use it. Just as keys of the piano make music when touched, anyone, even a beginner, can draw lines with this magic pen. We do not need to rub an ink stick back and forth, arrange the tip of the brush, nor does it require laborious practice to wield the brush. In addition, we do not need to wait for the ink to dry since this happens instantly, enough to be called 'the minion' of 'the age of the instant.' In spite of all these conveniences, I do not like it. I do not like the friction sound it makes when it glides over paper—the shrill cry of civilization. I also hate the pungent smell of the ink.

In contrast, the brush does not make any sound. I can feel the soft touch, as soft and tender as my mother's healing touch. I like the faint scent of the ink stick and the depth of the ink mark. I like the range and the flexibility I can enjoy when writing with a brush, since the size of the letters can range from as thin as a strand of hair, to a big letter, wider than the tube of the brush. Although and because the brush reguires a great amount of effort and discipline to the user, it makes one love and have affection for it. With the scope and flexibility that continue to thrill—, the brush is just like a classical scholar of integrity who would not easily yield.

Whereas the magic pen is the product of Western ingenuity focused on practicality and convenience, the brush carries the Oriental spirit in it. In my ink stone case, the two exist side by side, but this does not mean that I accept the logic of compromise expressed in the phrase 'Eastern spirit and Western vessel.'

Compromise or synthesis is nothing but another name of concealment and patching up. At a certain point in history, we have to make a sharp distinction between claims and opinions based on their gravity and order, while subjecting one to another—despite the considerable truth they may contain about various objective prepositions of the society or the age. And in such a case, practical partisanship is considered to be the true meaning of 'timely positioning' and the essence of moderation.

I still prefer the brush. Even for me who was educated in the city most of the time, the brush cannot simply be understood as an item of 'frivolous luxury,' being only connected to 'leisure or hobby.'

— August 8, 1977, DaeJeon Correctional Institute

A Grass Seed on the Window Pane of a Prison Cell

to the younger sister-in-law

옥창의 풀씨 한 알 · 202p

On the window pane of our prison cell,

A grass seed,

Which perhaps an ant has brought,

Is sprouting.

And now already waving its body

Of over an inch high,

It begins to teach us (the mystery of life).*

Chrysanthemum in the garden blooms yellow every autumn;

My mother's hair is getting whiter every year.

— August 29, 1978, DaeJeon Correctional Institute

---

* Quoted from *For the First Time*, p.38.

An Indian Chief's Letter

to my father

인디언의 편지 · 203p

Thank you very much for your letter dated the 8th. Hope family members including mother are well. We had a very warm winter last year. In the last few days, the spring rain has left the earth wet, but as the saying goes, 'on the path of spring, all living things prosper,' such wetness brings about flowers and leaves, doesn't it?

A few days ago, I read a letter from an American Indian to the American government. The letter contains these passages:

"How can you white men buy and sell the sky or the warmth of the earth?"

"If we do not sell the land, you will bring guns to us, ...But in fact, the fresh air and sparkling water are not our possessions."

"Just as a little baby loves the heartbeat of its mother, so do we love the land."

When we put such thoughts of the Indian alongside the white man's way of thinking—in which they consider everything as objects of possession, purchase and consumption—the shameful aspect of 'civilization' is clearly revealed.

Also contained in the letter is the following passage:

"The white men who take anything from the land if they think they need it, are aliens to the land."

"Your city pains the eyes of us Indian."

The logic of the city interprets nature as hostile, inconvenient, and primitive. Civilization is measured by the extent to which nature is excluded from human life, and thus, the measure of civilization depends on the distance we have secured from nature. The absurdity of civilization is that we are preoccupied with the life in which there is a vicious cycle of producing useless commodities in-between concrete walls, occupying ourselves with new desires and thirsts, and nevertheless, feeling more thirsty and hungry. To this, the letter from an Indian who has often sadly become synonymous with savagery and primitivism serves as a severe criticism of modern civilization. And from this, we must ask ourselves again about the meaning of both civilization and savagery. The descendants of the letter writer might be living on the outskirts of a city, their soil and wind taken from them, living without even a streak of polluted sunlight, standing in a queue to get some piece of civilization that the white men have invented and distributed.

Reading the short letter, I felt ashamed of the legacy of colonialism, which I could not entirely get rid of from the way of life I've been leading. Accepting Western culture and values as universal, and taking our own as peculiar, accidental, and marginal is the evidence of our colonized thoughts that remain as a deeply cut scar in our hearts.

I wonder what kind of world our ancestors intended to make. We have long lost, thrown away, and turned away from our values and cultural heritage. Now we live in a climate where 'the older people' are rapidly gotten rid of. Nevertheless, in our history, in our life, the precious soul that has been revealed in our ancestors' way of life is waiting to be re-illuminated.

The letter ends with the following passage:

"With all your power, ability, [and] devotion, love the land as God loves us and protect it for your children... Even the white men cannot be exempted from this common fate."

— February 25, 1979, DaeJeon Correctional Institute

Calligraphy

to my father

서도 · 205p

This winter the cold temperature appears to be so unpredictable that it is hard to say what kind of weather we are having. In the winter, we wear clothes in preparation for the coldest day. In severe cold, we wear the rough, unattractive, cotton-padded prison uniform, which though looks more 'beautiful' than a gentleman's suit to us. Here I am convinced that 'beauty' is ultimately defined by content rather than by outward appearances and design.

I have a similar experience with calligraphy. In calligraphy, the meaning of the letter should be good prior to the shape of the strokes, and the calligrapher is required to be a good-natured man. I prefer calligraphy to other forms which do not demonstrate the proximity between the human agency behind it and the work created. Calligraphy is based on a strong personal connection between the artist and the work. I like the common maxim that to produce good calligraphy work, one first has to be a good person—the unity of 'art' and 'human character,' —the art, serving to heighten human character and 'human character,' transforming itself into artistic value. Such unity is preserved only in calligraphy. How consoling for a calligrapher!

These days I have started reading *the Analects* again.

In a drafty room, we have an early dawn. Sitting below the window that glimmers with dawning, I read the old scholar's thoughts:

"Not sufficient with a friendship with a world-renowned scholar, I learn from reading the old."

It reminds me of the first verse of *Mencius* in which Mencius mentions the need to read the writings of old scholars when we feel that our friendship with old scholars is not enough to gain wisdom. Resolved to be awakened to this in the reality first, I try not to overread, though.

It is still too cold to begin writing calligraphy. I will let you know when I need more paper for calligraphy. Hope mother is well and strong.

— February 2, 1979, DaeJeon Correctional Institute

Like the Stream Opening Itself to the Sea

to my parents

바다로 열린 시냇물처럼 · 207p

Every July I have come to reflect on the days that have passed. This July marks the 12th year of my imprisonment. Just like the destitute who get narrow-minded and have a skewed view of things, I worry if I have become rather peculiar in my point of view in the same way as the cave-dweller who mistakes the fire in the cave for the sun in the east.

There was a discussion about where we can get the clearest view of Seoul, whether it is from the pagoda on top of Mt. Nam-San, from the city-hall, or from a manufacturing machine at YeoungDeungPo Industrial Complex. Unless we are fairies flying in the sky, we cannot get multiple views at the same time. We, who are deeply rooted in the soil, take the very place we live in as the look-out and adjust our thoughts based on our own circumstances.

Most people try to reduce their subjectivity and employ a more objective stance when making judgments. However, at the base of such effort lies the wrong assumption that subjectivity cannot serve a purpose and only objectivity guarantees fairness, that subjectivity cannot develop into objectivity, and that objectivity is not based on subjectivity.

I think, each should firmly hold on to the basis of his own life and widen the horizon of objectivity by expanding his own 'subjectivity.' What is most important in this case is the fact that the 'position' we take should be consistent with our whole self, just like the stream water opening its whole to the sea and flowing into it. After all, reducing the risk of being enclosed by our own thoughts is a matter of choosing the very basis of our own life.

This reminds me of a phrase by *Mencius*:

Those who temper spears are afraid if people are not hurt,

Those who make shields are afraid if people are hurt.

It is quite difficult to take timely positioning in the middle of historical moments, but nevertheless, I believe that we should not hesitate to stand at a dark corner that would lead to the wide sea of time and history.

It is extremely hot, but it has been a big help having rain every other day. I hope mother feels better after seeing me last time on a rainy day.

— July 28, 1980, DaeJeon Correctional Institute

The Low Place

to my elder sister-in-law

낮은 곳 · 209p

I had several busy days changing the placards and shibboleths for the 'new age.'

The difficulty of working high up on a ladder is, above all, that it is very hard to tell whether the letters on the signboard are straight or slanted. It is something like a blind man's helplessness in front of an elephant. I could manage to write the letters straight, but this was only possible by frequently asking others standing below on the ground.

'Just as green fruits change their sour and bitter flesh into sweet and fragrant juice by taking in sunlight', I, too, in this autumn, want to spread out my everyday painful experience onto the bright, warm roof of thoughts and store it in the granary as a precious harvest so that it will keep me through the winter.

— October 20, 1980, DaeJeon Correctional Institute

Emptiness Becomes Usefulness

to my father

없음이 곧 쓰임 • 210p

Though we did not experience severe cold, this winter was as cold as any other winter. I hope mother is doing all right and the whole family is well.

This is a line from *Laozi* about 'the usefulness of being empty':

When one makes pottery by kneading the clay thoroughly, the usefulness of the pot as a container is brought about by leaving the center of the pot empty.

I envy the encompassing and broad-minded wisdom that transforms 'emptiness' into 'usefulness'.

From various recent experiences, I reached a quite common-sensical conclusion that unless it is self-sufficient and thus complete in itself as a deed—whether it is good or bad—, we cannot judge a person as totally bad or totally good. Classifying a person either as completely bad or typically good is such a high level of abstraction involving stereotyping that it can hamper the true understanding of human beings. Looking for a typical person is nothing but looking for a person who does not exist in reality.

— from *For the First Time*

A Pair of Wooden Shoes and an Umbrella
to my younger sister-in-law

나막신에 우산 한 자루 • 211p

I used to think that I should live a simple life so that I can go free any time I want, whether it be an ordinary human life or a life in prison. But when I moved into a different prison cell, I had to take a heavy load of sundry goods I could well have left behind.

With a heavy load on my shoulders, quickening my pace to be in time for the arranged move, I could not help being worn down by my thoughts. I once heard a story about an old monk who asked his page boy to get him a few items of clothing and a walking stick in preparation for a long journey only to be found dead the next morning standing upright in his new clothes with the walking stick in his hand.

Far from following the wisdom of ancient people who were above possessions and worldly things, people who washed their hair with the rain and combed it with the wind, possessing only a pair of wooden shoes and an umbrella to their name, wasn't I afraid of being empty-handed after over 10 years of life in prison?

It is true that possessions make things convenient, but we may easily subject our soul to possessions since they have a tyrannical way of taking over our soul, not to mention space, and eating away our creative thoughts. Indeed, it is hard to have strict control of ourselves, living in a world in which we produce more needs than the goods to satisfy them. Thus, unless we bear in mind that the vessel can become useful only by being empty, and that a wealth of thought can only reside in an empty body, it is certain that all the ideas we nourish in this barren soil only leave their husks behind.

— April 27, 1981, DaeJeon Correctional Institute

Calligraphy and the Talent in Writing

to my elder sister-in-law

서도와 필재 · 213p

Most people think that handwriting is inborn and those without talent cannot transform themselves into a famous calligrapher. But I have the opposite opinion.

The writing of a talented person is outstanding, but it is limited to the skill itself, because such a person has come to totally depend on his talent. Meanwhile, the writing of a person without born talent shines with 'the beauty of discipline' suffused with the energy and sincerity he puts into the work, for he writes with his whole being.

If a gifted person writes steadily with all his might, his calligraphy might become state of the art like the monkey in the Chinese novel which wields a club, but this is only conceptually presupposed. In most cases, a gifted person indulges in his talent just like a duckling that enjoys floating on the water.

By nature, calligraphy requires the disciplined endurance of a tortoise rather than the talent of a rabbit. More so because the excellence of calligraphy is not found in the strokes of a letter, but is evaluated by the degree of enthusiasm put in the ink.

The same goes for human beauty. Beauty accumulated through wisdom and inner experience always wins over the beauty we are born with. I believe our view of life is not much different from this. Being honest in difficult times rather than being tempted to rely on short cuts and fortunes; —without bowing down our head to the strong and the powerful, but opening ourselves to truth and love, and choosing 'tactless stupidity' on our own is, I think, what makes our life meaningful.

— April 13, 1982, DaeJeon Correctional Institute

The Elements of Realism in Swearwords

to my younger sister-in-law

욕설의 리얼리즘 · 215p

One of the things that is abound in prison is swearing.

From morning to night, we live amongst a feast of overflowing swearwords. At the beginning of my prison life, I took the abusive language in such a naive way that I used to interpret its meaning word for word, ending up in an absurd plight. Now I am quite experienced to reach a state where I swallow the curses like I would sugar-coated pills.

Swearing is a cheap and stupid way of relieving stress or complaints, being a projection of sentiments beyond the limits of endurance. Nevertheless, in the same way that the word "apology" is derived from the concept of "apology," there are feelings or objects that need to be expressed through swearwords. For this reason, this place of imprisonment is likely to be the most obvious place for the production and exchange of swearwords.

In prison, swearwords are not swearwords any longer, for pleasure or joy is quite often expressed in the form of swearing. In such a case, the uniqueness of feeling is rather ironically emphasized with a poetic effect, which has long existed in the popular tradition of commoners who replaced swearwords for joyful greetings. I have been impressed by the wit which swearwords or slang expressions can carry. Figures of speech or satire that perfectly fit the situation, expressions that are carefully checked and controlled, without going too far, thus, capturing poignantly and accurately the tension of the topic in question, are in themselves wonderful works of art.

If we deconstruct situations into 'objects,' 'events' (that take place by the connection of various objects), and 'state' (that is formed by the interconnectedness of various events), swearwords are the conceptualization of 'events' or 'states,' and their artistic transformation can be called an activity of high level consciousness.

And in this sense, I find realism in swearwords, for they are based on the realistic recognition of the object and thus have both poignant sarcasm and comic relief, and they are completely different from intellectuals' rather abstract word play. I also found it fascinating that from the topics and figures of speech used in those swearwords, we can gain a ripened understanding of the customs of our time, and of the people's attitudes and human nature.

Nevertheless, we cannot deny that swearwords are only a product of the dark and thus, an unhappy language, whatever brilliant art of entertainment they carry inside themselves— just like we do not plant mushrooms in flower pots however pretty they may be.

— June 8, 1982, DaeJeon Correctional Institute

Similar Faces

to my younger sister-in-law

비슷한 얼굴 · 217p

After a long period of living together in the crowd, people come to have similar tones, similar cravings, and similar faces.

When looking at each other, we find similar faces as if we are looking into a mirror. Most people do not like being similar to another person, one ordinary person among many, because they take it as lack of individuality just like ready-made clothes, and thus, do not attach great value to the resemblance. For those of us who live in the age of individuality, thinking this way may be quite natural.

Then, is there an individual who does not resemble others at all, or an extraordinarily talented person? If there is, it is only by appearance. A 'pure individual' who does not have any communication with other human beings is just like Robinson Crusoe living alone on an island. Genius does not come from an individual or a moment, but from the cooperation and accumulation of collective wisdom over a long period of time.

What we forget is that we humans live 'together' as a part of each other's lives, taking in sunlight together and getting wet together, however high a wall is raised in-between.

With currency as the go-between, those who have a surplus of rice and a lack of salt and those who have a surplus of salt and a lack of rice can exchange their goods without meeting each other directly. Division of labor and gigantic enterprises, and the fetishism instigated by them make it difficult for us to realize that we are actually living 'together', because they separate and deprive us of the chance to meet each other.

The realization that we are 'in the same boat' connected by a common understanding and common fate is a wisdom that 'looks at both the trees and the forest'. It is an 'open-minded affection' towards all living things that does not ignore a buttercup or a small firefly. If they want me to be a tree, I would rather stand in the midst of the forest where numerous trees sing in chorus than be a tall and exuberant pine tree at the top of the mountain. If they want me to become a drop of water, I would certainly choose the sea as a place to stay. In the same way, I want to have a similar tone, similar desire and similar face to those who live in a low-land village.

— October 9, 1982, DaeJeon Correctional Institute

Meditation in Autumn

to my elder sister-in-law

가을의 사색 · 219p

Every autumn we collect the thoughts that we have raised for a year in the same way we harvest crops. Like any other year, there is nothing to show in this autumn, either. My empty mind is just like the old man's in Hemingway's *Old Man and the Sea* who returned to the port with only the bones of a fish. My year has been filled only with squatting and thinking, without doing any work with my whole body, and is as empty and useless as picking ice cubes to make beads. Furthermore, such thinking is not a part of my day-to-day meditation on an important topic, but pointless thoughts of miscellaneous affairs that would not go beyond the random exercise of thinking. It must be a very scanty harvest indeed. If I add some honest regret that I did not do my best in everything I achieved, this winter, the time of shutting myself in and waiting for spring, will be a longer and colder season.

Nevertheless, we know that after numerous autumns go by our regrets do not remain solely as regrets. Poverty rather than wealth, and pain rather than joy elevate us to confront the reality of our life and such reality in turn becomes a great antithesis against which we can coldly reflect on ourselves.

Such cold self-reflection looks unkind, but it is the very spring of courage with which we can look back upon ourselves regardless of the meager harvest.

In autumn, we usually collect and burn the fallen leaves and bury the ash around the root of the trees. We do not plant new trees, but fertilize the existing ones. Meditation in autumn can be described as this: it is not the desire to gain something new, but a fulfillment of promise with which we can arrange and accomplish what we already know.

Only in sofar as such a common promise is kept and fulfilled, our greed can be pursued, and that is the natural order of things. Perhaps the emptiness we feel in autumn is an awkward thing that comes from our rash greed.

A quiet harvest with which we find out and collect the promises we have forgotten changes into stepping stones that carry us through prison life which is as cold as the river on New Year's Eve.

As a mother, a wife, a daughter-in-law, and an elder sister-in-law, etc. in these numerous roles, I wish you a great harvest.

— November 18, 1982, DaeJeon Correctional Institute

Morning Bugle of a Winter Dawn

to my younger sister-in-law

겨울 새벽의 기상나팔 · 221p

30 minutes before the morning call, I woke a friend in deep sleep who was lying beside me. I woke him up with a soft pat with my hand. He was the bugler of the prison who went out to bugle the morning-call every dawn.

As he went out of the room, equipped with his uniform, socks, and hat, he wrapped up the 'mouthpiece' in his palm and warmed it on the one hand, and the bugle and a book to read at the interval between the first morning call bugle and the second door-opening bugle on the other. He went across the exercise ground in darkness lit only by a few outdoor lamps, climbed the steps of the church building, stood in front of the high window and blew the bugle. He blew his sigh deep from his heart and sprayed it into the sky of the dawn where even the star light was frozen. To everyone in the prison—to the farmer boy, to the factory worker, to the prisoner who had turned 25 years old, who sent a postcard to his step father, and who had made up his mind to earn money for his poor mother, the morning bugle in the early winter dawn is 'a sound made up of steel' that divided the frozen sky, tore through the dreams of the inmates, and signaled out another day of imprisonment.

If the culture of the prison is the culture of silence, the art of the prison lies in the pursuit of tragic beauty. These people at the edge of society are without exception the protagonists of tragedy who wrap their injured youth with blue prison uniforms like a soldier whose body is wrapped in horsehide, being killed on the battlefield.

They are indeed the main characters of the blue-black tragedy asking questions about the meaning of life; whether such a life is worth living, a life in which they have their black hair cut and scattered on the earth, a life without a blue sky to look up to, and a life without a gate to knock on at night, as was expressed in a Chinese saying, 'taking out their livers into a small gourd, and their guts into the front of an outer garment.' The possibility of an enormous tragedy to be transformed into something beautiful is in its 'honesty.' It is in the 'honesty' of the lowest people who bear the burden just as it is imposed on themselves, without imputing it onto others. Tragedies are related to the first-person narrative in which one cannot experience someone else's tragedy but only one's own. And such a character reinforces the dramatic effect of tragedy, ultimately leading to a new 'knowledge', which is 'beauty'.

Tragedy evokes in us not only how sharp a conflict is involved in our life and how its complicated structure is hidden in the everyday life we unconsciously pass by. It also makes us realize a new level of insight or a new horizon of understanding by frequently taking us from an audience seat to the backstage dressing room.

Whereas rapture enriches people's hearts, leaving indifference behind as burnt ash, sadness, like a vegetarian meal, purifies people's hearts by elevating them to 'beauty.' The deeper the night, the brighter the stars: the starlight that becomes brighter as the night gets deeper, I think, illuminates the 'wisdom' of the winter night sky. The essence of beauty lies in the golden chrysanthemums in the severe frost and the green plum flowers in the deep snow—as is described in old poems.

People beautify tragedy and cherish tragic beauty not with a 'warm heart' that would give consolation to the people in tragedy but with a 'profound thought' that helps them comprehend the depth of cold-hearted tragedy and 'cool-headedness.' Every time I go to wake up the fatigued young bugler from his deep sleep 30 minutes before the morning-call, I cannot help but hesitate. My hand stops two or three times before I touch his shoulder, not certain whether I should wake him up to the wretched reality of imprisonment that tears down the nest of dreams he is snugly settled in.

Some think of the New Year as just a point in time and call January the thirteenth month. If newness is thrown in front of us in its completion, then, I think, it cannot be regarded as new. We should not forget that all new things are new only when we have a new attitude towards them and that this New Year presents a new 'possibility' for us to fill with new things and new hope.

— January 17, 1983, DaeJeon Correctional Institute

Standing as a Clump of Short Field Grass
to my younger sister-in-law

한 포기 키 작은 풀로 서서 • 224p

Just like a fox and a crane who cannot eat food that is not contained in their own vessel, be it a bowl or a plate, people who have grown up in different environments cannot easily communicate with each other unless they use the same language. Language is a social promise and a public vehicle that is agreed upon, thus, barely carrying meaning that any single individuals endow. Just as the same pot can be used either as a pot for rice or for soup depending on the situation, so too can language be used by different people in different ways. One of the first difficulties people encounter—when they have grown up in different environments with different life experiences—is the difference in the use of language.

The difference may not be significant if we use a single word to mean different things; but the difference in judgment caused by interpreting a combination of multiple words becomes great since it involves a thought process which expands and links different meanings to make up the contents.

The most prominent example is in the difference between someone with an excellent educational background and someone with little education. The former cannot get away from the web of meaning he has woven with unnecessarily complicated expressions and microscopic thoughts, although he commands refined and calculated language and logic as if he is building blocks one by one. He takes pains to distinguish blue goblets from yellow ones ignoring the obvious fact that they are both goblets. By contrast, the latter's web of meaning is practical and narrow, straightforward and tangible. Nevertheless, too much simplification, a lack of logic, and an extreme overflow of emotion make it hard to tell a beard from an eyebrow. He can end up having monochromatic thoughts in which he throws the baby out with the bath water.

For more than ten years of my prison life, I have experienced various forms of wanderings and 'trials and errors' between these two contrary tendencies. For some time, I enjoyed complicated expressions and ideological thoughts and, as a result, became arrogant, thinking that such style is superior. Other times I learned coarse slang expressions and rattled them off, misunderstanding that I have obtained a group-perspective and thereby have reconstructed my own ideology. What is more, for a while I grew used to sitting complacently, enjoying the logic that 'the middle ground is just,' since I have compromised between the two positions. Then, at other times, I remember, I considered the middle ground as 'a seat of fiction,' a place of onlooking and of opportunism, and was startled into leaving the position in a hurry, being awakened to the fact that it is yet another type of wandering.

Of course in order to obtain one's own language and achieve one's own style of writing, it may be inevitable for an individual to go through prolonged wandering and drifting. Nevertheless, wandering itself does not accomplish such self-expression, nor does the length of wandering guarantee the height of accomplishment. After all, one's own language is gained by standing on 'firm ground' and taking root in the soil.

Prison is neither the ground nor a field. Rather it can be called an isolated island surrounded by a cliff of 15 inch-high brick walls with no mountain ranges or generous and slow-moving rivers. Perhaps the spiritual wandering of the prisoners is caused by the lonely thought that they do not have a piece of earth to take root inside the lonely island. And because they don't have this, most people, unlike us who have to stay for a long time, consider the prison as merely a temporary stop they can leave anytime. Such thinking is wrong. It is wrong because, with their minds and bodies struggling in their own hardships, they do not look at the lush grass growing in this place. It is a mistake that they cannot catch the quiet shout of the nameless grasses that gather together and form a field, along with the trodden weeds that live together, rubbing against each other.

'The leaves of grass that lie down and rise up prior to the wind' have heaped up a handful of the earth's warm temperature beneath them. Standing as a clump of short grass among these lush weeds, I hope to lean my body onto others, standing shoulder to shoulder, and continue to learn the secret of the barren soil until I gain my own language and finish my wanderings.

They say heavy snow makes spring leaves greener, but this winter was rather warm without much snow or cold. After the spring equinox, with 'the first rainfall of the year' ahead, the beautiful scenery of yesterday and today cleary shows spring, though not quite reliable.

— February 7, 1987, DaeJeon Correctional Institute

II

I Want to Walk

Mother I Saw in My Dream

to my mother

꿈에 뵈는 어머님 • 229p

Although it is the middle of March now, we had a late spiteful wind and rain mixed with snow last night. This spring may make the early spring flowers—the flowers that live true to the season, following it—shiver with cold again.

Very recently when my father came to see me before New Year's day, he used the weather conditions as an excuse for your not accompanying him, but I suspected that you were ill in bed. I looked anxiously at my father's back when he went out of the small gate after the visit. My father always goes a few steps ahead of you whenever you walk together, but that day, I could not spot you four or five steps behind him. Nevertheless, I thought you might have had an intermittent cold and thus tried to ignore my concern, but after getting my older brother's letter saying that you were seriously ill, I have seen you in my dreams night after night.

You always appear young and fair in my dream, but today when I woke up in the early morning and worked out your age, I was surprised to realize that you are really an old woman of 76. I have not realized how deeply my imprisonment for more than a decade has been hurting your body and mind, thinking that I am still 27! My stupidity of considering you as you were more than 10 years ago has become a cane whipping my calf.

"I am not afraid of dying at this age," you closed your mouth with this, but knowing that it is all because of me that you have heaped such regret deep in your heart, I feel a similar welling-up of feelings in my mind, wondering how to open my heart to you. Someday I want to talk to you about such pain piled up in our hearts: where it has originated, how we should take it, what kind of pain other people living in the contemporary world carry, how it is connected to mother's pain, (whether you can relate to the pain in numerous other people's hearts through your own pain), in the same way as the stream flows until it reaches the sea, and whether you can realize the truth and historicity of human life from individual pain, going beyond 'the limit of a mother's love for her son'.

Our meeting was short, and there is only a small space on this post card. Such insufficiency which always leaves me looking forward to the next visit, fatigues me a lot. Nevertheless, I cannot deny but accept that you have already overcome all this and has penetrated my heart more deeply than anyone else.

Like the old saying, "Nobody can beat parents for knowing their children," you not only know me best and know many friends of mine, but ruminates every word from your son in the court hearing, a son who walked out of the bosom of his mother's thoughts. Looking back on those days, I thought that perhaps you know me even better than I think you do. I think a mother's love is as far-reaching as to embrace all these with full confidence in her son.

Waiting makes us endure more things, look for things farther off, and prompts our eyes to keep shining in the darkness. I hope mother's waiting becomes an impetus to keep your body and soul strong.

The winter mother worried about has now passed and the spring sunlight, which is rather cruelly bright to the prisoners, is waking up the seeds of the grass below the surface.

— March 16, 1983, DaeJeon Correctional Institute

The Rain We Get Wet Together In

to my elder sister-in-law

함께 맞는 비 • 231p

The medicine we get after the wound has closed is too late to help. Rather it only reminds us of the pain we had experienced before. This is an example of time-crossed failure, but sometimes helping others as well as being helped by others can be harmful, not to mention that this is not 'help' at all.

Among the prisoners, there are some who are stubborn enough to refuse any help from others like a cake of soap or a toothbrush and live in isolation in prison without visitors, letters, or allowance in provisional holding. People rebuke the narrow-mindedness of such people saying that they do not know how to accept others' kindness, or pity them, thinking that they have a perverse mind caused by their wretchedness, or blame their dark mind for not even opening a window into it.

Is it because of their narrow, crooked, or dark mind that they stubbornly refuse others' kindness? To be fair, I think we have to slant the camera away from their faces and instead zoom in on those benefactors who want to treat them with favor.

We know from experience that there are various sources

of motivation behind the kindness of giving something -- even a toothbrush. There may be a motive to get a reward in exchange, or to get favor or cooperation in return, (though the return may not necessarily be material), or appease censure on them or mild resistance against them. In extreme cases, they may aim to get political mileage by securing their subservience or subordination of the recipients, or to gratify the self-serving motive of enjoying acclaim as a notable benefactor. In spite of his actions being motivated by charity, help coming from such a motive is not good at all. Without considering how such behavior can agitate the recipient's self-esteem and induce mental degradation, they still hasten to achieve their own purpose, and they commit callous hypocrisy in which they regard the recipient merely as their excuse and object of charity, and not as a human being whose feelings need to be respected.

Compared to this, we have a rather pure motive which is known as 'pity.' It originates from compassion and has long been considered a virtue. But even this has the limitation of blurring the objective essence of the matter. Subjectively, the limitation relates to escapism, as we try to appease our guilty conscience rather than seek to solve the real problems our friends are confronted with. Pity also makes the recipient look at things from the benefactor's perspective and causes his/her frustration and suppression at the same time. In this respect, pity, despite its being the first step of sympathy, must be considered inferior to, and distinguished from, 'sympathy.'

In imprisonment in which we incessantly give and take things, I, too, have experience of my favors being refused. At first, I blamed others' narrow-mindedness, but was surprised many times later, finding out that my underlying motive was not that pure, either. To tell the truth, the tenacity in which they refuse others' help is like sticking a hard wick of self-reliance in order to keep their integrity. Compared to a certain material power, such integrity plays a much more important role in paving one's own way.

Humans can only help themselves. Perhaps, helping others may be nothing more than helping oneself. In the same context, I like this saying of Aragon that "to teach is nothing but to say hope." Helping is not to lift an umbrella for others but to get wet together in the rain: I think, it is the confirmation of sympathy and the solidarity of walking together that we share, while getting wet together.

— March 29, 1983, DaeJeon Correctional Institute

Kkotsuni

to my elder sister-in-law

꽃순이 · 234p

'Kkotsuni' is the name of a stray cat that members of the music band found to keep watch over the music practice lab that used to turn into a rats' playground at night.

Now over a year after running away from its home, it has not only become a proud 'wild cat,' as if it mocks its old name Kkotsuni, but has also been seen at a distance to walk gallantly in the nights of the prison—a place studded with confrontations between cats and rats—showing off its ball as big as a pine cone.

When they first brought the cat, it was a pretty little cat and the name Kkotsuni was a perfect match. But when prison inmates began to raise it by hand and their unconditional fondling made it frail and dulled its feline senses, it soon lost its role of catching rats or taking them as its prey or enemy. When their original intention of having the cat watch the cupboard, washing, and books failed, people started harassing the innocent cat, treating it with contempt and abuse. They dropped the cat from high, kicked it with their feet, burned its beard with a briquette tong, put 'antiphlamine' on its nose. In the midst of these pranks and mistreatment under the guise of 'hard training,' its eyes have continued to shine fiercely until finally one night it ventured to go out through the vinyl window.

For a little cat, however, leaving home involved a series of other hardships and dangers. First of all, a puppy-sized black cat in the dressmaking factory did not accept this little cat as a friend but as an invader of its own territory. In the middle of the night, we could hear Kkotsuni's scream or see his pitiful state, roaming and limping around a nook.

Later, Kkotsuni returned a few times on his own feet. At times, his body was seen hunted and bound with a tennis net. But the most striking thing is that, while the cat was going through such vicissitudes of life, it slowly and completely escaped the band members' attention—the band members who were not as eager to show their love or hatred as before,—and accepted 'the cat's way.' Sometime ago, we were proud of the cat's change and growth, witnessing Kkotsuni tied in a fierce match with the black cat of the dressmaking factory.

Even now in the middle of the night, at the sound of the cat, three or four band members in my prison room kindly call it 'Kkotsun-a' in a knowing manner. Yet, Kkotsuni does not cast a look at the lingering attachment by his side, but only a perfunctory gesture of precaution. Perhaps, it may be a mistake to call it by its old name, 'Kkotsuni.'

I did not intend to write this story about Kkotsuni, but decided to add it after some thought. It is nothing else than this: the other day when I dropped by the wardens' lobby with a couple of band members, I saw Kkotsuni beg for its milk and canned food. I do not know how long it has been frequenting the wardens' lobby which is abound with things to eat. Kkotsuni that day was no longer 'the prince of the night' that I was proud of from a distance. It evoked in me the same feeling as when I met YoungJa, who had previously worked at a wig factory, in a red-light district of Jungdong. Nevertheless, regarding Kkotsuni's failure, as well as that of YoungJa in Jungdong or of all who live here, we cannot jump to a hasty conclusion without knowing whatever harsh realities and wanderings they might have gone through to have brought them there.

— July 14, 1983, DaeJeon Correctional Institute

Expressing Regret After Reading DaSan

to my father

독다산 유감 · 236p

I read a book written about DaSan Jung in his exile. Most of the subjects of the Cho-Sun Dynasty in exile built pavilions like the 'Pavilion for the Audience to the King' or the 'Pavilion of Longing for the King in the North' to express their everlasting loyalty and love for the king, but DaSan never built such pavilions nor expected that the royal court would send for him again. He took the precaution of remaining passive by only waiting to be released from exile and enduring the terrible weariness resulted from such passivity of life. He not only opened up a new horizon in his life through the love and positivity with which he embraced the miserable reality of a farmers' life, making it his own, but also planted the philosophy of realism for the people, renovating the stale confuscian theory of the Yi Dynasty.

Such love and care for the people never once abated in the 18 years from when he was sent into exile at the age of 39 in 1800 to when in 1818 he was released at the age of 57. Finally he accumulated such a store of knowledge that became the basis of the new philosophy of realism, which he propounded in 500 books of his own. including

Admonitions on Governing the people(Mokminsimseo). Of course, we cannot but point out certain limitations and biases in this DaSan school and his philosophy of realism. For one thing, at a time when the feudal ruling system began to collapse in the later Yi dynasty, and farmers presented their rough and unreserved resistance on the historical stage, his philosophy did not overcome the old feudal paradigms either by correcting or by complementing them. The argument for a high level of bureaucracy implied in the word, 'Governing' in the *Admonitions on Governing the People* and the conceptuality implied in the word 'admonitions' of the people's hearts cannot easily be pardoned.

Nevertheless, I believe such failings do not derive from DaSan's own limitation as an individual, but stem from those of the age in which he lived. Furthermore, he unreservedly took off all the opportunism and subservience of feudal ways of thinking which encouraged entrants to government service to become royalists, or naturalists withdrawing into nature when dismissed from it. He stepped down into the reality of farmers who were suffering from various types of exploitation. Dasan's career and thought truly set him apart as a valuable new paradigm of intelligence for the new age.

Vaguely fumbling through the details of DaSan's life in exile, I cannot but envy him. I envy him of the mountains, streams and other lankmarks he sauntered around including GoSeongAm Hermitage, BaekRyonSa Buddhist Temple, and GugangPo Port, not to mention his study where he wrote over 500 books, and his gift for making friend and attracting disciples.

The reason I envy him is neither to complain about the reality of my imprisonment, (which is worse than his,) nor to defend my sitting here, doing nothing. For creating something needs experiencing, and experiencing means taking on something with all one's heart and body. The reason that we cannot underestimate our experience itself, however under-qualified we may be.

What I envy is not the smoothness or toughness of the objective situation. What I truly envy is the 'leap' with which Dasan transformed his 18 years of exile into a bright creative space. And it is more so, because the 'leap,' unlike the hint of exuberance we feel in the word, does not refer to the 'logic of multiplication' that emerges all of a sudden one day.

— September 21, 1983, DaeJeon Correctional Institute

A Grain of Mung Bean Seed

to my younger sister-in-law

녹두 씨올 · 238p

On the 8th of last month, we went to GongJu for a field trip. I went to MuNyung Royal Tomb a few years ago, but I was quite impressed this time by UGeumChi I dropped on my way out, a critical battle place during the GapO Farmers' Revolution. There was a monument to the GapO Farmers' Revolution engraved on the pedestal, and the shrubs and thin grass around made a dreary scene, unique to the memorial site, among the fallen leaves rolling about in the autumn wind.

That night, I reread the account of the battle on UGeumChi from my book on Korean modern history. The number of farmers who took part in the battle in GongJu was known to have been in the region of 100,000 to 200,000, but I found from this reading that most of them were the farmers and their families who stood up against the ruling class, and the actual number of soldiers turned out to be fewer.

The farmer-soldier battle corps was said to be 20,000 all together, led by 10,000 Honam farmers including soldiers led by Jeon, BongJun. There was a corps led by Kim, BokYoung from Sesung Mt. at MokChon, and a corps from OkChunPo heading towards HyoPo, but they were defeated at the premier battle against the Japanese Corps and Korean Government Corps and could not join the battle at GongJu. Meanwhile, both the corps led by Sohn, HwaJung and the one led by Choi, MyungSun, proceeded up to HwaYak at JeonJu, defeating all the joint attacking forces of the Japanese and Korean government corps. They were stationed at NaJu in order to prepare for the battle against Japanese forces landing on the coast, and another corps led by Kim, GaeNam, a reserve force, remained at JeonJu. As such, the main force of farmers was divided and spread into three areas of GongJu, NaJu, and JeonJu, whereas the government force and Japanese corps were gathered together at one point in GongJu. The chief strategy of the farmers' corps was their effort to draw in and split the Korean government force deep into the countryside, but in the battle at GongJu, this strategy of concentration and scattering was reversed and this became a crucial weakness. Although such weakness was later overcome in the battle of the volunteer corps including the one led by Shin, DolSeok, it was only after sacrificing many lives.

Meanwhile the enemy force consisted of 10,000 soldiers in total, including 1,000 members of Japanese elite corps led by Lieutenant Minamio Shiro, 3,500 soldiers of Korean Central government force and 7,000 soldiers of local government force. They were superior in weapons and fire arms, but more so since the Japanese troops had the Korean governmental force under its strategic control, which made up for the shortfall in numbers. Moreover, the Japanese troop had gained a lot of experience in war, having quelled domestic riots in Japan, oppressed people in Taiwan, and launched war against China.

On December 4, 1894, the farmers' force carried out a furious battle, besieged UGeumChi on three sides and surrounded the 24 kilometers of the fortress. In the ensuing bloody battle which lasted 6 or 7 days, they won and lost 40 or 50 times in a row until they finally suffered a terrible defeat, being confronted with the enemy force, which was equipped with centralized force, advantageous location, strong fire arms and strategy. With UGeumChi battle as a turning point, the farmers' troop was repeatedly defeated at EunJin, Gumgu, TaeIn, and so forth, and had the curtain of history closed with their blood, unable to recover its fighting power.

GapO Farmers' Revolution stands as a cornerstone in the Asian People's Movement, in spite of its crushing defeat, and shines out as a forerunner of the struggle of the volunteer corps and in the Korean War for Independence that formed the main stream of Korean Modern History. In this sense, I was reminded of André Malraux's furious rebuke, saying "Who says that French Revolution ended in failure?"

A Korean poet wrote a poem dedicated to the death of General NokDu:

When I die, I will become a tansy bird,
And fly over all the land of this country
Pick a lump of sunlight in my mouth,
Bury it, plant it, and plant and bury it again

In every house, into every mud wall, and in every person's heart.

That day, we ate apples amidst four or five children's casual glances from afar, and came back with a blazing maple leaf, as blazing as if it bore witness to the bloody battle of those times. On my way back, I recited a couplet:

Among the mountains and rivers lies
People's outcry that man is heaven;
Where the mung bean flower bloomed,
The maple tree there is ablaze.

I got the news *via* my father when he visited me the day before yesterday. It was painful to hear from my gray-haired father that my mother had been hospitalized. I believe you sisters-in-law are taking good care of her. Thank you. Thank you also for the pocket money you sent me last month. I wrote a thank-you letter dated Oct. 22, but since you said you did not receive it, I'd like to express my gratitude again.

Now it seems like winter all of a sudden. The golden chrysanthemum that had warmed the cold territory of the prison with its golden blossoms dropped its petals and now, it is preparing for the cold winter, with only its roots.

— November 12, 1983, DaeJeon Correctional Institute

The Weight of Test

to my elder sister-in-law

시험의 무게 • 241p

Even now, among many dreams, I often dream of taking a test in my primary school days. The atmosphere in the room where the test takes place is always full of anxiety and restlessness: for example, when I ran through the empty play ground and long corridor, being late for the test, the door of the classroom was firmly closed and would not open, my classmates had all buried their faces into their answer sheets, the time kept running, and the sweat was running all over~, and suddenly I am being awakened from an old dark memory dating back more than 30 years.

Seeing that old scene of over 30 years ago and the pressure I felt in the dream reminded me of the immense psychological pressure which tests put on children in Korea.

The ideal type of education would be made possible by creating a learning environment in our everyday lives that wonderfully unites play, learning and labor into one. In Book 6 of *The Analects of Confucius*, this phrase appears: 'knowing' is inferior to 'liking,' and 'liking' is inferior to 'enjoying'; that is, whereas 'knowledge' is a state of understanding the existence of truth, and 'liking' is a state of taking interest in, but not yet possessing the truth, yet 'joy' is interpreted as the state of complete understanding of the truth, taking it as one's own and living it. If we take a close look at the process of thinking and creating something in joy, first, 'joy' involves 'play,' 'thinking' is led to 'learning,' and 'creating' includes 'labor.' The demand of forcing children to believe as the 'truth,' what is written on the blackboard in chalk or what is printed on the sheet of paper is, to use a strong expression, nothing but 'violence' on the part of the adults and contributes nothing to the joy of life. Under such preposterous pressure like tests, grades, and setting examples, numerous sprouts of possibilities are likely to be nipped. And in this context, we cannot but be sceptical of the type of human character that can be formed under such moral standards in today's schools.

Without recognizing the value of children with marked diversity and great creativity, we dismiss them derogatively as 'bad students' and push them away from the elite course early on. Instead we raise and praise passive weaklings who are obedient to the teacher and are only good at memorizing by rote and entrust them with a place of the pillar of society. We may get along with this in peaceful times but such a system is incapable of defending our fatherland in the midst of historical turmoil. I figured out the precise nature of 'honor student' only too late and went through a great downfall into an 'inferior student.' In my childhood, I was often afraid if the word 'honor' of an 'honor student' isolated me from my friends and, by deliberately doing some mischief, induced the teacher to scold me. Now I understand such mischievous actions were an expression of psychological confusion that haunted me between the so-called a 'superior student' and an 'inferior student.'

I hope U-Yong and Ju-Yong do not blindly aim to remain honor students with good test scores, but instead try to build strong characters full of firm conviction and originality.

That day, when I met them in front of their school, I had to take a flight back like a gust of wind promising (to drop by) 'next time' and excusing myself 'since your uncle is busy and you are little,' but I could tell from U-Yong's calm and Ju-Yong's lively faces that they were not weaklings at all. I think raising a boy is looking toward to the stars, the universe, and the future in the same way as cleaning the lens of a Hubble telescope.

— At the End of 1983, DaeJeon Correctional Institute

One-Footed Step

to my elder-sister-in-law

한 발 걸음 · 244p

There was a race between the fastest runner, a young man
in his twenties, and the slowest runner, an elderly man in his
fifties in our prison room. It was not a re-presentation of the
race in the fable between a rabbit and a turtle; it was a fair
race in that the young man ran with one foot and the old man
with his both feet. The result was something that reversed
our prediction: the old man won easily. It was the race that
made us realize the enormous difference between having one
foot and two feet. Luckily it was a race done just for fun after
tedious arguments among inmates who meant no harm, but
if it had really been the defeat of a one-footed disabled man,
the anguish would have been beyond expression.

One of the miseries we felt during our imprisonment
resembles walking alone on just one foot. That is, between
the two feet in our life, practice and cognition, we have to
do without the foot of practice. We can form cognition by
connecting ourselves to the external objects through practice,
and come to prove the truth in the process of putting
cognition into practice again. Practice is considered to be
the origin of cognition and, at the same time, the norm of its

truthfulness.

Repetition of such a process of 'practice → cognition → re-practice → re-cognition' leads to the development of practice and along with it, evolves cognition, from emotional one to rational cognition. Therefore, the very fact that leading a life without practice can have serious consequences. It means there will be a frustration of cognition and suspension of thought. It is in the same rationale that stagnant water becomes foul and thought without growth cannot help getting stained.

In the first years of my prison life, I was confronted with endless stains of thoughts, despite my continuous efforts to remove them. I realized that to keep my thoughts from getting stained is not about cleaning the stains but about allowing my thoughts themselves to grow. This was the realization that I had to stand up and walk.

It was a revalidation of common daily life as expressed in the passages such as, 'the more furrows we make by ploughing, the more shiny the blade of the plough becomes,' and 'running streams meet the sea,' but what they meant to me was completely different. The feeling of emptiness one has when one tries to stand up and walk, and the frustration of losing a leg makes one crumple and collapse into the same spot. The very first thing one can do when put into prison is to read books. But reading is different from practicing and it cannot become legs to walk with; it still equates to a one-footed walk. Furthermore, the reason why one finds reading boring is not because of the slowness in moving along in a one-footed walk, but because of the conceptualization of oneself caused by repeating the process of cognition ('cogniti on → cognition → cognition...). Thus, far from moving forward, one loses the solid ground of reality and gets conceptualized further into the air.

Finally I decided to walk on 'crutches' as all other disabled people do. The first crutch I chose was relying on the 'practice of the past,' by adopting other people's experience.

Since the wooden leg, though strong, cannot function the same as one's own leg with blood running through it, my two legs did not work well alongside each other and I had to suffer by moving slowly, stumbling across and falling down. Nevertheless as time went by and the crutch wore hand marks, such an awkward manner of walking managed to improve, increasing its speed and becoming steady.

For me, the experience of walking with the afore-mentioned crutch taught me an important lesson. The speedy and steady manner of walking was not made by the crutch following my own leg, but by the leg adjusting to the crutch. That is, my cognition got its step by learning the cognition of those whose experiences I took for my crutch and trying to resemble it. The very fact that it was my own leg making the progress, not the wooden crutch, was quite shocking to me since I had anticipated the opposite.

What is more surprising is that my fellow inmates' experience was not a mere trail of the past, but was strongly connected to, or constituted the present imprisonment, and assumed presence. The realization that the practice of the past is not a dead practice, but a breathing and living one, was as touching as though it made my blood run through the crutch, and enlivening my senses into it.

I have often thought deeply that we can apply practice not only to a substantial large-piece of work with dramatic structure, but to everywhere where people or tasks are involved.

Although people walk their lives with their own steps, they also seem to walk on the great territory of practice (of others) until they die and are buried underground, whether they get to the land by kicking it or by falling down on it.

Now in March, the long and cold winter is about to come to an end. Perhaps in some nooks under the prison wall spring has already come in the shape of a little germ of grass. Whatever it is, I think, spring does not come over the mountain from the south but rises through the frozen earth under the feet.

— March 1, 1984, DaeJeon Correctional Institute

A Closed Space, An Open Mind

to my elder sister-in-law

닫힌 공간, 열린 정신 • 247p

They say, new is good when it comes to clothes, and old friends are good when it comes to people. Now I wonder, in terms of a house, which one would be better, an old one or a new one? A house is different from clothes in that it is not built to fit the body; it is also different from people in that it does not yield to the passage of time, at least in the same way. Moving into a new prison, I think how many things there are to be tamed in the new building.

The little prince from the small planet says, "Taming is to enter into a relationship." Taming without establishing a relationship or being tamed into an unfair relationship is suppression by nature. The true meaning of establishing a relationship is sharing something with each other. Whether it is a wooden chair or some sublime spiritual value, sharing something means feeling sympathy with others while standing in front of the same window, and sensing the solidarity of fate that we are on board the same ship.

On this foothill of a mountain where there was no human trace at all until last year, it is now full of white walls squarely dividing numerous spaces. Sitting straight in a 6.138

square meter among those divided spaces, I think about the relationship that I have to establish with this cold space.

Numerous spaces and a man of 64kg weight that occupies only a tiny bit of it, high prison walls and the will to internalize the freedom of the blue sky that cannot be blocked by the walls, ...a relationship that is based on an intolerable contrast between a closed space and an open mind. Such a relationship is clearly ironic in that it is between the imprisoning space of the prison and me, an individual who should stand up against it. It points at a direction opposite to the one of being tamed; it shows, in other words, the relationship of conflict and tension. It may perhaps be something that comes prior to any relationship; it is a search for the relationship itself.

The relationship of tension and conflict is not only a condition of recognizing other subjects, but it is also the reality of all 'living' relationships. The complacency of being comfortably tamed after establishing a relationship has the appearance of 'completion of the relationship' or a 'well-ripened relationship,' but inside, it signals the collapse of the relationship that has brought it about, or the end of the collapse. I have witnessed such cases many times.

I think such tension and conflict I feel in this new prison does not uniquely derive from this particular prison or from some specific experience of my own. It rather derives from 'the nature of relationship in general' that has always resided in all relationships and happens to be momentarily expressed on some occasion. Therefore I try to understand such tension and conflict not as an independent object in itself, but rather as a perspective that I can arrive at of the nature of relationship in general. Thus, I want to take this precious opportunity honestly to recognize my existence and the existential condition I am in. I do not want to seek the capacity to endure and survive such tension and conflict in my lonely will. Such capacity can surely be obtained in those numerous spaces which are divided squarely by walls and where there are *full* of people.

I believe that strong solidarity not only of the prison inmates but also of all of us who exist amongst numerous people opens up the closed space and makes the blue sky breathe... so that it becomes the very power with which we step on the great continent that can sufficiently embrace tension and conflict. Perhaps, entering into a relationship begins with sharing the 'pain.'

Thank you for the money and watch you have sent me. The watch ticks on in the locked prison cell. It seems to me to be a foul play that 'time passes even in the closed space.'

Though I may be wearing a watch on my wrist, I will not become accustomed to, and thus anxious with time. For it takes ease for those with a life sentence to endure.

The 'April zephyr' generously blows warm breathes into the mountains, trees, earth, rocks, cements, worn sheets of paper, and even empty plastic bags. Wishing peace to all the family.

— April 26, 1981, DaeJeon Correctional Institute

Norma of Corruption

to my younger sister-in-law

타락의 노르마 · 250p

In old times, noble women were said to change their clothes in front of their slaves without hesitation. Perhaps they pretended that there was no body around them or they considered their slaves insignificant, even less significant than their cats or dogs. The slaves at that time, being shackled, probably could not properly see the point, either. Compared to them, today's prisoners can observe many things since they are free in their consciousness.

Just like the workers doing jobs in the manhole have a chance to see the hidden parts of the passers-by exposed, inmates who stay in the low place are given an unexpected perspective that helps them look directly into the shameful parts of other people's faces. Not to mention other people, the prison inmates themselves take off their clothes of manners, sense of honour and of culture the moment they enter into the prison, have their hair cut, and change their clothes into prison uniform. For this reason or that, we do not easily respect other people.

We have cultivated a very critical eyes upon all outward appearances against the so-called bare skin, not only on feigned looks and costume, but also on social position, property, educational background and career. Such a critical gaze that distinguishes humans themselves from the outward show they perform is indeed a rare insight, hard to gain in other places and thus, it becomes one of the precious assets we have, 'we' who have nothing much.

Nevertheless, since it is a way of judging a person by his most unhappy face and his darkest voice, it is likely to reveal the assessor's base intention of devaluing the person and justifying his own weakness. Although other people's flaws cannot save us from our own weaknesses, we try to find out their weaknesses and when finding one, we experience a sudden relief. This is nothing but a perverse mind that prevents us from growing up, not to mention not having some saving grace. Since many parts of a person are refracted by the situations he/she is in, it is nothing but an idealist's illusion to try to judge various concrete phenomena of the time against the purity of nature itself. There might also be an attitude of putting the blame on to others with a negative conclusion intended from the beginning.

Even in our imprisonment, there is a certain 'norma of corruption' that the prison uniform demands. Whether it is a value of mean or of assumption, this 'norma' regulates all those in prison uniform in advance. It does not stop with social prejudice against the prisoners. It influences even when prisoners look at themselves. It is indeed a stubborn rack from which one cannot escape either from the inside or from the outside. It is the very *norma* of corruption that makes the prisoners shed their manners or their sense of honour as if they take off worn-out clothes.

If we accept that many parts of a person are revealed when refracted upon situations, and that various situations reflect many parts of a person in return, we should nourish the humble thought that we have to blame both the person and the situations or to forgive both.

When judging a person, the very fact that the subject of our judgment is also a person makes it more difficult to judge. Humans are sure to turn their eyes to their own situations and scoop up only as much of the flowing water as their pail will contain. Unless one realizes such a limitation and characteristic, I think it very hard to widen his/her own thoughts and perspective.

Such a self-tormenting and cynical perspective contained in the ideology of imprisonment is the shade of prison life that should be abolished in whatever way possible. Nevertheless the free spirit—that takes off all the veils of existing morality, affectations, and falsehood brought about by the critical perspective and the outright anthropocentricism one cannot gain without imprisonment—is enough to compensate for all the heavy pressure of imprisonment. I believe such a free spirit embraces in it the potential for a new life in the same way as an egg promises a chick.

I feel 'the *norma* of corruption' of imprisonment as pleasant rather than being shameful, and the outrageous words and deeds shown beside us is felt, not to be offended, but to be pleased, thinking that they indicate a precious insight that shows the reality without falsehood.

Fortunately to my salvation, the new prison building has a mountain nearby. Not only is the shape of the mountain friendly but also the sharing of the mountain with rocks, trees and streams resembles the features of a man of virtue who combines sturdiness and gentleness. Moreover, the mountain of May, unlike that of March or April with faded color, is full of vigor with fresh verdure becoming greener every day, just like a person who is soon to begin work with his sleeves rolled up. Now I have to look around myself —myself who is surrounded by concrete walls and in large part by the mountain of May— to find out what new life sprouts within me.

— May 7, 1984, DaeJeon Correctional Institute

Creation of the 'MinJung'

to my elder sister-in-law

민중의 창조 · 253p

Thank you for the book, *The Clergymen Among the MinJung*, and the allowance you sent me. The book explains in a low voice what kind of life is meaningful by introducing 'the people of the shade,' who, having planted themselves into the lives of the alienated, suppressed and abandoned, sharing meager food with them, and showing mercy to them, help us nourish a perspective from which we can clearly look at the time we live in. While reading this book, I had persistent questions to myself like, "Who are the MinJung of our time?," "Where are the MinJung?"

It is very difficult to comprehend the firm reality of the MinJung regardless of the time or society, and unless we have a good grasp of the reality of the MinJung, we cannot comprehend the society and the time as a whole.

We know the MinJung well as a historical fact of the past, especially the MinJung when they clearly present themselves on the historical stage during an upheaval in society. But we also know that many people fail to find out the true entity of the MinJung in vivid situations of the present in contemporary society. It is indeed very difficult to find out the true substance of the MinJung in the field of fierce conflict —such as confrontations between tangled interests and ideologies, distortion of reality, exaggeration of the facts and the suppression of truth,— and to depend on their proper capacity.

At most, we can catch nothing but the 'shadow' of the MinJung, or we manage to bestow universal meaning on 'something that happened there at that time.' Such a false image in the name of the MinJung which our sentiment and pity have created makes us endlessly thirsty and tired. For it does not go even one step closer to the question about the reason for unhappiness, "Why so unhappy?" but it is degraded into an 'art of tears' that makes us endure and suffer everything. After all, it is something that, by giving consolation, leads us to the loss of life.

Living in a first-person situation of prison life over a decade, I have been thinking that the MinJung does not exist in a ready-made permanent form, but is always newly 'created.'

Unhappy people in the shade are neither the symbol of the MinJung, nor do they become the minimal bridge leading to the MinJung. It is in our *a priori* cognition of the MinJung as unhappy beings where the error of sentimentalism lies.

The MinJung is 'social potentiality condensed and expanded' which is created with the most basic contradiction of time as a momentum. Such potentiality is not in the hero with light footsteps that has shown up all at once on one occasion. Having been buried deep into the base of the history of the people as enormous potential, the memory of numerous successes and failures and of joys and sorrows is realized in its majestic appearance during the upheaval of the society.

However, consecrating the Minjung as such is, in fact, another type of sentimentalism. In the same way that we can reach the sea by following whatever stream flows into it, the root of the Minjung is stretched even to life in an alley however small and lonely it might be. This is the very nature of the MinJung, unique to it. What is missing is the all-encompassing spirit of the time and flexible artistry of the people concerned.

Many people lacking in capacity and consciousness, hovering around a false image of the MinJung, could not trust the MinJung. I try to interpret such failure as the result of the historical immaturity of our time and society rather than each individual's limitation. For an individual person's cognition and capacity is a social acquisition.

Two months have passed since we moved, but our surroundings are still cluttered with big and small chores, like sweeping, polishing, digging, filling and leveling. The birds' singing from the summer mountain in early dawn and the untainted voice of nature, as lively as the fresh verdure of May, revives our distressed bodies and minds from various noises and distractions.

— May 22, 1983, DaeJeon Correctional Institute

Six Days' Release Home on Leave

to my younger sister-in-law

엿새간의 귀휴 · 256p

Two of your letters delivered together last night, younger
sister-in-law, took my thoughts back to Seoul. Though the
meaning of release on leave is to take rest upon homecoming,
perhaps it is too early for me to feel at ease with this notion.
What I did during my momentary release was to live 16 years
of life in 6 days. It was hard work to bear the weight of the
load contained in the 16 years and to relive the pain of the
scar those years have inflicted. Above all, I had to turn my
eyes to where everybody's eyes were directed, that is, me
myself, and to look at myself.

Fortunately, the course of over 10 years has faded the
color and pain of the scar and my family has overcome the
enormous shock in a beneficial way so that we could talk
calmly about it as if we were just dealing with other people's
problems. It was a relief.

Nevertheless, despite how long it had been, still there
was something that was not weathered, but remained white
like the bone of sorrow and I carried it into my arm with a
light pain, feeling emptiness at the seemingly lost time. Since
I thought that I was quite experienced in living life resiliently,

while bearing a heavy load, it was unexpectedly tough and beyond my capacity, and I felt 'a certain yearning' that could barely be relieved even in my family's warm embrace. I might perhaps have felt thirst for something like a 'shelter of love' as you wrote in the letter.

If it were just a matter of love and rest, the loneliness I have experienced in the midst of the people—even when I wore the same clothes and mingled with them—harshly awakened me to the impropriety of such thirst, and consequently I have already acclimatized myself in this condition.

However, on my way back to prison, when I loosened my necktie, took off the worldly attire including my shirt, jacket, and pants one by one, and changed into my prison uniform in my brother's car, the particular pain I felt was so overwhelming that it refused the language of reason. Now I think it better that, after I returned here, I could replace 'rest' with an uncontrollable doze and never-sufficient sleep.

Thinking back, the pain and thirst I felt beyond my capacity during my homecoming leave was because of my impulsive and hacked thoughts. It was, I think, caused by 'the poverty of mind' which made me eager to be loved rather than to love, and to be understood rather than to understand.

The urge to explain oneself to others is, in a word, proof of one's lack of self-confidence, and at this point, it resolves itself into one's own personal problem.

Not to mention disturbing the routine of my younger

brother's busy life, I am afraid I have unintentionally stirred up many people, especially my young nephews, who did not understand what it was all about. I still vividly remember you, younger sister-in-law who was busy taking good care of me and doing uncommon things in the presence of the elderly people and guests, being the lowest member in the family hierarchy. Please convey my apology to your parents and your younger siblings for my 'poor expression of thanks and greetings' and promise better things next time. I promise you, of course, another opportunity to chat in the children's playground. The time we had for this was never sufficient.

I realized that surprisingly many people were waiting for me and watching me. Surely, I knew that such attention was the very power to help me endure this place and keep myself as I am.

— June 19, 1984, DaeJeon Correctional Institute

A Master at Work

to my elder sister-in-law

일의 명인 · 258p

First-class prisoners often join in with volunteer laboring during holidays. They do quite simple jobs like cleaning the long aisle you were surprised to notice, weeding, opening the drainage channels, or levelling the ground.

I have never missed the volunteer work we had during holidays. I never missed one, not only because many people working together is itself a 'school,' but also because I get the invaluable opportunity to learn from 'two great teachers.' These two teachers are the people of the shade who had neither learning nor wealth in the family, which meant that their prison life was relentlessly 'crushed into soup.' The reason I took these two as my teachers to guide my mind is because, through their silent action, I got to realize 'how 'work' has raised and transformed people.

First, these two people have an excellent capacity for 'finding' work. Things that are not considered 'work' to others including me are identified at a glance and receive attention. Nevertheless, unlike those who catch small fry and bustle with it, in timely fashion they discover a big and most necessary job that needs to be done and do it without the least condescension or distress. They indeed personify the stately features of 'the master at work' who has lived with work over a long period of time.

Second, these two people have a 'tender heart' so that they cannot pass by any work that requires attention. They have minds that cannot ignore any work wanting doing or leave any thing half done without feeling ill at ease. For them, work is not an external subject, but the very condition of existence that makes up their internal life. In a few casual steps, they are sure to straighten something; in their comings and goings for other tasks, they are sure to bring or take something with them. They never allow themselves to be empty-handed, even for a minute.

Third, these two people always take on the hardest menial work that calls for most laborers. Whereas some of the more educated people, not exactly because they want a less demanding job, prefer a role that distinguishes them from other people, these two put themselves in the center of the lowest place among the ill-assorted multitude. At this very point, they go beyond the 'expert' that teaches me skills of work, but become an example of the 'great teacher' who teaches and inspires 'human beings.' So, when they held a rag, I held a rag, and when they held a spade, I, too, picked up a spade. From the security of setting up my position beside them, I learned that such reliance actually empowered me.

For me, who grew up in schools with parents in the teaching profession, and thus, lacked direct experience of labor and the laborer's life, the meaning of my imprisonment and of meeting a few special teachers was truly tremendous.

We should blame our blindness which prevents us from realizing that the secrets of dialectics are commonly to be found in our daily labor—the dialectics in which the sea achieves its immensity at the lowest place and the individual flowers become a huge flower in a wreath.

I have not read the books you have sent because they were not allowed, but I appreciate your great kindness in sending them. I realize people and things are living in a village where it is hard to enter and leave.

— September 20, 1984, DaeJeon Correctional Institute

The Highest Form of Relationship
to my elder sister-in-law

관계의 최고 형태 · 261p

I read an article about 'Korean People' by a Japanese journalist. I spared some time to read it because one of my younger colleagues was asking about the article's real intention. It was a third-class piece of writing, far inferior to those written by a few democratic intellectuals of Japan I have read in the past. On this postcard, I do not intend to find fault with the content, or to dwell on the writer's national arrogance or twisted militarism. Reading this made me realize how hard it is to grasp and present some subjects.

Compared to dealing with a simple individual object or an individual person, it is tremendously difficult to recognize and describe a society, an age, or a people. With big subjects, the writer's observation or diligence does not help much. The writer's writing skills or sense is of no use, either. Without scientific thought, and system based on socio-historical understanding and a philosophical world view, one would be as helpless as touching the side of an elephant to try to determine its size, however many materials one makes use of or whatever profound knowledge one commands.

Even more important and critical than scientific thought, however, is the 'relationship' between the writer and his subject. Depending on the nature of that relationship, the depth of cognition and the comprehensiveness of perspective is decided. For instance, a relationship in which one merely looks on the subject as an on-looker indicates, in fact, an absence of relationship. Even if we replace the word 'on-looking' with a more refined one like, 'contemplation,' the result is still the same, since there is no cognition that starts from contemplation and ends in contemplation.

The illusion that we can recognize and describe the subject without ourselves being connected to it through the bond of love, or the blood of fate, that is, without a harmonious conjunction of the self and the subject, is simply a special type of error and deception with which today's journalism is flooded. By counterfeiting a fictional phase of the third way or the non-partisanship of neutrality and elevating its value, while devaluing all positions that have relationships with the subject as foul and inferior, journalism completely isolates human beings as mere spectators and dissipators of the truth. The characteristic of all types of spectators, whether they are consumers of goods, spectators on the stand, or viewers in front of the television set is their complete separation from the subject.

When the self and the subject are distinguished and isolated from each other, differences are always discovered and emphasized. For this reason, the more observation we have of the subject, the more differences we find, and the nearer we have access to the subject, the more distance we come across. Finally, we end up losing sight of the essence of the subject and at the same time, losing ourselves.

We know that cultural anthropology, the so-called 'advance guard of colonialism,' accompanied a cruel age of invasion in which numerous groups of people were objectified, and looked down on, while their folk customs and traditional culture were distorted, and their honest human lives were dismissed as savage, simply because they were different. Such thinking concealed their invasion under other names, and finally they ended up losing their human conscience, not to mention losing their subject.

We prisoners are objectified as well. We are categorized by the sins we have committed, or our crime types, and so forth, classified with various levels, and become subjects of study for different kinds of psychology like criminal psychology and abnormal psychology. They even get caught up in psychological warfare losing sight of the fact that the inmates they have objectified as their subjects live alongside them in the same period and are bound to them in different kinds of social relationships.

In the end, such study of classification and psychological observation is expected to discover and invent some new 'species of crime' who are as distant as Neandelthals, a totally different species from their own.

Various crimes thus discovered, having been committed by

this 'species of criminals' are considered to have nothing to do with the pseudo-scientific observers, and have absolutely no common bond or contemporaneity. The observers appropriate these 'crimes' for their own advantage, in order to self-defend, protect, and camouflage their own ethically treacherous mind, and thus create a vicious cycle of demoralizing themselves. Those who share the same age and the same society, by definition, are bound to have more things in common than differences, however different their situations are. Therefore I believe that the start of our cognition of a certain subject ought to be to begin with discovering the relationship we have established with that subject, something like the relationship of Malcolm X with black skin and of Franz Fanon with Algeria.

At every point in world history, we find the solemn grave consciousness in which the self embraces the subject and the subject is embodied into the self. Such identification with the subject, I think, clearly reveals the true features of our lives and at the same time helps us look honestly at ourselves.

"A warm heart is better than a cool head, a skilful hand is better than a warm heart, and a walking foot is better than a skilful hand. Love rather than observation, practice rather than love, to be on the same footing rather than practice is more important. To be in the same position, that is the highest form of relationship."[*]

— November 29, 1984, DaeJeon Correctional Institute

[*]   quoted from "Foot," *For the First Time*, p.162

The Rings of a Tree

to my elder sister-in-law

나이테 · 265p

"What the rings of a tree teach us is that a tree grows in winter, too, and the part that grows in winter is harder than the part that grows in summer."*

The trees that have their ankles buried and stand with their arms stretched in the midst of snow and wind without even a leaf that would gather a fistful of sunlight for them are cultivating their arms, their hearts and the next spring (even in winter.) They are passing winter in a wiser way than people who are bustling about.

I wish you, elder brother, U-Yong and Ju-Yong a bright and joyful New Year.

Thank you for sending the private supplies for me for the year.

— December 28, 1984, DaeJeon Correctional Institute

---

* Quoted from "The Rings of a Tree," *For the First Time*, p. 20

Prison Life in Summer

to my younger sister-in-law

여름 징역살이 · 266p

They say life is better for the poor in summer than in winter. Those of us who are in prison, though none the less poor, would choose winter over summer anytime, because of the crucial fact that nullifies any number of advantages summer may have—that is, prison life in summer makes you hate the person next to you.

The narrow bed space that forces you to sleep on your side degrades the person sleeping next to you into a 37 degree lump of heat. This is the harshest punishment of all that makes a dramatic contrast to the rather primitive friendship of winter in which you can overcome the bitter cold with the help of your fellow inmate's body temperature.

The very fact that in summer you hate the person nearest to you, and that you are hated by that person makes you very unhappy. Furthermore, that such hatred is not derived from your actions but from your existence itself turns unhappiness into despair. But above all what makes us most unhappy is that the object of our hatred is not grasped correctly by our reason but seized wrongly by peripheral senses, and the consequent self-abhorrence that we, knowing such mistakes, cannot correct the feeling and object of our hatred.

Such 'unjustified hatred' which we incite toward the nearest person is found not only in summer sleeping but also everywhere in the poor people's lives. Some rash people may take this as the matter of poor people's morality and tend to accuse their human nature. But we all know. We know that a downpour of rain we were expecting 'tomorrow' would do something to relieve the scorching heat and soon, the cool air of autumn will take away the unhappy hatred that we have directed at each other and make us realize the 'warm heart' of our near neighbor. And we know, too, that it would awaken us to cognition as clean and cool as the autumn stream.

As summer passes, various events during the week of my leave will be organized into card-sized photos, I believe. I am doing fine as always. Please send my greetings to your parents and your younger brothers and sisters.

— August 28, 1985, DaeJeon Correctional Institute

The Wisdom of Enduring Winter

to my elder sister-in-law

인동의 지혜 · 268p

When we get a sentence for over one and a half years, we have two winters to pass in prison. We call it 'double imprisonment,' for it is very difficult to endure.

When one is in solitary confinement, the cold is made worse since there is no other warmth except for one's own body temperature. Nevertheless, I have been in solitary confinement since last autumn. The reason that solitary confinement cannot be refused is that I do not think cold is the most difficult thing to endure in prison life. Although winter in prison is very cold, the saying, 'the wisdom of enduring winter,' as an outcome of numerous precedents of prison life over several decades, has long been passed on, in the same way as the folk remedies flourished in a doctorless village.

Whenever we come across such a weighty store of wisdom which the prisoners have gained on their chilled bodies over a long period of passive life, we feel the presence of their hard life jumps into our lives.

Thus, not only the winter cold confirms in us the strong life force manifesting in such hardship, but it also refreshes our thoughts as if giving a reward for chilling our body. For this reason I always prefer winter to summer, because winter cold refreshes our thoughts which are likely to be distressed by various little feelings and personal trivialities, and elevates them to a lofty spiritual world. Similar to 'poverty,' cold is only inconvenient. And inconvenience keeps us awake.

I want to heat myself up by filling up the cold space of this solitary cell of about 3. 3 square meters with a sharp awakening to the joys and sorrows of numerous neighbors and their history contained in us.

From the map appended to the geography book you sent, I looked into DaeChi-Dong where you recently moved to. I assume, since it is close to JamShil, it may shorten your commuting distance. Number 407 means you are on the fourth floor which I think will bring more sunlight into the flower pots unlike the house at IChon-Dong. I hope your face is full of sunlight, too.

— January 10, 1986, DaeJeon Correctional Institute

"I Want to Walk"

to my younger sister-in-law

나는 걷고 싶다 · 270p

Perhaps because we had plentiful rainfall last summer, this winter we have only had little snow. Although it is us who should have to cope with the severe cold after the snow, young inmates have eagerly waited for the coming of heavy snow, and as was expected, some time ago we had snow for three consecutive days and they made a snowman in a corner of the exercise area. The snowman standing in this spot had a quite startling phrase engraved on its chest with a piece of briquette:

"I want to walk."

The phrase that reminds us of our feet—that we have our feet, but we cannot walk with them—becomes a hard snowball and hits us on the forehead. The day after tomorrow being the first day of February, the snowman has melted, and we can hear the footsteps of approaching spring from afar.

— January 30, 1988, JeonJu Correctional Institute

What is the Young? And What is it to be the Mother?

to my father

새끼가 무엇인지, 어미가 무엇인지 · 271p

They brought down a little sparrow from the sparrow nest. Despite my earnest appeals, they climbed to that high place through the window and took out the sparrow without any difficulty. They said they wanted to tame it and play with it. It was a yellow-beaked fledgling which could not yet fly. While it was gasping with its heart beating fast from shock, its anxious mother flew about in a giddy hurling motion and would not leave.

"Look, please let the fledgling fly back to its mom."

"It cannot fly, can it?"

"Then put it back in its nest."

"Those from block no. 3 will take it, then. The bird in the block no. 2 was taken down, roasted, and eaten by them."

"..."

Opening my fist, I put it on the ground and out of blue, the mother sparrow flew down, not knowing what to do except rub its body on its young. Unable to fly together, or carry it up to the high nest, the sparrow scrambled to take it to a corner and tried to hide it;

"If it falls into a mouse hole, I am afraid it will become

prey to the rat."

That, too, was a terrible thing. We were the same in not knowing what to do. In the end, we brought it to the room, put it in a mouse cage we had happened to borrow, and placed it on the window sill.

Finding the little bird in no time, two mother birds promptly followed.

At first, they seemed to be cautious of the people, but soon, regardless of those around, they became fully absorbed with the young one. They took turns to continually carry food to the young. It was quite surprising, and a good thing to witness.

"That's great. However well we feed it, can we be compared to its mother? Let the mother raise it and when the yellow beak disappears, let it fly away."

As such, the young sparrow had to live on for some time with mothers feeding it in the mouse cage until it could fly. The mother sparrows regularly fed the young bird by carrying food in their mouths, taking the risk of getting caught themselves in the mouse cage and not being released at all.

What is the young and what is the mother, and what is life? ...

Looking at the sparrows, we felt pain in our hearts.

I thought of my mother, of course. I felt an ache in my heart thinking of my mother, mother who took good care of me in a valley at JeongReung, giving up eating and drinking herself. The memory which might well has grown fainter now

20 years later, still touches and pierces my heart with pain.

— May 30, 1988, JeonJu Correctional Institute

III

Tactless Honesty of Foolish People
Changes the World Little by Little

"Young Men, Step on Me and Rise"

Heo, Jun and His Teacher at the Ice Valley

청년들아 나를 딛고 오르거라 • 275p

I am sending this postcard from the foothill of a mountain in my hometown. It is the valley where the teacher Yu, EuiTae had his pupil Heo, Jun dissect his body.

It is the very Ice Valley mentioned in the novel, *DongEuiBoGam* (*The Manual of Oriental Medicine*). It is the valley where ice is covered during the three dogs' days period in May and June by lunar calendar, and where rather warm water runs in winter. In the time when anatomy of the human body was prohibited by national law, the teacher called his pupil to this Ice Valley.

In front of Heo, Jun was the body of his teacher, Yu, EuiTae who killed himself, lying on his back on the sedge mat and with his will beside him glowing in the yellow wax candle light. In his will, he wrote that he gave up his sick body, and since those who deal with illness cannot save life without knowing the inside of the human body, asked him to take this as an opportunity to vow that he would devote himself to medicine. Heo, Jun knelt down before the will.

I seem to see it as if Heo, Jun had revived himself in the midst of the darkness: after vowing to willingly submit himself to punishment if he showed reluctance to take up a medical career, or was lazy when trying to save sick people, or, coveted money or fame under the pretext of curing people, he was about to dissect his teacher's body.

Today instead of the torch of that day, blazing maple leaves lighten the darkness. Sitting on the jagged edge of a rock, I thought: Yu, EuiTae and Heo, Jun in the novel are fictional characters the novelist created in his imagination. Nevertheless, I believe it may convey the truth, however fictional and unreal it is, for the repository of fact is always too narrow and insufficient to carry the truth.

I cannot quite explain to myself why I came to this Ice Valley first, after 20 years' imprisonment and 7 years' seclusion. The greatest meaning of 'release' from prison is 'walking on one's own.' The right to go around on one's own is called 'the right to walk independently.' Being free to go where I had wanted to go gave such an exhilarating sense of release!

After my mother's death, my father who had survived alone for several years has now passed away. Rather empty-hearted, I took the train with no definite plans in mind. There was no ice in the Ice valley, since this was not May or June. But that was not very important. At the scene of heartbreaking succession of the teacher to his pupil, I could not help being deeply moved by the very seriousness of learning and teaching. We are inevitably someone's pupil and at the same time, some other's teacher. I think, to search for and clarify the so-called chain of learning and teaching, the link between the teacher and the pupil is to gain an accurate insight into ourselves.

It was perhaps in my middle school days that I followed my father to come to this place. I was amazed at my father who published a 440-page book at the age of 87, one year before he passed away. In his book, he said that we resemble our age more than our parents, but the very first discovery I made in my homecoming was that we take after the mountains and streams of our hometown first and foremost.

Even the trees and the color of soil, not to mention the contour of mountains, could not be more familiar. An awareness that the mountains and streams of childhood became one's own spiritual birthplace, although the expression 'symbiotics between the soil and the body' has been trivialized into advertisement copy since the rule of WTO! I think that the merging together of mountains and streams, and human beings, and of teachers and pupils presents a universal feature of human life.

Above the Ice Valley buried in darkness, the craggy tops that glowed with the evening sunset suddenly looked like Heo, Jun's face, or seemingly like his teacher Yu, Eui Tae's face. The message of the king who ordered the compilation of *The Manual of Oriental Medicine* is as follows:

"You must register in detail the medicinal herbs that grow abundantly in this country so that those without knowledge and money can easily recognize them and have everybody's illness cured."

For me, such perceptiveness and love for the people expressed in this passage is not restricted to the King Sun-Jo but extended to Heo, Jun's warmheartedness and his teacher's will.

The very writing of *The Manual of Oriental Medicine* was Heo, Jun's project, sure to be his own. Moreover, the completion of the book was the result of Heo, Jun's lonely work and was undertaken in exile on a distant isolated island. For 300 years it was the only medical manual available catering specially for our climate and body type and saved numerous people's lives until Lee, JeMa's theory of "The Four Types of Human Body" was issued.

Besides *The Manual of Oriental Medicine*, most of Heo, Jun's writings about the soul and heart were concerned with adapting difficult professional books into easy Korean. I guess King Sun-Jo's special promotion of Heo, Jun was an expression of his high esteem for Heo, Jun's love for the people and his notable career in the field.

Sitting in the darkness that enveloped the Ice Valley, I thought of the love and sacrifice of numerous people who had in different ways inspired Heo, Jun for his growth. I was reminded of Baek, Geo-I's poem "Chrysanthemum," in which he sang: "In order to bloom a golden chrysanthemum bright with the dew of an early morning, we had the first frost of the year last night." Rhyushin's pleading expressed in the phrase, "Young men, step on me and rise" struck me, too.

In the past, mothers thought of their life as somebody else's nutriment rather than of their own. Thus, the word, "nourishing mothers." Nevertheless, instead of putting ourselves in the middle of the chain of humanity, we try to realize ourselves with fashionable apparatus and euphemistic rhetoric and hide ourselves in them. A selfish and arrogant culture of today!

I seemed to hear your long sigh. I was reminded of you saying that we are meeting only as husks, losing ourselves amongst heaps of countless consumer goods and the empty aesthetics such goods create. What is worse, truly fearful is that we forget the 'invisible hand' that mass-produces such husks.

In this season of hypocrisy in which lofty moral language has been held captive by illegal profiteers, what to teach and what to learn has evoked a cold lesson of this Ice Valley. Althusser said, "play is the creation of a new audience. To complete the performance, to complete it in life, we need to create players who seek the meaning of its incompleteness."

I think, whether we walk on the stage or sit among the audience, we cannot but come back to the field of life, trying to find out the meaning of our life's incompleteness, and walk among the people who endeavour to reach completion of the silence and the discourse of life. I believe that after all what we realize is learned from the lives of numerous people who walk along with us before and after, right and left, and who teach us through their very own lives rather than by the luxurious garrulity of language.

This autumn which was cleaner and longer than in any previous years, but which you said you could not enjoy because it has winter trailing behind, is coming to an end. And your cold winter draws near.

— 1996, from *Trees, Oh, Trees*

The Pyramids We Have to Demolish

BanGuJung and ApGuJung

우리가 헐어야 할 피라미드 · 279p

Beside the River ImJin about 6km away to the west from
PaJu, there is a small pavilion called 'BanGuJung.' It was
the pavilion of Hwang, Hee, a great prime minister of Yi
Dynasty who was in the inner circle of King SeJong's court of
government officials. It was where he spent his old age in his
retirement after 18 years as prime minister until he lived out
his natural life in his 90th year, in the company of seagulls,
as the Chinese character in the name of the pavilion signifies.
As the autumnal season of maples is over and an early winter
approaches, it is as quiet as it had been 500 years ago, with
few visitors only.

You may remember a pavilion with the same name,
'ApGuJung' at GangNam in Seoul. It was built by Han,
MyungHoe, a schemer at King SeJo's time, and commemorated
after his own nickname. Both Chinese characters, 'Ban' in
'BanGujung' and 'Ap' in 'ApGuJung' have the same meaning of
'keeping company,' although they have different sounds.

These two pavilions are where the two prime ministers
spent their old age after retirement, keeping company with
seagulls, but now they are very different from each other.

Whereas 'BanGuJung' still shares its site with seagulls and welcomes migratory birds, all traces of 'ApGuJung' has been lost except for a small stone marker beside the 72th Dong Building of Hyundai Apartment, which merely indicates its original location.

I thought they made as dramatic contrast as did the lives of the two court officers, Hwang, Hee and Han, MyungHoe. Although both were raised to a position of supreme power as prime ministers, one has always been praised as a great lord or wise prime minister, whereas the other has always been called by derogatory names such as a schemer or a power-hungry courtier.

Behind the marvelous work of King SeJong always lay the discreetly hidden assistance of Hwang, Hee, the prime minister, content at times to be considered 'foolish' taking 'an almost invisible seat.' Even while he stayed beside the River ImJin after retirement, living alongside fishermen and taming his seagulls, nobody noticed that this was the former prime minister.

Although Han, MyungHoe married his two daughters into the queen's court and enjoyed being the first-rank courtier four times, he always lived with the premonition of a *coup d'etat*, premeditated murder, and the risk of major crimes. Though he was later exonerated himself from charges against him, he had met a terrible ending in which his corpse was dug up and beheaded.

Whether the prime minister Hwang, Hee had gone into

retirement at DooMoonDong or was sent into exile there, his life was always guided by principles, whereas Han, MyungHoe was a schemer who advanced himself to high office, was guided by self-interest and cleared away rivals.

Episodes relating to both were as different as they were. When two household servants of Hwang, Hee had a quarrel and came to him to tell tales about each other, he responded to the male servant, "You're right," and to the maid, "You're right, too" and sent them back. When his wife reproved his ambiguous positioning, he was well known to have retorted, "You, too, are right."

He was famous for refraining from saying 'you're wrong,' while saying 'yes, you're right' all the time, and tried to pursue great causes rather than stick to trifle matters. While Prime Minister Hwang, Hee was said to be a person with tolerance and humbleness, episodes related to Han, MyungHoe mostly showed the opposite. There is a famous episode in which Kim, SiSeup, one of the six famous loyal retainers in King SeJo's time, changed the letters in Han, MyungHoe's phrases, "When young, I tried to keep the gods of soil and grain of the State, when old, I enjoyed my life lying beside the river and lake." He changed the Chinese characters 'keep' into 'destroy' and 'enjoy' into 'defile,' thus changing the meaning of the phrase into "When young, I destroyed the gods of soil and grain of the State, when old, I defiled the river and lake." People added that Han, MyungHoe was greatly angered and defaced the phrase on the tablet.

As such the difference is great between BanGuJung and ApGuJung which are now less than two hours drive away from each other. What is at issue here may not simply be the difference of people's characters. We may understand it as a difference of political systems: whereas Hwang, Hee was a leading government minister in a cultured period, Han, MyungHoe belonged to a different age of royal despotism. The differences between these two men need to be placed in the context of two different political situations.

Nevertheless we should not forget that 'politics is about organizing and cultivating potential social capacity to its maximum.' I often thought that merely procuring power was nothing to do with politics, but often quite the opposite of this.

I could understand what you wrote: that is, building pyramids was not politics, but demolishing them was. I believe that we have to demolish all types of pyramids in order to restore the earth and to liberate labor.

History, whether we like it or not, will judge everything for sure. What we should do today is only to make a judgement necessary in this moment.

Although the present difference between ApGuJung and BanGuJung does not exactly reflect the judgment of history, we have to find the language that will best express the implications of such a difference. We have to figure out which pyramids we have to demolish and what the earth and labor are that we have to restore.

Whereas ApGuJung was downsized into a small mile stone amidst the surrounding concrete, BanGuJung stilll enjoys the company of seagulls beside the quiet River ImJin. Sitting in the BanGuJung pavilion, I looked down into the absent-minded meandering stream of the River ImJin, and felt as if it rendered the message that demolition of the DMZ would be the supreme political act for it would maximize the potential capacity of the people. BanGuJung was still innocently keeping company with the mountains and rivers of both South Korea and North Korea.

— 1996, from *Trees, Oh, Trees*

The Reason Why You Love Trees More

Pine Tree Forest at SoKwangRi

당신이 나무를 더 사랑하는 까닭 • 282p

Today I send this postcard from the pine tree forest at SoKwangRi which, you told me, was nestled at TaeBaekMountain Range. Entering into the pine tree forest shining in the morning sunlight, I was likely to know the reason why you loved trees more than people. Pine trees that experienced 200, 300, even 500 years of wind and frost packed up the valley. Supporting themselves for such a very long time on the rocks, they filled me with awe and admiration. What a shock to us—who run busily about—to see them stately standing on 'the land of only the size of a pair of shoes'! The pine tree forest teaches a strict lesson like a teacher who waits for me with a whip,— I, who did not achieve anything, despite spending much more than the pine tree.

I think of you who told me that I had to pay 100 won for every star I looked up last night. Today, I may have to pay some money for every pine tree I touch. I think, in fact, in Seoul, we pay more for something less than a pine tree. One day, I went to the scene of KyungBok Palace under restoration. I took it for granted that we should by all means restore the basic structure of the authentic Korean royal palace which the Japanese destroyed and transformed.

But today when I came to this pine tree forest at SoKwangRi, I regret such a thought. To restore the palace, I have heard that we needed two million logs, the enormous quantity of which amounts to 500 eleven-ton trucks of trees. I find it an unreasonable obstinacy on our part to completely restore the palace in pine wood since trees are becoming scarcer today. I can hardly dare imagine the scene of numerous pine trees being cut down and lying on the ground. It may be the same as cutting down several million years of so-called adversities.

It may not only be pine trees that we cut down thoughtlessly. We cut down valuable things to make goods that we can live without, and in reality we do not even hesitate to cut down people for the sake of our own selfish purposes. I am reminded of what you said that the only genuine producers on this earth are plants. Animals are perfect predators, and humans are merely the biggest and most unreasonable consumers of all.

Human production is nothing but consuming what plants have made or digging up what has been buried underground. It is as preposterous as calling cooked rice a production. It is humans who are the subjects of consumption rather than those of production and who, after all, have degenerated into objects of consumption. No place would highlight more clearly the stark violence of economics,—economics that defines nature only as elements of production—than here at

SoKwangRi.

It is an unwritten rule for the workers in the forest reserve not to stand on a stump of a big tree that has been cut. For the anger rising from the cut does harm to the people. How can it only be the pine trees that get angry? I seem to hear the outcry of all the mountains and rivers. As you said, pine trees are like our flesh and blood that, being closest to us, have gone through the same wind and frost.

They say that when a person is born, we exorcise him/her of evil spirits by hanging up a sacred straw festoon made of pine tree branches and when a person dies, we put him/her into the pine tree coffin and bury it into a pine tree field. And the breeze that passes through the pine trees appeases the sorrow of the person in the coffin. As the breeze passes through the pine trees, nothing enters deeper into our emotions than the pine color, pine fragrance, etc. Furthermore, the pine tree, as a symbol of lofty virtues, underpins our spirit, whether it is the straight base of the trunk of *Pinus densiflora erecta* or the bent and warped tree on the craggy hill. In these pines we can read the integrity of our forefathers.

From the past, we have nourished an aesthetics which is completely different from the aesthetics of commodity. All of a sudden I realized that what you truly love is not a pine tree, but some 'person' like a pine tree. I thought of numerous people who watch over the barren land. I thought of you who by now might be in the car and the pine trees in Mt. Nam San that, being confined into an isolated island, would feel thirsty.

Your story makes us sad that the pine trees in Mt. Nam San are about to give up their own survival and hang numerous pine cones to raise their descendants instead. It makes us gloomy that the land in which the pine cones may sprout has become infertile. But more frightening and shocking is the encroachment of acasias and other broad-leaved trees. No sooner have they nourished the barren soil with great difficulty than other tree competitors invade and drive out the pine trees. There is no place where the cold-hearted, brutal logic of relentless competition does not reach.

I came out of the mountain like a scolded child who had left the house. Picking up a pine cone and climbing down the forest, I started to think. I thought of a myth in which a boy who had been devoured by a giant was revived - because he had a pine cone in his hand. If you love a pine tree, you should love the pine cone, too. You have to trust the tenacious potentiality of numerous pine cones.

I send this postcard by writing a phrase I have once written in calligraphy: "When iron was first made, all the trees of the world trembled with fear. Then a thoughtful tree said, 'We do not have anything to be afraid of. Unless we become the handle, iron cannot hurt us.'"

— 1996, from *Trees, Oh, Trees*

Tactless Honesty of Foolish People Changes the World Little by Little

Princess PyungGang at OnDal Mountain Fortress

어리석은 자의 우직함이 세상을 조금씩 바꿔 갑니다 · 286p

I send this postcard today from OnDal Mountain Fortress at 2 Ha Ri, YoungChun Myun, TanYang County, North ChungCheong Province. I wonder how you will read this postcard sent from a historic site built 1400 years ago. OnDal Mountain Fortress is a small fortress with 683m around, but since it has a precipitous peak surrounded like a band, from a distance, it looks like a warrior with a rolled towel tied around his head. It is a strategic fortress with a savor of determined will. And so it did not allow an easy access.

Only a small path leads to the mountain fortress by cautiously opening itself out to the village of 2 Ha Ri. When we reach the middle slope of the mountain, there is a small pavilion called 'SaMoJung.' It is said to be the very place where Princess PyungGang led away the coffin of General OnDal by appeasing his spirit with her tears when it would not move from the earth after his death on the battlefield. It is the spot where people visiting the mountain fortress can meet Princess PyungGang.

I climbed the route from SaMoJung to the rest of the fortress with Princess PyungGang. With the River South

HanGang as the backdrop below and keeping a vigilant eye on SoBaek Mountain Range from afar, I knew right away that OnDal Mountain Fortress was not a fortress that simply lets people in and protects them in an emergency, but was an advanced base designed for recovering the lost territory taken by Silla. It commands a complete overview of the movement of the enemy, though without a lookout tower or a pavilion to defend the sky. Even now I can feel General Ondal's determination that he would not come back to his fatherland without restoring the territory extending to the west of JoRyung and JukRyung.

Looking at the SoBaek Mountain Range that runs in the sky, I was suddenly reminded of your dissatisfaction with the unification of Three Kingdoms by Silla. Considering your remark that by becoming one, the country should have got bigger, the Silla's unification by striking a compromise with the Tang Dynasty gave away the land to the north of River DaeDong. Thus it was not a unification in the true sense of the word, but it signified the loss of the enormous land of the Manchurian Plain.

Such a sense of loss, along with the sad love story of Princess PyungGang and OnDal makes me quite lonesome.

The story of OnDal and Princess PyungGang is often brought up to illustrate the period of social transition in which common people with accumulated wealth could elevate themselves both economically and politically in the process of reorganization of the ruling system. And often his name,

'OnDal, the Fool,' is referred to having been originated from the ruling class's precaution of and contempt for OnDal's obscure birth.

Nevertheless, I believe the story of OnDal and Princess PyungGang—which numerous people created together, and the underlying truth of which many more people have accepted over a long period of time. It conveys the emotion of the people of the time more accurately than any other actual facts. The people's wish and language is contained in Princess PyungGang's resolution of self-reliance with which she chose 'OnDal, the Fool,' of humble birth, but jumping over the indestructible wall of social position, to rise up to become an undaunted general. This is the reason why the tale of OnDal is not simply a story of loyalty of a brash country lad buried in the ideology of the society of the time.

I think a human being's greatest potential is in the leap to surpass the past, to jump over the wall of the society, and finally, to pass over him/herself. While walking on the OnDal Mountain Fortress with Princess PyungGang, I thought of you, looking for 'a person with ability who can make you comfortable and happy.' I felt sorry that you did not give up the dream of becoming a Cinderella.

Today modern society prizes the ability of 'competitiveness.' It can only be gained at the expense of other people's failure and collapse, and in a word, it is as cold-hearted as a hidden knife. Surely we should not complacently submit to the desire to embrace such ability. You may remember, for it was you who said, that the world is divided into two kinds of people; those who are wise and those who are foolish.

Wise people fit themselves to the world, and foolish people try to fit the world to themselves. But we should not forget that ironically the world gradually changes into a better one through the tactless stupidity of those foolish people.

Tactless stupidity, in fact, is the very basis and content of wisdom and sagacity. 'Complacency' ought to be an object of precaution, for it is a river that does not flow. On the contrary, 'discomfort' is running water. The running river is the water of memory that contains numerous sounds and scenes in it and at the same time, the water of hope that does not sleep, but goes forward toward some place of destination.

You mentioned that Princess PyungGang's life does not go beyond the limitation of patriarchy in that it shows an example of the husband's success. Nevertheless, 'to live' is to 'let others live.' It is keeping others alive. And you also added that you cannot become Princess PyungGang since you are not a princess, but 'keeping others alive' is 'keeping other's will to live.' It has nothing to do with worldly success.

In that sense, I think the story of Princess PyungGang does not merely offer a message about a woman's love, but rather 'a message of life' that goes beyond it. I wish someday you would come to this mountain fortress, and meet Princess PyungGang here where the curve of the blue South Han River stream has run for thousands of years.

The Fate of an Individual Person, the Fate of the People

개인의 팔자, 민족의 팔자 · 289p

The accident happened in the middle of DMZ at midnight
in the depths of winter. The sound of a gunfire that tore
through the frozen silence of DMZ snatched away 21years
of his life. In the middle of a squad's nighttime military
operation, someone fired accidentally and a person got shot
in his abdomen. Later investigations found that in fact it was
not an accidental firing. The shot was fired by a member of
the squad aimed at the platoon leader who attempted to go
north over the border. It was an attempt to foil the risky plan.
In the midst of confusion, another platoon member fired at
this person and he, not the originally targeted platoon leader,
fell down bleeding. After the firing, all the platoon members
scampered away like broken glass pieces, and with nobody
around, the place suddenly turned pitch black and deathly
silent. The wounded man barely managed to wrap his bloody
abdomen with his cartridge belt before passing out. When
he came round some time later, surrounded by silent rivers
and mountains in pitch-darkness, strong thirst gripped him.
Crawling on the frozen land with bloody fingernails toward
the faint sound of water, he lost consciousness again. That

was all he remembered.

Early next morning, he was found slumped on the ground a little to the north from DMZ. Carried away on a stretcher, he was sentenced to life imprisonment by a court martial, without being allowed to offer a defence and without a witness to speak for him. It was written in the verdict that he had to be shot because he 'attempted to go over the border to the North Korea' and had been 'in secret communication with the platoon leader.' In March 1989, he was released after 21years of imprisonment, having gone over 'double punishment' as a leftist long-term prisoner. He found the world he came back to had indeed changed a lot, but it was he who had changed much more. His father who had urged him to come home immediately from his long military service to take up farming had died without knowing that his son was in prison. Now his hometown was not a place to return to since he had neither family, nor land to farm. From the third day since his release, without time to reflect on his prison life, he carried a load of 120kg on his back in the cargo of containers in Pusan. One day, he came to see me to Seoul at 2 a. m. in the pouring rain and snow.

While in prison, he had one expectation. It was in fact a hopeless expectation that he would be proven innocent when the platoon leader who went over the border to the North Korea was dispatched to the South as a spy and arrested. As 21 years passed by, he slowly and sadly gave up such an expectation. Instead, he found some comfort from living alongside other prison inmates. With no hope of parole or special release, he spent the entire 21 years in prison. Those who are in prison do not expect parole; it is only the family outside who cling to that hope. While we are shocked at the 27 years imprisonment of Nelson Mandela in another country, in reality, we are ignorant of those long-term prisoners incarcerated for 40 years. Some people may think that the government releases too many prisoners on Liberation Day, Buddha's Birthday, or Christmas, but this is not true. A rough calculation explains: if 3 persons were released from 30 prisons a day upon completion of their term, there would only be 900 people in all who are released. If the government release them a month ahead of the time, then 2700 prisoners would be released at once on some occasion, but on special parole, not that many people are released in reality. This is the reason why prisoners themselves do not expect any special parole.

As an illustration of such situation, there is a sad story of a wife who left her husband, complaining "I cannot wait for you any longer since you are just in the same situation, while others get special parole for being well-behaved prisoners." Anyway, the afore-mentioned person's days were a series of questions and forbearance: "Isn't there any news that the platoon leader was arrested as a spy from the North?" "Everything that happened was my fate. So was the accidental firing. So was my crawling towards the North. Now we have to wait for reunification." Well, what is reunification to him?

What is the division of the country to him? It is something that illuminates the harsh reality of those 21 innocent years. What is reunification to us? As the wish of wishes of so many of our people, it is something that would illuminate the truth of our history.

But what we should do prior to this dreamed-of reunification is clarify the scar of division that cuts into our lives like splinters of a shell. It is not only to clarify our own position as regards reunification, but also to identify the fate of the country that lies deeply embedded in the fate of an individual person.

The standard by which we can judge whether a person's life is honest or not is the quantity of the period that is contained in that person's life. A life that avoids the pain of the period cannot really be called an honest life. Even more so with a life that selfishly takes advantage of the pain of the people. The fate of an individual is bound up with the fate of the people. The fate of the Republic of South Africa and that of Mandela, the fate of Latin America and that of Che Ghevara, the fate of colonized Korea and that of Yu, Kwan-Soon, the fate of politicians and collaborators at the top to nameless laborers including Young-Ja in the red-light district at the bottom, in all these instances the fate of an individual person is certainly deeply connected to the fate of the people. The failure or success of an individual person, though varied in degree, has everything to do with the fate of the people.

To find out the truth means to read how one's life is

connected to other people's lives, and further, to the fate of a whole society and people. The reason why we value truth is that it makes us honestly look at our present, makes us liquidate our past, and begin to confidently walk forward toward the future. For the discovery of truth is the true beginning of the future.

The day before yesterday, this ex-soldier and ex-prisoner began to work as a plumber on a construction site of an apartment complex. Whether the apartment becomes a luxurious one privately owned or an apartment on a fixed-term lease, he is struggling with copper pipes. Without caring what the completed apartment would look like, or without concerning himself with what Seoul is like where he is working, he is simply busy working.

— February 22, 1990, *Hankyoreh Daily Newspaper*

Spring in Nature, Spring in the World

산천의 봄, 세상의 봄 · 293p

Nature shows various signs of a new spring. Warm sunlight, beautiful flowers, swallows in the mild light are easy proof of its arrival. Apart from these signs, there was an ancient poet who tried to prove the arrival of spring by the full freshet of water from an ice-melt water pool.

Indeed, spring sunlight is not consistent because of the likelihood of spiteful late cold snaps; flowers bloom in all seasons and go beyond the seasonal barriers; and swallows are nothing but guests who arrive late for a meal already set on the table. Compared to them, ice-melt freshet water is said to signal a complete withdrawal of winter since the ice that has, up to that point, been stuck firm to the water and to the earth comes off completely. In the poet's mind in which he senses spring in the full flowing water rather than in the sunlight or flowers, there is a calm and cool understanding of the essence of spring, a far cry from the hasty enjoyment of spring landscapes.

In spite of the word, 'living water,' water is not life itself. It is a condition of life. For this reason, it is in the weeds that we find the surest evidence of a new spring every year.

The weeds indeed are proof of spring being not as vain as sunlight, nor as immature as the flowers, and nor as belated as the swallows. In the unspecified weeds, we meet the surest sign of spring for they resolutely sprout on their own in a place nobody looks at and without help from any person who cares for and raises them.

Weeds here refer to nameless grass, of course. Names are something given to them by humans, and once they have names, they have been put under human rule. Nameless weeds in an invisible place is victory itself gained by their own logic, their own existence, and their own strength. While the sunlight is the work of the sky, the flowers are the products of bushes or trees, and the swallows are guests from south of the river, the grass is the sum total of the elements of gold, tree, water, fire and earth, and the embodiment of all the spring. It has consistently grown its life deep in the history of the earth. Leaning on one another, shoulder to shoulder, the grass makes lush meadows in no time, without being taken away by the capricious wind and snow. It bears the place of life where the sunlight stays, the flowers bloom, and the swallows return. The grass is truly the most reliable vanguard of a new spring.

If the spring we find in the sunlight, flowers, and swallows is the spring for those who do not wait, if the spring we mark in the ice-melt freshet water is the spring for those who observe, the spring we sense in the nameless weeds of the field is the spring that numerous people know for sure through their body, while ploughing the spring earth.

In the same way as nature's spring, there are various expressions that prove spring's presence in the world. The sight of the students' backs going out of the school gate with their diploma, the meeting of friends who have come a long way to meet each other, the bright lustre of the tree after an iron saw has passed through; when such little joys of those short moments fill our hearts, then we come to discover a new meaning of life. When we share the pleasure of raising, meeting, and making something, and trust such sympathetic moments and enjoy them with other people, we know that the spring in the world emerges just like the spring in nature. Just as the grass of the field, along with the soil, raises spring, so does everyday's little joy coming together, forming a strong frame of the world and becoming love. Such small pleasure, since it is little, can be looked down on, and taken away, often in return for financial gain, but we know that, thanks to this, we can endure and we can begin again. History testifies that, too.

Politics is something that makes humans grow and come together. It is to help them trust each other in the pleasure of creation. Politics should have people join together in their hearts, and raise and mobilize such abilities as a way of maintaining society on proper footing. It is to open a new stage and to form a new framework. It is to change a wrong stage and to replace a wrong setting. We know that the flowers in the green house are unreal in a sense—green house where the weeds cannot intrude. We also know that birds in a cage cannot testify to the coming of a new spring. A large blossom that cannot support itself, but has to stay upright only with the help of a wooden stick makes us feel sorry. The blossom that is neither attached to the stem, nor to the root, but has been detached and simply belongs to others and to outsiders is not truly a flower. Now the present situation is: Seoul does not turn to the countryside, and industry does not need agriculture; the young and the old, the tenant and the landlord, the ruling party and the opposite party, man and woman, the poor and the rich, they do not respect each other; north and south, east and west, before and after, right and left, they, each of them insists that they are the center.

Where does the spring in the world come from? Spring in nature begins at the nearest spot to earth, for sure. It comes from the choir of wild grass that rises on its own after the ice has gone—the ice that was thoroughly stuck into the flesh of the earth during the winter. The spring in the world is no different from the spring in nature. It comes when disdain and distrust between a person and another person disappears. The spring in the world comes when the barrier of distrust and suppression between a group and another and between a person and another is removed and the potential that has been locked up amidst the distrust and suppression is liberated. Just like the spring in nature, it emerges from the midst of the cry of lush grass in the field. It comes without fail, confidently holding everything in its generous arms.

— March 8, 1990, *Hankyorhe Daily Newspaper*

A Warm Token and An Invisible Hand

따뜻한 토큰과 보이지 않는 손 • 296p

I bought a token in the ticket-booth of a bus stop at YoungDeungPo at dawn. It was a warm token. The body heat of the old man who has been waiting for a customer with a token in his hand is transmitted to my hand. I felt sorry as if I had stolen his warmth. A woman was sitting in the shop window of a red-light district at dawn. She was almost bare, sitting under the red lamp of an alley where there was no visitor. I felt sorry as if I had taken off her clothes. Following such feelings of regret, what stabs my forehead is the question: What made these people sit out on the street at dawn?

By this time, the early-morning market at NamDaeMoon and the labour market at SaDangDong might already have closed and several trains from ChungRyangRi Station and Seoul Station might have left full of passengers. What strikes our face like the gritty wind at an empty station is the question: What forced these people go out into darkness at such an early hour?

Some good but powerless people might feel sorry for such a hard life. Other people who insist without agonizing, might admire this as a strong life force of humans. Still others with the power to analyze, but with no practice may attribute the failure of socialism to this. And the last group of people who only produce without sharing, might praise the greatness of the market system and freedom referring to these people's industry.

Prior to attributing a social problem to an individual, or before explaining the present situation merely in terms of its outward appearance, we should ask questions of the invisible hands that force these people to come out into the unlit alleys at dawn. And we should question their history as well, starting from when they have driven to come out to the dark alley at dawn.

"If we call it sexual assault when one forces others to do something by using violence, by what name can we call the people who do the same by using money?" I cannot forget the heart-rending cry of a brother who had his sister's life ruined. If we call all deliberate enforcement exercised against others, 'violence,' then violence as a concept cannot just be limited to illegal violence involved in organized crime, rape, and burglary. For widespread violence is endemic in every corner of our society in the form of legal violence, or systematic violence. So long as there is no common purpose agreed upon between an individual and another individual, between a class and another class, and between people and other people, principles of coexistence and peace are basically a relationship of suppression and resistance, and thus a kind of violence, unless they accept difference.

When a stone is hit by another stone, we see a flash of light; when an egg hits a stone, it is broken into pieces, and when a stone presses onto grass, the grass is crushed. It does not matter whether it is a stone, or silence. There is no change in the nature of relationship. Whether it is a story of the fire cracker, or the cry of silence, it is only when it reveals a solid reality that it becomes truth.

A token is applied to a bus, the bus joins the cars that jam the streets, the cars come from a car factory, and the car factory exports, and is connected to America and further linked to the opening-up of the country, and by opening-up, we make the country dreary and less existential. And in this country, the old man in the ticket booth meets the hometown he left behind. When the red light in the brothel is turned off, the neon sign of the tavern gets brighter; when the neon sign is turned off, the light at the hilltop slum village shines as high as a building, when the electric light at that hilltop village is off, the light from a far-away factory can be seen. And under the light of this factory in which night shift laborers are working, the woman in the shop window meets the co-workers she left behind.

The distinctive feature of individual or social phenomena can be understood only in connection with the things they are linked with. But the true intrinsic feature is not on view to anybody, and rather tends to be invisible.

The person who feels sorry for the warm body temperature transmitted by a bus token has shown a touch of human feeling. But the position of the poor family concerning about the old man in the ticket booth in the aching winter wind form the entry point into the truth. The person who feels sad for the terrible life of the woman sitting in the shop window is a warm-hearted person. But the helplessness of the poor brother who cannot do anything for such a sister of his is the entry point into the truth.

It is a good and valid perspective to try to understand a phenomenon in its social context, indeed. But more important is not the perspective but the footing. One's standing is much more important, since human eyes, it may be said, are not fixed on their head but on their feet.

When we take a car, we feel irritated by the despotism of the buses; on the contrary, in a bus, we feel vexed at the egotism of the cars that privatize the space of the street. But we only feel vexed. Still walking through our own alleys and eating food from our own cookers in our kitchen all the time, we cannot gain a vantage point from which we can honestly look at the truth. When I mention that 'footing is important,' I mean 'footing' as the entry point into the truth, the entry point that transforms mere facts into the truth. And our cognition is not completed until we finally create the truth.

A bus token, a woman in the shop window, a bonfire in the early morning labour market, etc. all these individual facts we are confronted with are very important. In themselves these must be an aching shock to us that is sufficient to stab our foreheads. But each of these facts is nothing but a piece of a jigsaw puzzle. Truth is created only when such pieces are joined together to complete the whole picture. Truth is an enormous structure that contains innumerable individual facts. It reveals the reality of an invisible hand that forces those people to come out into darkness at dawn.

Facts are completed by creating truth and truth becomes alive by taking root in the facts. We should seek out the very place of their creation. It is the seat where factuality leaps to authenticity. Nevertheless, it cannot be discovered by an individual genius or a few warm-hearted people. It is only to be found by numerous people acting together. Nay, it is not to be found, but to be created, because truth is created from the facts, from countless facts. For truth should be created with the participation of all the people who walk on the same road and who share rice from the same pot. A big yard created by numerous facts coming from all the people is ultimately truth itself.

— March 23, 1990, *Hankyorhe Daily Newspaper*

The Beginning of Bamboo Shoots

죽순의 시작 · 300p

People plant many trees on arbor day every year, but no one plants a bamboo tree. A bamboo tree is not to be planted by some human hand, rather its shoot sprouts only from the root. The most distinguishing characteristic of the bamboo shoot— the bamboo shoot that finishes its life in the soil and starts a life of tree—is that the joints are very short. The very firmness that comes from these short joints in the end provides the power which will hold up the tall straight bamboo tree. Although the bamboo tree is later made into a bamboo spear that holds up a bonfire, and further into the skyscraper bamboo forest that blocks the strong wind by bending its entire body, it starts from the knarly bamboo shoot.

It is not only the bamboo tree. Most trees strengthen their stump with joints or knars. The same thing happens in everyday human life whether it is in the start of a new school, the reopening of an old academy, the beginning of a new job, or it is a new fire we set alight today in yesterday's work place, the very first essential thing that all beginners should do is to create short numerous joints.

In our lives which are not like a tree, what are the joints and how do we make them? Such a question is an urgent task for me to answer, as I am starting anew at the age of 50, as well as for those who have joined the many vigorous social movements that have risen up in this spring, and for ordinary people who intend to make new resolutions.

The reason why mundane affairs are difficult to manage is in the fact that, due to people's divided interests, a new venture will always start in the midst of strong resistance and suppression of the old. In itself this is less serious, but when we lose the minimum flexibility required for the old to learn and accept the new and to achieve improvement, then we are immediately confronted with a destructive crisis. And at such a time, the bamboo shoot becomes only a good prey for predators to feed on.

To be sure, the joints of the bamboo shoot learn from the root. The joints indicate the gesture of adversity in which the root stretches into the dark earth. As an outcome of hard times, they show traces of resistance. At times they may carry the scars of defeat.

Of course we know the life of strong will who rises up and overcomes frustration and defeat. Reading from everywhere in our history, we also come to know the dialectics of success and failure in which sad failure in people's struggle emerges as the dynamics which make a final brilliant triumph possible, having been buried at the bottom of long-lasting history of people.

Setting up goals and processes that fit current objective conditions and the capacity to handle them is the science of the joints, and organizing an achievable goal and winning a fight is the very lesson of the short joint. Not unlike the lesson from *The Art of War*, fighting a good war means winning an enemy who can easily be won. This of course is not the same as the meanness of choosing a weak enemy from the beginning.

As is mentioned in a well-known epigram, "a flash in the pan," whether it is a political party, a group, or an individual, a boisterous and bright beginning is in many cases likely to end up revealing the dull weak finish that has lurked inside. Those who dig up dandelion roots know this. They know however short and unimpressive spring grass may look, its roots stretch deep into the earth. Many trees push down roots into the soil as deep as their height. The bamboo forest keeps wide roots that would go as deep into the earth as all the bamboo trees' heights combined.

More importantly, bamboo trees together share the same root. The very secret of bamboo trees forming a forest is in such sharing of roots. Once the bamboo trees form a forest, then it is no longer a story of an individual tree. It starts a history of the forest that is made up of the solidarity between individual joints of a tree and its roots. It keeps the soil even in the flooding area, turns the flow of the river, keeps snakes at bay, and offers shade and shelter to tigers with its shade. And by that time, though its evergreen leaves are blown by the wind, it can tell when it should lull its leaves to sleep from when it should stand up to the wind with its whole body. Though it may be cut and remain a stump, it keeps itself in soft pipe music; though it may be torn into strips under the edge of the sword, it prevails as the wind that dries the salty sweat of the laboring brow. Before planting a tree in the planting season, we have to think for a moment about which root should we plant ourselves on and how many joints should we grow on our stumps.

— April 6, 1990, *Hankyorhe Daily Newspaper*

Humane Person, Humane Society

인간적인 사람, 인간적인 사회 · 303p

They say those who earn a living by moving their bodies are wasteful, whereas those who earn a living by moving their money are thrifty. But the money the former group earns by moving their bodies is, apart from satisfying immediate needs, not sufficient enough to have extra leftover to accumulate.

Being too wasteful of money signifies easy spending. And the reason for such easy spending is, judging from what I have observed, because some people rely entirely on their labor. They do not think that their labor is exhaustible. They think that they 'can just go on earning.' And another reason, I think, is perhaps because they have close human relationships.

The human relationships formed by labouring people is so deep seated in their lives that they not only work together but spend together as well. The two things go together. Therefore easy spending on the part of those who earn their living by moving their bodies becomes a social need itself in the same way as wearing shoes that are a bit larger than the feet. It cannot really be called a character flaw.

It can rather be seen as a very human characteristic in

that they trust in their own ability and take it for granted that they should live together in harmony with other people. But the word 'earning' is often used quite ambiguously. We call it 'earning' when we get paid for hard work; we apply the term to a non-manual income, such as profits from interest on lending money or profits from real estate speculations. We casually use the word 'earning' even in the case of deceiving and robbing others of their money.

What is the real meaning of 'earning' then? According to a strict economic definition, 'earning' is the portion we get from extra values produced and divided whether it is in the form of interest, benefits, or income without labor. Those who are not directly involved in a productive activity are in effect making part of other people's income their own by whatever methods they use. Therefore, strictly speaking, the word 'earning' should be limited to those situations in which something of direct value has been produced. We ought to change the word 'earn' in the expression, 'money earns money,' into another word.

A Mr Huh who lived in the countryside came to Seoul to visit his second son who worked in a tailor shop and bought a suit for himself.

"Son, how much is this suit?"

"200,000 won, sir. 100,000 won for the cloth and 100,000 won for the labor charge."

Mr Huh went to his eldest daughter who worked in the textile factory.

"Daughter, how much is the cloth for this suit?"

"100,000 won, father. 50,000 won for the thread and 50,000 won for the labor."

Mr Huh this time went to his younger daughter who worked in the spinning mill.

"Daughter, how much does the thread cost for this suit?"

"50,000 won, dad. 20,000 won for the wool and 30,000 won for the labor."

Mr Huh went back to the countryside again and asked his eldest son who raised lambs.

"Son, how much does the wool cost used for a suit?"

"20,000 won, sir. 10,000 won for the lamb and 10,000 won for the labor."

A lamb is born of a lamb and the price of the lamb is the labor charge for raising the lamb.

In the end, the price of the suit Mr Huh wore turned out to be decided by the labor charge of 4 sisters and brothers.

This episode deals not only with a suit but by extension what the reality of clothing, feeding, and sheltering costs society for its nourishment and support.

On May Day, the first of May, we hear laborers' desparate cry demanding their rights on the one hand, and the authority's equal demand for the enforcement of 'law and economic controls' on the other. Hatred, mistrust and collective cynicism common to almost all sections of the society, not only in the field of labor but also in matters relating to the land, housing, schools, and the press, endlessly frustrate creativity and the will of all of us.

Merely 0.2% of the people 'earn' about 80 trillion won without labor in a year: on the one hand poverty and suppression alienate people, on the other hand, such 'surplus' and 'self-indulgence' ceaselessly deprave them. It is impossible to reach an agreement of national sympathy out of such collective distrust and cynicism if we leave the process of unfair concentration of capital as it is.

Progress in society is not achieved by economic wealth only; it is decided by the reality of the people and the relationship they have with one another. If people's trust in their own ability and their creation of a life—which they make together and share with others—cultivate a new man and a new society, then, for this very reason, the goals and ideals of the democratic labor movement deemed to be very humane and progressive.

A farmer shows a striking case of politico-economics by saying that animals are mere consumers and microorganisms, mere aids. He emphasizes that the only genuine producers on the earth are plants. In the same way that growing a tree helps preserve nature, so trusting the producers in society and raising them to be healthy and strong is the surest way to keep society itself in good heart, and further is the only way to save many people from alienation and depravity at the same time.

— May 3, 1990, *Hankyorhe Daily Newspaper*

Human Faces

사람의 얼굴 · 306p

When I listen to the Korean song 'Homesickness,' I think of the River Yuchon around my hometown where I grew up in my childhood. When I listen to another Korean song, 'Climbing Upon the Old Hill,' the only hill I am reminded of is a small hill behind my home village.

The River Yuchon and the small hill behind my home village are places the poets of those songs have never seen or even heard of. In the same way, among those who listen to those songs, nobody would think of the river and the hill that I was reminded of. Even those who grew up with me and shared memory of the same river and hill would not associate the river or the hill with the same songs that I do.

It does not stop with songs. While reading a word in a sentence, we instantly create a scene, a mental image associated with the word. Being engrossed in the meaning of words and thus, not having enough time to reflect, such a world of association spreads far and wide, just like panoramic background image.

For instance, when we ask people what 'scene' can be associated with the word 'nation,' there will be endless answers. Some may associate 'nation' with the country's national flag, others with the place where the commemorative ceremony is held for the uprising on March 1st, and still others with the Olympic Games of 1988, with totem poles, or with rural market places.

It is not only with the word 'nation,' but also with more concrete words such as 'pine tree,' 'pig,' 'car,' 'rice,' 'clothes,' etc.; the scenes associated with them differ greatly from person to person.

In an effort to relieve my tedious long solitary confinement, I once examined the world of association of the words I encounter and use. I checked the worlds of association one by one, as if I was trying to delve into the background of my thoughts. And I found it very surprising.

For example, when I read the word 'joblessness,' the scene that came to my mind was inseparable from concepts I have read in economics textbooks, like 'Keynesian joblessness,' 'Malthusian joblessness,' 'relative population surplus,' 'the rate of joblessness,' and so forth. I have associated the word with economic concepts and theories. I could not help being shocked that such obviously social concepts as 'war,' 'capital,' and 'merchandising goods' seemed to have been deprived of the social relationship that is the essence of their sociality. Even these words with concrete connotations pointed to superficial and formal worlds of association.

From the word 'war,' I was likely to associate with TV screen images showing electronic games played out with patriot missiles and scud missiles; from the word 'capital,' a bank safe; and from the word 'consumer goods,' the display windows of department stores. In short, there was hardly an instant when I could directly associate words with 'people,' the well spring of emotional sympathy.

The shock I felt when I realized for the first time that there was no human face in my raft of association was overwhelming. It felt something like severe loneliness and helplessness. It was a more helpless and more desperate loneliness than I had ever felt in my solitary prison cell in the depths of winter. I felt as if I stood in barren reclaimed land without any co-workers by my side, or without seasoned and trusted tools, but with only a few books and pencils.

If the cool head (reason) that social science students require does not accommodate humans and their relationships with other people, then the result could be nothing more than a pure fiction. Furthermore, if a cool head is not obtained by having an underlying warm heart, my world of ideas can only be called hard-hearted.

I was gaining only the husk from what I had read and thought, and even from what I had experienced through my whole body. I was building only a castle in the air with such a husk. I made a resolution to plant people's faces one by one into my impersonal and cold world of association. I wished to fill an enormous conceptual world of association with rich human details.

First and foremost, I made the conscious decision to imagine a friend in my mind when I hear or read the word 'joblessness.' When 1kg of rice cost 800 won, the unemployed man was ashamed of buying 500 won worth of rice and managed to sustain himself with Ramyon.

In winter, when he stayed in a cold room due to not having enough money to buy briquettes, what tormented him most was not the cold outside, but the glance of the shop owner who looked at him suspiciously wondering whether he bought coal from other stores. When his days' earning was not sufficient to feed all the members of his family, he did not go home since he dared not look at his younger siblings, but sold some of his blood to the university hospital on a cold winter dawn, after sleeping uncomfortably curled up in a cheap dormitory.

The man who, in the recovery room, was eating dry custard and, scribbled on the wall with his finger which was spotted with blood running down his wrist. I decided to think of the friend, and the scribble on the wall he wrote with his blood.

To get rid of conceptuality seems primarily not to make the world of association conceptual. I think, from the word, 'architecture,' it would be less conceptual if we come up with 'forklift,' or 'hammer' or, best of all, 'carpenter' whom we know well rather than the image of a 'building.'

The more abstract the words like 'honesty' or 'conscience,' the more helpless they become in conveying people's lives unless they are associated with people, and accordingly, the more difficult to be humane.

And what is more important, the kind of people associated in our thoughts reflects our own social position and determines the character of our thoughts. Only when the most humane people form the basis of our thinking are we in a position to reflect on and be linked properly to the urgent tasks of today and the many paradoxes of our own society.

Only when such lofty concepts as 'freedom' and 'equality' are filled with images that realistically link them with people, and the people's relationship with one another, can we be liberated from an idle ideological argument or inhumane fetishism.

It is not difficult to think of the aunt and our home town from a pack of dates she sent us. But it is difficult to associate an apple we bought at a supermarket with a particular apple orchard. Furthermore, it may almost be impossible to be reminded of the hard toil of the sweaty laborers who work in a car factory, just by looking at the numerous cars that fill our city streets.

In our minds that do not carry a human face in their associations and in our lives where human relationships have been banished, what would take the place of humans? It is frightening only to think of it.

On the way upward to Mt. Bukhan, two middle-aged men passed by, and I heard them saying "That is not a squirrel. What is it called? (Anyway) I've heard the tail is quite expensive." How twisted our thoughts have become and how barren and fragmented our life is!

We have to discover human faces in the forces that produce and maintain today's material achievement and that permeate through spiritual culture, and realize that our lives are maintained in our interactions with them.

I might have planted people into the world of my associations in an effort to put such an awareness within my reach. But sitting straight in a cold solitary prison cell and delving into the background of my thoughts, sweeping off the various dry grasses preyed on my mind, and even after planting my friends in the empty space, my efforts did not progress far enough. It only left a terrible hole.

Every detail of my terrible failure is too complicated to put down here in words. Looking back, what I did was a necessary thing, but it happened too rashly.

For one thing, I lacked the number of friends whom I could use as a way of underpinning so many concepts. Even if I had enough friends, I may not have been able to place all their faces, merely for the emotional familiarity with them. Due to the familiarity of individual faces, the concepts may have become trivialized or even changed their meaning so as to strengthen their subjectivity. Even the friend who took a seat in my mental concept of 'joblessness' could not illuminate the essential nature of the joblessness of the 1980s.

All too often my effort to pay attention to the rich emotions and sociality surrounding human beings degraded into my interest only in individual people and led me to fail to reach the pinnacle of the sensibility of the period through human beings. And most disappointing of all is that this kind of task simply cannot be adequately fulfilled, while sitting in solitary confinement. It was just like grass that would not take root with even after three or four attempts at planting. In short, I should have met them in the field of life, shoulder to shoulder, and not simply have planted them in my head.

After all, the effort to change my world of association has brought me little consolation for a moment, and rather has left more discomfort and pain behind.

An individual persons' emotion and reality might first carry lean sympathy, but it turned out to be incapable of helping me draw a solid structural reality of our time.

Each person is no doubt someone's friend and belongs to some body's family, but as long as he/she continues to remain only a friend or a family member, our thoughts cannot be extrapolated beyond the sentimental level towards a wider horizon.

Whether it is a world of association, or it is inside the stiff tension of reality, we have to proceed from the people we meet and connect them to the frame of social structure that regulates them.

We may have to start from an individual who is close to us, but if we do not proceed to place this individual and his role in the context of society, we may not be able to recognize the heroes who would transform the paradoxes we are confronted with. Furthermore, we may not even trust our instinct for such capacity.

Nevertheless, I will go on cherishing my friends. For I love the friends I have met, while warming myself in the cold winter in my solitary confinement where whatever practice of comfort is completely absent. However trivial an object may be there deep inside the individual, love embraces it and nourishes it until it is enlarged.

True affection is to walk into the middle of the sharpest paradox of our time, and to be struck frequently by the keenest blade of the sword in the field. That is the only way for our thoughts to step securely on to a material base, and for our lives to take root in the solid earth, and at last for us to complete the integration of ourselves as the 'people of our time' and the 'people of our society.'

Walking always starts with humans and passes through other humans.

— May, 1991, *Social Criticism*

Hardship Is Easier to Share Than Pleasure

어려움은 즐거움보다 함께하기 쉽습니다 · 313p

'Is hardship easier than pleasure to share?'

When asked such a question, we instinctively think it easier to share pleasure. For to share hardship means taking on part of what might be a considerable amount of pain. Pleasure is something to enjoy together without experiencing any pain at all.

Although it is a story of a time when the two Chinese countries of Oh and Wol competed with each other for the dominion of the area around the River Yanz, BumRyo who helped King GuChun of Wol to revenge the humiliation at Mt. HyoGye thought the opposite to be true. He considered King GuChun to be a person with "whom we can share hardship together, but not pleasure" and then left him. Of course, BumRyo's judgment is on the individual person GuChon, but it would equally fit the nature of ordinary people in general, as is expressed in the old saying, "it's difficult to share a rice cake, though it is not so with work."

There might be various reasons for the difficulty of sharing pleasure, but one of the most important reasons is that pleasure makes one self-indulgently and selfishly enjoy from the beginning to the end. And indulgence is nothing but a preoccupation with oneself. Although it may start from celebrating other's pleasure, it ends up with being preoccupied with one's own feelings and interests, where the notion of 'being together' is minimized. Often where pleasure is concerned, we come to lose any exchange of warmth as though we shake hands without taking off our gloves. It is a meeting quite different from the shaking of bare hands in which we come to feel if 'my hand is cold, your hand is warm, and if your hand is cold, mine is warm.' The Chinese Phrase, 'ToSaGuPang', meaning 'after using other's help in one's difficulty, one throws him away' is also what BumRyo left behind. Illicit unions based only on self-interest produce exclusion. So is the beginning and the ending of self-indulgence like bubbles on water.

'New Year's Day' means a 'strange day,' a day on which we feel strange. The expression carries an implication of the need to be prudent. This year we have had a truly strange beginning. We feel strange at the cold economic wave that has brought the winter wind. It is rather difficult to anticipate what kind of hardship will follow this one. In fact, such economic cold wave is not really strange at all. It is a situation which we have caused ourselves, but which we tried to ignore.

There is a single streak of consolation, even in this cold wave. We get a glimmer of consolation from the fact that the bubble will in time be removed, and when the bubble is taken away, the dust will be removed along with it. So we get comfort from the fact that hardship is easier to share than pleasure. Hardship makes us miss those we can share it with. And if we can look straight at the reality we are in, it could provide truly precious reflection on it and comfort for us.

I do not think it desirable to attempt another 'miracle of the Han River' this year, for it is no different from an old, empty catchword, 'to make a bubble in the economy.' It may be as helpless as taking away the foam without removing the stain. In the same way as we long for a good administrator of state when the country is going through times of hardship and a good wife when a household is poor, we have to start by realizing the importance of human beings. We have to realize that the most precious value of life comes from people. We have to rediscover those groups and sub-groups we have completely forgotten and, together with them, build a fortress in which we can endure hardships together. We have to build a fortress of warm-hearted people in order to defend the value of life; we have to construct a strong fortress which can withstand the enormous torrential wave of cold-hearted international financial capital.

Indeed, we have to meet this new year with keen awakening to the stern reality of the world around us and try to desperately return to basics and first principles. We have to start this year by reuniting with our old friends we have long forgotten.

— January 23, 1998, *JungAng Daily Newspaper*

Sharing, Such a Beautiful Life!

나눔, 그 아름다운 삶 • 316p

"When possessions increase, people scatter and when possessions scatter, people come together." That expression has long been a proverb about the relationship between possessions and people. If we do not share possessions with others, people will not gather around us; on the contrary, if we give away our possessions to others, people will gather around us. Such is one long-lasting belief. And this saying shows the true character of our culture of the past that has cherished people more than possessions.

Now that phrase has become an outdated one, so people gather around possessions, and scatter when possessions are scarce.

What is the reason for such a reversal in the relationship between people and possessions? It is simply because we have come to value possessions more than people.

Then, why do we think possessions more important than people? It is a useless question to ask, since we can buy any number of people with possessions.

It may perhaps be extremely stupid to ask questions about something that is as plain as can be. Nevertheless, stupid questions sometimes bring about wise answers, for they contain penetrating reflections on our life and our society.

With a reversed proverb in front of us, we have to think about 'possessions' first. We may have to think in what way 'possessions' of the past are different from those of today.

The 'possessions' of the past were expendable goods in the same way as grains are, meanwhile today's possessions take the form of capital. The difference between real possessions and capital is tremendous. Possessions are the object of consumption, but capital is itself a means of increasing value. Capital's rationale is to increase. In its nature, it is indivisible.

Possessions are for human use, but capital aims at increasing its value. One more decisive difference is that whereas possessions cannot be accumulated indefinitely, capital can be indefinitely stored.

As today's most valued possession, capital is different in nature and form from possessions in the past. It is characterized by endless self-aggrandizement, and it takes the form of indefinite accumulation. The biggest difference between real possessions and capital is that possessions have practical usage, whereas capital's only value is that of exchange.

Whereas possessions complete its mission by being used for human beings, capital repeats and circulates the process of its own ceaseless multiplication by being exchanged with others. It is far from being a common denominator. And at this point, we have only to think of today's reversed saying that 'where possessions gather, people gather.'

Today's expression that 'where possessions gather, people gather,' can be understood as capital creating employment and, in this sense it has indeed become the most common form of the gathering of people.

Here we have to think once more about the gathering of people around capital, whether it is to be called a genuine meeting of people or not, because capital never takes on a human character. The same is true when capital seeks out creative people. Whatever the case, what capital needs after all is only the labor force necessary for value increase. For this reason, today's saying, 'when/where possessions gather, people gather' is nothing but fiction.

Today's possessions are unable to gather people in any meaningful sense. All the aches and pains of people in our time are caused by the conflicts they go through in the work place—the work place where the realization of human value is demoated to the heated struggle of labor liberation.

And in that respect, the old saying, "Only when possessions scatter, people gather," still remains a golden maxim. Gathering people by scattering possessions is not a petty story limited to the sharing of possessions. That may also be a story about our social structure and about our life as human beings.

Encouraging a genuine sharing in social structure is certainly not a small subject that only appeals to charity or sympathy. It requires a change in the nature of capital into that of "possessions" in the old sense and bringing such possessions into reach and use of more people. For constructing a more humane society, by drawing out the discourse of 'sharing' from the audience seat, ought to be the prime aim of the new age.

Today's harsh realities allow the logic of capital and the market to ruin all our human values in the name of 'New Liberalism.' But sharing is a more positive and sensitive alternative agenda for individuals and society. We are probably living in a society in which sharing is not possible in the true sense of the word. We may be living in a barren society where only old, hard-pressed ladies selling sushi can practice 'sharing.' Nevertheless, the more difficult sharing is in practice, the more necessary it is to press honest, forthright and perhaps foolish questions about it.

We have to throw apparently naive questions at ourselves, like 'what do humans live for?' or 'what is money?' We know that the most exhilarating joy comes from human beings and from human interaction, and the most painful sorrow derives from the same source. Nevertheless, we may be panting along a narrow alley where all too often we cannot look back upon the most basic things.

After all, it may not be possessions that we have to share. For possessions and capital just cannot be shared in the conventional sense of dividing things up. They might have been formed just because we had not shared. What we can share may ultimately depend on increase and is limited to something that can be doubled by sharing itself, and not halved. And in this sense, sharing truly becomes love, and gathering, service to people.

Love and service? It is not a loss. Not a bit. For loving and serving are infinitely human. They enrich the resources of our society and embellish our life more beautifully. And they adorn not just the appearance of our society but the very structure of it.

— May 4, 2000, *DongA Daily Newspaper*

The Whistle of a Train in My Memory

내 기억 속의 기차 이야기 · 320p

There is a train I remember only by its whistle. In my 20 years of imprisonment, I spent 15 years at the DaeJeon Correctional Institute. It was heart-breaking to hear the whistle of the night train every night, DaeJeon prison being located close to HoNam Railway. For a prisoner to hear the sound of the train was indeed a heart-rending pain and longing. I thought, "the train with its lightened windows carries people to each person's hometown." It became so strong around the time of traditional holidays that I got sick for longing for the outside world. For about 20 years, the whistle of the train fixed itself into my mind as the sound of homecoming, of going on trips, and of returning to family and loved ones, surely the sound of poetic emotion.

It seems not entirely unrelated to this memory that after I was released from prison, I have tried to take the train, though it was often inconvenient. Especially when the train passes by DaeJeon, I become quite emotional, "Now I am sitting on the train I remember only by the whistle I used to hear."

Recently hearing the news that the railroad that had long been disconnected between South and North Korea would be linked up again, I get guite emotional. This was an emotion very different from the sentimental feeling I had kept in my mind; the feeling that 'Now an enormous world is opening up' made me wonder whether I had not been too complacent in my personal emotion until now.

In 1997, I had an opportunity to travel around the world, with a project sponsored by JungAng Daily Newspaper. My first destination was Spain, a place 16 hours' journey time away. I had thought, 'If a railway has opened from Seoul to P'yang, and if I travel to Spain, passing through China and then Russia, what rich emotion would fill the journey?' Now the very railway in my wish is opening up to the world.

The restoration of the disconnected railway underlines the meaning of reunification. This may not only mean unification of the people. It may also mean opening up a broad view of history that helps us remove the narrow framework in which Korean history has up to now been confined by Japan and America and move us forward directly toward the continent and the world. It will mean establishing a new relationship with the wide world which we have previously been disconnected from.

In such a stream of historical change, recollecting my prison sentiment might perhaps be a shameful thing. Nevertheless, however sentimental such a memory may be, I do not think it too trivial to be forgotten. A recent Japanese movie, entitled "The Railway Man" supports my opinion. In the movie, a simple but beautiful human life around a small railway station in a poor area of the countryside is wonderfully described and touches many people's hearts. Korean modern history has unilaterally run through modernization and economic growth, and looking back on such progress, we feel pain that humanity has either lost its place or has been pushed to the edge.

On reflection, the longing we have nurtured at the scene of small cosmos flowers at a rural railway station or along the long-stretched railroad can lead us to the deepest human truth that any material prosperity or the speed of modern life can never provide. There we catch glimpses of a beautiful life which cannot be exchanged with anything whatsoever.

In the New Millennium, such human truth and humane logic should never be forgotten or marginalized, but should be properly evaluated and reilluminated so that it should fully inspire us in the search for a new civilization and in our way to reunification that is breathlessly stretching out before us. I hope such wishes are wholly carried on the new train that runs toward the new age.

— September, 2000, *Railroad*

Life That Shares Pain

아픔을 나누는 삶 · 323p

While I was travelling around the world and finishing my journey in Sweden, I had to summarize the Welfare State, Sweden in a drawing. I still remember how I struggled until late at night to finish it. I have started to reconsider why it was so difficult to do that. Perhaps it was because my impression of Sweden was unexpectedly complicated.

I was envious when contrasting the harsh realities of Korean life where nothing can be taken for granted, and the high-ranking social welfare system Sweden is proud of, with its various welfare institutes, hospitals, parks, schools, etc. Nevertheless, I felt heavy in my mind because I found it embarrassing to summarize their comfortable but somewhat lifeless life in a drawing.

For instance, if a man who had argued with his wife began to talk about his quarrel to a colleague, the latter would politely cut short his story, recommending him to go to consult a professional counsellor. The professional counsellor would of course suggest a much more rational solution than his colleague was qualified to propose. But it would make for a very dreary scene. An old lady at a well-equipped social welfare institute for the aged would not let me go, though I was a total stranger-traveller. She looked quite lonely, and she missed people. There was a counselling program running in that institute, of course. Nevertheless, I kept asking myself what would make it a really good facility if such up-to-date and conveniently located facilities as this looks so depressingly cold-hearted.

In one word, the dreariness I felt in Sweden might come from a certain lack of sharing pain amongst the residents there. I think fast solutions to the experience of pain is not always desirable. Sharing it might be more important than an instant cure. Getting wet in the rain together would probably be more truly helpful than holding an umbrella for the person in pain. My heart was heavy.

I believe that the sharing of our pain and collaborating in efforts to heal it goes beyond the particular issue of an individual's pain, but enables us to directly confront society and its systems that give rise to pain in the first place. This thought coincides with oriental medicine that looks upon illness as a physiological problem and accordingly tries to strengthen the whole human body, rather than focus narrowly on sickness as a clinical phenomenon calling for the clinical treatment of its revealed symptoms.

Recently a new theory has been brought to my attention which is based on family-related welfare system. I have very positive expectations of this approach in that it draws on existing patterns of human relationships which help us cope with socially induced problems face-to-face, although I do not expect any visible effect in this attempt.

The phrase, "virtue is not lonely, since we always have neighbors" means that those who practice virtue have neighbors. "If someone lives a life of practicing virtue to others until at least into his fifties, he should not be concerned about his life afterward" seems to be a more appropriate interpretation.

In the last chapter of *Lao-tzu*, a phrase appears, "Wise men do not accumulate possessions for their private use; since they have already shared with others, they are alike in having the same sufficiency." Of course, it might be a little too much to expect ordinary people to behave in the same way as wise men. Nevertheless such "wise men" provide us with an ideal goal at which to aim.

Operational problems in any welfare system originate from social structures and systems which prevent the sharing of both pain and possessions. These are the uncomfortable realities in social structures and human relationships.

Korea's welfare problems and their relationship to our country's system might be thought too obvious to mention. All the material surplus of our country goes only into capital accumulation and its ferocious agenda of self-multiplication. Not much space is left for human relationships and human affection.

Nonetheless non-market spaces and non-capitalistic relationships do exist in good shape everywhere in our society and are capable of expansion. We have to openly discuss all these things more in our radical discourse and apply it to making social change a living reality. We need a clearer idea of the process needed for reaching our goal, rather than on hastily achieving the goal itself, and find the true meaning of the process. I hope my rather mixed feelings about systems and practices in Sweden are not mere sentiments brought about to comfort harsh realities in Korean welfare system.

— September, 2000, *Social Welfare Trend*

Beautiful Defeat

아름다운 패배 · 326p

Looking at you meeting the New Year, I am reminded of the extravagant New Millennium festival held exactly a year ago. It might only have happened yesterday with its fireworks embroidering the night sky. I look at your heavy step that leaves for your work place at the beginning of the New Year. Perhaps you represent all of us who enter the New Year.

Looking back, last year was a year spotted with the struggles of numerous people who wanted to keep their rights and interests in all sectors of industry, medicine, agriculture, education, finance, etc. Both to those who leave their work place and to those who are left behind, restructuring roused apprehension rather than hope. Honest communication about what kind of restructuring and trust in the ways proposed for making it happen disappeared. Painful struggles and refusal to take responsibility appear to lie ahead, the very reality of the New Year with which we are confronted. Confused about whether the year 2000 or the year 2001 marks the start of the New Millennium, we certainly appear to be starting the New Year without having anything new, and we feel stupefied about what we should do and how we should proceed.

You said that you have to take your chances on everything and see whether you win or lose. And you also said that once started, you have to win the fight. But to our regret, the tragedy of fighting is that, obviously, not everybody involved can win. The reason why I feel appalled at the sight of you who go out to the battle field is because I know that your fighting is a lonely fight and that, because it is a lonely fight, you would finally be wounded and defeated. Your enemy is very stubborn. You are standing against layers and layers of walls such as capital, power, public opinion, the invisible market, and multi-national capital.

I would rather wish for you 'a beautiful defeat,' one that might be a defeat today but a victory tomorrow. A beautiful defeat can perhaps be a victory for all the people. For this reason, I told you to take pains concerning the way to be defeated. I asked you to bear in mind what, not who, you are going to fight against. Never choose an individual enemy. For all the burdens of the restructuring of the four domains of enterprise, public, labor and finance are on your shoulders and encircle you. For that very reason, we have to clarify 'what' we are fighting against as our enemy and make widely known our reason for fighting.

You told me that you did not understand the reason why only enterprise should survive these days. You also confessed to me that you did not know the reason why public enterprise and financial institutions should yield a good profit. You said that you did not trust the logic that in a social system divided at a ratio of 20 to 80, 20 should survive first so that the other 80 might also survive someday. I just like you, do not understand such logic in which national burden is transferred to ordinary people's load under the name of the public. It is not only you and me. It is the same with all those who silently endure the pain of our system.

You have continuously to raise questions: What is the purpose of economic development? What is the purpose of people's lives? You have to try to reveal what we have completely forgotten. You have to insist that unless we have genuine renovation, and not simply intervention, and unless we have reforms not just of the profit structure but of the very basis of the people's economy, we will surely be confronted with a massive economic crisis. Your fight should be a fight that declares such basic principles. It should not be a lonely defeat but a beautiful defeat that will evoke people's sympathy and move them, and that in the end, will surely succeed.

The story of defeat we share at the beginning of a New Year might seem appalling. But I believe that you should read this as a story of victory and not one of defeat.

I wish you a Happy New Year. Just like all beginnings, the New Year should start anew to make itself new. You have to plant new seeds 'here' and 'today.' I am writing down a passage I have written to you before.

As It Was in the Beginning

Like a little bird that meets the sky for the first time,
Like a new sprout that treads on the earth for the first
time,
We, even in a winter evening,
When the day fades and darkness spreads,
We always start a new day,
As of a new morning,
As of a new spring,
And as of a new beginning."
(from *For the First Time*)

— January 4, 2001, *JungAng Daily Newspaper*

1부

한 포기 키 작은 풀로 서서

수도꼭지의 경제학

The Economics of Taps · 13p

C교도소 4동 상층의 세면장에는 수도꼭지가 8개 있었습니다. 그러나 사용할 수 있는 꼭지는 2개뿐이었습니다. 나머지 6개는 T자형의 손잡이를 뽑아 버리고 스패너로 단단히 조여 놓았기 때문에 먹통이었습니다. 맨손으로는 그것을 풀 수가 없도록 해놓았습니다. 물을 절약하기 위해서임은 말할 나위도 없습니다. 재소자는 너나없이 "물 본 기러기"이기 때문이었습니다.

교도소에서 귀하기로 말할 것 같으면 밥과 맞먹는 것이 물입니다. 단 한번도 물을 물 쓰듯 써 보지 못한 우리들로서는 너무나도 당연한 욕심입니다. 하루 세 끼 설거지에서부터 세수, 빨래는 물론이고 목욕은 감히 생심을 못한다 하더라도 냉수마찰은 어떻게든 하고 싶기도 합니다. 기회만 있으면 방에 있는 주전자나 물통은 물론이고 그릇이란 그릇마다 물을 채워 놓는 것이 일이었습니다. 물을 많이 챙겨 놓은 날은 마음 흐뭇하기가 흡사 그득한 쌀 뒤주를 바라보는 심정이었습니다. 그만큼 물이 귀했습니다.

여름철은 말할 필요도 없고 겨울이라고 해서 찬물 목욕이나 담요 빨래를 시켜만 준다면 마다할 사람이 없는 처지이고 보면 물을 가운데에 둔 관官과 재소자의 줄다리기가 사철 팽팽하지 않을 수 없는 것입니다.

8개의 수도꼭지 중에서 2개만 남기고 나머지 6개를 먹통으로 잠가 버리는 것은 어느 교도소건 관례가 되다시피한 통상적인 통제의 방법

　　　　　　　　1부　한 포기 키 작은 풀로 서서

이었습니다. 이것은 이를테면 원천을 봉쇄하는 가장 확실한 방법이기 때문입니다.

이러한 방법이 언뜻 가장 완벽한 것 같지만 사실은 그렇지 못하였습니다. 어느새 엄청난 누수가 일어나고 마는 것입니다.

맨 먼저 일어난 사건은 성하게 남겨 둔 수도꼭지의 손잡이가 분실되기 시작하는 사건이었습니다. 처음 몇 번은 관에서 없어진 손잡이를 다시 갖다가 꽂아 놓았습니다. 그러나 다시 꽂기가 무섭게 이내 없어지고 말았습니다. 수도꼭지는 어느 것이나 마찬가지로 윗부분의 나사 한 개만 풀면 손잡이가 쉽게 분해될 수 있는 얼개였으며, 손잡이만 가지면 먹통 꼭지를 틀어서 얼마든지 물을 얻을 수 있기 때문이었습니다.

손잡이의 분실 사건이 계속되자 이제는 아예 나머지 성한 꼭지의 손잡이마저 분리하여 담당 교도관이 책상 서랍에 보관하였습니다. 이제는 물을 합법적으로 쓰기 위해서도 절차를 밟아야 했습니다. 숨겨 둔 손잡이의 가치는 더욱 커졌습니다. 다른 출역사동의 세면장에 있는 수도꼭지의 손잡이가 분실되기 시작하였고 공장이건 목욕탕이건 심지어 직원 화장실에 이르기까지 수도꼭지가 분실되지 않는 곳이 없었습니다.

우리 방에도 물론 비밀리에 입수하여 감추어 두고 사용하는 수도꼭지가 한 개 있었습니다. 그리고 제법 끝발이 센 K군이 자기 혼자만 사용하는 손잡이가 한 개 더 있었습니다. 4동 상층의 11개 사방 가운데 수도꼭지를 한두 개 감추어 두고 있지 않은 방은 하나도 없었을 것입니다. 그리고 '잘 나가는 방'에는 두어 개씩 보유하고 있기도 하였습니다. 심지어는 2개 또는 3개씩의 개인용 꼭지를 가지고 있는 사람도 있었습니다. 혹시 분실할 수도 있고 검방이나 검신 때 발각되어 압수될지도 모르기 때문에 여벌로 한두 개쯤 더 가질 필요가 있는 것입니다.

수도꼭지는 어느덧 친한 친구나 평소 신세를 진 사람에게 귀한 선물이 되기도 하였고 더러는 상품이 되어 다른 물건과 교환되기도 하였습니다. 수도꼭지는 이제 수도꼭지 이상의 가치를 갖게 되었습니다. 수도꼭지는 물을 떠나서도 가치를 지니게 되었습니다.

4동 상층에 몰래 감추어 두고 사용하는 수도꼭지가 모두 몇 개인지 정확하게는 알 수 없지만 대충 계산해 보더라도 11개 방마다 한두개씩 그리고 끝발 있는 재소자가 네댓 명이라 치면 거진 20여 개의 수도꼭지가 있는 셈이 됩니다. 세면장에 설치되어 있는 8개의 수도꼭지에 비하면 무려 두어 갑절이나 됩니다. 그럼에도 불구하고 수도꼭지는 여전히 부족하였습니다. 우선 그 방에 몰래 감추어 두고 쓰는 것이기 때문에 그 꼭지의 관리자한테 일일이 허락을 받아야 하였고, 개인용을 빌리기도 한두 번이지 미안하고 속상하는 일이었습니다.

4동 상층의 1백여 명의 재소자가 불편이나 불평 없이 물을 쓸 수 있기 위해서는 대체 몇 개의 수도꼭지가 있어야 하는지 계산해 보았습니다. 1인당 1개에다 분실이나 압수에 대비한 여벌 1개씩 도합 2백여 개의 수도꼭지가 필요하다는 계산입니다. 8개의 수도꼭지에 비하여 무려 2, 30배의 수도꼭지가 필요한 셈입니다. 이처럼 많은 양이 있더라도 물의 사용은 일단 불법임에는 변함이 없습니다. 실제로 담당 교도관에게 적발되어 수도꼭지를 압수당하고 경을 친 사람도 더러 있었습니다. 대개는 담당 교도관에서 밉게 보인 사람이거나 만만하게 보인 약한 사람이었습니다. 그러나 사람들은 그를 일컬어 '재수 없어' 걸렸다고 했습니다.

어쨌건 원천을 봉쇄하여 물을 통제하려던 애초의 계획은 수포로 돌아가고 8개의 수도꼭지를 모두 열어 놓는 것보다 더 많은 물이 누수되고 있었습니다. 스패너로 단단히 묶어 둔 6개의 먹통 수도꼭지도 아무 소용이 없었습니다. 맨손인 사람에게만 철벽일 뿐 수도꼭지를 가지고 있는 사람한테는 수청 기생처럼 쉽게 몸을 풀었음은 말할 필요가 없었습니다.

이처럼 수많은 수도꼭지에도 불구하고 대부분의 사람들에게는 물은 여전히 부족하였고 불편하였습니다. 물의 필요는 수도꼭지에 대한 욕심으로 바뀌어 남들의 비난을 받았고 스스로도 부끄러웠습니다.

이 이야기는 물론 징역살이의 이야기이고 교도소 안에나 있는 '물 본 기러기'들의 물 욕심에 대한 이야기이기도 합니다. 그러나 나는 지금도 서울의 도처에서 문득문득 그 씁쓸한 수도꼭지의 기억을 상기하게 됩니다. 수많은 자동차들로 체증을 이룬 도로의 한복판에서 걷는 것보다 더 느리게 꿈틀대는 버스 속에 앉아 있을 때 나는 예의 그 수도꼭지를 생각합니다. 분양 아파트의 모델 하우스에 붐비는 인파 속에서 나는 먹통 수도꼭지 앞에서 마른 침을 삼키던 예의 그 갈증을 생각합니다.

8개의 수도꼭지로 될 일이 20개, 30개의 수도꼭지로도 안 되는 일은 교도소가 아닌 바깥 세상에도 얼마든지 있습니다. 자동차도 그렇고 아파트도 그렇고 땅도 그렇고 대학 입시도 그렇고 화려한 백화점의 수많은 상품들도 그렇습니다. 나는 낯선 서울 거리를 걸으며 버릇처럼 수도꼭지를 상기합니다. 맨손으로 수도꼭지를 비틀다가 하얗게 핏기가 가신 엄지와 검지의 통증을 생각합니다. 그리고 그때마다 잘못된 소유, 잘못된 사유가 한편으로 얼마나 엄청난 낭비를 가져오며, 다른 한편으로 얼마나 심한 궁핍을 가져오는가를 생각합니다. 망망대해 위를 날으는 목마른 기러기를 생각합니다.

죄수의 이빨

계수님께

A Prisoner's Teeth • 18p

치과에 가서 이빨을 뽑으면 뽑은 이빨을 커다란 포르말린 유리병에 넣습니다. 얼마 동안이나 모았을까 두어 됫박은 족히 됨직한 그 많은 이빨들 속에 나의 이빨을 넣고 나면 마음 뒤끝이 답답해집니다.

지난번에는 물론 많이 흔들리는 이빨이기도 했지만, 치과에 가지 않고 실로 묶어서 내 손으로 뽑았습니다. 뽑은 이빨을 호주머니에 넣고 다니다가 어느날 운동시간에 15척 담 밖으로 던졌습니다. 일부분의 출소입니다. 어릴 때의 젖니처럼 지붕에 던져서 새가 물고 날아갔다던 이야기보다는 못하지만 시원하기가 포르말린 병에 넣는 것에 비할 바가 아닙니다.

10년도 더 된 이야깁니다만 그때도 치과에 가지 않고 공장에서 젊은 친구와 둘이서 실로 묶어 뽑았습니다. 그러나 그때는 담 곁에 갈 수가 없어서 바깥으로 내보낼 방법이 없었습니다. 궁리 끝에 마침 우리 공장에서 작업하고 있던 풍한방직 여공들의 작업복 주머니에 넣어서 제품과 함께 실려 내보낸 일이 있습니다. 지금 생각하면 매우 미안한 일입니다. 아무리 종이로 예쁘게(?) 쌌다고 하지만 '죄수의 이빨'에 질겁했을 광경을 생각하면 민망스러운 마음 금할 길이 없습니다.

나는 징역 사는 동안 풍치 때문에 참 많은 이빨을 뽑았습니다. 더러는 치과의 그 유리병 속에 넣기도 하고, 더러는 교도소의 땅에 묻기도 하고 또 어떤 것은 담밖으로 나가기도 했습니다.

생각해보면 비단 이빨뿐만이 아니라 우리가 살아간다는 것이 곧 우리들의 심신의 일부분을 여기, 저기, 이 사람, 저 사람에게 나누어 묻는 과정이란 생각이 듭니다. 무심한 한마디 말에서부터 피땀어린 인생의 한 토막에 이르기까지 혹은 친구들의 마음 속에, 혹은 한 뙈기의 전답田畓 속에, 혹은 타락한 도시의 골목에, 혹은 역사의 너른 광장에……, 저마다 묻으며 살아가는 것이라 느껴집니다.

돌이켜보면 나의 경우는 나의 많은 부분을 교도소에 묻은 셈이 됩니다. 이것은 흡사 치과의 포르말린 병 속에 이빨을 담은 것처럼 답답한 것이기도 합니다.

교도소가 닫힌 공간이라면, 그래서 포르말린 병처럼 멎은 공간이라면 그러한 느낌도 당연한 것이라 할 수 있습니다. 그러나 또 한편 돌이켜보면 교도소는 세상으로부터 동떨어진 곳이 아닐 뿐 아니라 도리어 우리 사회, 우리 시대와 가장 끈끈하게 맺어져 있는, 그것의 어떤 복판을 이루고 있는 것이 사실입니다.

이를테면 피라미드를 거꾸로 세웠을 경우 그 꼭지점이 땅에 닿는 자리, 즉 피라미드의 전 중압全重壓이 한 점을 찌르는 바로 그 지점에 교도소가 위치하고 있습니다. 이처럼 교도소는 사회의 모순 구조와 직결된 공간임으로 해서 전 사회를 향하여 활짝 열려 있는 공간이라 믿고 있습니다.

그럼에도 불구하고 교도소에 묻은 나의 20여 년의 세월이 쓸쓸하게 느껴지는 까닭은 무엇인가. 포르말린 병의 그 답답함이 연상되는 까닭은 무엇인가. ……징역살이라 하여 한시도 끊임없이 내내 자신을 팽팽하게 켕겨놓을 수도 없지만 어느새 느슨해져버린 의식과 비어버린 가슴에 새삼 놀라게 됩니다. 이것은 깨어 있지 못한 하루하루의 누적이 만들어놓은 공동空洞입니다. 피라미드의 전 중압이 걸려 있는 자리에서 나타나는 의식의 공동화空洞化 — 역시 교도소가 만만치 않음을 실감케 합니다.

묻는다는 것이 파종播種임을 확신치 못하고, 나눈다는 것이 팽창임을 깨닫지 못하는, 아직도 청산되지 못한 나의 소시민적 잔재가 치통보다 더 통렬한 아픔이 되어 나를 찌릅니다.

계수님께 편지 쓸 때면 으레 약간의 망설임이 없지 않습니다. 징역이야기만 가득한 나의 편지가 계수님의 생활에 무엇이 되어 나타나는지, 공연히 계수님의 방 창유리나 깨뜨려 찬바람 술렁이게 하는 것이나 아닌지, 걱정이 없지 않습니다. 그러나 계수님의 편지와 그 편지에 실려오는 계수님의 면모와 생활자세는 이러한 나의 망설임이나 걱정을 시원하게 없애줍니다.

1987. 5. 28.

이웃의 체온
계수님께

The Body Temperature of Neighbors • 21p

수인들은 늘 벽을 만납니다.

통근길의 시민이 'stop'을 만나듯, 사슴이 엽사를 만나듯, 수인들은 징역의 도처에서 늘 벽을 만나고 있습니다. 가련한 자유의 시간인 꿈속에서마저 벽을 만나고 마는 것입니다. 무수한 벽과 벽 사이, 운신도 어려운 각진 공간에서 우리는 부단히 사고의 벽을 헐고자 합니다. 생각의 지붕을 벗고자 합니다. 흉회쇄락胸懷灑落, 광풍제월光風霽月. 그리하여 이윽고 '광야의 목소리'를, 달처럼 둥근 마음을 기르고 싶은 것입니다.

아버님 서한에 육년래六年來의 혹한酷寒이라고 하였습니다만 그런 추위를 실감치 않았음은 웬일일까. 심동深冬의 빙한氷寒, 온기 한 점 없는 냉방에서 우리를 덮어 준 것은 동료들의 체온이었습니다. 추운 사람들끼리 서로의 체온을 모으는 동안 우리는 냉방이 가르치는 '벗'의 의미를, 겨울이 가르치는 '이웃의 체온'을 조금씩 조금씩 이해해가는 것입니다.

이제 입춘도 지나고 머지않아 강물이 풀리고 다사로운 춘풍에 이른 꽃들이 필 무렵, 겨우내 우리의 몸속에 심어 둔 이웃들의 체온이 송이송이 빛나는 꽃들로 피어날는지……. 인정人情은 꽃들의 웃음소리.

구정 때 보낸 편지와 영치금 잘 받았습니다. 염려하는 사람이 한 사람 더 늘었다는 기쁨은 흡사 소년들의 그것처럼 친구들에게 자랑하고 싶고 보이고 싶고…….

　제수와 시숙의 사이가 '어려운 관계'라고들 하지만, 그것은 우리 시
대의 것은 아니라고 믿습니다. 현재로서는 물론, 동생을 가운데 둔 관계
이며 '생활의 공유'를 기초로 하지 않은, 또 그만큼 인간적 이해가 부족
한 관계라는 사실을 없는 듯 덮어 두자는 것은 아닙니다. 그러나 앞으로
는 어차피 가족의 일원으로서 생활을 공유하지 않을 수 없다는 장래의
유대를 미리 가불하기도 하고, 또 편지를 쓰면 '소식의 공유'쯤 당장부
터도 가능하다는 점에서 '어려운 관계'의 그 어려움이 차차 가시리라
생각합니다. 서로의 건투를 빕니다.

서도의 관계론關係論
아버님께

Theory of Relationship in Calligraphy • 23p

제가 서도書道를 운위하다니 당구堂狗의 폐풍월吠風月 짝입니다만 엽서 위의 편언片言이고 보면 조리條理가 빈다고 허물이겠습니까.

일껏 붓을 가누어 조신해 그은 획이 그만 비뚤어 버린 때 저는 우선 그 부근의 다른 획의 위치나 모양을 바꾸어서 그 실패를 구하려 합니다.

이것은 물론 지우거나 개칠改漆하지 못하기 때문이기도 하지만 실상 획의 성패란 획 그 자체에 있지 않고 획과 획의 '관계' 속에 있다고 이해하기 때문입니다. 하나의 획이 다른 획을 만나지 않고 어찌 제 혼자서 '자'字가 될 수 있겠습니까. 획도 흡사 사람과 같아서 독존獨存하지 못하는 '반쪽'인 듯합니다. 마찬가지로 한 '자'가 잘못된 때는 그 다음 자 또는 그 다음다음 자로써 그 결함을 보상하려고 합니다. 또 한 '행'行 의 잘못은 다른 행의 배려로써, 한 '연'聯의 실수는 다른 연의 구성으로 써 감싸려 합니다. 그리하여 어쩌면 잘못과 실수의 누적으로 이루어진, 실패와 보상과 결함과 사과와 노력들이 점철된, 그러기에 더 애착이 가는, 한 폭의 글을 얻게 됩니다.

이렇게 얻은 한 폭의 글은, 획, 자, 행, 연 들이 대소, 강약, 태세太細, 지속遲速, 농담濃淡 등의 여러 가지 형태로 서로가 서로를 의지하고 양보하며 실수와 결함을 감싸 주며 간신히 이룩한 성취입니다. 그 중 한 자, 한 획이라도 그 생김생김이 그렇지 않았더라면 와르르 얼개가 전부

196

무너질 뻔한, 심지어 낙관落款까지도 전체 속에 융화되어 균형에 한몫 참여하고 있을 정도의, 그 피가 통할 듯 농밀한 '상호 연계'와 '통일' 속에는 이윽고 묵과 여백, 흑과 백이 이루는 대립과 조화, 그 '대립과 조화' 그것의 통일이 창출해 내는 드높은 '질'質이 가능할 것입니다. 이에 비하여 규격화된 자, 자, 자의 단순한 양적 집합이 우리에게 주는 느낌은 줄 것도 받을 것도 없는 남남끼리의 그저 냉랭한 군서群棲일 뿐 거기 어디 악수하고 싶은 얼굴 하나 있겠습니까.

유리창을 깨뜨린 잘못이 유리 한 장으로 보상될 수 있다는 생각은, 사람의 수고가, 인정이 배제된 일정액의 화폐로 대상代償될 수 있다는 생각만큼이나 쓸쓸한 것이 아니겠습니까. 획과 획 간에, 자와 자 간에 붓을 세우듯이, 저는 묵을 갈 적마다 인人과 인 간間의 그 뜨거운 '연계' 위에 서고자 합니다.

춥다가 아직 덥기 전의, 4월도 한창 때, 좋은 시절입니다.

두 개의 종소리

아버님께

Two Kinds of Bell—Sounds · 25p

새벽마다 저는 두 개의 종소리를 듣습니다. 새벽 4시쯤이면 어느 절에
선가 범종梵鍾소리가 울려오고 다시 한동안이 지나면 교회당의 종소리
가 들려옵니다. 그러나 이 두 종소리는 서로 커다란 차이를 담고 있습니
다. 교회종이 높고 연속적인 금속성임에 비하여, 범종은 쇠붙이 소리가
아닌 듯, 누구의 나직한 음성 같습니다. 교회종이 새벽의 정적을 휘저어
놓는 틈입자闖入者라면, 꼭 스물아홉 맥박마다 한 번씩 울리는 범종은
'승고월하문'僧敲月下門의 '고'敲처럼, 오히려 적막을 심화하는 것입니
다. 빌딩의 숲 속 철제의 높은 종탑에서 뿌리듯이 흔드는 교회 종소리가
마치 반갑지 않은 사람의 노크 같음에 비하여, 이슬이 맺힌 산사山寺 어
디쯤에서 땅에 닿을 듯, 지심地心에 전하듯 울리는 범종소리는 산이 부
르는 목소리라 하겠습니다. 교회 종소리의 여운 속에는 플래시를 들고
손목시계를 보며 종을 치는 수위의 바쁜 동작이 보이는가 하면, 끊일 듯
끊일 듯하는 범종의 여운 속에는 부동不動의 수도자가 서 있습니다.

범종소리에 이끌려 도달한 사색과 정밀靜謐이 교회 종소리로 유리
처럼 깨어지고 나면 저는 주섬주섬 생각의 파편을 주운 다음, 제3의 전
혀 엉뚱한 소리—기상 나팔소리가 깨울 때까지 내쳐 자 버릴 때가 많습
니다. 그러나 고달픈 수정囚情들이 잠든 새벽녘, 이 두 개의 종소리 사이
에 누워 깊은 생각에 잠길 수 있다는 것은 작지만 기쁨이 아닐 수 없습

니다.

저는 불제자佛弟子도 기독도基督徒도 아닙니다. 이것은 제가 '믿는다'는 사고 형식에는 도시 서툴기 때문이라고 생각됩니다. 제게도 사람을 믿는다거나 어떤 법칙을 믿는 등의 소위 '믿는다'는 사고 양식이 없는 것은 아니지만 그런 경우의 믿음은 어디까지나 그 사람의 인격이나 객관화된 경험에 대한 이해와 평가의 종합적 표현일 뿐 결코 '이해에 기초하지 않은 믿음'을 일방적으로 수용하는 태도와는 별개의 것이라 생각됩니다. 결국 범종과 교회종에 대한 포폄褒貶이 저의 종교적 입장과는 인연이 먼 것이며 그렇다고 일시적인 호오好惡나 감정의 경사傾斜에도 관계가 없는 것입니다. 이것은 아마 지금까지 저의 내부에 형성된 의식意識의 표출이었는지 모르겠습니다. 그렇기 때문에 저는 이 두 개의 종소리 사이에 누워 저의 의식 속에 잠재해 있을 몇 개의 종소리에 귀 기울여 봅니다. 외래 문물의 와중에서 성장해 온 저희 세대의 의식 속에는 필시 꺼야 할 이질異質의 종소리들이 착종錯綜하고 있음에 틀림없습니다.

매직펜과 붓
아버님께

'Magic Pen' and Calligraphy Brush • 27p

오늘이 입추立秋. 기승을 부리던 더위도 어젯밤에 폭우를 맞더니 정말 오늘부터는 가을로 접어들려는지 아침 햇살이 뜨겁지 않습니다.

우송해 주신 먹과 화선지 그리고 아버님의 하서 모두 잘 받았습니다. 어머님께옵서도 안녕하시고 가내 두루 평안하실 줄 믿습니다.

저는 주로 붓으로 글씨를 쓰고 있습니다만 가끔 '매직펜'으로 줄을 긋거나 글씨를 쓸 일이 생깁니다. 이 매직펜은 매직잉크가 든 작은 병을 병째 펜처럼 들고 사용하도록 만든 편리한 문방구文房具입니다. 이것은 붓글씨와 달라 특별한 숙련이 요구되지 않으므로, 초보자가 따로 없습니다. 마치 피아노의 건반을 아무나 눌러도 정해진 음이 울리듯, 매직펜은 누가 긋더라도 정해진 너비대로 줄을 칠 수 있습니다. 먹을 갈거나 붓끝을 가누는 수고가 없어도 좋고, 필법筆法의 수련 같은 귀찮은 노력은 더구나 필요하지 않습니다. 그뿐만 아니라 휘발성이 높아 건조를 기다릴 것까지 없고 보면 가히 인스턴트 시대의 총아라 할 만합니다. 그러나 저는 이 모든 편의에도 불구하고 이것을 좋아하지 않습니다. 종이 위를 지날 때 내는 날카로운 마찰음—기계와 기계의 틈새에 끼인 문명의 비명 같은 소리가 좋지 않습니다. 달려들듯 다가오는 그 자극성의 냄새가 좋지 않습니다.

붓은 결코 소리내지 않습니다. 어머님의 약손같이 부드러운 감촉이,

수줍은 듯 은근한 그 묵향墨香이, 묵의 깊이가 좋습니다. 추호秋毫처럼 가늘은 획에서 필관筆管보다 굵은 글자에 이르기까지 흡사 피리 소리처럼 이어지는 그 폭과 유연성이 좋습니다. 붓은 그 사용자에게 상당한 양의 노력과 수련을 요구하지만 그러기에 그만큼의 애착과 사랑을 갖게 해줍니다. 붓은 좀체 호락호락하지 않는 매운 지조의 선비 같습니다.

매직펜이 실용과 편의라는 서양적 사고의 산물이라면 붓은 동양의 정신을 담은 것이라 생각됩니다. 저의 벼룻집 속에는 이 둘이 공존하고 있습니다만, 이것은 제가 소위 '동도서기'東道西器라는 절충의 논리를 수긍하는 뜻이 아닙니다.

절충이나 종합은 흔히 은폐와 호도糊塗의 다른 이름일 뿐, 역사의 특정한 시점에서는 그 사회, 그 시대가 당면하고 있는 객관적 제조건에 비추어, 비록 상당한 진리를 내포하고 있는 주장이라 하더라도 그 경중, 선후를 준별하고 하나를 다른 하나에 종속시키는 실천적 파당성派黨性이 도리어 '시중'時中의 진의이며 중용의 본도本道라고 생각됩니다.

저는 역시 붓을 선호하는 쪽입니다. 주로 도시에서 교육을 받아 온 저에게 있어서 붓은 단순한 취미나 여기餘技라는 공연한 사치로 이해될 수는 없는 것입니다.

옥창의 풀씨 한 알
계수님께

A Grass Seed on the Window Pane of a Prison Cell • 30p

우리 방 창문 턱에
개미가 물어다 놓았는지
풀씨 한 알
싹이 나더니
어느새
한 뼘도 넘는
키를 흔들며
우리들을
가르치고 있습니다.

정국추추황 자모년년백

庭菊秋秋黃 慈母年年白

(뜰의 국화는 가을마다 노랗고
어머니의 머리는 해마다 희어지네.)

인디언의 편지
아버님께

An Indian Chief's Letter • 31p

8일부 하서 받았습니다. 그간 어머님을 비롯하여 가내 두루 평안하시리라 믿습니다. 금년은 매우 따뜻한 겨울이었습니다. 연일 봄비가 내려 주위가 축축합니다만, 춘도생 만물영春道生 萬物榮, 이 축축함이 곧 꽃이 되고 잎이 되는 것이 아니겠습니까.

며칠 전에는 1885년에 아메리카의 한 인디언이 미국 정부에 보낸 편지를 읽었습니다. 그 속에는 이런 구절들이 있습니다.

"당신(백인)들은 어떻게 하늘을, 땅의 체온을 매매할 수 있습니까."

"우리가 땅을 팔지 않겠다면 당신들은 총을 가지고 올 것입니다. ……그러나 신선한 공기와 반짝이는 물은 기실 우리의 소유가 아닙니다."

"갓난아기가 엄마의 심장의 고동소리를 사랑하듯 우리는 땅을 사랑합니다."

어머니를 팔 수 없다고 하는 이 인디언의 생각을, 사유와 매매와 소비의 대상으로 모든 것을 인식하는 백인들의 사고 방식과 나란히 놓을 때 거기 '문명'의 치부가 선연히 드러납니다.

또 다음과 같은 구절도 있습니다.

"땅으로부터 자기들이 필요하다면 무엇이나 가져가 버리는 백인들은 (땅에 대한) 이방인입니다."

"당신네 도시의 모습은 우리 인디언의 눈을 아프게 합니다."

1부 한 포기 키 작은 풀로 서서

자연을 적대적인 것으로, 또는 불편한 것, 미개한 것으로 파악하고 인간 생활로부터 자연을 차단해 온 성과가 문명의 내용이고, 차단된 자연으로부터의 거리가 문명의 척도가 되는 '도시의 물리物理', 철근 콘크리트의 벽과 벽 사이에서 없어도 되는 물건을 생산하기에 여념이 없는, 욕망과 갈증의 생산에 여념이 없는, 생산할수록 더욱 궁핍을 느끼게 하는 '문명의 역리逆理'에 대하여, 야만과 미개의 대명사처럼 되어 온 한 인디언의 편지가 이처럼 통렬한 문명 비평이 된다는 사실로부터 우리는 문명과 야만의 의미를 다시 물어야 옳다고 생각됩니다. 편지의 후예들은 지금쯤 그들의 흙내와 바람마저 잃고 도시의 어느 외곽에서 오염된 햇볕 한 조각 입지 못한 채 백인들이 만들어 낸 문명(?)의 어떤 것을 분배받고 있을지 모를 일입니다.

저는 이 짤막한 편지를 읽으며 저의 세계관 속에 아직도 청산되지 못한 식민지적 잔재가 부끄러웠습니다. 서구적인 것을 보편적인 원리로 수긍하고 우리의 것은 항상 특수한 것, 우연적인 것으로 규정하는 '사고의 식민성'은 우리들의 가슴에 아직도 자국 깊은 상처로 남아 있습니다.

저는 우리의 조상들이 만들려고 하였던 세계가 어떠한 것이었는지 몹시 궁금해집니다. 우리는 오랫동안 우리의 것을 잃고, 버리고, 외면해 왔습니다. 지금은 '노인'마저 급속히 없어져 가고 있는 풍토입니다. 그러나 우리의 역사, 우리의 생활 속에는 아직도 조상의 수택手澤이 상신尙新한 귀중한 정신이 새로운 조명을 기다리고 있다고 믿습니다.

그 편지는 다음과 같은 구절로 끝맺고 있습니다.

"당신의 모든 힘과 능력과 정성을 기울여, 당신의 자녀들을 위하여 땅을 보존하고 또 신이 우리를 사랑하듯 그 땅을 사랑해 주십시오. …… 백인들일지라도 공동의 운명으로부터 제외될 수는 없습니다."

서도

아버님께

Calligraphy · 34p

이번 겨울은 한온寒溫이 무상하여 앞 날씨를 측량키 어렵습니다. 저희
는 제일 추운 날씨를 표준하여 옷들을 입고 있습니다. 호한㷔寒에는 볼
품이 없어도 솜이 든 저희들의 수의囚衣가 신사들의 옷보다 훨씬 '아름
다워' 보입니다. '아름다움'이란 바깥 형식에 의해서라기보다 속 내용
에 의하여 최종적으로 규정되는 법임을 확인하는 심정입니다.

서도書道의 경우에도 이와 비슷한 경험이 있습니다. 자획字劃의 모
양보다는 자구字句에 담긴 뜻이 좋아야 함은 물론 특히 그 '사람'이 훌
륭해야 한다는 점이 그렇습니다. 작품과 인간이 강하게 연대되고 있는
서도가, 단지 작품만으로 평가되는 인간 부재의 다른 분야보다 마음에
듭니다. 좋은 글씨를 남기기 위하여 결국 좋은 사람이 될 수밖에 없다는
평범한 상식이 마음 흐뭇합니다. 인간의 품성을 높이는 데 복무하는
'예술'과 예술적 가치로 전화되는 '인간의 품성'과의 통일, 이 통일이
서도에만 보존되고 있다고 한다면 아무래도 근묵자近墨者의 자위이겠
습니까.

요즈음은 다시 『논어』를 들었습니다. 외풍이 센 방에는 새벽이 일찍
옵니다. 새벽 창 밑에 앉아 고인의 지성을 읽어 봅니다.

이우천하지선사위미족 우상론고지인

以友天下之善士爲未足 又尙論古之人

천하의 선비로서도 부족하여 고인을 읽는다는 『맹자』의 일절이 상기됩니다. 항상 생활 속에서 먼저 깨닫기로 하고 독서가 결코 과욕이 되지 않도록 부단히 절제하고 있습니다.

아직 손 시려 글씨 쓰지 못합니다. 종이 필요하면 말씀드리겠습니다. 어머님 강건하시길 빕니다.

바다로 열린 시냇물처럼

부모님께

Like the Stream Opening Itself to the Sea • 36p

해마다 7월이 되면 어느덧 지나온 날을 돌아보는 마음이 됩니다. 금년 7월은 제가 징역을 시작한 지 12년이 되는 달입니다. 궁벽한 곳에 오래 살면 관점마저 자연히 좁아지고 치우쳐, 흡사 동굴 속에 사는 사람이 동굴의 아궁이를 동쪽이라 착각하듯이 저도 모르는 사이에 이러저러한 견해가 주관 쪽으로 많이 기운 것이 되어 있지나 않을까 하는 걱정이 있습니다.

서울을 가장 정직하게 바라볼 수 있는 조망대가 어디인가를 놓고도 남산 팔각정이다, 시청이다, 영등포 공단의 어느 작업기 앞이다, 시비가 없지 않습니다. 훨훨 날아다니는 하늘의 선녀가 아닌 다음에야 여러 개의 조망대를 한꺼번에 가질 수는 없고 어디든 땅에 뿌리를 내리고 살 수밖에 없는 우리들로서는 제가 사는 터전을 저의 조망대로 삼지 않을 수 없기 때문에 어차피 자신의 처지에 따른 강한 주관에서부터 생각을 간추리지 않을 수 없다고 믿습니다.

대다수의 사람들은 이 주관의 양을 조금이라도 더 줄이고 객관적인 견해를 더 많이 수입하려고 합니다. 그러나 이러한 노력의 바닥에는, 주관主觀은 궁벽하고 객관客觀은 평정한 것이며, 주관은 객관으로 발전하지 못하고, 객관은 주관을 기초로 하지 않는다는 잘못된 전제가 깔려 있음을 알 수 있습니다.

저는, 각자가 저마다의 삶의 터전에 깊숙이 발목 박고 서서 그 '곳'

에 고유한 주관을 더욱 강화해 가는 노력이야말로 객관의 지평을 열어
주는 것임을 의심치 않습니다. 그러나 이 경우 가장 중요한 것은 그 '곳'
이, 바다로 열린 시냇물처럼, 전체와 튼튼히 연대되고 있어야 한다는 사
실입니다. 그러므로 사고의 동굴을 벗어나는 길은 그 삶의 터전을 선택
하는 문제로 환원될 수 있다고 생각됩니다.

『맹자』의 일절이 상기됩니다.

시인유공불상인 함인유공상인 무장역연 고술불가불신야

矢人惟恐不傷人 函人惟恐傷人 巫匠亦然 故術不可不愼也

(활 만드는 사람은 사람이 상하지 않을까 두려워하고

방패를 만드는 사람은 사람이 상할까 두려워한다.)

스스로 시대의 복판에 서기도 어려운 일이 아닐 수 없습니다만 시대
와 역사의 대하로 향하는 어느 가난한 골목에 서기를 주저해서도 안 되
리라 믿습니다.

한창 더울 때입니다만 하루 걸러 내리는 비가 큰 부조扶助입니다. 지
난 접견 때는 우중雨中에 돌아가시느라 어머님 발길이 더 무거웠으리라
짐작됩니다.

낮은 곳
형수님께

The Low Place · 38p

그동안 '새시대'의 구호와 표어로 갈아붙이느라 몹시 바쁜 날들의 연속이었습니다.

사다리를 올라가 높은 곳에서 일할 때의 어려움은 무엇보다도 글씨가 바른지 삐뚤어졌는지를 알 수 없다는 것입니다. 코끼리 앞에 선 장님의 막연함 같은 것입니다. 저는 낮은 곳에 있는 사람들에게 부지런히 물어봄으로써 겨우 바른 글씨를 쓸 수 있었습니다.

'푸른 과실이 햇빛을 마시고 제 속의 쓰고 신 물을 달고 향기로운 즙으로 만들듯이' 저도 이 가을에는 하루하루의 아픈 경험들을 양지바른 생각의 지붕에 널어, 소중한 겨울의 양식으로 갈무리하려고 합니다.

1부 한 포기 키 작은 풀로 서서

없음〔無〕이 곧 쓰임〔用〕
아버님께

Emptiness Becomes Usefulness · 39p

큰 추위는 없었습니다만 그런대로 겨울땜은 한 것 같습니다. 어머님 평안하시고 가내 무고하리라 믿습니다.

'당무유용'當無有用.『노자』老子의 일절입니다.

연식이위기 당기무 유기지용

挻埴以爲器 當其無 有器之用

흙을 이겨서 그릇을 만드는 경우, 그릇으로서의 쓰임새는 그릇 가운데를 비움으로써 생긴다.

'없음'〔無〕으로써 '쓰임'〔用〕으로 삼는 지혜. 그 여백 있는 생각, 그 유원幽遠한 경지가 부럽습니다.

최근의 몇 가지 경험에서 자주 생각 키우는 느낌입니다만 선행이든 악행이든 그것이 일회 완료의 대상화된 행위가 아니고 '좋은 사람' 또는 '나쁜 사람'과 같이 그것이 '사람'인 경우에는 완전한 악인도 전형적인 선인도 존재하지 않는다는 지극히 평범한 상식이 확인됩니다. 그러한 사람은 형이상학적으로 존재하는 하나의 추상된 도식이기 때문에 도리어 인간 이해를 방해하는 관념이라 생각됩니다. 전형적 인간을 찾는 것은, 없는 것을 찾는 것이 됩니다.

나막신에 우산 한 자루

계수님께

A Pair of Wooden Shoes and an Umbrella • 41p

인생살이도 그러하겠지만 더구나 징역살이는 언제든지 떠날 수 있는 단촐한 차림으로 살아야겠다고 생각하였습니다. 그러나 막상 이번 전방 때는 버려도 아까울 것 하나 없는 자질구레한 짐들로 하여 상당히 무거운 이삿짐(?)을 날라야 했습니다.

입방 시간에 쫓기며 무거운 짐을 어깨로 메고 걸어가면서 나는 나를 짓누르는 또 한 덩어리의 육중한 생각을 짐 지지 않을 수 없었습니다. 내일은 '머-ㄴ길'을 떠날 터이니 옷 한 벌과 지팡이를 채비해 두도록 동자더러 이른 어느 노승이 이튿날 새벽 지팡이 하나 사립 앞에 짚고 풀발선 옷자락으로 꼿꼿이 선 채 숨을 거두었더라는 그 고결한 임종의 자태가 줄곧 나를 책망하였습니다.

섭갹담등躡屩擔簦, 즐풍목우櫛風沐雨. 나막신에 우산 한 자루로 바람결에 머리 빗고 빗물로 머리 감던 옛사람들의 미련 없는 속탈俗脫은 감히 시늉할 수 없는 것이라 하더라도 10여 년 징역을 살고도 아직 빈 몸을 두려워하고 있었던 것은 아니었을까.

있으면 없는 것보다 편리한 것도 사실이지만 완물상지玩物喪志, 가지면 가진 것에 뜻을 앗기며, 물건은 방만 차지함에 그치지 않고 우리의 마음속에도 자리를 틀고 앉아 창의創意를 잠식하기도 합니다.

이기利器를 생산한다기보다 '필요' 그 자체를 무한정 생산해 내고 있는 현실을 살면서 오연傲然히 자기를 다스려 나가기도 쉽지 않음을 알 수 있습니다. 그러나 그릇은 그 속이 빔[虛]으로써 쓰임이 되고 넉넉함은 빈 몸에 고이는 이치를 배워 스스로를 당당히 간수하지 않는 한, 척박한 땅에서 키우는 모든 뜻이 껍데기만 남을 뿐임이 확실합니다.

서도와 필재筆才

형수님께

Calligraphy and the Talent in Writing · 43p

대부분의 사람들은, 글씨란 타고나는 것이며 필재筆才가 없는 사람은 아무리 노력하여도 명필이 될 수 없다고 생각합니다. 그러나 저는 정반대의 생각을 가지고 있습니다.

필재가 있는 사람의 글씨는 대체로 그 재능에 의존하기 때문에 일견 빼어나긴 하되 재능이 도리어 함정이 되어 손끝의 교巧를 벗어나기 어려운 데 비하여, 필재가 없는 사람의 글씨는 손끝으로 쓰는 것이 아니라 온몸으로 쓰기 때문에 그 속에 혼신의 힘과 정성이 배어 있어서 '단련의 미'가 쟁쟁히 빛나게 됩니다.

만약 필재가 뛰어난 사람이 그 위에 혼신의 노력으로 꾸준히 쓴다면 이는 흡사 여의봉 휘두르는 손오공처럼 더할 나위 없겠지만 이런 경우는 관념적으로나 상정될 수 있을 뿐, 필재가 있는 사람은 역시 오리새끼 물로 가듯이 손재주에 탐닉하게 마련이라 하겠습니다.

결국 서도는 그 성격상 토끼의 재능보다는 거북이의 끈기를 연마하는 것인지도 모릅니다. 더욱이 글씨의 훌륭함이란 글자의 자획에서 찾아지는 것이 아니라 묵 속에 갈아 넣은 정성의 양에 의하여 최종적으로 평가되는 것이기에 더욱 그러리라 생각됩니다.

사람의 아름다움도 이와 같아서 타고난 얼굴의 조형미보다는 그 사람의 지혜와 경험의 축적이 내밀한 인격이 되어 은은히 배어나는 아름다움이 더욱 높은 것임과 마찬가지입니다. 뿐만 아니라 인생을 보는 시각

1부 한 포기 키 작은 풀로 서서

도 이와 다르지 않다고 믿습니다. 첩경과 행운에 연연해하지 않고, 역경에서 오히려 정직하며, 기존旣存과 권부權富에 몸 낮추지 않고, 진리와 사랑에 허심탄회한……. 그리하여 스스로 선택한 '우직함'이야말로 인생의 무게를 육중하게 해주는 것이라 생각합니다.

욕설의 리얼리즘

계수님께

The Elements of Realism in Swearwords • 45p

교도소에 많은 것 중의 하나가 '욕설'입니다.

아침부터 밤까지 우리는 실로 흐드러진 욕설의 잔치 속에 살고 있는 셈입니다. 저도 징역 초기에는 욕설을 듣는 방법이 너무 고지식하여 단어 하나하나의 뜻을 곧이곧대로 상상하다가 어처구니없는 궁상窮狀에 빠져 헤어나지 못하기 일쑤였습니다만 지금은 그 방면에서도 어느덧 이력이 나서 한 알의 당의정糖衣錠을 삼키듯 '이순'耳順의 경지에 이르렀다 하겠습니다.

욕설은 어떤 비상한 감정이 인내력의 한계를 넘어 밖으로 돌출하는, 이를테면 불만이나 스트레스의 가장 싸고 '후진' 해소 방법이라 느껴집니다. 그러나 사과가 먼저 있고 사과라는 말이 나중에 생기듯이 욕설로 표현될 만한 감정이나 대상이 먼저 있음이 사실입니다. 징역의 현장인 이곳이 곧 욕설의 산지産地이며 욕설의 시장인 까닭도 그런 데에 연유하는가 봅니다.

그러나 이곳에서 욕설은 이미 욕설이 아닙니다. 기쁨이나 반가움마저도 일단 욕설의 형식으로 표현되는 경우가 허다합니다. 이런 경우는 그 감정의 비상함이 역설적으로 강조되는 시적 효과를 얻게 되는데 이 것은 반가운 인사를 욕설로 대신해 오던 서민들의 전통에 오래전부터 있어 온 것이기도 합니다. 저는 오래전부터 욕설이나 은어에 담겨 있는 뛰어난 언어 감각에 탄복해 오고 있습니다. 그 상황에 멋지게 들어맞는 비유나 풍자라든가, 극단적인 표현에 치우친 방만한 것이 아니라 약간 못미치는 듯한 선에서 용케 억제됨으로써 오히려 예리하고 팽팽한 긴장감을 느끼게 하는 것 등은 그것 자체로서 하나의 훌륭한 작품입니다.

'사물'과, 여러 개의 사물이 연계됨으로써 이루어지는 '사건'과, 여러 개의 사건이 연계됨으로써 이루어지는 '사태' 등으로 상황을 카테고리로 구분한다면, 욕설은 대체로 높은 단계인 '사건' 또는 '사태'에 관한 개념화이며 이 개념의 예술적(?) 형상화 작업이라는 점에서 그것은 고도의 의식 활동이라 할 수 있습니다.

저는 바로 이 점에 있어서, 대상에 대한 사실적 인식을 기초로 하면서 예리한 풍자와 골계滑稽의 구조를 갖는 욕설에서, 인텔리들의 추상적 언어 유희와는 확연히 구별되는, 적나라한 리얼리즘을 발견합니다. 뿐만 아니라 욕설에 동원되는 화재話材와 비유로부터 시세時世와 인정, 풍물에 대한 뜸 든 이해를 얻을 수 있다는 사실이 매우 귀중하게 여겨집니다.

그러나 버섯이 아무리 곱다 한들 화분에 떠서 기르지 않듯이 욕설이 그 속에 아무리 뛰어난 예능을 담고 있다 한들 그것은 기실 응달의 산물이며 불행의 언어가 아닐 수 없습니다.

비슷한 얼굴

계수님께

Similar Faces • 47p

여러 사람이 맨살 부대끼며 오래 살다보면 어느덧 비슷한 말투, 비슷한 욕심, 비슷한 얼굴을 가지게 됩니다.

서로 바라보면 거울 대한 듯 비슷비슷합니다. 자기가 다른 사람과 비슷하다는 사실, 여럿 중의 평범한 하나에 불과하다는 사실은 대부분의 사람들이 못마땅하게 여깁니다. 기성품처럼 개성이 없고 값어치가 훨씬 떨어지는 것으로 받아들입니다. '개인의 세기世紀'에 살고 있는 우리들의 당연한 사고입니다.

그러면 다른 사람과 조금도 닮지 않은 개인이나 탁월한 천재가 과연 있는가. 물론 없습니다. 있다면 그것은 외형만 그럴 뿐입니다. 다른 사람과 아무런 내왕來往이 없는 '순수한 개인'이란 무인도의 로빈슨 크루소처럼 소설 속에나 있는 것이며, 천재란 그것이 어느 개인이나 순간의 독창이 아니라 오랜 중지衆智의 집성이며 협동의 결정임을 우리는 알고 있습니다.

우리들이 잊고 있는 것은 아무리 담장을 높이더라도 사람들은 결국 서로가 서로의 일부가 되어 함께 햇빛을 나누며, 함께 비를 맞으며 '함께' 살아가고 있다는 사실입니다.

화폐가 중간에 들면, 쌀이 남고 소금이 부족한 사람과, 소금이 남고 쌀이 부족한 사람이 서로 만나지 않더라도 교환이 이루어집니다. 천 갈래 만 갈래 분업과 거대한 조직, 그리고 거기서 생겨나는 물신성物神性

은 사람들의 만남을 멀리 떼어 놓기 때문에 '함께' 살아간다는 뜻을 깨닫기 어렵게 합니다.

같은 이해利害, 같은 운명으로 연대된 '한 배 탄 마음'은 '나무도 보고 숲도 보는' 지혜이며, 한 포기 미나리아재비나 보잘것없는 개똥벌레 한 마리도 그냥 지나치지 않는 '열린 사랑'입니다. 한 그루의 나무가 되라고 한다면 나는 산봉우리의 낙락장송보다 수많은 나무들이 합창하는 숲 속에 서고 싶습니다. 한 알의 물방울이 되라고 한다면 저는 단연 바다를 선택하고 싶습니다. 그리하여 가장 많은 사람들이 모여 사는 나지막한 동네에서 비슷한 말투, 비슷한 욕심, 비슷한 얼굴을 가지고 싶습니다.

가을의 사색

형수님께

Meditation in Autumn • 49p

해마다 가을이 되면 우리들은 추수라도 하듯이 한 해 동안 키워 온 생각들을 거두어 봅니다. 금년 가을도 여느 해나 다름없이 손에 잡히는 것이 없습니다. 공허한 마음은 뼈만 데리고 돌아온 '바다의 노인' 같습니다. 봄, 여름, 가을, 언제 한번 온몸으로 떠맡은 일 없이 그저 앉아서 생각만 달리는 일이 부질없기가 얼음 쪼아 구슬 만드는 격입니다. 그나마 내 쪽에서 벼리를 잡고 엮어 간 일관된 사색이 아니라 그때그때 부딪쳐 오는 잡념잡사雜念雜事의 범위를 넘지 못하는 연습 같은 것들이고 보면 빈약한 추수가 당연할 수밖에 없습니다. 그 위에 정직한 최선을 다하지 못한 후회까지 더한다면 이제 문 닫고 앉아 봄을 기다려야 할 겨울이 더 길고 추운 계절로만 여겨집니다.

그러나 우리는 숱한 가을을 보내고 맞는 동안 가을에 갖는 우리의 회한이 결코 회한으로만 끝나지 않음을 압니다. 풍요보다는 궁핍이, 기쁨보다는 아픔이 우리를 삶의 진상眞相에 맞세워 주는 법이며, 삶의 진상은 다시 위대한 대립물이 되어 우리 자신을 냉정하게 바라보도록 합니다. 자기 자신에 대한 냉정한 인식은 일견 비정한 듯하나, 빈약한 추수에도 아랑곳없이 스스로를 간추려 보게 하는 용기의 원천이기도 합니다.

가을에 흔히 사람들은 낙엽을 긁어모아 불사르고 그 재를 뿌리쨤에 묻어 줍니다. 이것은 새로운 나무의 식목이 아니라 이미 있는 나무를 북

1부   한 포기 키 작은 풀로 서서

돋우는 시비施肥입니다. 가을의 사색도 이와 같아서 그것은 새로운 것을 획득하려는 욕심이 아니라 이미 알고 있는 것들을 다짐하고 챙기는 '약속의 이행'입니다.

이 평범한 일상의 약속들이 다짐되고 이행된 다음, 나중에야 비로소 욕심이 충족되더라도 되는 것이 응당한 순서이리라 생각됩니다. 가을에 갖는 우리들의 공허한 마음이란 기실 조급한 욕심이 만들어 놓은 엉뚱한 것이라 해야 하겠습니다.

혹시나 잊고 있는 약속들을 찾아서 거두는 조용한 추수의 사려 깊음은 시내에 놓인 징검돌이 되어 이곳의 우리들로 하여금 섣달 냇물같이 차가운 징역을 건네줍니다.

엄마의 자리, 아내의 자리, 며느리의 자리, 형수의 자리……. 숱한 자리마다 올 가을에 큼직큼직한 수확 있으시기 바랍니다.

겨울 새벽의 기상나팔

계수님께

Morning Bugle of a Winter Dawn • 51p

기상 30분 전이 되면 나는 옆에서 곤히 잠든 친구를 깨워 줍니다. 부드러운 손찌검으로 조용히 깨워 줍니다. 그는 새벽마다 기상 나팔을 불러 나가는 교도소의 나팔수입니다.

옷, 양말, 모자 등을 챙겨서 갖춘 다음 한 손에는 '마우스피스'를 감싸 쥐어 손바닥의 온기로 데우며 다른 손에는 나팔과, 기상 나팔 후부터 개방開房 나팔 때까지 서서 읽을 책 한 권 받쳐 들고 방을 나갑니다. 몇 개의 외등外燈으로 군데군데 어둠이 탈색된 운동장을 가로질러서 교회당 계단을 꺾어 올라 높다란 2층 창 앞에 서서 나팔을 붑니다. 가슴에 맺힌 한숨 가누어서 별빛 얼어붙은 새벽 하늘에 뿜어냅니다. 성씨 다른 아버지께 엽서를 띄우는, 엄마 불쌍해서 돈 벌어야겠다는…… 농農돌이, 공工돌이, 이제는 스물다섯 징懲돌이……. 얼어붙은 새벽 하늘을 가르고, 고달픈 재소자들의 꿈을 찢고, 또 하루의 징역을 외치는 겨울 새벽의 기상 나팔은 '강철로 된 소리'입니다.

교도소의 문화가 침묵의 문화라면 교도소의 예술은 비극미悲劇美의 추구에 있습니다. 전장에서 쓰러진 병정이 그 주검을 말가죽에 싸듯이 상처난 청춘을 푸른 수의에 싸고 있는 이 끝동네 사람들은 예외 없이 비극의 임자들입니다.

검은 머리 잘라서 땅에 뿌리고, 우러러볼 청천靑天 하늘 한 자락 없이, 오늘밤 두들겨 볼 대문도 없이, 간 꺼내어 쪽박에 담고 벨 꺼내어 오지랖에 싸고, 이렇게 사는 것도 사는 것이냐며 삶 그 전체를 질문하는, 검푸른 비극의 임자들입니다. 비극이, 더욱이 이처럼 엄청난 비극이 미적인 것으로 승화될 수 있는 가능성은 그 '정직성'에서 찾을 수 있습니다. 저한테 가해지는 중압을 아무에게도 전가하지 않고 고스란히 짐 질 수밖에 없는, 가장 낮은 곳에 사는 사람의 '정직함'에 있습니다. 비극은 남의 것을 대신 체험할 수 없고 단지 자기 것밖에 체험할 수 없는 고독한 일인칭의 서술이라는 특질을 가지며 바로 이러한 특질이 그 극적 성격을 강화하는 한편 종내에는 새로운 '앎'— '아름다움'—을 마련해 주는 것입니다.

비극은 우리들이 무심히 흘려버리고 있는 일상 생활이 얼마나 치열한 갈등과 복잡한 얼개를 그 내부에 감추고 있는가를 깨닫게 할 뿐 아니라 때로는 우리를 객석으로부터 무대의 뒤편 분장실로 인도함으로써 전혀 새로운 인식평면認識平面을 열어 줍니다.

열락悅樂이 사람의 마음을 살찌게 하되 그 뒤에다 '모름다움'을 타 버린 재로 남김에 비하여 슬픔은 채식菜食처럼 사람의 생각을 맑게 함으로써 그 복판에 '아름다움'[知]을 일으켜 놓습니다. 야심성유휘夜深星愈輝, 밤 깊을수록 광채를 더하는 별빛은 겨울 밤하늘의 '지성'이며, 상국설매霜菊雪梅, 된서리 속의 황국黃菊도, 풍설風雪 속의 한매寒梅도 그 미의 본질은 다름 아닌 비극성에 있는 것이라 생각됩니다.

사람들이 구태여 비극을 미화하고 비극미를 기리는 까닭은, 한갓되이 비극의 사람들을 위로하려는 '작은 사랑'[warm heart]에서가 아니라, 비극의 그 비정한 깊이를 자각케 함으로써 '새로운 앎'[cool head]을 터득하고자 한 오의奧義를 알 듯합니다. 그러나 기상 30분 전 곤히 잠든 친구를 깨울 적마다 나는 망설여지는 마음을 어쩌지 못합니다. 포근히 몸 담고 있는 꿈의 보금자리를 헐어 버리고 참담한 징역의 현실로 끌어내는 나의 손길은 두 번 세 번 망설여집니다.

새해란 실상 면면한 세월의 똑같은 한 토막이라 하여 1월을 13월이라 부르는 사람도 있지만, 만약 새로움이 완성된 형태로 우리 앞에 던져진다면 그것은 이미 새로움이 아니라 생각됩니다. 모든 새로움은 그에 임하는 우리의 심기心機가 새롭고, 그 속에 새로운 것을 채워 나갈 수 있는 하나의 '가능성'으로서 주어지는 새로움임을 잊지 말아야 할 것입니다.

한 포기 키 작은 풀로 서서

계수님께

Standing as a Clump of Short Field Grass • 55p

자기의 그릇이 아니고서는 음식을 먹을 수 없는 여우와 두루미의 우화처럼, 성장 환경이 다른 사람들끼리는 자기의 언어가 아니고서는 대화가 여간 어렵지 않습니다. 언어란 미리 정해진 약속이고 공기公器여서 제 마음대로 뜻을 담아 쓸 수가 없지만 같은 그릇도 어떤 집에서는 밥그릇으로 쓰이고 어떤 집에서는 국그릇으로 사용되듯 사람에 따라 차이가 나게 마련입니다. 성장 과정과 경험 세계가 판이한 사람들이 서로 만날 때 맨 먼저 부딪치는 곤란의 하나가 이 언어의 차이입니다.

같은 단어를 다른 뜻으로 사용하는 경우는 그런대로 작은 차이이고, 여러 단어의 조합에 의한 판단 형식의 차이는 그것의 내용을 이루는 생각의 차이를 확대한다는 점에서 매우 큰 것이라 하겠습니다.

가장 두드러진 예를 든다면 아마 '책가방 끈이 길고 먹물이 든 사람'과 그렇지 못한 사람 간의 차이라고 생각됩니다. 전자는 대체로 벽돌을 쌓듯 정제精製되고 계산된 언어와 논리를 구사하되 필요 이상의 복잡한 표현과 미시적 사고로 말미암아 자기가 쳐 놓은 의미망意味網에 갇혀 헤어나지 못합니다. 도깨비이기는 마찬가지임에도 불구하고 구태여 파란색 도깨비와 노란색 도깨비를 구별하느라 수고롭습니다. 이에 비하여 후자의 그것은 구체적이고 그릇이 커서 손으로 만지듯 확실하고 시원시원하기는 합니다. 그러나 지나친 단순화와 무리無理, 그리고 감정의 범람이 심하여 수염과 눈썹을 구별치 않고, 목욕물과 함께 아이까지 내다 버리는 단색적 사고를 면치 못하는 경향이 있습니다.

나는 십수년의 징역을 살아오는 동안 이 두 가지의 상반된 경향의 틈새에서 여러 형태의 방황과 시행착오를 경험해 왔음이 사실입니다. 복잡한 표현과 관념적 사고를 내심 즐기며, 그것이 상위의 것이라 여기던 오만의 시절이 있었는가 하면, 조야粗野한 비어를 배우고 주워섬김으로써 마치 군중 관점群衆觀點을 얻은 듯, 자신의 관념성을 개조한 듯 착각하던 시절도 있었습니다. 뿐만 아니라 양쪽을 절충하여 '중간은 정당하다'는 논리 속에 한동안 안주하다가 중간은 '가공架空의 자리'이며 방관이며, 기회주의이며, 다른 형태의 방황임을 소스라쳐 깨닫고 허둥지둥 그 자리를 떠나던 기억도 없지 않습니다.

물론 어느 개인이 자기의 언어를 얻고, 자기의 작풍作風을 이루기 위해서는 오랜 방황과 표류의 역정歷程을 겪지 않을 수 없는 것이라 하더라도, 방황 그 자체가 이것을 성취시켜 주는 것이 아니며, 방황의 길이가 성취의 높이로 나타나는 것도 아닙니다. 최종적으로는 어딘가의 '땅'에 자신을 세우고 뿌리내림으로써 비로소 이룩되는 것이라 믿습니다.

교도소는 대지大地도 벌판도 아닙니다. 휘달리는 산맥도 없고 큰 마음으로 누운 유유한 강물도 없는 차라리 15척 벽돌 벼랑으로 둘린 외따른 섬이라 불립니다. 징역 사는 사람들이 겪는 정신적 방황은 대개가 이처럼 땅이 없다는 외로운 생각에 연유되는 것인지도 모릅니다. 그래서 대부분의 사람들은, 오랜 세월을 이곳에서 살아야 하는 우리들과는 달리, 아무렇게나 잠시 머물렀다가 떠나가면 그만인 곳으로 여기는지도 모릅니다. 그러나 이것은 자신의 고달픈 처지에 심신이 부대끼느라 이곳에 자라고 있는 무성한 풀들을 보지 못하는 잘못된 생각입니다. 이름도 없는 풀들이 모이고 모여 밭을 이루고 밟힌 잡초들이 서로 몸 비비며 살아가는 그 조용한 아우성을 듣지 못하는 생각입니다.

1부 한 포기 키 작은 풀로 서서

초상지풍초필언 수지풍중초부립草上之風草必偃 誰知風中草復立. '바람보다 먼저 눕고' 바람보다 먼저 일어나는 풀잎마다 발 밑에 한 줌씩의 따뜻한 땅의 체온을 쌓아 놓고 있습니다. 나는 이 무성한 잡초 속에 한 포기 키 작은 풀로 서서 몸 기대며 어깨를 짜며 꾸준히 박토薄土를 배우고, 나의 언어를 얻고, 나의 방황을 끝낼 수 있기를 바랍니다.

폭설이 내린 이듬해 봄의 잎사귀가 더 푸른 법이라는데 이번 겨울은 추위도 눈도 없는 난동暖冬이었습니다. 입춘 지나 우수雨水를 앞둔 어제 오늘이, 풍광風光은 완연 봄인데 아직은 믿음직스럽지 못합니다.

2부

나는 걷고 싶다

꿈에 뵈는 어머님

어머님께

Mother I Saw in My Dream • 61p

3월 중순인데도 뒤늦게야 해살맞은 바람에다 엊그제 저녁은 진눈깨비 섞인 비까지 흩뿌립니다. 올봄도 계절을 정직하게 사는 꽃들이 늦추위에 떠는 해가 되려나 봅니다.

세전歲前에 아버님 혼자 오셨을 때 아버님께선 날씨 탓으로 돌리셨지만 저는 어머님이 몸져 누우신 줄 짐작하였습니다. 접견 마치고 혼자 소문所門을 나가시는 아버님을 이윽고 바라보았습니다. 아버님은 어머님과 함께 걸으실 때도 언제나 네댓 걸음 앞서 가시지만 그날은 아버님의 네댓 걸음 뒤에도 어머님이 계시지 않았습니다. 그렇더라도 설마 치레 잦은 감기몸살이겠거니 하고 우정 염려를 외면해 왔습니다만 막상 형님 편에 그것이 매우 위중한 것임을 알고부터는 연일 꿈에 어머님을 봅니다.

꿈에 뵈는 어머님은 늘 곱고 젊은 어머님인데 오늘 새벽 잠 깨어 새삼스레 어머님 연세를 꼽아 보니 일흔여섯, '극노인'極老人임에 놀라지 않을 수 없었습니다. 제가 징역 들어오고 난 최근의 십수년이 어머님의 심신을 얼마나 깊게 할퀴어 놓은 것인지도 모르고 제 나이를 스물일곱인 줄 알듯이, 어머님도 매양 그전처럼만 여겨 온 저의 미욱함이 따가운 매가 되어 종아리를 칩니다.

"인제 죽어도 나이는 아까울 게 없다" 하시며 입 다물어 버리신 그 뒷말씀이 기실 저로 인하여 가슴에 응어리진 한恨임을 모르지 않기 때문에 제게도 어머님께 드리고 싶은 말씀이 응어리가 되어 쌓입니다. 언젠가는 어머님과 함께 어머님의 이 응어리진 아픔에 대하여 이야기 나누고 싶습니다. 이 아픔은 어디에서 연유하는 것이며, 우리는 이를 어떻게 받아들여야 하는가, 같은 세월을 살아가는 다른 사람들은 어떤 아픔을 속에 담고 있으며 그것은 어머님의 그것과 어떻게 상통相通되는가, 냇물이 흘러흘러 바다에 이르듯 자신의 아픔을 통하여 모든 어머니들이 가슴에 안고 있는 그 숱한 아픔들을 만날 수는 없는가, 그리하여 한 아들의 어머니라는 '모정母情의 한계'를 뛰어넘어, 개인의 아픔에서 삶의 진실과 역사성을 깨달을 수는 없는가…….

접견은 짧고 엽서는 좁아 언제나 다음을 기약할 뿐인 미진함은 저를 몹시 피곤하게 합니다. 그러나 한편 생각해 보면 어머님께선 이미 이 모든 것을 달관하고 계실 뿐 아니라 누구보다도 깊이 저를 꿰뚫어 보고 계심에 틀림없다는 생각이 듭니다.

지자막여부知子莫如父. 자식을 아는 데는 부모를 덮을 사람이 없다는 옛말처럼, 어머님은 이 세상의 누구보다도 저를 잘 아시고 또 저의 친구들을 숱하게 아실 뿐 아니라 빠짐없이 공판정에 나오셔서 어느덧 어머님의 생각의 품 바깥으로 걸어 나와 버린 아들의 이야기를 한마디도 놓치지 않으시려던 그때의 모습을 회상하면, 아마 어머님은 제가 어머님을 알고 있는 것보다 더 많이 저를 알고 계심을 깨닫게 됩니다. 어머님의 모정은 이 모든 것을 포용할 수 있을 만큼 품이 넓고 그 위에 아들에 대한 튼튼한 신뢰로 가득 찬 것이라 믿습니다.

기다림은 더 많은 것을 견디게 하고 더 먼 것을 보게 하고, 캄캄한 어둠 속에서도 빛나는 눈을 갖게 합니다. 어머님께도 기다림이 집념이 되어 어머님의 정신과 건강을 강하게 지탱해 주시기 바랍니다.

어머님께서 걱정하시던 겨울도 가고 창밖에는 갇힌 사람들에게는 잔인하리만큼 화사한 봄볕이 땅속의 풀싹들을 깨우고 있습니다.

함께 맞는 비
형수님께

The Rain We Get Wet Together In • 64p

상처가 아물고 난 다음에 받은 약은 상처를 치료하는 데 사용하기에는 너무 늦고, 도리어 그 아프던 기억을 상기시키는 역할을 하는 경우가 있습니다. 이것은 단지 시기가 엇갈려 일어난 실패의 사소한 예에 불과하지만, 남을 돕고 도움을 받는 일이 경우에 따라서는 도움이 되기는커녕 더 큰 것을 해치는 일이 됩니다.

함께 징역을 살아가는 사람 중에는 접견도, 서신도, 영치금도 없이 받은 징역을 춥게 살면서도 비누 한 장, 칫솔 한 개라도 남의 신세를 지지 않으려는 고집 센 사람들이 많이 있습니다. 모르는 사람들은 이러한 사람들을 두고 남의 호의를 받아들일 줄 모르는 좁은 속을 핀잔하기도 하고, 가난이 만들어 놓은 비뚤어진 심사를 불쌍하게 여기기도 하고, 단 한 개의 창문도 열지 않는 어두운 마음을 비난하기도 합니다.

남의 호의를 거부하는 고집이 과연 좁고 비뚤고 어두운 마음의 소치인가. 우리는 공정한 논의를 위하여 카메라를 반대편, 즉 베푸는 자의 얼굴에도 초점을 맞추어 조명해 볼 필요가 있다고 생각합니다.

칫솔 한 개를 베푸는 마음도 그 내심을 들추어 보면 실상 여러 가지의 동기가 그 속에 도사리고 있음을 우리는 겪어서 압니다. 이를테면 그 대가를 다른 것으로 거두어들이기 위한 상략적商略的인 동기가 있는가 하면, 비록 물질적인 형태의 보상을 목적으로 하지는 않으나 수혜자 측의 호의나 협조를 얻거나, 그의 비판이나 저항을 둔화시키거나, 극단적인 경우 그의 추종이나 굴종을 확보함으로써 자기의 신장伸張을 도모하는 정략적政略的인 동기도 있으며, 또 시혜자라는 정신적 우월감을 즐기는 향락적享樂的인 동기도 없지 않습니다. 이러한 동기에서 나오는 도움은 자선이라는 극히 선량한 명칭에도 불구하고 그 본질은 조금도 선량한 것이 못됩니다. 도움을 받는 쪽이 감수해야 하는 주체성의 침해와 정신적 저상沮喪이 그를 얼마나 병들게 하는가에 대하여 조금도 고려하지 않고 서둘러 자기의 볼일만 챙겨 가는 처사는 상대방을 한 사람의 인간적 주체로 보지 않고 자기의 환경이나 방편으로 삼는 비정한 위선입니다.

이러한 것에 비하여 매우 순수한 것으로 알려진 '동정'이라는 동기가 있습니다. 이것은 측은지심惻隱之心의 발로로서 고래古來의 미덕으로 간주되고 있습니다. 그러나 이 동정이란 것은 객관적으로는 문제의 핵심을 흐리게 하는 인정주의의 한계를 가지며 주관적으로는 상대방의 문제 해결보다는 자기의 양심의 가책을 위무慰撫하려는 도피주의의 한계를 갖는 것입니다. 뿐만 아니라 동정은 동정받는 사람으로 하여금 동정하는 자의 시점에서 자신을 조감케 함으로써 탈기脫氣와 위축을 동시에 안겨 줍니다. 이 점에서 동정은, 공감의 제일보라는 강변强辯에도 불구하고 그것은 공감과는 뚜렷이 구별되는 값싼 것임에 틀림없습니다.

여러 가지를 부단히 서로 주고받으며 살아가는 징역 속에서, 제게도 저의 호의가 거부당한 경험이 적지 않습니다. 처음에는 상대방의 비좁은 마음을 탓하기도 하였지만, 순수하지 못했던 나 자신의 저의를 뒤늦게 발견하고는 스스로 놀란 적이 한두 번이 아니었습니다. 사실, 남의 호의를 거부하는 고집에는 자기를 지키려는 주체성의 단단한 심지가 박혀 있습니다. 이것은 얼마간의 물질적 수혜에 비하여 자신의 처지를 개척해 나가는 데 대개의 경우 훨씬 더 큰 힘이 되어 줍니다.

사람은 스스로를 도울 수 있을 뿐이며, 남을 돕는다는 것은 그 '스스로 도우는 일'을 도울 수 있음에 불과한지도 모릅니다. 그래서 저는 "가르친다는 것은 다만 희망을 말하는 것이다"라는 아라공의 시구를 좋아합니다. 돕는다는 것은 우산을 들어 주는 것이 아니라 함께 비를 맞으며 함께 걸어가는 공감과 연대의 확인이라 생각됩니다.

꽃순이

형수님께

Kkotsuni • 67p

'꽃순이'는 밤이면 쥐들의 놀이터가 되는 악대 실습장을 지키게 하기 위하여 악대부원들이 겨우겨우 구해 온 고양이의 이름입니다.

지금은 가출(?)해 버린 지 일 년도 더 넘어서 몰라볼 만큼 의젓한 한 마리의 '도둑고양이'로 바뀌었을 뿐 아니라 꽃순이라는 이름을 비웃기나 하듯 솔방울만한 불알을 과시하며 '쥐와 고양이의 대결'로 점철된 교도소의 밤을 늠름하게 걷는 모습을 먼 빛으로 가끔 볼 수 있을 따름입니다.

처음 고양이를 데려왔을 때는 꽃순이라는 이름이 어울리는 귀여운 새끼고양이였습니다. 사람들의 손에 의한 부양과 사람들의 무분별한 애완은 금방 고양이를 무력하게 만들고, 고양이로서의 자각을 더디게 하여 아무리 기다려도 쥐들을 자기의 먹이나 적으로 삼을 생각을 않았습니다. 쥐들로부터 찬장과 빨래, 책 등을 지키게 하려던 애초의 의도가 무산되자 이제는 사람들의 경멸과 학대가 영문 모르는 새끼고양이를 들볶기 시작했습니다. 높은 데서 떨어뜨려지기도 하고 발길에 채이기도 하고, 연탄불 집게에 수염이 타기도 하고, 안티플라민이 코에 발리기도 하는 등……, 강훈強訓이란 이름의 장난과 천대 속에 눈만 사납게 빛내다가 드디어 어느날 밤 비닐 창문을 뚫고 최초의 가출을 시작하였습니다.

그러나 어린 고양이에게 가출은 또 다른 고생과 위험의 연속이었습니다. 우선 강아지만한 양재공장의 검은 고양이가 자기의 영지에 침입한 이 새끼고양이를 받아들이지 않았습니다. 우리는 한밤중에 꽃순이의 자지러지는 비명을 듣기도 하고 다리를 절며 후미진 곳으로 도는 처량한 모습을 보기도 하였습니다.

그후 꽃순이는 몇 차례 제 발로 돌아오기도 하고 어떤 때는 테니스 네트로 수렵을 당하여 묶여 지내기도 하였습니다. 그러나 가장 뜻깊은 사실은, 이처럼 파란만장한 역사를 겪는 동안 이제는 사랑도 미움도 시들해져 버린 악대부원들의 관심 밖으로 서서히 그리고 완전히 걸어 나와 '고양이의 길'을 걸어갔다는 사실입니다. 얼마 전에는 꽃순이가 양재공장의 검은 고양이와 격렬한 한판 승부에서 비기는 현장을 목격하고 꽃순이의 변모와 성장을 대견해 하기도 하였습니다.

지금도 밤중에 고양이 소리가 나면 우리 방의 악대부원 서너 명은 얼른 창문을 열고 지나가는 고양이를 향해 "꽃순아!" 하고 상냥한 목소리로 아는 척을 합니다. 그러나 꽃순이는 사람들의 기척에 잠시 경계의 몸짓을 해보일 뿐 이쪽의 미련은 거들떠보지도 않습니다. '꽃순이'라는 옛날의 이름으로 부르는 쪽이 잘못이었는지도 모릅니다.

꽃순이에 대한 다음의 이야기는 쓰지 않으려고 하였습니다만 생각 끝에 덧붙여 두기로 하였습니다. 그것은 며칠 전 악대부원 몇 사람과 함께 지도원 휴게실에 들렀다가 거기서 우유며 통조림을 얻어먹고 있는 꽃순이를 본 사실입니다. 언제부터 먹을 것이 많은 이 지도원실을 드나들었는지 알 수 없지만 그날의 꽃순이는 먼 빛으로 보며 대견해했던 '밤의 왕자'가 아니었습니다. '가발공장에 다니던 영자를 중동中洞 창녀촌에서 보았을 때의 심정'을 안겨 주는 것이었습니다. 그러나 '꽃순이의 실패'도 '중동의 영자'나 이곳에 사는 모든 사람들의 실패와 마찬가지로 그가 겪었을 모진 시련과 편력을 알지 못하는 '남'들로서는 함부로 단언할 수 없는 것임은 물론입니다.

독다산讀茶山 유감有感

아버님께

Expressing Regret After Reading DaSan • 70p

유배지의 정다산丁茶山을 쓴 글을 읽었습니다. 이조를 통틀어 대부분의
유배자들이 배소配所에서 망경대望京臺나 연북정戀北亭 따위를 지어 임
금에 대한 변함없는 충성과 연모를 표시했음에 비하여 다산은 그런 정
자를 짓지도 않았거니와 조정이 다시 자기를 불러 줄 것을 기대하지도
않았습니다. 그는 해배解配만을 기다리는 삶의 피동성과 그 피동성이
결과하는 무서운 노쇠老衰를 일찍부터 경계하였습니다. 그는 오히려 농
민의 참담한 현실을 자신의 삶으로 안아 들이는 애정과 능동성을 통하여
자신의 삶에 새로운 지평을 열었을 뿐 아니라, 나아가 이조의 묵은 사변
思辨에 신신新新한 목민牧民의 실학實學을 심을 수 있었다 하겠습니다.

다산의 이러한 애정과 의지는 1800년 그가 39세로 유배되던 때부터
1818년 57세의 고령으로 해배될 때까지의 18년이란 긴 세월 동안 한시
도 흐트러진 적이 없었으며 마침내 『목민심서』牧民心書 등 500권의 저
술을 비롯하여 실학의 근간을 이룬 사색의 온축蘊蓄을 이룩하였습니다.
물론, 다산학茶山學과 실학에 대해서는 일정한 한계와 편향이 없지 않음
이 지적될 수 있다고 생각됩니다. 이를테면 이조 후기, 봉건적 지배 질
서가 무너지기 시작하고, 농민들이 그 거칠고 적나라한 저항의 모습을
역사의 무대에 드러내는 이른바 '민강民强의 시대'에, 봉건 질서의 청산
이 아닌 그것의 보정補整·개량이라는 구궤舊軌를 벗어나지 못하였다고
하겠습니다. 목민심서의 '목'牧 자에 담긴 관학적官學的 인상印象과 '심'

心 자에서 풍기는 그 관념성 역시 그냥 지나쳐 버릴 수 없는 것이라 생각합니다.

그러나 이는 다산 개인의 한계로서가 아니라 다산이 살던 그 시대 자체의 역사적 미숙으로 받아들여져야 하리라고 믿습니다. 더구나, 나아가 벼슬자리에 오르면 왕권주의자가 되고 물러나 강호江湖에 처하면 자연주의자가 되기 일쑤인 모든 봉건 지성의 시녀성과 기회주의를 둘 다 시원히 벗어던지고, 갖가지의 수탈 장치 밑에서 허덕이는 농민의 현실 속에 내려선 다산의 생애와 사상은 분명, 새 세기의 새로운 양식의 지성에 대한 값진 전범典範을 보인 것이라 할 수 있습니다.

저는 다산 선생의 유배 생활을 아득히 더듬어 보면서 실로 부러움을 금치 못합니다. 그가 거닐었던 고성암, 백련사, 구강포의 산천이며, 500여 권의 저술을 낳은 산방山房과 서재, 그리고 많은 지기知己와 제자들의 우의가 그렇습니다.

그러나 다산 선생의 유배 생활을 부러워하는 것은 그만 못한 저의 징역 현실을 탓하려 함이 아니며 더구나 저의 무위無爲를 두호斗護하려 함도 아닙니다. 왜냐하면 무엇을 만든다는 것은 먼저 무엇을 겪는다는 것이며, 겪는다는 것은 어차피 '온몸'으로 떠맡는 것이고 보면 적성積成이 없다 하여 절절한 체험 그 자체를 과소평가할 수 없는 것이기 때문입니다.

그러기에 제가 정작 부러워하는 것은 객관적인 처지의 순역順逆이 아닙니다. 생사별리生死別離 등 갖가지 인간적 고초로 가득 찬 18년에 걸친 유형의 세월을 빛나는 창조의 공간으로 삼은 '비약'飛躍이 부러운 것입니다. 그리고 비약은 그 어감에서 느껴지는 화려함처럼 어느날 갑자기 나타나는 '곱셈의 논리'가 아니라는 점에서 더욱 그렇습니다.

녹두 씨울

계수님께

A Grain of Mung Bean Seed • 73p

지난 8일에는 공주로 사회참관을 다녀왔습니다. 무녕왕릉은 연전年前에도 다녀온 일이 있었습니다만 이번에는 그곳을 돌아 나오면서 갑오농민혁명의 최대 격전지였던 '우금치'를 찾았던 일이 매우 인상 깊었습니다. 그곳에는 '갑오농민혁명기념비'甲午農民革命紀念碑라 부조浮彫된 그리 크지 않은 비가 석대石臺 위에 서 있고, 주위의 잡목과 성근 잔디는 때마침 추풍에 구르는 낙엽들로 해서 잊혀져 가고 있는 유적지 특유의 스산한 풍경을 만들고 있었습니다.

저는 이날 저녁 제가 가진 근대사의 우금치 공방전에 관한 부분을 다시 읽어 보았습니다. 종전에는 소위 공주전투에 참가한 농민군의 수가 10~20만으로 알려져 왔으나 그 대부분은 편의대便衣隊의 봉기 농민과 그 가족들이었고 실제의 병력은 훨씬 적은 것으로 밝혀졌습니다.

농민군의 전투부대는 전봉준이 인솔한 4,000명을 포함한 호남농민군 1만을 주축으로 한 도합 2만이었다고 합니다. 그외에 목천木川 세성산細城山의 김복용 부대와, 효포孝浦에 진출한 옥천포 부대가 있었으나 이들은 우금치 전투의 전초전에서 일본군과 관군의 선제 기습공격으로 괴멸되었기 때문에 공주전투에는 참가하지 못하였으며, 일찍이 전주화약全州和約에 이르기까지 연전연승해 온 손화중, 최명선 부대는 일본군의 해안 상륙에 대비하여 나주에 주둔하였고, 김개남 부대는 후비後備부대로서 전주에 남아 있었습니다. 이처럼 농민군 주력이 공주, 나주,

전주 세 방면으로 분산된 반면 관군과 일본군은 공주 일점一點에 그 전력을 집중시키고 있었습니다. 원래 농민군의 전략상의 강점은 관군을 광범한 농촌, 농민들 속으로 깊숙이 분산, 유인하여 타격하는 운동전運動戰에 있음에도 불구하고 공주전투에서는 이 집중과 분산의 전략이 역전되어 있었다는 것이 결정적 결함으로 지적되고 있습니다. 이러한 결함은 후일 신돌석 부대 등 농민 출신 의병장의 의병투쟁에서 발전적으로 극복되게 되지만 이는 너무나 값비싼 희생을 치른 교훈이라 하겠습니다.

이에 비하여 상대편은 미나미오 시로南小四郎 소좌가 이끄는 일본군 정예 1,000명, 그리고 관군으로는 중앙 영병中央 營兵 3,500명, 지방영병 7,000명으로 도합 1만여 명이었습니다. 그들은 화력과 장비에 있어서 월등할 뿐 아니라 특히 일본군은 관군을 그들의 작전 지휘 아래 두어 병력의 부족을 충분히 보강하였을 뿐 아니라 일본 국내에서의 내란 진압, 대만에서의 민중 탄압, 청일전쟁 등 풍부한 실전 경험을 갖추고 있었습니다.

1894년 12월 4일 농민군은 이곳 우금치를 삼면에서 포위하여 30리의 장사진으로 그 처절한 격전을 전개하였습니다. 뺏고 빼앗기기 40, 50차를 거듭한 6~7일간의 혈전에서, 결국 일본군의 집중된 전력과 지리地利, 우세한 화력과 작전에 정면 승부를 건 농민군이 무참한 패배를 당하게 됩니다. 이곳 우금치의 전투를 분수령으로 하여 농민군은 끝내 그 세를 만회하지 못한 채 은진, 금구, 태인 등지에서 패배에 패배를 거듭, 농민군의 피로써 그 막을 내리게 됩니다.

갑오농민전쟁은 그 참담한 패배에도 불구하고 19세기 아시아 민족운동의 큰 봉우리로서, 그리고 그 이후 한국 근대사의 골간을 이루는 의병투쟁, 독립전쟁의 선구로서 찬연히 빛나고 있다는 점에서 저는 "누가

프랑스 혁명을 실패로 끝났다고 하는가?"라는 앙드레 말로의 노기 띤 반문을 상기하게 됩니다.

어느 시인은 녹두장군의 죽음에 다음과 같이 헌시獻詩하고 있습니다.

나는 죽어 쑥국새 되리라.
이 강산 모든 땅 위를 날며, 햇살 빛덩이를 찍어 물어,
집집마다 토담마다 가슴마다 묻고 심고 심고 묻는…….

그날 우리는 무심한 아이들 네댓 명 멀찌감치 서서 지켜보는 가운데 사과를 먹고 당시의 혈전을 증거 하듯 붉게 타는 단풍잎 한 장 가지고 돌아왔습니다. 돌아오는 차 속에서 절구絶句 한 짝 읊어 보았습니다.

산함려성인내천 녹두화처풍사연
山含黎聲人乃天 綠豆花處楓似然
(산천에는 사람이 하늘이라는 민중의 함성이 배어 있고
녹두꽃 피었던 곳에는 단풍이 불타듯 붉도다.)

그저께 아버님 다녀가신 편에 소식 잘 들었습니다. 빈백빔白의 아버님께 듣는 어머님의 입원 소식은 마음 아픈 일입니다. 형수님, 계수님께서 잘 간호하시리라 믿습니다. 지난 달에 보내 주신 돈 받고 10월 22일 편지 드렸습니다만 못 받으셨다니 다시 적었습니다.

이제 성큼 겨울로 다가선 느낌입니다. 교도소의 차가운 땅을 그 밝은 금빛 꽃송이로 따뜻이 데워 주던 황국黃菊도 인제는 꽃을 떨어 버리고 뿌리로만 남아서 겨울을 맞이할 채비를 하고 있습니다.

시험의 무게

형수님께

The Weight of Test • 77p

지금도 이따금 꾸는 꿈 중에 국민학교 때의 시험장 광경이 있습니다. 꿈에 보는 시험장은 언제나 초조하고 불안한 분위기로 가득 찬 것입니다. 이를테면 시험 시간에 대지 못하여 아무도 없는 운동장, 긴 복도를 부랴부랴 달려왔으나 교실문은 굳게 닫혀 열리지 않고 급우들은 제 답안지에 얼굴을 박고 있을 뿐, 시간은 자꾸 흐르고, 땀도 흐르고……. 그러다 깜짝 잠이 깨면 30년도 더 지난 아득한 옛날의 기억입니다.

30년도 더 된 옛일이 지금도 꿈이 되어 가위 누르는 것을 보면 어린 이들의 마음을 누르는 시험의 무게가 얼마나 가혹한 것이었던가를 다시 생각케 합니다.

가장 이상적인 교육은 놀이와 학습과 노동이 하나로 통일된 생활의 어떤 멋진 덩어리 ─ 일감 ─ 을 안겨 주는 것이라 합니다. 『논어』「옹야편」雍也篇에 '지지자 불여호지자 호지자 불여락지자'知之者 不如好之者 好知者 不如樂之者라는 구절이 있습니다. 안다는 것은 좋아하는 것만 못하고 좋아하는 것은 그것을 즐기는 것만 못하다 하여 '지'知란 진리의 존재를 파악한 상태이고, '호'好가 그 진리를 아직 자기 것으로 삼지 못한 상태로 보는 데에 비하여 '낙'樂은 그것을 완전히 터득하고 자기 것으로 삼아서 생활화하고 있는 경지로 풀이되기도 합니다.

즐거운 마음으로 무엇을 궁리해 가며 만들어 내는 과정을 살펴보면, 우선 그 즐거움은 놀이이며, 궁리는 학습이고, 만들어 내는 행위는 곧 노동이 됩니다. 이러한 생활 속의 즐거움이나 일거리와는 하등의 인연도 없이 칠판에 백묵으로 적어 놓은 것이나 종이에 인쇄된 것을 '진리'라고 믿으라는 '요구'는 심하게 표현한다면 어른들의 폭력이라 해야 합니다. 이런 무리한 요구에 억눌려 자라지 못하는 무수한 가능성의 싹들을 생각하면 시험과 성적과 모범 등……, 이러한 학교의 도덕적 규준이 만들어 내는 품성이 과연 어떠한 것인가에 대하여 회의를 품지 않을 수 없게 됩니다.

창의성 있고 개성 있는 어린이, 굵은 뼈대를 가진 어린이를 알아보지 못하고 도리어 불량 학생이란 흉한 이름을 붙여 일찌감치 엘리트 코스에서 밀어내 버리고, 선생님 말 잘 듣고 고분고분 잘 암기하는 수신형受信型의 편편약골을 기르고 기리어 사회의 동량棟樑의 자리를 맡긴다면 평화로운 시기는 또 그렇다 치더라도 역사의 격동기에 조국을 지켜 나가기에는 아무래도 미덥지 못하다 생각됩니다. 저는 훨씬 나중에야 그 '우등'의 본질을 보다 정확하게 파악하고 열등생으로의 대전락大轉落(?)을 경험하게 되지만, 어린 시절 우등생이라는 명예(?)가 어쩐지 다른 친구들로부터 나를 소외시키는 것 같아 일부러 심한 장난을 저질러 선생님의 꾸중을 자초하던 기억이 있습니다. 이러한 장난들은 우등생과 열등생 사이를 넘나들던 정신적 갈등의 표현이었음을 지금에야 깨닫게 됩니다.

저는 우용이와 주용이가 시험 성적이 뛰어난 우등생에 그치지 않고 동시에 자기의 주견主見과 창의에 가득 찬 강건한 품성을 키워 가기 바랍니다.

그날 학교 앞에서 잠시 삼촌을 보여 줄 때 '우용이, 주용이는 아직 어리고 삼촌은 또 바빠서' 다만 '다음'을 약속하고 바람같이 떠나고 말았습니다만 우용이의 침착하고, 주용이의 발랄한 인상에서 결코 약골이 아님을 읽을 수 있었습니다. 소년을 보살피는 일은 천체망원경의 렌즈를 닦는 일처럼 별과 우주와 미래를 바라보는 일이라 생각됩니다.

한 발 걸음
형수님께

One-Footed Step · 80p

우리 방에서 가장 빨리 달리는 20대의 청년과 가장 느린 50대의 노년이 경주를 하였습니다. 토끼와 거북이의 우화를 실연實演해 본 놀이가 아니라 청년은 한 발로 뛰고 노년은 두 발로 뛰는 일견 공평한 경주였습니다. 결과는 예상을 뒤엎고 50대 노년이 거뜬히 이겼습니다. 한 발과 두 발의 엄청난 차이를 실감케 해준 한판 승부였습니다. 우김질 끝에 장난 삼아 해본 경주라 망정이지 정말 다리가 하나뿐인 불구자의 패배였다면 그 침통함이란 이루 형언키 어려웠을 것입니다.

그런데 징역살이에서 느끼는 불행 중의 하나가 바로 이 한 발 걸음이라는 외로운 보행입니다. 실천과 인식이라는 두 개의 다리 중에서 '실천의 다리'가 없기 때문입니다. 사람은 실천 활동을 통하여 외계의 사물과 접촉함으로써 인식을 가지게 되며 이를 다시 실천에 적용하는 과정에서 그 진실성이 검증되는 것입니다. 실천은 인식의 원천인 동시에 그 진리성의 규준이라 합니다.

이처럼 '실천→인식→재실천→재인식'의 과정이 반복되어 실천의 발전과 더불어 인식도 감성적 인식에서 이성적 인식으로 발전해 갑니다. 그러므로 이 실천이 없다는 사실은 거의 결정적인 의미를 띱니다. 그것은 곧 인식의 좌절, 사고의 정지를 의미합니다. 흐르지 않는 물이 썩고, 발전하지 못하는 생각이 녹슬 수밖에 없는 이치입니다.

제가 징역 초년, 닦아도 닦아도 끝이 없는 생각의 녹을 상대하면서 깨달은 사실은 생각을 녹슬지 않게 간수하기 위해서는 앉아서 녹을 닦고 있을 것이 아니라 생각 자체를 키워 나가야 한다는 사실이었습니다. 요컨대 일어서서 걸어야 한다는 것입니다.

"이랑 많이 일굴수록 쟁깃날은 빛나고", 유수봉하해流水逢河海, 흐르는 물은 바다를 만난다는 너무나 평범한 일상의 재확인이었습니다만 이것이 제게 갖는 뜻은 결코 예사로운 것이 아니었습니다. 그러나 막상 일어나서 걷고자 할 경우의 허전함, 다리 하나가 없다는 절망은 다시 그 자리에 주저앉게 합니다.

징역 속에 주저앉아 있는 사람들이 맨 처음 시작하는 일이 책을 읽는 일입니다. 그러나 독서는 실천이 아니며 독서는 다리가 되어 주지 않았습니다. 그것은 역시 한 발 걸음이었습니다. 더구나 독서가 우리를 피곤하게 하는 까닭은 그것이 한 발 걸음이라 더디다는 데에 있다기보다는 '인식→인식→인식……'의 과정을 되풀이하는 동안 앞으로 나아가기는커녕 현실의 튼튼한 땅을 잃고 공중으로 공중으로 지극히 관념화해 간다는 사실입니다.

그래서 결국 저는 다른 모든 불구자가 그러듯이 목발을 짚고 걸어가기로 작정하였습니다. 제가 처음 목발로 삼은 것은 다른 사람들의 경험 즉 '과거의 실천'이었습니다.

목발은 비록 단단하기는 해도 자기의 피가 통하는 생다리와 같을 수 없기 때문에 두 개의 다리가 줄곧 서로 차질을 빚어 걸음이 더디고, 뒤뚱거리고, 넘어지기 일쑤였습니다. 그러나 이 어색한 걸음새도 세월이 흐르고 목발에 손때가 묻으면서 그럭저럭 이력이 나고 보속步速과 맵시(?)가 붙어 갔습니다.

그런데 이 경우의 소위 이력이란 것이 제게는 매우 귀중한 교훈을 주는 것입니다. 그것은 목발이 생다리를 닮아서 이루어진 숙달이 아니라 반대로 생다리가 목발을 배워서 이루어진 숙달이라는 사실입니다. 다시 말하자면 나의 인식이 내가 목발로 삼은 그 경험들의 임자들의 인식을 배우고 그것을 닮아감으로써 비로소 걸음걸이를 얻었다는 사실입니다. 목발의 발전에 의한 것이 아니라 생다리의 발전에 의한 것이라는 사실은 사전事前에는 반대로 예상했던 것이었던 만큼 실로 충격적인 것이었습니다.

더욱 놀라운 것은 함께 살아가고 있는 징역 동료들의 경험들이 단지 과거의 것으로 화석화되어 있지 않고 현재의 징역 그 자체와 튼튼히 연계되거나 그 일부를 구성하고 있음으로 해서 강렬한 현재성을 띠고 있다는 사실입니다. 과거의 실천이란 죽은 실천이 아니라 살아서 숨 쉬고 있는 것이라는 사실의 발견은 나의 목발에 피가 통하고 감각이 살아나는 듯한 감동을 안겨 주는 것이었습니다.

실천이란 반드시 극적 구조를 갖춘 큰 규모의 일만이 아니라 사람이 있고 일거리가 있는 곳이면 어디든지 흔전으로 널려 있다는 제법 익은 듯한 생각을 가져 보기도 합니다.

사람은 각자 저마다의 걸음걸이로 저마다의 인생을 걸어가는 것이겠지만, 땅을 박차서 땅을 얻든, 그 위에 쓰러져 그것을 얻든, 죽어서 땅 속에 묻히기까지는 거대한 실천의 대륙 위를 걸어가게 마련이라 생각됩니다.

3월, 길고 추웠던 겨울이 끝나려 하고 있습니다. 어쩌면 옥담 밑 어느 후미진 곳에 봄은 벌써 작은 풀싹으로 와 있는지도 모를 일입니다. 어떻든 봄은 산 너머 남쪽에서 오는 것이 아니라 발 밑의 언땅을 뚫고 솟아오르는 것이라 생각됩니다.

닫힌 공간, 열린 정신

형수님께

A Closed Space, An Open Mind • 84p

옷은 새 옷이 좋고 사람은 헌 사람이 좋다고 하는데, 집의 경우는 어느 쪽이 좋은지 생각중입니다. 집은 옷과 달라서 우리 몸에 맞추어 지은 것이 아니며, 집은 사람과 달라서 시간이 흘러도 양보해 주지 않습니다. 새 교도소에 이사 와서 보니 새집은 역시 길들일 것이 많습니다.

소혹성에서 온 어린 왕자는 '길들인다는 것은 관계를 맺는 것'이라고 합니다. 관계를 맺음이 없이 길들이는 것이나 불평등한 관계 밑에서 길들여진 모든 것은, 본질에 있어서 억압입니다. 관계를 맺는다는 것의 진정한 의미는 무엇을 서로 공유하는 것이라 생각됩니다. 한 개의 나무 의자든, 높은 정신적 가치든, 무엇을 공유한다는 것은 같은 창문 앞에 서는 공감을 의미하며, 같은 배를 타고 있는 운명의 연대를 뜻하는 것이라 생각됩니다.

작년까지만 하더라도 인적이 없던 이 산기슭에 지금은 새하얀 벽과 벽에 의하여 또박또박 분할된 수많은 공간들로 가득 찼습니다. 저는 그 중의 어느 각진 1.86평 공간 속에 곧추앉아서 이 냉정한 공간과 제가 맺어야 할 관계에 대하여 생각해 봅니다.

수많은 공간과 그것의 지극히 작은 일부를 채우는 64kg의 무게, 높은 옥담과 그것으로는 가둘 수 없는 저 푸른 하늘의 자유로움을 내면화하려는 의지……. 한마디로 닫힌 공간과 열린 정신의 불편한 대응에 기초하고 있는 이러한 관계는 교도소의 구금拘禁 공간과 제가 맺어야 할 역설적 관계의 본질을 선명하게 밝혀 줍니다. 그것은 길들여지는 것과는 반대 방향을 겨냥하는 이른바 긴장과 갈등의 관계입니다. 그것은 관계 이전의 어떤 것, 관계 그 자체의 모색이라 해야 할 것입니다.

긴장과 갈등으로 팽팽히 맞선 관계는 대자적對者的 인식의 한 조건일 뿐 아니라 모든 '살아 있는' 관계의 실상입니다. 관계를 맺고 난 후의 편안하게 길들여진 안거安居는 일견 '관계의 완성' 또는 '완숙한 관계'와 같은 외모를 하고 있지만 그 내부에는 그것을 가져다 준 관계 그 자체의 붕괴가 시작되고 있음을, 이미 붕괴가 끝나 가고 있음을 허다히 보아 왔기 때문입니다.

저는 새 교도소에 와서 느끼는 이 갈등과 긴장을 교도소 특유의 어떤 것, 또는 제 개인의 특별한 경험 내용에서 연유된 것이라 생각하지 않고, 사물의 모든 관계 속에 항상 있어 온 '관계 일반의 본질'이 우연한 계기를 만나 잠시 표출된 것으로 생각합니다. 그래서 저는 이 긴장과 갈등을 그것 자체로서 독립된 대상으로 받아들이기보다 도리어 이것을 통하여 관계 일반의 본질에 도달할 수 있는 하나의 시점으로 이해하려 합니다. 그리하여 제 자신과 제 자신이 놓여 있는 존재 조건을 정직하게 인식하는 귀중한 계기로 삼고자 합니다. 그러나 저는 이 긴장과 갈등을 견딜 수 있고 이길 수 있는 역량을 제 개인의 고독한 의지 속에서 구하려 하지 않습니다. 그것은 새하얀 벽과 벽에 의하여 또박또박 분할된 그 수많은 공간마다에 사람들이 가득 차 있다는 사실에서 무엇보다도 확실하게 얻어질 수 있기 때문입니다.

비단 갇혀 있는 사람들뿐만 아니라 우리들이 많은 사람들 속에 존재하고 있다는 튼튼한 연대감이야말로 닫힌 공간을 열고, 저 푸른 하늘을 숨쉬게 하며……, 그리하여 긴장과 갈등마저 넉넉히 포용하는 거대한 대륙에 발 딛게 하는 우람한 힘이라 믿고 있습니다. 관계를 맺는다는 것은 '아픔'을 공유하는 것에서부터 시작하는 것인가 봅니다.

보내 주신 돈과 시계 잘 받았습니다. 잠겨 있는 옥방 안에서도 시계는 잘 갑니다. '막힌 공간에 흐르는 시간'……, 흡사 반칙反則 같습니다.

팔목에 시간을 가지고 있더라도 시간에 각박해지지 않도록 노력하겠습니다. 어차피 무기징역은 유유한 자세를 필요로 합니다.

4월의 훈풍은 산과 나무와 흙과 바위와 시멘트와 헌 종이와 빈 비닐봉지에까지 아낌없이 따뜻한 입김을 불어넣어 주고 있습니다. 가내의 평안을 빕니다.

타락의 노르마
계수님께

옛날의 귀부인들은 노예가 있는 옆에서 서슴없이 옷을 갈아입었다 합니다. 옆에 아무도 없는 것〔傍若無人〕으로 치든가 고양이나 강아지가 있는 것쯤으로 생각했던가 봅니다. 그러나 당시의 노예들은 생각마저 묶여 있어서 제대로 바라보지도 못하였으리라 생각됩니다. 그에 비하면 오늘의 수인들은 그 의식이 훨씬 자유롭기 때문에 많은 것을 관찰하는 셈입니다.

맨홀에서 작업중인 인부에게 길가는 사람들의 숨긴 곳이 노출되듯이, 낮은 자리를 사는 수인들에게는 사람들의 치부를 직시할 수 있는 의외의 시각이 주어져 있습니다. 비단 다른 사람들뿐만 아니라 재소자 자신들도 징역 들어와 머리 깎고 수의로 옷 갈아입을 때 예의, 염치, 교양……, 이런 것들도 함께 벗어 버리는 사람이 대부분입니다. 이러저러한 까닭으로 해서 우리는 사람들을 쉽게 존경하지 않습니다.

꾸민 표정, 걸친 의상은 물론 지위, 재산, 학벌, 경력 등 소위 알몸이 아닌 모든 겉치레에 대하여 지극히 냉정한 시선을 키워 두고 있습니다. 인간과 그 인간이 걸치고 있는 외식外飾을 구별하는 이 냉정한 시선은 다른 곳에서는 여간해서 얻기 어려운 하나의 통찰임에 틀림없으며 그렇기 때문에 별로 가진 것이 없는 우리들에게는 귀중한 자산資産의 하나가 아닐 수 없습니다.

그러나 이것은 그 사람의 가장 불우한 모습과, 그 사람의 가장 어두

운 목소리로 그를 판단하는 것이며, 자칫 사람을 판단함에 있어 가학적
加虐的 악의를 드러내기 쉬우며 그럼으로써 자기 자신의 결함을 합리화
하려는 것입니다. 타인의 결함이 자기의 결함을 구제해 줄 수 없음에도
불구하고 사람을 그 결함에서 먼저 인식하여 비슷한 것이라도 발견되
면 서둘러 안도의 심정이 되는 것은 남은 고사하고 자기 자신의 성장을
가로막는 고약한 심사가 아닐 수 없습니다. 사람의 많은 부분은 상황에
따라 굴절되어 표현되기 때문에 그때그때의 구체적인 현상을 어떤 순
수한 본질에 비추어 규정하려는 태도는 이상주의적 환상이 아니면 처
음부터 부정적인 결론을 의도하는 비난 그 자체라 해야 합니다.

우리가 살고 있는 징역살이만 하더라도 거기에는 수의가 요구하는
일정한 '타락의 노르마'가 있습니다. 그것이 어떤 평균치이건, 또는 하
나의 가정치假定値이건 이 '노르마'는 수의를 입은 모든 사람을 사전적
事前的으로 규정합니다. 이것은 사회가 수인들을 보는 선입관에 그치지
않고 수인들이 자기 자신을 바라보는 경우에도 작용하는 이른바 안에
서도 밖에서도 벗어나기 어려운 완고한 형틀입니다. 수인들로 하여금
징역 속에서 예의나 염치를 헌옷 벗듯 손쉽게 벗어 버리게 하는 것도 바
로 이 '타락의 노르마'입니다.

사람의 많은 부분이 상황에 따라 굴절되어 표현됨과 동시에 반대로
상황이 사람의 많은 부분을 굴절시킨다는 사실을 수긍한다면 우리는
상황과 인간을 함께 타매唾罵하거나 함께 용서할 수밖에 없다는 겸손한
생각을 길러야 합니다.

사람을 판단하는 것은, 그 판단의 주체가 또한 사람이라는 사실이
그것을 더욱 어렵게 하고 있습니다. 사람은 누구나 자신의 처지에 눈이
달리게 마련이고 자신의 그릇만큼의 강물밖에 뜨지 못합니다. 이러한
자신의 제한성과 특수성을 올바로 깨닫지 못하는 한 자기의 생각과 견

해를 넓혀 나가기는 몹시 어렵다고 생각됩니다.

징역의 이데올로기(?) 속에 격납格納되어 있는 이 가학적이고 냉소적인 시각은 어떤 형태로든 청산되어야 할 징역의 응달입니다. 그러나 징역이 아니면 얻기 어려운 냉정한 시각과 그 적나라한 인간학으로 해서 기존의 도덕적 베일, 분식粉飾과 허위로부터 시원하게 벗어난 자유로운 정신은 징역의 모든 중압을 보상해 주고도 남는 값진 것이 아닐 수 없습니다. 이 자유로운 정신은 계란이 병아리를 약속하듯 새로운 것에로의 가능성을 안고 있다고 믿습니다.

나는 징역에 고유한 '타락의 노르마'가 부끄러운 것이기보다 오히려 쾌적한 것으로 느껴지고, 우리들의 옆에서 행해지는 방약무인傍若無人의 언행이 노엽다기보다 가식 없는 실체를 보여 주는 소중한 통찰로 생각됩니다.

새 교도소는 가까이 산이 있다는 사실이 커다란 구원입니다. 산의 모양도 정다울 뿐 아니라 암석과 수목이 서로 사이좋게 산을 나누어 흡사 강유剛柔를 겸비한 군자의 풍모입니다. 더욱이 5월의 산은, 어딘가 바랜 듯하던 빛깔의 3, 4월 산과 달리, 하루가 다르게 더해 가는 신록으로 하여 바야흐로 소매 걷어붙이고 무언가 시작하려는 듯한 활기로 가득 차 있습니다. 콘크리트 벽에 둘러싸여 있기도 하지만 더 크게는 5월의 산에 둘러싸여 있는 나에게는 과연 어떤 새로움이 싹트고 있는지 살펴보아야겠습니다.

민중의 창조
형수님께

Creation of the 'MinJung' • 91p

형수님께서 보내 주신 『민중 속의 성직자들』 그리고 돈 잘 받았습니다. 그들을 말미암음으로써 우리가 사는 시대를 더욱 선명하게 바라볼 수 있는 시각을 키워 주는 '응달의 사람들', 소외되고 억눌리고 버려진 사람들 속에 자기 자신을 심고 그들과 함께 고반苦飯을 드는 사람과 자비의 이야기들은 뜻있는 삶이 어떤 것인가를 크지 않는 목소리로 말해 주고 있습니다. 이 책을 읽는 동안 저의 뇌리를 줄곧 떠나지 않는 것은 "우리 시대의 민중은 누구인가?", "우리 사회의 민중은 어디에 있는가?"라는 집요한 자문自問입니다.

어느 시대, 어느 사회든 민중의 든든한 실체를 파악한다는 것은 매우 어려운 일이 아닐 수 없으며, 민중의 실체를 파악하지 못하는 한 그 시대, 그 사회를 총체적으로 인식할 수 없는 법입니다.

우리는 과거의 역사적 사실로서의 민중, 특히 격변기의 역사 무대에 그 모습을 확연히 드러낸 경우의 민중에 대해서는 잘 알고 있습니다. 그러나 당대 사회의 생생한 현재 상황 속에서 민중의 진정한 실체를 발견해 내는 데는 많은 사람들이 실패하고 있음을 우리는 알고 있습니다. 착종錯綜하는 이해관계와 이데올로기의 대립, 현실의 왜곡, 사실의 과장, 진실의 은폐 등 격렬한 싸움의 현장에서 민중의 참모습을 발견해 내고 그것의 합당한 역량을 신뢰하기는 지극히 어려운 일이 아닐 수 없습니다.

기껏 잡은 것이 민중의 '그림자'에 불과하거나 '그때 그곳의 우연'

에다 보편적인 의미를 입히고 있는 등……, 감상과 연민이 만들어 낸 민중이란 이름의 허상이 우리들을 한없이 피곤하고 목마르게 합니다. 그것은 '왜 불행한가?'라는 불행의 원인에 대한 질문에로는 한 걸음도 나아가지 못하고 모든 것을 참으며 모든 것을 견디게 하는 '눈물의 예술'로 그 격이 떨어져 있기 때문입니다. 결국 그것은 위안을 줌으로써 삶을 상실케 하는 것이기 때문입니다.

저는 십수년의 징역살이 그 일인칭의 상황을 살아오면서 민중이란 결코 어디엔가 기성既成의 형태로 존재하는 것이 아니라 항상 새로이 '창조'되는 것이라 생각해 오고 있습니다.

응달의 불우한 사람들이 곧 민중의 표상이 아님은 물론, 민중을 만날 수 있는 최소한의 가교假橋가 되어 주지도 않습니다. 민중을 불우한 존재로 선험先驗하려는 데에 바로 감상주의의 오류가 있는 것입니다.

민중은 당대의 가장 기본적인 모순을 계기로 하여 창조되는 '응집되고 증폭된 사회적 역량'입니다. 이러한 역량은 단일한 계기에 의하여 단번에 나타나는 가벼운 걸음걸이의 주인공이 아닙니다. 장구한 역사속에 점철된 수많은 성공과 실패, 그 환희와 비탄의 기억들이 민족사의 기저基底에 거대한 잠재력으로 묻혀 있다가 역사의 격변기에 그 당당한 모습을 실현하는 것입니다.

그러나 민중을 이렇게 신성시하는 것도 실은 다른 형태의 감상주의입니다. 어떠한 시냇물을 따라서도 우리가 바다로 나아갈 수 있듯이 아무리 작고 외로운 골목의 삶이라 하더라도 그곳에는 민중의 뿌리가 뻗어 와 있는 것입니다. 이것이 바로 민중 특유의 민중성입니다. 부족한 것은 당사자들의 투철한 시대정신과 유연한 예술성입니다.

그 허상의 주변을 서성이며 민중을 신뢰하지 못하고 있는 많은 사람들의 실패가 설령 그들 각인의 의식과 역량의 부족에 연유된 것이라 할

지라도, 저는 그들 개인의 한계에 앞서 우리 시대, 우리 사회 자체의 역사적 미숙으로 이해하려고 합니다. 왜냐하면 개인의 인식과 역량은 기본적으로는 사회적 획득물이기 때문입니다.

이사온 지 두 달입니다만 아직도 쓸고 닦고 파고 메우고 고르고……, 크고 작은 일들로 주변이 어수선합니다. 그러나 새벽의 여름 산에서 들려오는 산새소리, 때묻지 않은 자연의 육성은 갖가지 인조음에 시달려 온 우리의 심신을 5월의 신록처럼 싱싱하게 되살려 줍니다.

엿새간의 귀휴
계수님께

Six Days' Release Home on Leave • 94p

어제 저녁 두 통 한꺼번에 배달된 계수님의 편지는 나의 생각을 다시 서울로 데려갑니다. 귀휴歸休란 돌아가 쉰다는 뜻인데도 아직 마음 편히 쉬기에는 일렀던가 봅니다. 귀휴 기간 동안 내가 해야 했던 것은 우선 엿새 동안에 지난 16년의 세월을 사는 일이었습니다. 16년 세월에 담긴 중량重量을 짐 지는 일이며, 그 세월이 할퀴고 간 상처의 통증을 되살리는 일이었습니다. 그리고 만나는 모든 사람들의 시선이 향하고 있는 곳—나 자신을, 나도 또한 바라보지 않을 수 없었습니다.

다행히 십수년의 세월은 그 빛깔이나 아픔을 훨씬 묽게 만들어 주었고 가족들도 그 엄청난 충격을 건강하게 극복해 두고 있어서 어떤 것은 마치 남의 일 대하듯 담담하게 이야기 나눌 수 있었습니다. 기쁜 일입니다.

그러나 그 오랜 세월에도 불구하고 풍화風化되지 않고 하얗게 남아 있는 슬픔의 뼈 같은 것이 함몰된 세월의 공허와 더불어 잔잔한 아픔으로 안겨 오기도 하였습니다. 짐 지고 서서 사는 일에는 어지간히 이력이 났거니 생각해 온 나로서는 의외다 싶을 정도로 힘겨웠고 가족들의 따뜻한 포용에도 좀체 풀리지 않는 '어떤 갈증'에 목말라 하기도 했습니다. 아마 계수님이 편지에 적은 '애정의 안식처'에 대한 갈구였는지도 모릅니다.

그러한 애정과 안식의 문제라면, 세상 사람들과 같은 옷 입고 섞여 보아도 결코 사라지지 못하던 소외감이 그러한 갈구의 부당함을 준열히 깨우쳐 주었고 나 자신 이전에 이미 정리해 두고 있었던 일이기도 하였습니다.

그러나 교도소로 돌아오는 형님의 차 안에서 넥타이 풀고, 와이셔츠, 저고리, 바지 등 세상의 옷들을 하나하나 벗어 버리고 다시 수의로 갈아입을 때, 그때의 유별난 아픔은 냉정한 이성의 언어를 거부하는 감정의 독립 같은 것이었습니다. 결국 이곳에 돌아와 자도자도 끝이 없는 졸음과 잠으로 대신할 수밖에 없었던 '휴식'이 차라리 잘된 일이라 생각됩니다.

돌이켜 생각해 보면 귀휴 기간 동안에 내가 힘 부쳐 했던 아픔과 갈증은 나 자신의 조급하고 밭은 생각 때문이란 반성을 갖게 됩니다. '사랑하기보다는 사랑받으려 하고 이해하기보다는 이해받으려 하는' '마음의 가난'에 연유한 것이라 생각됩니다.

남에게 자기를 설명하려고 하는 충동은 한마디로 자기 자신에 대한 자신감의 결여를 반증하는 것이라는 점에서 그것은 어차피 나 자신의 개인적인 문제로 귀착되는 것입니다.

바쁜 동생의 생활 질서를 깨뜨려 놓았음은 물론 아무것도 모르는 꼬마들만 빼놓고, 여러 사람들을 본의 아니게 교란하지나 않았나 무척 송구스럽습니다. 늘 뒷켠으로 한 걸음 물러선 자리에서, 계수님의 표현대로 제일 아랫서열이기 때문에, 항상 어른들과 손님들의 울타리 바깥에서 무언가 내게 주려고 부지런히 오가며 애쓰던 계수님의 표정이 눈에 선합니다. 친정부모님과 동생들께도 나의 '부족한 말씀과 인사'에 대하여 양해받아 주시고 다음을 약속해 주시기 바랍니다. 계수님과도 물론 어린이 놀이터에서의 부족했던 이야기 다시 약속합니다.

의외로 많은 사람들이 나를 기다리고, 지켜보고 있음을 알 수 있었습니다. 이것이 곧 나로 하여금 이곳을 견디게 하고 나 자신을 지켜나가게 해주는 힘임을 모르지 않습니다.

일의 명인名人
형수님께

A Master at Work • 97p

1급수들은 휴일을 이용하여 노력봉사를 하는 일이 가끔 있습니다. 형수님이 보시고 놀라던 그 긴 복도를 청소하기도 하고, 잡초를 뽑거나 빗물로 메인 배수로를 열기도 하고 땅을 고르는 등 비교적 간단한 작업입니다.

　저는 휴일에 작업이 있기만 하면 빠지는 일이 없습니다. 여러 사람이 함께 일을 하면 그 자체가 하나의 '학교'가 되게 마련이지만 특히 제게는 두 사람의 훌륭한 '스승'을 배울 수 있는 귀중한 기회이기 때문에 절대로 빠지는 일이 없습니다. 이 두 사람의 스승은 학식도 없고 집안 형편도 어려워 징역살이도 자연 '국으로 찌그러져' 사는 응달의 사람입니다. 제가 이 두 사람을 스승으로 마음 두고 있는 까닭은 '일'이 사람을 어떻게 키워 주고 사람을 어떻게 개조하는가를 이분들의 말없는 행동을 통하여 깨닫기 때문입니다.

　첫째 이 두 사람은 일을 '발견'하는 눈이 매우 탁월합니다. 저는 물론이고 다른 사람들의 눈에는 미처 일거리로 보이지 않는 것도 이 두 사람의 눈길이 닿으면 마치 조명을 받은 피사체처럼 대뜸 발견되고 맙니다. 그것도 자잘한 잔챙이를 낚아서 바지런 떠는 그런 부류와는 달리 별로 힘들이는 기색이나 생색내는 일도 없이 큼직큼직한 일거리, 꼭 필요한 일머리를 제때에 찾아내는 솜씨란 과연 오랜 세월을 일과 더불어 살아 온 '일의 명인名人'다운 풍모를 느끼게 합니다.

둘째로 이 두 사람은 일을 두고 그냥 지나치지 못하는 '가녀린 심정'을 가지고 있습니다. 주변에 일손을 기다리는 일거리가 있거나 비뚤어져 있는 물건이 한 개라도 있으면 그만 마음이 불편해서 견디지 못하는 그런 심정의 소유자입니다. 이분들에게 있어서 일이란 외부의 어떤 대상이 아니라 삶의 내면을 이루는 존재 조건 그 자체임을 알 수 있습니다. 무심히 걷는 몇 발자국의 걸음 중에도 항상 무엇인가를 바루어 놓고 말며, 다른 일로 오가는 중에도 반드시 무얼 하나씩 들고 가고 들고 옵니다. 잠시 동안도 빈손일 때가 없습니다.

셋째로 이 두 사람은 여러 사람과 함께 일하는 경우에는 언제나 제일 많은 사람이 달라붙는 말단의 바닥일을 골라잡습니다. 일부의, 더러는 먹물이 좀 들어 있는 사람들이, 반드시 힘이 덜 들어서가 아니라, 약간 독특한 작업상의 위치를 선호하여 자신을 다른 사람들과 일정하게 구별하려는 경향이 있음에 비하여 이 두 사람은 언제나 맨 낮은 자리, 그 무한한 대중성 속에 철저히 자신을 세우고 있습니다. 바로 이 점에서 이 두 사람은 제게 다만 일솜씨만을 가르치는 '기술자'의 의미를 넘어서 '사람'을 가르치는 사표師表가 되고 있습니다. 그래서 저는 이 두 사람이 걸레를 잡으면 저도 걸레를 잡고, 이 두 사람이 삽을 잡으면 저도 얼른 삽을 잡습니다. 이분들의 옆에 항상 나 자신의 자리를 정함으로 해서 깨달은 사실은 여러 사람들 속에 설 때의 그 든든함이 우리를 매우 힘 있게 만들어 준다는 것입니다.

교편을 잡으시던 부모님 슬하에서 어려서부터 줄곧 학교에서 자라 노동의 경험은 물론, 노동자들과의 생활마저 부족했던 제게 징역과 징역 속의 여러 스승이 갖는 의미는 실로 막중한 것이 아닐 수 없습니다.

바다가 가장 낮은 자리에서 그 큼을 이루고 꽃송이가 다발을 이루어 큰 꽃이 되는 그 변증법의 비밀이 실은 우리의 가장 비근한 일상의 노동

속에 흔전으로 있는 것임에 새삼 우리들 자신의 맹목을 탓하지 않을 수 없습니다.

　보내 주신 책 두 권은 열독이 허가되지 않아 읽지는 못하였습니다만 보내 주신 마음은 잘 읽고 있습니다. 사람도 물건도 출입이 어려운 마을에 살고 있음을 알겠습니다.

관계의 최고 형태
형수님께

The Highest Form of Relationship • 100p

어느 일본인 기자가 쓴 '한국인'에 관한 글을 읽었습니다. 젊은 동료 한 사람이 그 글의 진의眞意를 물어 와서 일부러 시간을 내어 읽어 본 것입니다만 제가 읽어 본 일본의 몇몇 민주적인 지식인의 글에 비하면 그 격이 훨씬 떨어지는 3류의 것이었습니다. 저는 이 작은 엽서에서 그 글의 내용을 탓하려고도 않으며 또 그 글에 숨어 있는 필자의 민족적 오만이나 군국주의의 변태變態를 들추려고도 않습니다. 한마디로 그 글은 우리가 어떤 대상을 인식하거나 서술한다는 것이 얼마나 어려운 일인가를 다시 한번 깨닫게 해준 반면反面의 교사였습니다.

우리가 인식하거나 서술하려는 대상이 비교적 간단한 한 개의 사물이나 일개인인 경우와는 달리 사회나 민족이나 한 시대를 대상으로 삼을 경우 그 어려움은 실로 막중한 것이 아닐 수 없습니다. 대상이 이처럼 거대한 총체인 경우에는 필자의 관찰력이나 부지런함 따위는 별로 도움이 되지 않습니다. 하물며 필자의 문장력이나 감각은 아무 소용이 없습니다. 사회·역사 의식이나 철학적 세계관에 기초한 과학적 사상체계가 갖추어져 있지 않는 한, 아무리 많은 자료를 동원하고 아무리 해박한 지식을 구사한다 하더라도 결국은 코끼리를 더듬는 장님 꼴을 면치 못할 것입니다.

그러나 이러한 과학적 사고보다 더 중요하고 결정적인 것은 바로 대상과 필자의 '관계'라 생각합니다. 대상과 필자가 어떠한 관계로 연결되는가에 따라서 얼마만큼의 깊이 있는 인식이, 또 어떠한 측면이 파악되는가가 결정됩니다. 이를테면 대상을 바라보기만 하는 관계, 즉 구경하는 관계 그것은 한마디로 '관계 없음'입니다. 구경이란 말 대신 '관조'라는 좀더 운치 있는 어휘로 대치하더라도 마찬가지입니다. 세상에는 관조만으로 시작되고 관조만으로서 완결되는 인식이란 없기 때문입니다.

대상과 자기가 애정의 젖줄로 연결되거나, 운명의 핏줄로 맺어짐이 없이, 즉 대상과 필자의 혼연한 육화肉化 없이 대상을 인식·서술할 수 있다는 환상, 이 환상이야말로 우리 시대에 범람하는 저널리즘이 양산해 낸 특별한 형태의 오류이며 기만입니다. 저널리즘은 항상 제3의 입장, 중립의 불편부당이라는 허구의 위상을 의제擬制하여 거기에 높은 가치를 부여하고, 대상과 관계를 가진 모든 입장을 불순하고 저급한 것으로 폄하함으로써 사람들로 하여금 구경꾼, 진실의 낭비자로 철저히 소외시킵니다. 상품의 소비자, 스탠드 위의 관객, TV 앞의 시청자 등…… 모든 형태의 구경꾼의 특징은 대상과 인식 주체 간의 완벽한 격리에 있습니다.

이처럼 대상과 인식 주체가 구별, 격리되어 있는 경우에는 시종 양자의 차이점만이 발견되고 부각됩니다. 그러기 때문에 대상을 관찰하면 할수록 자기와는 점점 더 다른 무엇으로 나타나고, 가까이 접근하면 할수록 더욱더 멀어질 뿐입니다. 그리하여 종내에는 대상을 잃어버림과 동시에 자기 자신마저 상실하고 마는 것입니다.

우리는 소위 문화인류학이 식민주의의 첨병尖兵으로서 세계의 수많은 민족을 대상화하여 그들의 민속과 전통문화 그리고 그들의 정직한 인간적 삶을, 자기들의 그것과 다르다는 이유로, 자기들의 침탈을 다른 이름으로 은폐할 목적으로, 야만시하고 왜곡해 왔으며, 그러한 부당한 왜곡이 결국은 대상의 상실뿐 아니라 자신의 인간적 양심을 상실케 함으로써 그토록 잔혹한 침략의 세기世紀를 연출해 내었던 사실을 알고 있습니다.

징역 사는 우리들 재소자도 대상화되고 있기는 마찬가지입니다. 죄명별, 범죄 유형별……, 여러 가지 표식標識에 따라 분류되기도 하고, 범죄심리학, 이상심리학, 심리전 등 각종 심리학의 연구 대상이 되기도 하는데, 이 경우 대부분의 연구자들에게서는 그들이 대상으로 삼고 있는 재소자들이 그들과 동시대를 살고, 동일한 사회관계 속에 연대되고 있다는 거시적인 깨달음을 기대하기가 어렵습니다.

그러므로 그러한 분류 연구나 심리학적 관찰은 결국 그들과는 전혀 딴판인 이를테면 '종'種을 달리하는 네안데르탈인만큼이나 멀리 떨어진 '범죄 인종'犯罪人種을 발견해 내고 만들어 내도록 예정되어 있는 것입니다.

그리하여 발견된 범죄 인종의 여러 가지 패륜은 그들 자신과는 하등의 인연도 없는, 수십만 년의 거리가 있는 것이란 점에서 그들 자신의 윤리적 반의叛意를 자위하고 두호斗護하고 은폐하는 데 역용逆用됨으로써 결국 그들 자신을 패륜화하는 악순환을 낳기도 합니다. 시대와 사회를 공유하고 있는 사람들은 각자의 처한 위치가 아무리 다르다 하더라도 차이점보다는 공통점이 더 많은 법입니다. 그러므로 우리의 어떤 대상에 대한 인식의 출발은 대상과 내가 이미 맺고 있는 관계의 발견에서부터 시작되어야 한다고 믿습니다. 검은 피부에 대한 맬컴 엑스의 관계, 알제리에 대한 프란츠 파농의 관계…….

주체가 대상을 포옹하고 대상이 주체 속에 육화된 혼혈의 엄숙한 의식을 우리는 세계의 도처에서, 역사의 수시隨時에서 발견합니다. 이러한 대상과의 일체화야말로 우리들의 삶의 진상을 선명하게 드러내 주는 동시에 우리 스스로를 정직하게 바라보게 해주는 것이라 생각됩니다.

　머리 좋은 것이 마음 좋은 것만 못하고, 마음 좋은 것이 손 좋은 것만 못하고, 손 좋은 것이 발 좋은 것만 못한 법입니다. 관찰보다는 애정이, 애정보다는 실천적 연대가, 실천적 연대보다는 입장의 동일함이 더욱 중요합니다. 입장의 동일함 그것은 관계의 최고 형태입니다.

나이테
형수님께

The Rings of a Tree • 104p

나무의 나이테가 우리에게 가르치는 것은 나무는 겨울에도 자란다는
사실입니다. 그리고 겨울에 자란 부분일수록 여름에 자란 부분보다 훨
씬 단단하다는 사실입니다.

햇빛 한 줌 챙겨 줄 단 한 개의 잎새도 없이 동토凍土에 발목 박고 풍
설風雪에 팔 벌리고 서서도 나무는 팔뚝을, 가슴을, 그리고 내년의 봄을
키우고 있습니다. 부산스럽게 뛰어다니는 사람들에 비해 겨울을 지혜
롭게 보내고 있습니다.

형님, 우용이, 주용이 밝고 기쁜 새해가 되길 기원합니다.

한 해 동안의 옥바라지 감사드립니다.

여름 징역살이

계수님께

Prison Life in Summer • 105p

없는 사람이 살기는 겨울보다 여름이 낫다고 하지만 교도소의 우리들은 없이 살기는 더합니다만 차라리 겨울을 택합니다. 왜냐하면 여름 징역의 열 가지 스무 가지 장점을 일시에 무색케 해버리는 결정적인 사실—여름 징역은 자기의 바로 옆사람을 증오하게 한다는 사실 때문입니다.

모로 누워 칼잠을 자야 하는 좁은 잠자리는 옆사람을 단지 37℃의 열덩어리로만 느끼게 합니다. 이것은 옆사람의 체온으로 추위를 이겨나가는 겨울철의 원시적 우정과는 극명한 대조를 이루는 형벌 중의 형벌입니다.

자기의 가장 가까이에 있는 사람을 미워한다는 사실, 자기의 가장 가까이에 있는 사람으로부터 미움받는다는 사실은 매우 불행한 일입니다. 더욱이 그 미움의 원인이 자신의 고의적인 소행에서 연유된 것이 아니고 자신의 존재 그 자체 때문이라는 사실은 그 불행을 매우 절망적인 것으로 만듭니다. 그러나 무엇보다도 우리 자신을 불행하게 하는 것은 우리가 미워하는 대상이 이성적으로 옳게 파악되지 못하고 말초 감각에 의하여 그릇되게 파악되고 있다는 것, 그리고 그것을 알면서도 증오의 감정과 대상을 바로잡지 못하고 있다는 자기 혐오에 있습니다.

자기의 가장 가까운 사람을 향하여 키우는 '부당한 증오'는 비단 여름 잠자리에만 고유한 것이 아니라 없이 사는 사람들의 생활 도처에서

266

발견됩니다. 이를 두고 성급한 사람들은 없는 사람들의 도덕성의 문제로 받아들여 그 인성人性을 탓하려 들지도 모릅니다. 그러나 우리는 알고 있습니다. 오늘 내일 온다온다 하던 비 한줄금 내리고 나면 노염老炎도 더는 버티지 못할 줄 알고 있으며, 머지않아 조석의 추량秋凉은 우리들끼리 서로 키워 왔던 불행한 증오를 서서히 거두어 가고, 그 상처의 자리에서 이웃들의 '따뜻한 가슴'을 깨닫게 해줄 것임을 알고 있습니다. 그리고 추수秋水처럼 정갈하고 냉철한 인식을 일깨워 줄 것임을 또한 알고 있습니다.

다사多事했던 귀휴 1주일의 일들도 이 여름이 지나고 나면 아마 한 장의 명함판 사진으로 정리되리라 믿습니다. 변함없이 잘 지내고 있습니다. 친정부모님과 동생들께도 안부 전해 주시기 바랍니다.

인동忍冬의 지혜

형수님께

The Wisdom of Enduring Winter • 107p

형기刑期가 1년 6월 이상이 되면 그 속에 겨울이 두 번 들게 됩니다. 겨울이 두 번 드는 징역을 '곱징역'이라 합니다. 겨울 징역이 그만큼 어렵기 때문에 붙여진 이름이라 생각됩니다.

특히 자기 체온 외에는 온기 한 점 찾을 수 없는 독거獨居는 그 추위가 더합니다. 그럼에도 저는 지난 가을 이래 독거하고 있습니다. 제가 구태여 독거를 마다하지 않는 것은 추위가 징역살이의 가장 큰 어려움이라고는 생각지 않기 때문입니다. 교도소의 겨울이 대단히 추운 것이긴 하지만 그 대신 이곳에는 오래전부터 수많은 징역 선배들이 수십 번의 겨울을 치르면서 발전시켜 온 '인동忍冬의 지혜'가 마치 무의촌의 토방土方처럼 면면히 구전되어 오고 있습니다.

이 숱한 지혜들에 접할 때마다 그 긴 인고의 세월 속에서 시린 몸으로 체득한 그 지혜들의 무게와 그 무게가 상징하는 힘겨운 삶이 싱싱한 현재성을 띠고 우리의 삶 속에 뛰어듭니다.

겨울 추위는 이처럼 역경에서 발휘되는 강한 생명력을 확인하고 신뢰하게 합니다. 뿐만 아니라 겨울 추위는 몸을 차게 하는 대신 생각을 맑게 해줍니다. 그래서 저는 언제나 여름보다 겨울을 선호합니다. 다른 계절 동안 자잘한 감정에 부대끼거나 신변잡사에 얽매여 있던 생각들이 드높은 정신 세계로 시원하게 정돈되고 고양되는 것도 필경 겨울에 서슬져 있는 이 추위 때문이라 믿습니다. 추위는 흡사 '가난'처럼 불편

268

할 따름입니다. 그리고 불편은 우리를 깨어 있게 합니다.

저는 한 평 남짓한 독거실의 차가운 공간을 우리의 숱한 이웃과 역사의 애환으로 가득 채워 이 겨울을 통렬한 깨달음으로 자신을 달구고 싶습니다.

지리부도를 펴놓고 새로 이사한 대치동을 찾아보았습니다. 잠실에서 가까워 형수님의 잠실 출근(?)길이 줄었다 싶습니다. 407호면 4층, 이촌동 집과는 달라 화분에 햇빛 가득 담기리라 생각됩니다. 형수님의 얼굴에도 햇빛 가득 담기길 바랍니다.

나는 걷고 싶다

계수님께

"I Want to Walk" • 109p

작년 여름 비로 다 내렸기 때문인지 눈이 인색한 겨울이었습니다. 눈이 내리면 눈 뒤끝의 매서운 추위는 죄다 우리가 입어야 하는데도 눈 한번 찐하게 안 오나, 젊은 친구들 기다려 쌓더니 얼마 전 사흘 내리 눈 내리는 날 기어이 운동장 구석에 눈사람 하나 세웠습니다. 옥뜰에 서 있는 눈사람. 연탄 조각으로 가슴에 박은 글귀가 섬뜩합니다.

"나는 걷고 싶다."

있으면서도 걷지 못하는 우리들의 다리를 깨닫게 하는 그 글귀는 단단한 눈뭉치가 되어 이마를 때립니다. 내일모레가 2월 초하루. 눈사람도 어디론가 가고 없고 먼 데서 봄이 오는 기척이 들립니다.

새끼가 무엇인지, 어미가 무엇인지

아버님께

What is the Young? And What is it to be the Mother? • 110p

참새집에서 참새새끼를 내렸습니다. 날새들 하늘에 두고 보자며 한사코 말렸는데도 철창 타고 그 높은 데까지 올라가 기어이 꺼내 왔습니다. 길들여서 데리고 논다는 것입니다. 아직 날지도 못하는 부리가 노란 새 끼였습니다. 손아귀 속에 놀란 가슴 할딱이고 있는데 사색이 된 어미참새가 가로세로 어지럽게 날며 머리 위를 떠나지 못합니다.

"저것 봐라. 에미한테 날려 보내 줘라."

"날도 못하는디요?"

"그러믄 새집에 도로 올려 줘라."

"3사 늠들이 꺼내갈 껀디요? 2사 꺼는 위생늠들이 꺼내서 구워 먹어 뿌렀당께요."

"……."

손을 열어 땅에다 놓았더니 어미새가 번개같이 내려와 서로 몸 비비며 어쩔 줄 모릅니다. 함께 날아가 버리지도 못하고, 그렇다고 그 높은 새집까지 안고 날아오를 수도 없고, 급한대로 구석으로 구석으로 데리고 가 숨박는데,

"저러다가 쥐구멍에 들어갔뿌리믄 쥐밥 된당께."

그것도 끔찍한 일입니다. 어쩔 수 없기는 우리도 마찬가지입니다. 결국 방으로 가지고 왔습니다. 마침 빌어 두었던 쥐덫에 넣어 우선 창문 턱에 얹어 놓았습니다.

어느새 알아냈는지 어미새 두 마리가 득달같이 쫓아왔습니다.

처음에는 방 안의 사람 짐승을 경계하는 듯하더니 금세 아랑곳하지 않고 오로지 새끼한테 전념해 버립니다. 쉴새없이 번갈아 먹이를 물어 나릅니다. 놀라운 일입니다. 그리고 다행한 일입니다.

"거 참 잘됐다. 우리가 아무리 잘 먹여야 에미만 하겠어? 에미가 키우게 해서 노랑딱지 떨어지면 훨훨 날려 보내 주자."

이렇게 해서 새끼참새는 날 수 있을 때까지 당분간 쥐덫 속에서 계속 어미새의 부양을 받으며 살아야 합니다. 먹이를 물어 나르던 어미새는 쥐덫에 갇혔다가 놓여 나는 혼찌검을 당하고도 조금도 변함이 없습니다.

새끼가 무엇인지, 어미가 무엇이지, 생명이 무엇인지…….

참새를 바라보는 우리의 마음이 아픕니다.

저는 물론 어머님을 생각했습니다. 정릉 골짜기에서 식음을 전폐하시고 공들이시던 어머님 생각에 마음이 아픕니다. 20년이 지나 이제는 빛바래도 좋을 기억이 쩡하고 가슴에 사무쳐 옵니다.

3부

어리석은 자의 우직함이
세상을 조금씩 바꿔 갑니다

청년들아 나를 딛고 오르거라

얼음골 스승과 허준

"Young Men, Step on Me and Rise" • 115p

이 엽서는 고향의 산기슭에서 띄웁니다. 스승 유의태가 제자 허준으로 하여금 자신의 시신을 해부하게 하였던 골짜기입니다.

소설 『동의보감』의 바로 그 얼음골입니다. 오뉴월 삼복三伏에는 얼음으로 덮이고 겨울에는 오히려 더운 물이 흐르는 계곡입니다. 인체의 해부가 국법으로 금지돼 있던 시절, 스승은 이 얼음골로 제자 허준을 불러들였던 것입니다.

스승의 부름을 받고 찾아간 허준의 앞에는 왕골자리에 반듯이 누운 채 자진自盡한 스승의 시체와 시체 옆에 남겨진 유서가 황촉불에 빛나고 있었습니다. 사람의 병을 다루는 자가 신체의 내부를 모르고서 생명을 지킬 수 없기에 병든 몸이나마 네게 주노니 네 정진의 계기로 삼으라고 적은 유서. 그 앞에 무릎을 꿇어앉은 허준.

의원의 길을 괴로워하거나, 병든 이를 구하기를 게을리 하거나, 이를 빙자해 돈이나 명예를 탐하거든 어떠한 벌이라도 달게 받을 것을 맹세한 다음 스승의 시신을 칼로 가르던 허준의 모습이 어둠 속에서 되살아나는 듯합니다.

오늘은 그날의 횟불 대신 타는 듯한 단풍이 어둠을 밝히고 있습니다. 나는 바위너덜에 앉아 생각했습니다. 소설 속의 유의태와 허준의 이야기는 물론 소설가가 그려 낸 상상의 세계이며, 사실이 아닐 수도 있습니다. 그러나 그것이 비록 사실은 아니라 하더라도 '진실'임에는 틀림

없다고 믿습니다. 사실이라는 그릇은 진실을 담아내기에는 언제나 작고 부족한 것이기 때문입니다.

내가 20년의 징역살이와 7년여의 칩거 후에 가장 먼저 찾아온 곳이 이곳 얼음골이라는 사실이 내게도 잘 설명이 되지 않습니다. 갇힌 사람들에게 '출소'의 가장 큰 의미는 '독보'獨步입니다. 혼자서 다닐 수 있는 권리를 그곳에서는 '독보권'이라 하였습니다. 가고 싶은 곳에 혼자서 갈 수 있다는 것은 참으로 가슴 설레는 해방감이었습니다.

이제 어머님에 이어 홀로 남아 계시던 아버님마저 세상을 떠나셨습니다. 나는 차라리 허전한 마음으로 기차를 타고 무작정 떠나왔습니다. 오뉴월이 아닌 가마볼 얼음골에는 이미 얼음이 없었습니다. 그러나 그것은 그리 중요한 일이 아닙니다. 스승과 제자가 서로를 처절하게 승계하는 현장에서 나는 배우고 가르치는 일의 엄정함 하나만으로도 가슴 넘치는 감회를 금할 수 없습니다. 우리는 어차피 누군가의 제자이면서 동시에 스승이기도 합니다. 이 배우고 가르치는 이른바 사제師弟의 연쇄를 더듬어 확인하는 일이 곧 자신을 정확하게 통찰하는 길이라 생각합니다.

중학교 때던가 나는 이곳에 아버님을 따라온 적이 있습니다. 여든일곱에 440여 쪽의 책을 출간하시고 여든여덟에 세상을 떠나신 아버님이 생각납니다. 아버님은 그 책에서 사람은 그 부모를 닮기보다 그 시대를 더 많이 닮는다고 하였지만 내가 고향에 돌아와 맨 처음 느낀 것은 사람은 먼저 그 산천을 닮는다는 발견이었습니다.

산의 능선은 물론 나무와 흙빛까지 그토록 친근할 수가 없었습니다. 신토불이身土不二란 말이 세계무역기구(WTO) 체제 이후 한낱 광고 문안으로 왜소화되어 버렸지만 어린 시절의 산천이 바로 자신의 정서적 모태가 되고 있다는 깨달음이었습니다. 산천과 사람, 스승과 제자의 원융圓融. 이것이 바로 삶의 가장 보편적인 모습이 아닐까 생각됩니다.

어둠에 묻혀 가는 얼음골 위로 석양을 받아 빛을 발하고 있는 암봉巖峰이 문득 허준의 얼굴처럼 보이기도 하고 스승 유의태의 얼굴처럼 다가오기도 합니다. 『동의보감』의 찬술을 명한 왕의 교서에 다음과 같은 구절이 있습니다.

"우리나라에서 많이 나는 약재를 자세하게 적어서 지식이 없는 사람, 가난한 사람들도 쉽게 이해할 수 있고 누구나 병을 고칠 수도 있도록 하여야 한다."

이 글에 나타난 민족 의식과 백성들에 대한 애정은 선조왕의 것이 아니라 허준의 마음이고 허준을 가르친 스승의 뜻이라고 생각됩니다.

『동의보감』의 찬술 자체가 허준의 기획이었고, 허준의 집필이었음에 틀림없다고 할 수 있습니다. 더구나 『동의보감』의 완성은 오로지 허준 혼자만의 외로운 작업이었고 그나마 절해고도의 유배지에서 이루어졌기 때문입니다. 300년 후 이제마李濟馬의 사상의학이 나오기까지 우리 풍토와 체질에 맞는 유일한 의학서로서 수많은 사람들의 목숨을 구해 낸 책이었습니다.

『동의보감』 외에도 허준이 심혈을 기울인 저술은 대부분이 난해한 전문 서적을 한글로 쉽게 풀어쓰는 일이었습니다. 서출인 의원 허준에 대한 선조의 파격적인 가자加資는 이와 같은 허준의 백성에 대한 애정과 경륜을 높이 사서 내린 것이라 짐작됩니다.

나는 얼음골에 쌓이는 어둠 속에 앉아서 한 사람의 허준이 있기까지 그의 성장을 위하여 바쳐진 수많은 사람의 애정과 헌신에 대하여 생각하였습니다. 한 송이의 금빛 국화가 새벽 이슬에 맑게 피어나기 위하여 간밤의 무서리가 내리더라는 백거이白居易의 시 「국화」가 생각납니다. '청년들아 나를 딛고 오르거라'던 루쉰의 얼굴이 떠오르기도 하였습니다.

옛날의 어머니들은 자기가 무엇이 되겠다는 생각보다는 저마다 누군가의 자양이 되는 것을 삶으로 생각하였습니다. 그래서 자모慈母라 하였습니다. 사람과 사람의 연쇄 가운데에다 자신을 세우기보다는 한 벌의 패션 의상과 화려한 언술로 자기를 실현하고, 또 자기를 숨기려 하는 것이 오늘의 문화입니다.

당신의 장탄식이 들리는 듯합니다. 무수한 상품의 더미와 그 상품들이 만들어 내는 미학에 매몰된 채 우리는 다만 껍데기로 만나고 있을 뿐이라던 당신의 말이 생각납니다. 정작 두려운 것은 그러한 껍데기를 양산해 내고 있는 '보이지 않는 손'을 잊고 있는 것이라 할 것입니다.

고매한 도덕적 언어들이 수천억 원의 부정한 축재로 여지없이 무너져 내리는 이 위선의 계절에 우리는 과연 무엇으로 가르치고 무엇으로 배우는가 하는 생각이 얼음골의 차가운 교훈으로 남습니다. 알튀세는 연극이란 새로운 관객의 생산이라고 하였습니다. 관람을 완성하기 위하여, 삶 속에서 완성하기 위하여, 그 미완성의 의미를 추구하기 시작하는 배우의 생산이라고 하였습니다.

우리는 무대 위를 걷든, 객석에 앉아 있든 어차피 삶의 현장으로 돌아와 저마다 그 미완성의 의미를, 그 침묵과 담론의 완성을 천착해 가는 사람들 속을 걸어갈 수밖에 없다고 생각됩니다. 화사한 언어의 요설이 아니라 결국은 우리의 앞뒤좌우에 우리와 함께 걸어가는 수많은 사람들의 삶으로써 깨닫고, 삶으로써 가르칠 뿐이라 믿습니다.

여느 해보다 청명하고 길었던 가을이 끝나고 있습니다. 등 뒤에 겨울을 데리고 있어서 가을을 즐기지 못한다던 당신의 추운 겨울이 다가오고 있습니다.

우리가 헐어야 할 피라미드

반구정과 압구정

The Pyramids We Have to Demolish • 121p

파주에서 서쪽으로 시오리十五里 임진강가에 반구정伴鷗亭이라는 작은
정자가 있습니다. 세종조의 명상이며 청백리의 귀감인 방촌 황희厖村 黃
喜 정승의 정자입니다. 18년간의 영상직을 치사致仕하고 90세의 천수를
다할 때까지 이름 그대로 갈매기를 벗하며 그의 노년을 보낸 곳입니다.
단풍철도 지난 초겨울이라 찾는 사람도 없어 한적하기가 500년 전 그
대로다 싶었습니다.

당신은 아마 똑같은 이름의 정자를 기억할 것입니다. 서울 강남의
압구정狎鷗亭이 그것입니다. 압구정은 세조의 모신謀臣이던 한명회韓明
澮가 그의 호를 따서 지은 정자입니다. 반구정의 '반'伴과 압구정의 '압'
狎은 글자는 비록 다르지만 둘 다 '벗한다'는 뜻입니다.

이 두 정자는 다같이 노老재상이 퇴은하여 한가로이 갈매기를 벗하
며 여생을 보내던 정자입니다만 남아 있는 지금의 모습은 참으로 판이
합니다. 반구정이 지금도 갈매기를 벗하며 철새들을 맞이하고 있음에
반하여 압구정은 이미 그 자취마저 없어지고 현대아파트 72동 옆의 작
은 표석으로 그 유허임을 가리키고 있을 따름입니다.

정자의 주인인 황희 정승과 한명회의 일생만큼이나 극적인 대조를
보인다는 생각이 들었습니다. 두 사람 모두 일인지하 만인지상이라는
영상의 자리에 올랐던 재상이었음에도 불구하고 한 사람은 언제나 명
상名相·현상賢相의 이름으로 칭송되는가 하면 또 한 사람은 권신權臣·

모신謀臣의 이름으로 역사에 남아 있기 때문입니다.

세종조의 찬란한 업적 뒤에는 언제나 황희 정승의 보필이 있었으되 사람들은 오히려 그를 몽매하다고 할 만큼 눈에 띄지 않는 자리에 있었고, 심지어는 물러나 임진강가에서 야인어부들과 구로鷗鷺를 길들일 때에도 그가 당대의 재상이었음을 아무도 몰랐을 정도였습니다.

한명회는 그의 두 딸을 왕비로 들이고 정난공신 1등, 익대공신 1등 등 네 차례나 1등 공신이 되지만 그 뒤에는 언제나 쿠데타와 모살과 옥사獄事가 도사리고 있었습니다. 후에 신원되기는 하였지만 부관참시剖棺斬屍의 화를 입은 권력자였습니다.

황희 정승은 두문동에 은거하기도 하고 유배되기도 하지만 언제나 자신의 원칙에 따라 진퇴했던 반면, 한명회는 스스로 실력자에게 나아가 그를 앞질러 헤아리고 처리해 나간 모신이었습니다.

두 사람에게 얽힌 일화도 판이하기는 마찬가지입니다. 황희 정승의 집안 노비 두 사람이 서로 다투다가 그를 찾아와 서로 상대방의 잘못을 일러바치자 사내종에게도 '네 말이 옳다' 계집종에게도 '네 말이 옳다' 하며 돌려보냈다고 합니다. 이를 지켜보던 부인이 그 무정견을 나무라자 '부인의 말도 옳다'고 했다는 일화는 잘 알려진 이야기입니다.

언언시시言言是是 정승이라 불릴 정도로 그는 시是를 말하되 비非를 말하기를 삼갔고, 소절小節에 구애되기보다 대절大節을 지키는 재상이었다고 합니다. 황희 정승이 겸허하고 관후한 일화의 주인공으로 회자됨에 비하여 한명회에 관한 일화는 그와 정반대인 것이 대부분입니다. 생육신의 한 사람인 김시습이 강정江亭에 걸려 있는 한명회의 '청춘부사직 백수와강호'靑春扶社稷 白首臥江湖라는 시구의 부扶를 망亡으로, 와臥를 오汚로 고쳐 써서 '젊어서는 사직을 망치고 늙어서는 강호를 더럽힌다'는 뜻으로 바꾸어 버린 일화는 유명합니다. 사람들은 한명회가 대로大怒하여 이를 찢어 버렸다는 후일담까지 곁들여 놓았습니다.

차로 2시간도 채 못 되는 거리에 남아 있는 반구정과 압구정의 차이가 이와 같습니다. 그것은 물론 그 인품의 차이만이 아닐 수도 있습니다. 황희가 문화통치기의 재상이었고, 한명회는 의정부 중심의 합의제를 타파하고 강력한 왕권체제로 회귀하던 시기의 재상이라는 정치체제상의 차이로 이해할 수도 있습니다. 상황의 차이로 환원시킬 수도 있습니다.

그러나 우리가 잊지 말아야 할 것은 '정치란 사회의 잠재적 역량을 최대한으로 조직해 내고 키우는 일'이라는 것입니다. 권력의 창출 그 자체는 잠재적 역량의 계발과 무관하거나 오히려 그 반대라고 생각합니다.

피라미드의 건설이 정치가 아니라 피라미드의 해체가 정치라는 당신의 글귀를 이해할 수 있습니다. 땅을 회복하고 노역을 해방하기 위해서는 먼저 모든 형태의 피라미드를 허물어야 한다고 믿기 때문입니다.

역사는 우리가 맡기지 않더라도 어김없이 모든 것을 심판하게 마련입니다. 우리의 몫은 우리가 내려야 할 오늘의 심판일 따름입니다.

반구정과 압구정의 남아 있는 모습이 그대로 역사의 평가는 아니라 하더라도 우리는 그것의 차이가 함의하는 언어를 찾아야 한다고 믿습니다. 우리가 해체해야 할 피라미드는 과연 무엇인지, 우리가 회복해야 할 땅과 노동은 무엇인지를 헤아려야 할 것입니다.

압구정이 콘크리트 더미 속 한 개의 작은 돌멩이로 왜소화되어 있음에 반하여 반구정은 유유한 임진강가에서 이름 그대로 갈매기를 벗하고 있습니다. 나는 바람 부는 반구정에 앉아서 임진강의 무심한 물길을 굽어보았습니다. 분단의 제거야말로 민족의 역량을 최대화하는 최선의 정치임을 이야기하는 듯 반구정은 오늘도 남북의 산천과 남북의 새들을 벗하고 있었습니다.

당신이 나무를 더 사랑하는 까닭

소광리 소나무숲

The Reason Why You Love Trees More • 126p

오늘은 당신이 가르쳐 준 태백산맥 속의 소광리 소나무숲에서 이 엽서
를 띄웁니다. 아침 햇살에 빛나는 소나무숲에 들어서니 당신이 사람보
다 나무를 더 사랑하는 까닭을 알 것 같습니다. 200년 300년, 더러는
500년의 풍상을 겪은 소나무들이 골짜기에 가득합니다. 그 긴 세월을
온전히 바위 위에서 버티어 온 것에 이르러서는 차라리 경이였습니다.
바쁘게 뛰어다니는 우리들과는 달리 오직 '신발 한 켤레의 토지'에 서
서 이처럼 우람할 수 있다는 것이 충격이고 경이였습니다. 생각하면 소
나무보다 훨씬 더 많은 것을 소비하면서도 무엇 하나 변변히 이루어 내
지 못하고 있는 나에게 소광리의 솔숲은 마치 회초리를 들고 기다리는
엄한 스승 같았습니다.

어젯밤 별 한 개 쳐다볼 때마다 100원씩 내라던 당신의 말이 생각납
니다. 오늘은 소나무 한 그루 만져 볼 때마다 돈을 내야겠지요. 사실 서
울에서는 그보다 못한 것을 그보다 비싼 값을 치르며 살아가고 있다는
생각이 듭니다. 언젠가 경복궁 복원 공사 현장에 가본 적이 있습니다.
일제가 파괴하고 변형시킨 조선 정궁의 기본 궁제를 되찾는 일이 당연
하다고 생각하였습니다.

그러나 막상 오늘 이곳 소광리 소나무숲에 와서는 그러한 생각을 반
성하게 됩니다. 경복궁의 복원에 소요되는 나무가 원목으로 200만재,
11톤 트럭으로 500대라는 엄청난 양이라고 합니다. 소나무가 없어져

가고 있는 지금에 와서도 기어이 소나무로 복원한다는 것이 무리한 고집이라고 생각됩니다. 수많은 소나무들이 베어져 눕혀진 광경이라니 감히 상상할 수가 없습니다. 그것은 이를테면 고난에 찬 몇 백만 년의 세월을 잘라 내는 것이나 마찬가지입니다.

우리가 생각 없이 잘라 내고 있는 것이 어찌 소나무만이겠습니까. 없어도 되는 물건을 만들기 위하여 없어서는 안 될 것들을 마구 잘라내고 있는가 하면 아예 사람을 잘라 내는 일마저 서슴지 않는 것이 우리의 현실이기 때문입니다. 우리가 살고 있는 이 지구 위의 유일한 생산자는 식물이라던 당신의 말이 생각납니다. 동물은 완벽한 소비자입니다. 그 중에서도 최대의 소비자가 바로 사람입니다.

사람들의 생산이란 고작 식물들이 만들어 놓은 것이나 땅속에 묻힌 것을 파내어 소비하는 것에 지나지 않습니다. 쌀로 밥을 짓는 일을 두고 밥의 생산이라고 할 수 없는 것이나 마찬가지입니다. 생산의 주체가 아니라 소비의 주체이며 급기야는 소비의 객체로 전락되고 있는 것이 바로 사람입니다. 자연을 오로지 생산의 요소로 규정하는 경제학의 폭력성이 이 소광리에서만큼 분명하게 부각되는 곳이 달리 없을 듯합니다.

산판일을 하는 사람들은 큰 나무를 베어 낸 그루터기에 올라서지 않는 것이 불문율로 되어 있다고 합니다. 잘린 부분에서 올라오는 나무의 노기가 사람을 해치기 때문입니다. 어찌 노하는 것이 소나무뿐이겠습니까. 온 산천의 아우성이 들리는 듯합니다. 당신의 말처럼 소나무는 우리의 삶과 가장 가까운 자리에서 우리와 함께 풍상을 겪어온 혈육 같은 나무입니다.

사람이 태어나면 금줄에 솔가지를 꽂아 부정을 물리고 사람이 죽으면 소나무 관 속에 누워 솔밭에 묻히는 것이 우리의 일생이라 하였습니다. 그리고 그 무덤 속의 한恨을 달래 주는 것이 바로 은은한 솔바람입니다. 솔바람뿐만이 아니라 솔빛·솔향 등 어느 것 하나 우리의 정서 깊숙이 들어와 있지 않는 것이 없습니다. 더구나 소나무는 고절高節의 상징으로 우리의 정신을 지탱하는 기둥이 되고 있습니다. 금강송의 곧은 등치에서뿐만 아니라 암석지의 굽고 뒤틀린 나무에서도 우리는 곧은 지조를 읽어 낼 줄 압니다.

오늘날의 상품 미학과는 전혀 다른 미학을 우리는 일찍부터 가꾸어 놓고 있었습니다. 나는 문득 당신이 진정 사랑하는 것이 소나무가 아니라 소나무 같은 '사람'이라는 생각이 들었습니다. 메마른 땅을 지키고 있는 수많은 사람들이란 생각이 들었습니다. 문득 지금쯤 서울 거리의 자동차 속에 앉아 있을 당신을 생각했습니다. 그리고 외딴 섬에 갇혀 목말라 하는 남산의 소나무들을 생각했습니다.

남산의 소나무가 이제는 더이상 살아남기를 포기하고 자손들이나 기르겠다는 체념으로 무수한 솔방울을 달고 있다는 당신의 이야기는 우리를 슬프게 합니다. 더구나 그 솔방울들이 싹을 키울 땅마저 황폐해 버렸다는 사실이 우리를 더욱 암담하게 합니다. 그러나 그보다 더 무서운 것이 아카시아와 활엽수의 침습이라니 놀라지 않을 수 없습니다. 척박한 땅을 겨우겨우 가꾸어 놓으면 이내 다른 경쟁수들이 쳐들어와 소나무를 몰아내고 만다는 것입니다. 무한경쟁의 비정한 논리가 뻗어 오지 않는 곳이 없습니다.

나는 마치 꾸중 듣고 집 나오는 아이처럼 산을 나왔습니다. 솔방울 한 개를 주워 들고 내려오면서 생각하였습니다. 거인에게 잡아 먹힌 소년이 솔방울을 손에 쥐고 있었기 때문에 다시 소생했다는 신화를 생각하였습니다. 당신이 나무를 사랑한다면 솔방울도 사랑해야 합니다. 무수한 솔방울들의 끈질긴 저력을 신뢰해야 합니다.

언젠가 붓글씨로 써 드렸던 글귀를 엽서 끝에 적습니다. "처음으로

쇠가 만들어졌을 때 세상의 모든 나무들이 두려움에 떨었다. 그러나 어느 생각 깊은 나무가 말했다. 두려워할 것 없다. 우리들이 자루가 되어 주지 않는 한 쇠는 결코 우리를 해칠 수 없는 법이다."

어리석은 자의 우직함이 세상을 조금씩 바꿔 갑니다

온달산성의 평강공주

Tactless Honesty of Foolish People Changes the World Little by Little • 130p

오늘은 충청북도 단양군 영춘면 하2리에 있는 온달산성에서 엽서를 띄웁니다. 1,400년 전의 과거로부터 띄우는 이 엽서가 당신에게 어떻게 읽혀질지 망설여집니다. 온달산성은 둘레가 683미터에 불과한 작은 산성입니다만 깎아지른 산봉우리를 테를 메우듯 두르고 있어서 멀리서 바라보면 흡사 머리에 수건을 동여맨 투사 같습니다. 결연한 의지가 풍겨오는 책성幘城입니다. 그래서 쉽게 접근을 허락하지 않는 성이었습니다.

다만 하2리 마을 쪽으로 앞섶을 조심스레 열어 산성에 이르는 길을 내주고 있었습니다. 산 중턱에 이르면 사모정思慕亭이라는 작은 정자가 있습니다. 전사한 온달장군의 관이 땅에서 떨어지지 않자 평강공주가 달려와 눈물로 달래어 모셔 간 자리라 전해지고 있습니다. 이 산성을 찾아오는 사람들이 평강공주를 만나는 자리입니다.

나는 사모정에서 나머지 산성까지의 길을 평강공주와 함께 올라갔습니다. 아래로는 남한강을 배수의 진으로 하고 멀리 소백산맥을 호시虎視하고 있는 온달산성은 유사시에 백성들을 입보入保시키는 성이 아니라 신라에 빼앗긴 실지를 회복하기 위한 전초기지였음을 단번에 알 수 있습니다. 망루나 천수각天守閣이 없어도 적병의 움직임이 한눈에 내려다보이는 조망眺望이었습니다. 조령과 죽령 서쪽 땅을 되찾기 전에는 다시 고국에 돌아오지 않겠다는 그의 결의가 지금도 느껴집니다.

나는 반공半空을 휘달리는 소백산맥을 바라보다 문득 신라의 삼국 통일을 못마땅해 하던 당신의 말이 생각났습니다. 하나가 되는 것은 더 커지는 것이라는 당신의 말을 생각하면 대동강 이북의 땅을 당나라에게 내주기로 하고 이룩한 통일은 분명 더 작아진 것이라는 점에서 그것은 통일이 아니라 광활한 요동 벌판의 상실에 불과한 것인지도 모릅니다.

이러한 상실감은 온달과 평강공주의 애절한 사랑의 이야기와 더불어 이 산성을 찾은 나를 매우 쓸쓸하게 합니다.

온달과 평강공주의 이야기는 부富를 축적한 당시의 평민 계층이 지배 체제의 개편 과정에서 정치·경제적 상승을 할 수 있었던 사회 변동기의 사료史料로 거론되기도 합니다. 그리고 '바보 온달'이란 별명도 사실은 온달의 미천한 출신에 대한 지배 계층의 경멸과 경계심이 만들어 낸 이름이라고 분석되기도 합니다.

그러나 나는 수많은 사람들이 함께 창작하고 그후 더 많은 사람들이 오랜 세월에 걸쳐서 승낙한 온달장군과 평강공주의 이야기를 믿습니다. 다른 어떠한 실증적 사실史實보다도 당시의 정서를 더 정확히 담아 내고 있다고 생각하기 때문입니다. 완고한 신분의 벽을 뛰어넘어 미천한 출신의 바보 온달을 선택하고 드디어 용맹한 장수로 일어서게 한 평강공주의 결단과 주체적 삶에는 민중들의 소망과 언어가 담겨 있기 때문입니다. 이것이 바로 온달 설화가 당대 사회의 이데올로기에 매몰된 한 농촌 청년의 우직한 충절의 이야기로 끝나지 않는 까닭이라고 생각됩니다.

인간의 가장 위대한 가능성은 이처럼 과거를 뛰어넘고 사회의 벽을 뛰어넘어 드디어 자기를 뛰어넘는 비약에 있는 것이라고 할 수 있기 때문입니다. 나는 평강공주와 함께 온달산성을 걷는 동안 내내 '능력 있고 편하게 해줄 사람'을 찾는 당신이 생각났습니다. '신데렐라의 꿈'을 버리지 못하고 있는 당신이 안타까웠습니다.

현대 사회에서 평가되는 능력이란 인간적 품성이 도외시된 '경쟁적 능력'입니다. 그것은 다른 사람들의 낙오와 좌절 이후에 얻을 수 있는 것으로, 한마디로 숨겨진 칼처럼 매우 비정한 것입니다. 그러한 능력의 품속에 안주하려는 우리의 소망이 과연 어떤 실상을 갖는 것인지 고민해야 할 것입니다. 당신은 기억할 것입니다. 세상 사람은 현명한 사람과 어리석은 사람으로 분류할 수 있다고 당신이 먼저 말했습니다.

현명한 사람은 자기를 세상에 잘 맞추는 사람인 반면에 어리석은 사람은 그야말로 어리석게도 세상을 자기에게 맞추려고 하는 사람이라고 했습니다. 그러나 역설적이게도 세상은 이런 어리석은 사람들의 우직함으로 인하여 조금씩 나은 것으로 변화해 간다는 사실을 잊지 말아야 한다고 생각합니다.

우직한 어리석음, 그것이 곧 지혜와 현명함의 바탕이고 내용입니다. '편안함' 그것도 경계해야 할 대상이기는 마찬가지입니다. 편안함은 흐르지 않는 강물이기 때문입니다. '불편함'은 흐르는 강물입니다. 흐르는 강물은 수많은 소리와 풍경을 그 속에 담고 있는 추억의 물이며 어딘가를 희망하는 잠들지 않는 물입니다.

당신은 평강공주의 삶이 남편의 입신立身이라는 가부장적 한계를 뛰어넘지 못한 것이라고 하였습니다만 산다는 것은 살리는 것입니다. 살림(生)입니다. 그리고 당신은 자신이 공주가 아니기 때문에 평강공주가 될 수 없다고 하지만 살림이란 '뜻의 살림'입니다. 세속적 성취와는 상관없는 것이기도 합니다.

그런 점에서 나는 평강공주의 이야기는 한 여인의 사랑의 메시지가 아니라 그것을 뛰어넘은 '삶의 메시지'라고 생각합니다. 나는 당신이 언젠가 이 산성에 오기를 바랍니다. 남한강 푸른 물굽이가 천년세월을 변함없이 감돌아 흐르는 이 산성에서 평강공주와 만나기를 바랍니다.

개인의 팔자, 민족의 팔자

The Fate of an Individual Person, the Fate of the People • 134p

그의 사건은 한겨울의 한밤중 비무장지대의 한복판에서 일어났습니다. DMZ의 얼어붙은 정적을 찢는 한 발의 총성이 그의 21년을 앗아갔습니다. 영문도 모르고 따라나선 분대 규모의 야간 작전중에 누군가의 M1 소총이 오발되면서 그의 하복부를 좌우로 관통했습니다. 나중에 밝혀졌지만 그것은 오발이 아니라 소대장의 월북 기도를 간파한 분대원이 소대장을 겨냥한 저격이었습니다. 애꿎게도 소대장이 아닌 그가 피를 뿌리며 쓰러졌습니다. 총성과 함께 분대원들은 유리 조각처럼 흩어지고 주위는 아무도 없고, 아무 소리도 없는 칠흑 같은 적막으로 변했습니다. 칠흑 같은 적막 속에서 피가 쏟아지는 하복부를 가까스로 탄띠로 동인 다음 정신을 잃었습니다. 얼마 뒤 다시 의식을 회복했을 때는 적막한 산천, 칠흑 같은 어둠 그리고 심한 갈증만 엄습해 올 뿐이었습니다. 희미한 물소리를 향해 피 묻은 손톱으로 언 땅을 긁으며 기어가다 다시 의식을 잃었습니다. 이것이 기억의 전부입니다.

이튿날 새벽 군사분계선에서 북쪽으로 약간 벗어난 지점에서 쓰러져 있는 그가 발견되었습니다. 들것에 실려 다니며 단 한마디의 대꾸도, 단 한 사람의 증인도 없는 재판에서 무기징역을 선고받았습니다. 판결문에는 소대장과 "내응하여 월북을 기도하다" 피격당해 체포된 것으로 되어 있습니다. 좌익 장기수라는 '곱징역'을 고스란히 치르고, 1989년 3월, 21년 만에 마흔 다섯의 나이로 만기 출소했습니다. 21년 만에 돌아

온 세상은 참 많이 변하였습니다. 세상도 변하였지만 세상보다 더 변한 것은 바로 자기 자신이었습니다. 감옥에 갇혀 있는 줄도 모르고 군대 생활을 왜 그렇게 오래하느냐며 당장 집으로 돌아와서 농사나 지으라고 성화시던 아버지도 돌아가신 지 이미 오래고, 가족도 없고 농토도 없는 고향은 그가 돌아갈 곳이 못 되었습니다. 출소 사흘째부터 부산 부두 컨테이너 하역장에서 이제는 징역 대신 120kg의 짐을 지다가 새벽 2시 눈비 맞으며 서울로 찾아왔습니다.

징역 사는 동안 그에게는 한 가닥 기대가 있었습니다. 월북한 소대장이 간첩으로 남파되어 체포되면 사실이 밝혀지리라는 기약 없는 기대가 그것이었습니다. 그러나 21년 동안 그러한 기대는 서서히 그리고 결정적으로 버리게 됩니다. 그보다는 오히려 그처럼 무고하게 옥살이를 하고 있는 수많은 수인들이 함께 살고 있다는 사실이 위로였습니다. 가석방이나 특별 사면에 대한 기대도 없이 고스란히 21년을 살았습니다. 사면을 기대하는 쪽은 도리어 바깥의 가족들일 뿐 막상 징역살이를 하고 있는 당사자들은 별로 기대하지 않습니다. 만델라의 27년에 대해서는 경악하면서도, 우리의 40년 장기수에 대해서는 무지한 것이 우리의 현실이기 때문입니다. 광복절·불탄절·성탄절 등에 죄수들을 너무 많이 풀어 준다고 생각하는 사람도 있겠지만, 만기 출소자가 하루 평균 3명이라면 30여 개 교도소에서 매일 90명이 출소합니다. 만약 그들을 한 달 앞당겨 석방한다면 무슨 이름 있는 날 한꺼번에 2천7백 명을 석방할 수 있습니다. 이것이 갇힌 사람들이 특별 가석방을 기대하지 않는 이유입니다.

"다른 사람들은 모범수가 되어 모두 석방되는데 당신은 징역 속에서도 여태 그 모양이니 더 이상 기다릴 수 없다"며, 고무신을 거꾸로 신고 떠나 버린 어느 아내의 딱한 이야기도 있습니다. "그 소대장 간첩으로 잡혔다는 소식 아직 없어?", "다 팔자소관이지요. 오발탄도 그렇지요. 하필이면 북쪽으로 기어간 것도 그렇지요. 이제 통일될 때나 기다려야지요." 그에게 있어서 통일이란 무엇인가? 그에게 있어서 분단이란 무엇인가? 그것은 무고한 21년 세월의 진실을 밝히는 일입니다. 마찬가지로 우리에게 통일이란 무엇인가? 물론 통일은 민족의 비원이고 우리역사의 진실을 밝히는 일이 아닐 수 없습니다.

그러나 이러한 대의에 앞서 우리가 해야 하는 일은 자기의 삶 속에 파편처럼 박혀 있는 분단의 상처를 확인하는 일입니다. 이것은 단지 통일에 대한 자신의 입장을 확인하는 일일 뿐 아니라 개인의 팔자 속에 깊숙이 들어와 있는 민족의 팔자를 확인하는 일이기 때문입니다.

한 사람의 일생이 정직한가 정직하지 않은가를 준별하는 기준은 그 사람의 일생에 담겨 있는 시대의 양률이라고 할 수 있습니다. 시대의 아픔을 비켜 간 삶을 정직한 삶이라고 할 수 없으며 더구나 민족의 고통을 역이용하여 자신을 높여 간 삶을 정직하다고 할 수 없음은 물론입니다. 개인의 팔자는 민족의 팔자와 결코 무관할 수 없습니다. 남아공과 만델라의 팔자, 라틴아메리카와 체 게바라의 팔자, 식민지 조국과 유관순의 팔자. 위로는 그룹 총수의 팔자에서부터 아래로는 이름 없는 노동자와 창녀촌의 영자에 이르기까지 개인의 팔자 속에는 어김없이 민족의 팔자가 깊숙이 들어와 있습니다. 개인의 실패나 성공도 정도의 차이는 있지만 민족의 팔자와 결코 무관할 수 없는 것이 우리의 삶이고 우리 민족의 역사입니다.

진실을 밝힌다는 것은 자기의 삶이 다른 사람의 삶과 어떻게 연결되어 있으며, 나아가 우리 사회와 민족의 운명과 어떻게 연결되어 있는가를 읽어내는 것을 의미합니다. 그러나 우리가 진실을 소중하게 여기는 까닭은 그것이 우리의 현재를 정직하게 바라보게 할 뿐 아니라 진실은 과거를 청산하고 동시에 미래를 향하여 나아가는 일의 시작이기 때문입니다. 진실의 발견이 미래의 참된 시작이기 때문입니다.

그저께부터 그는 아파트 건설 공사장의 배관공으로 일 나가고 있습니다. 임대 주택이 될지 호화 주택이 될지 아랑곳없이 동파이프와 씨름하고 있습니다. 완공된 아파트 단지의 모습이 어떤 것인지, 그가 일하고 있는 서울의 모습이 어떤 것인지 아랑곳없이 일하고 있습니다.

산천의 봄, 세상의 봄

Spring in Nature, Spring in the World • 139p

새봄을 증거 하는 산천의 표정은 여러 가지입니다. 따스한 볕, 아름다운 꽃, 훈광 속의 제비가 우선 가장 쉬운 새봄의 증거입니다. 그러나 이러한 것과는 달리 얼음이 녹아서 그득히 고여 있는 물에서 봄을 확인하는, 이른바 해빙의 출수出水로 봄을 증거 했던 옛 시인이 있습니다.

　봄볕은 흔히 늦추위의 심술 때문에 한결같지 못하고, 꽃은 봄·여름·가을·겨울 할 것 없이 사시장철로 피어 이미 봄의 경계를 훌쩍 넘어서고 있으며, 제비는 고작 차려 놓은 밥상에 뒤늦게 끼어드는 손님일 뿐입니다. 이에 비해, 흙 살 속속들이 박혀 있던 얼음들이 빠져나오는 해빙의 출수야말로 겨울의 집단적 철수撤收라 할 수 있을 것입니다. 볕이나 꽃에서 봄을 확인하기보다 그득히 고여 있는 물에서 봄을 깨닫는 시인의 마음에는 분명 성급한 상춘과는 구별되는 봄에 대한 차분하고 냉철한 이해가 담겨 있다고 할 수 있습니다.

　그러나 생수生水라는 말이 있기는 하지만 물은 아무래도 생명은 아닙니다. 생명의 조건일 뿐입니다. 그런 점에서 우리는 새봄의 가장 확실한 증거를 잡초에서 확인합니다. 볕처럼 무상하지 않고, 꽃처럼 철없지 않고, 제비처럼 뒤늦지 않은 봄의 증거를 해마다 잡초에서 확인합니다. 아무도 보지 않는 곳에서 누구 하나 거두고 가꾸어 주는 사람 없이 오로지 저 혼자의 힘으로 돋아나는 이름 없는 잡초에서 가장 확실한 봄을 만납니다.

잡초는 물론 이름 없는 풀입니다. 이름은 사람들이 붙이는 것이고, 이름이 붙었다는 것은 사람들의 지배하에 들어갔다는 뜻입니다. 눈에 뜨이지 않는 곳의 이름 없는 풀은 자신의 논리, 자신의 존재 그리고 자신의 힘으로 쟁취한 승리 그 자체입니다. 더구나 볕이 하늘의 일이고, 꽃이 나무 위의 성과이고, 제비가 강남의 손님인 데 반하여, 풀은 시종일관 흙의 역사 속에서 생명을 키워 온 금목수화토金木水火土의 총화이면서 모든 봄의 육신입니다. 서로서로 기대어 어깨를 짜며 금세 무성한 풀밭을 이루어 철없는 풍설의 해코지에도 결코 물러서는 법 없이, 어느덧 볕을 머물게 하고 꽃을 피우고 제비를 돌아오게 합니다. 이 들풀이야말로 가장 믿음직한 새봄의 전위前衛입니다. 볕, 꽃, 제비에서 발견하는 봄이 기다리지 않는 사람들의 봄이라면, 해빙의 출수에서 발견하는 봄이 관찰하는 사람들의 봄이라면, 이름 없는 들풀에서 깨닫는 봄이야말로 대지를 일구는 수많은 사람들이 몸으로 확인하는 봄입니다.

산천의 봄과 마찬가지로 세상의 봄을 증거 하는 표정도 여러 가지입니다. 졸업장을 들고 추억의 교정을 나서는 아이들의 뒷모습, 먼 길을 마다 않고 찾아온 만남, 대팻날이 지나간 자리에 얼굴 내미는 나무결의 밝은 윤기潤氣. 이 짧은 순간들이 안겨 주는 작은 기쁨들이 가슴에 차오를 때 우리는 삶의 의미를 새롭게 확인합니다. 키우고, 만나고, 만들어 내는 기쁨을 공감하고 이 공감을 사람들과 더불어 신뢰할 때 산천의 봄처럼 세상의 봄이 시작됩니다. 산천의 들풀이 흙과 더불어 봄을 키우듯이 일상의 작은 기쁨은 모이고 모여 세상을 튼실하게 받쳐 주는 뼈대가 되고 사랑이 됩니다. 이러한 기쁨은 작은 것이기 때문에 업신여겨지고, 또 돈이 되기 때문에 빼앗기기도 하지만, 우리는 이로써 견디고 이로써 다시 시작해 왔음을 역사는 증거 하고 있습니다.

정치란 사람을 자라게 하고 사람을 만나게 하는 일입니다. 그리고 만들어 내는 일의 기쁨을 서로 신뢰하게 하는 일입니다. 사람을 그 가슴에서 만나게 하고 사회를 그 뼈대에서 지탱하고 있는 이러한 역량들을 일으켜 세우고 사회화社會化하는 일이 정치의 본연本然입니다. 그러한 판을 열고 그러한 틀을 짜는 일입니다. 잘못된 판, 잘못된 틀을 새롭게 바꾸는 일입니다. 잡초가 근접하지 못하게 하는 비닐하우스 속의 꽃이 철없음을 우리는 알고 있습니다. 새장 속의 새가 새봄을 증거 하지 못함을 우리는 알고 있습니다. 저 혼자서는 그 큰 머리를 지탱할 수 없어 목발을 짚고 서 있는 큰 꽃송이는 우리를 마음 아프게 합니다. 줄기의 것도 뿌리의 것도 아닌 꽃, 그것은 남의 것, 외부의 것, 그리고 이미 꽃이 아닙니다. 서울은 농촌을 향하지 않고 공업은 농업을 필요로 하지 않습니다. 노자勞資·임차賃借·여야與野·남녀男女·빈부貧富는 서로 존경하지 않으며, 남북南北·동서東西·전후前後·좌우左右는 저마다 중심이라 주장합니다.

세상의 봄은 어디서부터 오는가? 산천의 봄은 분명 흙에서 가장 가까운 곳에서 시작됩니다. 흙살 속속들이 박힌 얼음이 빠지고 제 힘으로 일어서는 들풀들의 합창 속에서 옵니다. 세상의 봄도 산천의 봄과 다를 리 없습니다. 사람과 사람 사이에 박힌 경멸과 불신이 사라질 때 옵니다. 집단과 집단, 지역과 지역 사이에 박혀 있는 불신과 억압이 사라지고 불신과 억압의 자리에 갇혀 있는 역량들의 해방과 함께 세상의 봄은 옵니다. 산천의 봄과 마찬가지로 무성한 들풀의 아우성 속에서 옵니다. 모든 것을 넉넉히 포용하면서 기어코 옵니다.

따뜻한 토큰과 보이지 않는 손

A Warm Token and An Invisible Hand · 144p

새벽 영등포 버스 정류장 가판대에서 토큰 한 개를 샀습니다. 따뜻한 토큰이었습니다. 토큰을 손에 들고 손님을 기다리고 있던 할아버지의 체온이 나의 손으로 옮아 왔습니다. 할아버지의 체온을 뺏은 듯 죄송한 마음이 들었습니다. 새벽 사창가 유리 진열장 속에 여자가 앉아 있었습니다. 손님도 없는 골목의 홍등 밑에 거의 벗은 몸으로 앉아 있었습니다. 여자의 옷을 뺏은 듯 죄송한 마음이 들었습니다. 그러나 이 죄송한 마음에 이어 우리의 이마를 찌르는 것은 무엇이 이 사람들을 새벽 거리에 나앉게 하는가 하는 물음입니다.

남대문 새벽 시장과 사당동 인력 시장의 이 시간은 이미 파장 무렵이고 청량리역과 서울역은 벌써 승객들을 가득 싣고 몇 차례나 열차가 떠난 뒤입니다. 텅 빈 광장의 모래바람처럼 우리의 얼굴을 때리는 것은 무엇이 이 사람들을 어둠 속으로 나서게 하는가 하는 물음입니다.

선량하나 무력한 사람들은 그 힘겨운 삶을 마음 아파하기도 하고, 주장하나 고민하지 않는 사람들은 인간의 강인한 생명력에 경탄을 금치 못하기도 하고, 분석하나 실천하지 않는 사람들은 이로써 사회주의의 실패를 설명하기도 하고, 생산하나 나누지 않는 사람들은 이들의 근면을 들어 시장과 자유의 위대함을 예찬하기도 합니다.

사회 문제를 개인의 문제로 환원하거나 현재를 현상만으로 설명하기 이전에 우리는 먼저 그들로 하여금 불꺼진 새벽 골목에 나서게 하는 보이지 않는 손을 질문하지 않으면 안 됩니다. 그리고 그들이 새벽 골목에 나서기까지의 역사를 생각하지 않으면 안 됩니다.

"폭력을 사용하여 강제하는 경우를 성폭행이라고 한다면 똑같은 행위를 폭력 대신 돈으로 강제하는 경우 이를 어떤 이름으로 불러야 하는가?" 누이를 망쳐 버린 못난 오라비의 한 맺힌 질문을 잊을 수 없습니다. 상대방의 뜻에 반하여 자기의 의도를 관철시키기 위한 모든 강제를 폭력이라고 한다면 폭력은 조직 폭력이나 강도, 강간과 같은 불법적 폭력에 한정할 수 없을 것입니다. 더 큰 폭력이 합법적 폭력, 제도적 폭력의 형식으로 우리 사회의 곳곳에 구조화되어 있기 때문입니다. 개인과 개인, 계층과 계층, 민족과 민족이 합의된 목표를 공유하지 못하고 있는 한, 다름과 차이를 승인하는 공존과 평화의 원리가 정착되지 않는 한 그것은 기본적으로 억압과 저항의 관계이며 본질에 있어서 폭력이 아닐 수 없습니다.

돌이 돌을 치면 불꽃이 튀고, 계란이 돌을 치면 박살이 나고, 돌이 풀을 누르면 풀이 눕습니다. 그것이 불꽃이든 침묵이든 상관없습니다. 관계 그 자체의 본질에는 조금도 변함이 없습니다. 불꽃에 관한 이야기든, 아우성과 침묵에 관한 이야기든 그것이 다만 돌멩이를 가리킬 때에만 진실이 됩니다.

토큰은 버스를 만나고, 버스는 도로를 메운 승용차를 만나고, 승용차는 자동차 공장을 만나고, 자동차 공장은 수출과 미국과 개방을 만나고 개방은 황량한 농촌을 만납니다. 이 농촌에서 가판대의 할아버지는 두고 온 고향을 만납니다. 사창가의 홍등을 끄면 술집의 네온이 붉고, 네온을 끄면 산동네 불빛이 빌딩처럼 높고, 산동네 전등불을 끄면 멀리 공장의 불빛이 보입니다. 그리고 이 공장의 야근 불빛 아래 진열장 속의 여자는 두고 온 동료를 만납니다.

개인이나 사회 현상은 그것이 맺고 있는 사회적 연관 속에서만 그것의 참모습이 파악될 수 있습니다. 그러나 참모습은 아무에게나 보여 주는 것이 아니며 아무나 참모습을 볼 수 있는 것도 아닙니다.

토큰에 배어 있는 따뜻한 체온에 마음 아파하는 사람은 인정 있는 사람입니다. 그러나 가판대의 손 시린 겨울바람을 걱정하는 가난한 가족들의 자리가 진실의 참여점〔entry point〕입니다. 새벽 진열장 속에 앉아 있는 여자의 참혹한 삶을 마음 아파하는 사람은 가슴이 따뜻한 사람입니다. 그러나 그 누이를 어찌할 수 없는 못난 오라비의 무력함이 진실로 통하는 참여점입니다.

하나의 현상을 그 사회적인 연관 속에서 파악하는 관점觀點은 매우 훌륭한 것입니다. 그러나 더욱 중요한 것은 관점이 아니라 입장立場입니다. 발 딛고 있는 자리가 훨씬 중요합니다. 사람의 눈은 머리에 달려 있는 것이 아니라 발에 달려 있기 때문입니다.

승용차를 타면 버스의 횡포에 속상하고, 반대로 버스를 타면 도로공간을 사유화하고 있는 승용차의 이기심에 속상합니다. 그러나 그저 속상하기만 할 뿐 변함없이 저마다의 골목을 걸어가고, 저마다의 솥에서 밥을 얻고 있는 한 사실을 정직하게 바라볼 수 있는 자리를 얻지 못합니다. 입장이 중요하다고 하는 것은 사실을 진실로 이끌어 주는 참여점으로서의 입장이 중요하다는 뜻입니다. 우리의 인식은 진실의 창조에 이르러 비로소 인식이 완성되기 때문입니다.

한 개의 토큰, 진열장 속의 여자, 새벽 인력 시장의 모닥불 등 우리가 만나는 개개의 사실들은 매우 중요합니다. 그것은 그것만으로도 충분히 우리의 이마를 찌르고도 남는 아픈 충격임에 틀림없습니다. 그러나 그러한 사실들은 어디까지나 하나하나의 조각 그림일 뿐입니다. 진실은 그러한 조각 그림이 모여서 전체 그림이 완성될 때 비로소 창조됩니다. 진실은 사실들의 배후에서 개개의 사실들을 만들어 내는 거대한 구조를 보여 줍니다. 새벽 어둠 속으로 나서게 하는 보이지 않는 손의 실상을 드러냅니다.

사실은 진실을 창조함으로써 완성되고 진실은 사실에 뿌리내림으로써 살아 있는 것이 됩니다. 우리가 찾아가야 하는 곳이 바로 그 창조의 자리입니다. 사실성寫實性이 진정성眞正性으로 비약하는 창조의 자리입니다. 그러나 이것은 어느 개인의 천재나 몇몇 사람의 따뜻한 가슴이 찾아낼 수 있는 것이 아닙니다. 그것은 수많은 사람이 참여함으로써 비로소 찾을 수 있는 것입니다. 찾아내는 것이 아니라 만들어 내는 것입니다. 왜냐하면 진실은 사실로부터 창조되는 것이되 언제나 수많은 사실로부터 창조되는 것이기 때문입니다. 진실은 같은 길을 걸어가는 모든 사람들과 그리고 한솥밥을 나누는 모든 사람들의 참여에 의해서 창조되어야 하기 때문입니다. 모든 사람들의 수많은 사실로부터 창조되는 너른 마당이 바로 진실이기 때문입니다.

죽순의 시작

해마다 식목일에 많은 나무를 심지만 대나무를 심는 사람은 없습니다. 대나무는 누가 심어 주어서 자라는 나무가 아니라 오직 뿌리에서만 그 죽순이 나오기 때문입니다. 땅속의 시절을 끝내고 나무를 시작하는 죽순의 가장 큰 특징은 마디가 무척 짧다는 점입니다. 이 짧은 마디에서 나오는 강고함이 곧 대나무의 곧고 큰 키를 지탱하는 힘이 됩니다. 훗날 횃불을 에워싸는 죽창이 되고, 온몸을 휘어 강풍을 막는 청천青天 높은 장대 숲이 될지언정 대나무는 마디마디 옹이진 죽순으로 시작합니다.

대나무뿐만 아니라 대부분의 나무들은 마디나 옹이로 먼저 밑둥을 튼튼하게 합니다. 이것은 사람들의 일상사에서도 마찬가지라고 생각됩니다. 새 학교를 시작하든, 묵은 학원을 다시 시작하든, 새 직장을 시작하든, 어제의 일터에 오늘 다시 불을 지피든, 모든 시작하는 사람들이 맨 먼저 만들어 내어야 하는 것은 바로 이 짧고 많은 마디입니다.

나무가 아닌 우리들의 삶에 있어서 마디는 과연 무엇이며 또 우리는 그것을 어떻게 만들어 내어야 하는가. 이러한 물음은 새봄과 함께 세차게 일어나는 우리 사회의 여러 부문 운동에 있어서는 말할 것도 없고, 새로운 뜻을 심고자 하는 평범한 사람들, 그리고 지천명知天命의 나이에 세상을 시작하는 내게도 절실한 과제가 아닐 수 없습니다.

세상사가 어렵다고 하는 까닭은 서로 다른 이해관계 때문에 새로운 것은 언제나 낡은 것의 완강한 저항과 억압 속에서 시작하지 않을 수 없기 때문입니다. 이러한 경우는 그래도 덜한 경우이고, 낡은 것이 새로운 것을 부단히 배우고 수용함으로써 자기 개선을 해 나갈 수 있는 최소한의 탄력성마저 상실해 버린 단계가 되면 이는 아예 초전박살의 살벌한 위기 구조가 되고 맙니다. 이때 죽순은 다만 좋은 먹이가 될 뿐입니다.

죽순의 마디는 분명히 뿌리에서 배운 것입니다. 캄캄한 땅속을 뻗어 가던 어렵던 시절의 몸짓입니다. 역경의 산물이며 동시에 저항의 흔적입니다. 그것은 차라리 패배의 상처 그 자체인지도 모릅니다.

좌절과 패배를 딛고 일어선 의지의 인생을 우리는 물론 알고 있으며, 처절한 패배로 막을 내린 민중 투쟁마저도 유구한 민족사의 밑바닥에 묻혀 있다가 이윽고 찬란한 승리의 원동력이 되었던 승패의 변증법을 우리는 역사의 도처에서 읽어서 압니다.

객관적 조건과 주체적 역량에 맞는 목표와 단계를 설정하는 일이 곧 마디의 과학이라 생각하며, 달성할 수 있는 목표, 이길 수 있는 싸움을 조직하는 일이 바로 짧은 마디의 교훈이라 생각됩니다. 손자병법이 가르치는 바도 다르지 않은데, 이를테면 전쟁을 잘 한다는 것은 쉽게 이길 수 있는 상대를 이기는 것이라고 했습니다. 이것은 약한 상대를 고르라는 비열함이 아님은 물론입니다.

용두사미란 경구를 모르는 사람이 없듯이 정당이든 단체든 개인이든 거대하고 요란한 출발은 대체로 속에 허약함을 숨기고 있는 허세인 경우가 허다합니다. 민들레의 뿌리를 캐어 본 사람은 압니다. 하찮은 봄 풀 한 포기라도 뽑아 본 사람은 땅속에 얼마나 깊은 뿌리를 뻗고 있는가를 압니다. 모든 나무는 자기 키만큼의 긴 뿌리를 땅속에 묻어 두고 있는 법입니다. 대숲은 그 숲의 모든 대나무의 키를 합친 것만큼의 광범한 뿌리를 땅속에 간직하고 있는 것입니다.

그리고 더욱 중요한 것은 대나무는 뿌리를 서로 공유하고 있다는 사실입니다. 대나무가 반드시 숲을 이루고야 마는 비결이 바로 이 뿌리의 공유에 있는 것입니다. 대나무가 숲을 이루고 나면 이제는 나무의 이야기가 아닙니다. 개인의 마디와 뿌리의 연대가 이루어 내는 숲의 역사를 시작하는 것입니다. 홍수의 유역에서도 흙을 지키고 강물을 돌려놓기도 하며 뱀을 범접치 못하게 하고 그늘을 드리워 호랑이를 기릅니다. 그때쯤이면 사시청청 잎사귀까지 달아 바람을 상대하되 잎사귀로 사귀어 잠재울 것과 온몸으로 버틸 것을 적절히 가릴 줄 압니다. 설령 잘리어 토막 지더라도 은은한 피리 소리로 남고, 칼날 아래 갈갈이 찢어지더라도 수고하는 이마의 소금 땀을 들이는 바람으로 남습니다. 식목의 계절에 저마다 한 그루의 나무를 심기 전에 잠시 생각해 보아야 합니다. 나는 어느 뿌리 위에 나 자신을 심고 있는가. 그리고 얼마만큼의 마디로 밑둥을 가꾸어 놓고 있는가.

인간적인 사람, 인간적인 사회

Humane Person, Humane Society • 153p

몸을 움직여서 먹고사는 사람은 대체로 쓰임새가 헤픈 반면에 돈을 움직여서 먹고사는 사람은 쓰임새가 여물다고 합니다. 그러나 몸을 움직여 버는 돈이란 그저 먹고사는 데서 이쪽저쪽일 뿐 따로 쌓아 둘 나머지가 있을 리 없습니다.

쓰임새가 헤프다는 것은 다만 그 씀씀이가 쉽다는 뜻에 불과합니다. 쓰임새가 쉬운 까닭도 내가 겪어 본 바로는 첫째 자신의 노동력을 믿기 때문입니다. 쓰더라도 축난다는 생각이 없습니다. '벌면 된다'는 생각입니다. 그리고 또 하나의 이유는 끈끈한 인간관계를 가지고 있기 때문이라고 생각됩니다.

일하는 과정에서 맺은 인간관계가 생활 깊숙이 자리 잡고 있어서 함께 써야 할 사람들이 주위에 많기 때문입니다. 더불어 일하고 더불어 써야 하기 때문입니다. 따라서 몸을 움직여 먹고사는 사람의 쓰임새가 헤프다는 것은 이를테면 구두가 발보다 조금 크다는 정도의 필요 그 자체일 뿐 결코 인격적인 결함이라 할 수는 없습니다.

스스로의 역량을 신뢰하고, 더불어 살아가는 삶을 당연하게 여긴다는 점에서 오히려 지극히 인간적인 품성이라 할 것입니다. 다만 이러한 내용이 쉽사리 드러나지 않는 까닭은 이른바 '번다'는 말의 뜻이 애매하기 때문이라고 생각됩니다. 힘들여 일한 대가로 돈을 받은 경우에도 돈을 벌었다고 하고, 돈놀이나 부동산 투기로 얻은 불로소득의 경우에도 돈을 벌었다고 합니다. 심지어는 남을 속이거나 빼앗은 경우도 돈을 벌었다는 말로 표현하고 있습니다.

도대체 '번다'는 말의 본뜻은 무엇인가. 경제학이 가르치는 바에 따르면 사람들이 버는 모든 소득은 노임이든 이자든 이윤이든 불로 소득이든, 오로지 생산된 가치물에서 나누어 받는 것입니다. 가치물을 생산하지 않는 사람은 어떤 경로를 통해서건 타인의 소득을 자기의 소득으로 만드는 것입니다. 그러므로 '번다'는 말은 가치를 생산함으로써 받는 돈에 국한해야 할 것입니다. '돈이 돈을 번다'는 말의 '번다'고 하는 단어는 다른 말로 바꾸어야 마땅합니다.

시골에 사는 허 서방이 서울에 올라와서 양복점에서 일하는 둘째아들한테서 양복 한 벌을 해 입었다.

"애, 이 옷이 얼마냐?"

"20만 원입니다. 10만 원은 옷감값이고 10만 원은 품값이지요."

허 서방은 방직공장에 다니는 큰딸을 찾아갔다.

"애, 양복 한 벌 감의 값이 얼마냐?"

"10만 원입니다. 5만 원은 실값이고 5만 원은 품값이지요."

허 서방은 이번에는 방적공장에 다니는 작은딸을 찾아갔다.

"애, 양복 한 벌 감에 드는 실값이 얼마냐?"

"5만 원입니다. 2만 원은 양모값이고 3만 원은 품값이지요."

허 서방은 도로 시골로 내려가서 양을 키우는 큰아들한테 물었다.

"애, 양복 한 벌 감에 드는 양모값이 얼마냐?"

"2만 원입니다. 만 원은 양값이고 만 원은 품값이지요."

양은 양이 낳고 양값이란 양을 기르는 품값이다.

허 서방이 입은 20만 원의 양복은 결국 4남매의 품값이다.

이 이야기는 양복뿐만이 아니라 사회를 양육하고 지탱하는 의식주의 실체가 과연 무엇인가를 이야기해 줍니다.

5월 1일 노동절을 전후하여 한편에서는 노동자들의 주장이 뜨겁게 일어나고 있으며, 다른 한편에서는 '법과 경제'의 이름으로 이를 강력하게 다스리고 있습니다. 노동 현장뿐만 아니라 토지·주택·학교·언론 등 사회의 거의 모든 부문에 일상화되어 있는 증오와 불신과 집단적 냉소가 우리 모두의 창의와 의욕을 한없이 천대하고 있습니다.

국민의 불과 0.2%가 한 해 동안 80조여 원의 불로소득을 '벌고' 있으며, 한편에서는 그 빈궁과 억압이 사람을 소외시키고, 다른 한편에서는 그 잉여와 방종이 사람을 부단히 타락시키고 있습니다. 이와 같은 자본의 부당한 축적 과정을 그대로 둔 채 이 집단적 불신과 냉소를 국민적 공감으로 합의해 내기란 불가능한 일입니다.

사회의 진보는 경제적 부로 이룩되는 것이 아니라, 결국은 사람과 그 사람들이 맺고 있는 '관계'의 실상에 따라 결정되는 법입니다. 자신의 역량에 대한 신뢰와, 더불어 만들고 함께 나누는 삶의 창출이 새로운 사람, 새로운 사회를 키우는 것이라면 바로 이 점에 있어서 민주 노동운동의 목표와 이상은 지극히 인간적이며 진보적이라 하지 않을 수 없습니다.

동물은 철저한 소비자일 뿐이며 미생물은 단지 보조자임에 비하여 지구 위의 유일한 생산자는 오직 식물이라는 한 농사꾼의 이야기는 실로 놀라운 정치경제학입니다. 나무를 키우는 일이 자연을 지키는 일이듯이 사회의 생산자를 신뢰하며 그를 건강하고 힘 있게 키우는 일이야말로 사회를 지키는 가장 확실한 길이며 나아가 수많은 사람들의 소외와 타락을 동시에 구제하는 유일한 길이라 할 것입니다.

사람의 얼굴

Human Faces • 157p

〈가고파〉란 노래를 들을 때 나는 내가 어린 시절에 자랐던 유천강을 생각합니다. 〈옛 동산에 올라〉란 노래를 들을 때마다 나의 머리 속에 변함없이 떠오르는 동산은 언제나 고향의 작은 뒷산입니다.

유천강이나 고향의 작은 뒷산은 이 노랫말을 지은 시인이 생전 보지도 듣지도 못한 곳입니다. 이 노래를 부르거나 듣는 사람들 가운데 내가 떠올리는 강이나 산을 연상하는 사람은 아무도 없을 것입니다. 심지어 어린 시절 이 강과 산을 함께 나누며 자라 온 나의 친구나 형제들 가운데에도 나와 같은 연상을 하는 사람은 아무도 없을 것입니다.

비단 노래뿐만이 아닙니다. 무심히 글을 읽다가 문장 속에서 잠시 만나는 한 개의 단어에서도 우리들에게는 그것과 함께 연상되는 장면이 있게 마련입니다. 글뜻에 마음이 빼앗겨 미처 돌이켜 볼 여유가 없어서 그렇지 이러한 연상 세계는 마치 영상의 배경처럼 우리가 구사하는 모든 개념의 바탕에 펼쳐져 있습니다.

이를테면 '민족'이란 단어를 읽을 때 연상되는 장면을 물어보면 사람마다 각각 다른 장면을 이야기해 줍니다. 어떤 사람은 태극기를, 어떤 사람은 3·1절 기념식장을, 어떤 사람은 88올림픽을, 장승을, 시골 장터를 연상하고 있습니다.

민족이란 단어뿐만이 아니라 더욱 구체적인 단어의 경우도 사람마다 그 연상의 세계가 가지각색이기는 마찬가지입니다. 소나무, 돼지, 자동차, 쌀, 옷…….

　나는 오랜 독거 생활의 무료를 달랠 생각으로 시작한 것이기는 하지만 내가 사용하거나 만나는 모든 단어의 연상 세계를 조사해 나간 시절이 있었습니다. 내 생각의 배후를 파헤치는 심정으로 하나하나 점검해 본 적이 있습니다. 그리고 매우 놀라운 것을 발견했습니다.

　예를 들어 '실업'이란 단어를 읽을 때 나의 머리 속을 스쳐 지나가는 장면은 경제학 교과서에서 읽은 이러저러한 개념이었습니다. 케인스적 실업, 맬서스적 실업, 상대적 과잉 인구, 실업률…… 메마른 경제학 개념과 이론들이 연상되는 것이었습니다. '전쟁', '자본', '상품'과 같이 고도의 사회성을 띠고 있는 개념도 그 사회관계의 본질인 사회적 관계가 사상되고 있음은 물론이고 구체성을 담고 있는 개념마저도 그 연상 세계가 감각적이고 형식적인 것임에 놀라지 않을 수 없었습니다.

　'전쟁'이라는 단어에서는 이제 패트리어트 미사일과 스커드 미사일이 펼치는 전자 오락 게임과 같은 텔레비전 화면이 연상되기 십상이며 '자본'에서는 은행의 금고가, '상품'에서는 백화점 쇼윈도가 연상되게 마련입니다. 한마디로 정서적 공감의 원초가 되는 '사람'이 연상되는 경우는 거의 없습니다.

　이처럼 나의 머리 속에 사람의 얼굴이 담겨 있지 않다는 사실을 처음으로 깨달았을 때의 충격은 엄청난 것이었습니다. 그것은 심한 무력감과 외로움 같은 것이었습니다. 한겨울의 독방보다도 더 무력하고 통절한 외로움이었습니다. 더불어 함께 일할 동료도 없이, 손때 묻은 연장 하나 없이, 고작 몇 권의 책과 연필을 들고 척박한 간척지에 서 있는 느낌이었습니다.

　사회과학도에게 요구되는 냉철한 이성(cool head)이 사람과, 사람과의 관계를 배제하는 것이 아니라면 이것은 거대한 허구가 아닐 수 없습니다. 더구나 냉철한 이성이 따뜻한 가슴[warm heart]을 바탕으로 하여 얻어지는 것이라면 나의 관념 세계는 실로 비정한 것이 아닐 수 없습니다.

나는 내가 읽고 생각한 것, 심지어 내가 온몸으로 겪은 것에서마저도 껍데기만 얻고 있었을 뿐이었고 껍데기로 누각을 짓고 있었을 뿐이었습니다. 나는 나의 메마르고 비정한 연상 세계에 사람의 얼굴을 하나하나 심어 나가기로 작정하였습니다. 관념적인 연상 세계를 풍부한 구체성으로 채우고 싶었습니다.

나는 우선 '실업'이란 말을 듣거나 읽을 때 의식적으로 내가 잘 아는 친구를 떠올리기로 하였습니다. 그는 쌀 1kg에 800원 하던 때에 500원어치의 쌀을 달라고 하기가 부끄러워 라면으로 끼니를 때우는 사람이었습니다.

연탄을 살 돈이 없어 아예 냉방으로 지내던 겨울에 그를 괴롭히던 것은 추위가 아니라 혹시 다른 가게에서 연탄을 사고 있지나 않나 하고 의심스럽게 바라보는 가겟집 아주머니의 시선이 고통스럽던 친구였습니다. 하루 종일 번 돈이 식구들의 끼니를 에울 만큼이 되지 못하면 차마 자기만 바라고 있는 동생들을 볼 면목이 없어 집으로 들어 가지 못하고 싸구려 합숙소에서 새우잠을 자고 새벽 어둠 속 대학병원에서 피를 팔던 친구였습니다.

회복실에 누워 메마른 카스테라를 먹으며 팔목을 타고 흘러내리는 피를 손가락에 찍어 벽에다 낙서를 하던 친구. 그 친구를 생각하기로 작정하였습니다. 그가 썼던 벽 위의 낙서를 생각하기로 하였습니다.

관념성을 벗는다는 것은 일차적으로 이 연상의 세계가 관념적이지 않아야 할 것 같았습니다. '건축'이라는 단어에서 '빌딩'이 연상되는 것보다는 '포크레인'이나 '망치'가 연상되는 것이 덜 관념적이고 포크레인이나 망치보다는 자기가 잘 아는 '목수'가 연상되는 경우가 보다 덜 관념적이라고 생각됩니다.

더구나 '정직'이라든가 '양심'과 같이 추상적인 단어일수록 그것과 더불어 사람이 연상되지 않는 한 그것이 사람들의 삶을 담아내는 일에 있어서는 무력할 수밖에 없는 것이며, 그것이 인간적인 것으로 되기는 더욱 어려운 것입니다.

그리고 더욱 중요한 것은 연상되는 사람이 어떠한 사람인가에 따라서 사고의 성격 즉 그의 사회적 입장이 정해진다는 사실입니다. 그리고 그 시대 그 사회의 가장 민중적인 사람들이 사고의 밑바탕을 자리 잡고 있어야만 그의 사상도 시대적 과제와 사회적 모순을 온당하게 반영하고 그것과 튼튼히 연결될 수 있다는 사실입니다.

그리하여 '자유'나 '평등'과 같은 고매한 개념도 사람과, 사람과의 관계를 사실적으로 표현해 내는 그림으로 그 내용이 채워질 때 비로소 우리는 관념의 유희와 비인간적인 물신성으로부터 해방될 수 있는 것이라 생각됩니다.

고향에서 숙모님이 보내 주신 대추 한 되를 앞에 놓고 숙모님의 모습과 고향의 산천을 떠올리기는 어렵지 않지만 수퍼에서 구입한 사과 한 개를 손에 들고 과수원을 연상하기는 어렵습니다. 더구나 거리마다 넘치는 무수한 자동차를 바라보며 자동차 공장의 기름땀에 젖은 노동자들의 수고를 생각하기는 거의 불가능에 가깝다고 할 것입니다.

사람의 얼굴이 담겨 있지 않은 우리의 머리와 사람과의 관계가 사라져 버린 우리들의 삶 속에 사람 대신 무엇이 그 자리를 차지하고 들어앉아 있는지…… 참으로 섬뜩하지 않을 수 없습니다.

북한산 등반 길에서 어느 중년의 남자 두 사람이 이야기하며 지나갔습니다. "저게 다람쥐는 아니고 이름이 무어라더라? 꼬리가 꽤 비싸다던데?" 우리들의 생각은 얼마나 삐뚜로 놓여 있으며 우리들의 삶은 얼마나 삭막하고 산산히 조각나 있는가.

모든 물질적 성과와 모든 정신적 문화의 밑바탕에서 그것을 만들어 내고 그것을 지탱하고 있는 사람들의 얼굴을 발견해 내고 그 사람들과의 관계 위에서 영위되고 있는 나의 삶을 깨닫지 않으면 안 되는 것입니다.

나는 그러한 깨달음을 가까이 두기 위하여 나의 연상 세계에 사람들을 심으려 했는지도 모릅니다. 그러나 독거실의 냉기 속에 곧추앉아서 사고의 배후를 파헤치고, 나의 뇌리 속에 틀고 앉은 잡다한 관념의 검불을 쓸어 내고, 그 자리에 나의 친구들을 심으려던 나의 시도는 결국 이렇다 할 진척을 보지 못한 채 참담한 구멍만 뚫어 놓고 말았습니다.

그 참담한 실패의 전모를 글로써 적기에는 그 과정이 너무나 복잡합니다. 돌이켜 보면 그것은 필요한 일이기는 하였으나 성급한 것이었습니다.

나에게는 우선 그 많은 개념들의 밑바닥에 들어앉힐 친구들이 부족했습니다. 그리고 설령 내게 수많은 친구가 있었다고 하더라도 그 친구들의 얼굴을 내게 정서적 친근감을 준다는 이유만으로 그 자리에 들어앉힐 수도 없었습니다. 친근한 개인으로 말미암아 도리어 그 개념이 왜 소화하거나 심지어는 다른 내용으로 변질되어 버림으로써 거꾸로 주관성이 강화되기도 하였습니다. 뿐만 아니라 '실업'이라는 개념의 밑바닥에 들어앉힌 친구만 하더라도 그가 1980년대의 실업의 본질적 성격을 제시해 주지는 못했습니다.

사람이 담지擔持하고 있는 그 풍부한 정서와 사회성에 주목했던 나의 노력이 사람을 통하여 당대 감수성의 절정에 이르기는커녕 한낱 개별 인간에 대한 관심으로 전락되기도 하였습니다. 그리고 가장 절망적인 것은 도대체 독거실에 앉아서는 될 일이 아니었습니다. 세 번 네 번 심어도 뿌리내리지 않는 풀이었습니다. 한마디로 머리 속에 심을 것이 아니라 삶의 현장에서 어깨동무로 만나야 하는 것이었습니다.

연상 세계를 바꾸려던 나의 노력은 결국 나에게 작은 위안만을 한동안 가져다주었을 뿐 더욱 침통한 고민을 안겨 주었습니다.

개별 인간의 정서와 현실이 우선은 핍진한 공감을 안겨 줄지는 모르지만 그것은 우리 시대의 견고한 구조적 실상에 대하여는 극히 무력할 뿐이었습니다.

'사람'이란 누구나 누구의 친구이고 누구의 가족일 터이지만 그것이 우리의 사고 속에 계속 친구나 가족으로서만 남아 있는 한 우리의 사고가 감상적 차원을 넘어 드넓은 지평으로 나아가기는 어려운 것이라고 생각됩니다.

그곳이 연상의 세계이든, 그곳이 현실의 팽팽한 긴장 속이든 우리는 우리가 만나는 사람으로부터 그 사람을 규정하고 있는 사회 구조적 얼개를 향하여 다시 나아가지 않으면 안 되는 것이라고 생각됩니다.

어차피 한 사람의 절친한 개인으로부터 출발하지 않을 수 없다 하더라도 그 개인을 매개로 하여 사회적 개인으로 나아가지 않는 한 우리는 당면한 모순을 변혁해 낼 주인공의 얼굴을 만날 수는 없는 것입니다. 더구나 그 역량에 대한 신뢰를 가질 수는 더욱 없는 것이라고 믿습니다.

그럼에도 불구하고 나는 나의 친구들을 소중히 간직할 것입니다. 일체의 실천이 배제된 독거실에서 추운 겨울밤을 뜨겁게 달구며 해후한 나의 친구들을 나는 사랑합니다. 애정은 아무리 보잘것없는 대상도 자신의 내부로 깊숙이 안아 들여 더욱 큰 것으로 키워 내기 때문입니다.

그리고 진정한 애정은 우리 시대의 가장 첨예한 모순의 한복판으로 걸어 나가는 일, 그리고 그 현장의 첨예한 칼끝으로부터 부단히 상처받는 일인지도 모릅니다. 그것이야말로 우리의 생각을 확실한 물적 토대 위에 발 딛게 하는 길이며, 우리의 삶을 튼튼한 대지 위에 뿌리내리게 하는 길이며, 이윽고 우리들로 하여금 '우리 시대의 사람', '우리 사회의 사람'으로 완성해 가는 길이기 때문입니다.

그리고 그 길은 언제나 사람에서 비롯되고 언제나 사람에게로 통하는 것이기 때문입니다.

어려움은 즐거움보다 함께하기 쉽습니다

Hardship Is Easier to Share Than Pleasure · 165p

"어려움을 함께하는 일이 쉬운가, 즐거움을 같이하는 일이 쉬운가."

이러한 질문을 받고 우리는 즐거움을 나누는 일이 훨씬 쉽다고 생각합니다. 어려움을 함께하기 위해서는 상당한 정도의 고통을 분담할 수밖에 없지만 하등의 고통 분담도 없이 함께할 수 있는 것이 즐거움이기 때문입니다.

그러나 일찍이 양자강 유역에서 오월吳越이 패권覇權을 다투던 때의 이야기입니다만 월왕越王 구천句踐을 도와 회계산會稽山의 치욕을 설욕케 한 범려范蠡의 생각은 이와 반대입니다. 그는 월왕 구천을 평하여 "어려움은 함께할 수 있어도 즐거움은 같이할 수 없는 사람"이란 말을 남기고 그를 떠납니다. 범려의 이러한 판단은 물론 구천이란 개인을 두고 내린 것이라고 할 수 있습니다. 그러나 비단 구천뿐만이 아니라 우리들에게는 평범한 사람들의 성정이 대체로 그러하다는 경험이 없지 않습니다. 일감을 나누기보다 떡을 나누기가 더 어렵다는 옛말이 그렇습니다.

즐거움을 함께하기 어려운 이유는 물론 여러 가지가 있겠지만 가장 중요한 이유는 무엇보다도 즐거움은 다만 즐거움 그 자체에 탐닉耽溺하는 것으로 시종하기 때문입니다. 그리고 탐닉은 자기 자신에 대한 몰두입니다. 그것이 타인에 대한 축하에서 비롯된 경우에도 결국은 자기 감정, 자기의 이해관계에 대한 몰두로 변합니다. '함께'의 의미가 그만큼

왜소해집니다. 마치 장갑을 벗지 않고 나누는 악수처럼 체온의 교감을 상실하고 있는 것이 대체로 즐거움의 부근附近입니다. 내 손이 따뜻하면 네 손이 차고, 네 손이 따뜻하면 내 손이 차가운 줄을 알게 하는 맨손의 악수와는 분명 다른 만남입니다. 토사구팽兎死拘烹이란 성어成語도 범려가 떠나면서 남긴 말입니다. 이해利害로 맺은 야합野合이 팽烹을 낳습니다. 탐닉과 거품의 처음과 끝이 그러합니다.

설날이란 '낯선 날'이란 뜻이라고 합니다. 새해를 맞아 스스로 삼가는 마음을 담고 있습니다. 올해는 참으로 낯선 한 해를 맞고 있습니다. 겨울 바람과 함께 몰아치는 경제 한파가 낯설기만 합니다. 지금의 고통 뒤에 또 어떤 고통이 뒤따를지 짐작하기 어렵습니다. 생각하면 이러한 경제 한파는 결코 낯선 것이 아닙니다. 우리들 스스로가 만들어 낸 것이며 알면서도 외면하고 있었던 것에 불과합니다.

이 한파 속에도 한 가닥의 위로가 없지 않습니다. 거품이 빠진다는 사실에서 위로를 받습니다. 거품이 빠지면서 때도 함께 빠지기 때문입니다. 어려움은 즐거움보다 함께하기 쉽다는 사실에서 위로를 받습니다. 어려움은 그것을 함께할 사람을 그리워하게 하기 때문입니다. 그리하여 우리의 실상을 분명하게 직시할 수 있게 된다면 그것은 참으로 소중한 반성이고 위로가 아닐 수 없습니다.

새해를 맞아 다시 '한강의 기적'을 만들어 내자는 호소는 바람직하지 않다고 생각합니다. 또다시 거품을 만들자는 구호와 다름없기 때문입니다. 거품만 빼고 때는 빼지 말자는 은밀한 책략이 될 수 있기 때문입니다. 나라가 어려우면 어진 재상을 생각하고 집이 어려우면 좋은 아내를 생각하는 것처럼〔國亂思良相 家貧思賢妻〕 우리는 모름지기 사람을 깨닫는 일에서부터 시작해야 할 것입니다. 가장 귀중한 삶의 가치란 바로 사람으로부터 건너오는 것임을 깨닫는 일에서부터 시작하여야 할 것입니다. 까마득히 잊었던 사람을 발견하고 그 사람들과 함께 어려움을 견딜 수 있는 진지陣地를 만들어야 할 것입니다. 참다운 삶의 가치를 지켜 주는 따뜻한 진지를 만들어 내고, 막강한 국제 금융 자본의 한파에도 무너지지 않는 견고한 진지를 만들어 가야 합니다.

그리하여 올해는 우리들로 하여금 근본으로 '돌아가도록' 하는 통절한 각성의 한 해로 맞이하여야 할 것입니다. 잊었던 벗을 다시 만나는 해후의 나날로 만들어 가야 할 것입니다.

3부 어리석은 자의 우직함이 세상을 조금씩 바꿔 갑니다

나눔, 그 아름다운 삶

Sharing, Such a Beautiful Life! · 168p

"재물財物이 모이면 사람이 흩어지고 재물이 흩어지면 사람이 모인다."
이 말은 재물과 사람의 관계에 관한 우리들의 오랜 금언이었습니다. 재물을 다른 사람들에게 베풀지 않으면 그의 주변에는 사람들이 모이지 않고 반대로 여러 사람을 위하여 자기의 재물을 베풀면 그의 주변에 사람들이 모인다는 것이 우리들의 믿음이었습니다. 그리고 이 금언은 재물보다는 사람을 더 귀중하게 생각해 온 우리의 문화이기도 하였습니다.

그러나 이 말은 이제 참으로 옛말이 되었습니다. 지금은 오히려 재물이 모여야 사람이 모이고 재물이 흩어지면 사람도 흩어진다고 믿고 있는 것이 오늘의 현실입니다.

재물과 사람의 관계가 이처럼 역전된 까닭은 무엇인가. 그것은 물론 사람보다 재물을 더 귀하게 여기기 때문입니다.

그렇다면 재물을 사람보다 더 귀하게 여기는 까닭은 무엇인가. 이것은 참으로 부질없는 질문입니다. 재물만 있으면 사람은 얼마든지 살 수 있기 때문입니다.

너무도 당연한 것에 대하여 의문을 갖는다는 것은 그 자체가 어리석기 짝이 없는 것인지도 모릅니다. 그러나 어리석은 물음이 현명한 답변을 주기도 합니다. 어리석은 질문은 때때로 우리의 삶에 대한 성찰과 사회에 대한 반성을 담기도 합니다.

뒤바뀐 금언을 놓고 우리가 생각해 보아야 하는 것은 먼저 '재물'에 관한 것입니다. 과거의 재물과 현재의 재물에 어떤 차이가 있는가 하는 점입니다.

과거의 재물은 이를테면 곡식과 같은 소비재 형태의 재물이었음에 비하여 오늘의 재물은 자본입니다. 재물과 자본의 차이는 엄청난 것입니다. 재물은 소비의 대상이지만 자본은 그 자체가 가치 증식의 수단입니다. 자본은 자기를 불리기 위한 것입니다. 결코 나눌 수 없는 성질을 갖는 것입니다.

재물은 사람의 사용을 위한 것이지만 자본은 자본 그 자체의 가치 증식을 목적으로 하기 때문입니다. 그리고 또 한 가지의 결정적 차이는 재물은 무한히 쌓아 둘 수 없지만 자본은 무한히 쌓아 둘 수 있다는 사실입니다.

오늘의 재물인 자본은 이처럼 과거의 재물과 그 성격에 있어서도 판이하고 그 형태도 확연히 달라졌습니다. 끊임없이 자기를 불려 나가야 하는 본질을 갖고 있으면서 단 한 개의 계좌만으로서도 무한히 쌓아 놓을 수 있는 형태를 취하고 있는 것이 바로 오늘의 재물인 자본의 실체입니다. 그러나 재물과 자본의 가장 큰 차이는 재물이 사용 가치임에 반하여 자본은 교환 가치라는 사실입니다.

재물은 결국 사람을 위하여 쓰임으로써 자기의 소임을 다하게 되는데 반하여 자본은 사람을 위하여 사용되는 것이 아니라 다른 것과 교환하여 자기를 끊임없이 불려 가는 과정을 반복하고 순환할 뿐이라는 사실입니다. 바로 이 점에서 우리는 "재물이 모이면 사람이 모인다"는 오늘날의 뒤바뀐 금언을 다시 생각하지 않을 수 없습니다.

재물이 모이면 사람이 모인다는 오늘날의 금언은 곧 자본이 고용을 창출한다는 뜻으로 이해될 수 있습니다. '자본에 의하여 고용된 취업'이 오늘날 사람이 모이는 가장 보편적인 형식이 되고 있는 것이 사실입니다.

그러나 이 경우에 자본을 중심으로 하여 모인 사람에 대하여 다시 한번 생각해 볼 필요가 있습니다. 자본을 중심으로 모인 것이 과연 진정한 인격으로서의 만남인가. 자본은 결코 인격을 요구하지 않습니다. 창의력이 있는 사람을 요구하는 경우에도 마찬가지입니다. 어떠한 경우든 결국 자본은 가치 증식에 필요한 노동력을 필요로 할 뿐입니다. 그렇기 때문에 재물이 모이면 사람이 모인다는 오늘날의 금언은 결국 허구일 수밖에 없습니다.

오늘날의 재물은 진정한 인격으로서의 사람을 모으지 못하고 있다고 해야 합니다. 인간적 가치 실현이 좌절된 직장에서 수많은 사람들이 겪고 있는 갈등에서부터 노동 해방의 치열한 투쟁에 이르기까지 우리 시대의 모든 사람들이 짐 지고 있는 고통과 아픔이 바로 여기서 연유하는 것임을 우리는 알고 있습니다.

그런 점에서 "재물이 흩어져야 사람이 모인다"는 옛말은 오늘날에도 여전히 금언으로 남아 있다고 할 수 있습니다. 재물을 흩어서 사람을 모으는 일은 단지 재물의 분배에 국한된 작은 이야기가 아닙니다. 그것은 어쩌면 우리 사회의 구조에 대한 이야기이기도 하고 삶과 인간에 대한 이야기이기도 합니다.

나눔이 실천될 수 없는 사회적 구조 속에서 나눔을 주장하는 것은 동정이나 자선을 호소하는 작은 담론이 아닙니다. 그것은 자본의 성격을 재물로 바꾸고 그 재물을 다시 사람의 소용에 닿게 하고자 하는 사회 운동과 인간 운동으로 이어질 수밖에 없기 때문입니다. '나눔'의 담론을 분식粉飾의 방조적 공간으로부터 인간적인 사회 건설의 실천적 현장으로 이끌어 내는 일이야말로 새로운 시대의 실천적 과제인지도 모릅니다.

자본의 논리와 시장의 논리가 신자유주의라는 이름으로 우리의 모든 인간적 가치를 황폐화시키고 있는 오늘의 현실 속에서 '나눔'은 사회와 인간을 읽을 수 있는 대단히 민감한 고리가 아닐 수 없습니다. 우리는 참으로 나누지 못하는 사회를 살고 있는지도 모릅니다. 역경을 겪어 온 김밥 할머니만이 나눔을 실천하고 있는 삭막한 사회를 우리는 살고 있는지도 모릅니다. 그러나 이러한 상황일수록 우리는 더욱 우직하고 어리석은 질문을 던져 볼 필요가 있습니다.

　　사람은 무엇으로 사는가? 돈이란 무엇인가? 하는 어리석은 질문을 스스로에게 던져 볼 필요가 있는 것입니다. 가장 뜨거운 기쁨은 사람으로부터 얻는다는 것을 우리는 알고 있으며 마찬가지로 가장 침통한 아픔도 바로 사람으로부터 온다는 것을 알고 있습니다. 그럼에도 불구하고 우리는 가장 근본적인 것을 돌이켜 볼 수 없는 숨 가쁜 골목을 달리고 있는지도 모릅니다.

　　생각하면 우리가 나누어야 할 것은 재물이 아닙니다. 자본이든 재물이든 그것은 근본적으로 나눌 수 없는 것입니다. 그것은 어쩌면 이미 나누지 않았기 때문에 형성된 것일 수도 있기 때문입니다. 우리가 나눌 수 있는 것은 나눔으로써 반으로 줄어드는 것이 아니라 나눔으로써 두 배로 커지는 것에 국한될 수밖에 없습니다. 그런 점에서 나눔은 사랑이어야 하고 모임은 봉사이어야 합니다.

　　사랑과 봉사, 그것은 조금도 상실이 아니기 때문입니다. 그리고 사랑과 봉사야말로 한없이 인간적인 것이기 때문입니다. 우리 사회의 재물을 더 풍성하게 하고 우리를 더욱 아름답게 가꾸어 주는 것이기 때문입니다. 그리고 그것은 우리 사회를 그 구조에서부터 가꾸어 주는 것이기 때문입니다.

내 기억 속의 기차 이야기

The Whistle of a Train in My Memory • 173p

소리로만 기억되는 기차가 있었습니다. 20년간 갇혀 있으면서 그 중 15년을 대전교도소에서 보냈습니다. 대전교도소는 호남선 철길과 가까운 곳에 있어서 가장 가슴 아프게 하는 것이 밤마다 들려오는 열차 소리였습니다. 갇혀 있는 처지에서 듣는 기차 소리는 가슴 저미는 아픔과 그리움이었습니다. '차창에 불 밝힌 저 기차는 저마다의 고향으로 사람들을 싣고 가고 있구나' 하는 상념에 젖게 합니다. 특히 명절이 가까워 올 때면 그런 생각이 더욱 간절해져 바깥 세상을 향한 그리움을 앓게 됩니다. 근 20년 기차 소리는 그렇게, 바깥으로 향하는, 가족들 혹은 그리운 이들에게 돌아가는 귀환의 의미로, 어쩌면 시적인 정서로 내 마음에 자리 잡았습니다.

출옥 후 번거롭기는 하지만 가능하면 기차를 이용하는 것도 그 기억과 무관하지 않으리라고 생각됩니다. 특히 대전쯤을 지날 때면 '예전에 소리로만 듣던 기차에 내가 앉아 있구나' 하는 생각이 들어 감회가 남다릅니다.

최근 남북 간에 끊어진 열차가 이어진다는 소식을 들으면서 또 다른 감개에 젖게 됩니다. 가슴에 담고 있던 감상적인 정서와는 사뭇 다른 정서, '엄청난 세계가 열리는구나' 하는 생각에 그동안 내가 너무 개인적인 정서에 칩거해 있지 않았나 하는 반성을 하게 됩니다.

97년 1년간 중앙일보사에서 기획한 세계 기행을 할 기회가 있었습니다. 첫 여행지로 찾아간 곳이 스페인이었는데 비행기로 무려 16시간이나 걸려 도착한 곳이었습니다. '만약 서울~평양 간 철길이 열리고 중국을, 러시아를 거쳐서 스페인에 도착했더라면 그 길이 얼마나 풍부한 여행의 정서로 가득 차겠는가' 하는 생각을 했었는데 바로 그 철길이 지금 열리고 있습니다.

끊어진 철길의 복구는 당연히 우리들에게 통일의 의미로 다가옵니다. 그러나 그것은 단지 민족의 통일만을 의미하는 것은 아닐 것입니다. 그 길은 우리의 역사가 일본과 미국을 통한 세계와의 관계 형성이라는 그런 좁은 틀을 벗어 버리고 대륙과 세계로 바로 나아갈 수 있는 역사의 큰 길이 열린다는 것을 의미합니다. 그런 점에서 그것은 끊어진 철길의 복구가 아니라 끊어진 세계와의 관계를 복구하고 새롭게 정립하는 범상치 않은 의미를 갖는다고 생각합니다.

이처럼 역사적인 변화의 물결 속에서, 감옥 시절에 간직했던 기차에 대한 감상을 떠올린다는 것은 부끄러운 추억입니다. 그러나 또 한 편 생각해 보면 그러한 추억이 비록 감상적이라고 하더라도 결코 지워 버려야 할 하찮은 추억이라고 생각하지는 않습니다. 최근에 상영된 일본 영화 '철도원'은 궁벽한 시골의 작은 간이역에 얽힌 인간의 삶과 그 시절의 진솔한 이야기를 아름답게 그려 내고 있습니다. 근대화와 경제 성장이라는 일방 궤도를 숨 가쁘게 달려온 우리의 현대사를 돌이켜 보면 진솔한 인간적 공간이 그 설 자리를 잃었거나 주변으로 밀려나 버린 아픔을 안겨 줍니다.

생각해 보면 우리의 삶에 있어서 간이역의 키 작은 코스모스와 먼 곳으로 이어진 철길을 바라보며 키우는 그리움이야말로 어떠한 물질적 풍요나 속도라 하더라도 결코 가져다줄 수 없는 인간적 진실입니다. 어떠한 것과도 바꿀 수 없는 아름다운 삶의 내용이며 꿈이 아닐 수 없습니다.

뉴 밀레니엄의 새로운 문명을 모색하는 과정에서도, 그리고 숨 가쁘게 진행되고 있는 통일의 도정에서도 이러한 인간적 진실이 온당하게 평가받고 재조명되어야 할 것입니다. 그것은 망각되고 주변화된 인간적 진실, 인간적 논리를 다시 세우는 일이기도 하기 때문입니다. 새 세기를 향하여 달리는 새로운 열차에는 우리의 인간적 소망이 가득히 실리길 바랄 뿐입니다.

아픔을 나누는 삶

Life That Shares Pain • 176p

해외 기행 때의 일입니다. 스웨덴 기행을 끝내면서 복지 국가 스웨덴을 한 장의 그림으로 만들어야 할 차례였습니다. 늦은 밤까지 애를 먹었던 기억이 있습니다. 복지 선진국 스웨덴을 그림으로 그리기가 어려웠던 까닭을 지금 다시 생각해 봅니다. 그것은 아마 스웨덴에서 받은 나의 인상이 의외로 착잡하였기 때문이었을 겁니다.

각종 복지관, 병원, 공원, 학교 등 스웨덴이 자랑하는 수준 높은 복지 제도는 기초 생활도 보장되지 못하고 있는 우리의 현실을 생각하면 사실 부러운 것이 한두 가지가 아니었습니다. 그럼에도 불구하고 나의 심정은 매우 복잡한 것이었습니다. 안락한 삶이되 어딘가 노쇠하고 무기력한 삶. 이것을 그림으로 표현한다는 것이 내게는 참으로 망연하였습니다.

한 가지 예를 들면 아내와의 다툼에 대하여 동료에게 이야기를 꺼내면 이야기를 채 잇기도 전에 정중하게 그 문제는 전문 상담인과 상담하라고 권유하면서 이야기를 잘라 버립니다. 물론 전문 상담자는 그의 동료보다 훨씬 더 합리적인 해결 방법을 제시해 줄 것이 틀림없습니다. 그러나 이것은 삭막한 풍경이 아닐 수 없습니다. 훌륭한 시설을 갖춘 노인 복지관의 할머니는 생면부지의 여행자인 나를 붙잡고 놓아주려 하지 않았습니다. 사람을 그리워하는 노년의 생활은 무척 삭막해 보였습니다. 물론 복지관에 상담 프로그램이 실시되고 있기는 하였습니다. 그러나 나는 내내 훌륭한 시설이란 무엇인가 반문해 보았습니다. 편리하게 설치되어 있는 첨단 시설들이 오히려 비정한 모습으로 내게 비쳐 오는 것이었습니다.

한마디로 스웨덴에서 느낀 삭막함은 사람들 사이에 아픔의 공유가 없다는 사실에서 오는 것이었는지도 모릅니다. 아픔은 그것의 신속한 해결만이 전부가 아니라고 생각됩니다. 아픔은 신속한 해결보다는 그 아픔의 공유가 더 중요하지 않을까. 우산을 들어 주는 것보다 함께 비를 맞는 것이 진정한 도움이 아닐까. 생각은 매우 착잡하였습니다.

아픔의 공유와 그 아픔의 치유를 위한 공동의 노력. 그러한 공동의 노력은 그 과정에서 당면의 아픔만을 문제삼는 것이 아니라 그 아픔을 만들어 내는 근본적인 사회적 구조를 대면하게 해준다고 믿습니다. 이 것은 질병을 국소적 병리 현상으로 진단하고 대증요법對症療法으로 처치하는 의학보다는 질병을 생리 현상生理現象으로 파악하고 인체의 생명력을 높이는 동의학東醫學의 사고와 맥을 같이하는 것이라 할 수 있습니다.

최근 연복지緣福祉 개념을 구성하여 서구적 복지 개념을 반성하는 이론도 제시되고 있습니다만 나는 그러한 시도에서 어떤 가시적 성과를 기대하기보다는 그러한 이론적 접근이 인간관계를 주목하게 하고 사회 구조의 문제를 대면하게 한다는 점에서 매우 긍정적 기대를 갖고 있습니다.

덕불고 필유린德不孤 必有隣은 물론 덕을 베푸는 사람에게는 반드시 이웃이 있다는 의미입니다. "적어도 50세까지 베푸는 삶을 산다면 그 이후의 삶은 걱정하지 않아도 된다"는 해석이 사회 구조를 반성하는 폴이로서 더욱 적절한 해석이라고 생각합니다.

『노자』의 마지막 장에는 "성인은 사사로이 쌓아 두지 않는다. 이미 남을 위하여 베풀었으므로 오히려 자기에게 넉넉하게 있는 것이나 다름없다"(聖人不積 旣以爲人己愈有 旣以爲人己有多)는 구절이 있습니다. 물론 범인에게 성인의 도리를 요구하는 것은 무리라고 생각됩니다. 그러나 이 경우의 성인은 이상적 목표를 의미하는 것으로 받아들일 수 있습니다.

생각하면 오늘날의 복지 문제는 함께 아픔을 나누지 않고 그 가진 바를 남을 위하여 베풀 수 없는 사회 구조에서 비롯되는 것이 아닐 수 없습니다. 궁극적으로는 사회 구조와 인간관계의 문제가 아닐 수 없습니다.

그러나 최소한의 기초 생활마저 해결하지 못하고 있는 우리의 열악한 복지 현실에서 사회 구조의 문제나 인간관계의 문제를 거론한다는 것은 너무나 비현실적인 접근인지도 모릅니다. 더구나 모든 물질적 여유가 나누어지기는커녕 남김없이 자본화되어 치열한 자기 증식自己增殖을 추구하고 있는 것이 우리의 현실입니다. 비자본적 공간에 남아 있는 '작은 인정'만을 나누고 있는 것이 우리의 현실입니다.

그러나 우리 사회에는 비시장적非市場的 공간과 비자본주의적非資本主義的인 관계가 도처에 건재하고 있으며 얼마든지 확장될 수 있는 가능성이 있다는 사실이 간과되어서는 안 될 것입니다. 그러한 가능성을 키워 나가는 것이 진정한 사회 변화의 내용이 되고 새로운 문명적 담론으로 자리 잡아야 하는 것도 사실입니다. 성급한 목표 달성보다는 그 목표에 이르는 과정, 그 과정 속에서 진정한 의미를 찾아야 하는 것 또한 사실이 아닐 수 없습니다. 나는 스웨덴에서 느꼈던 착잡한 상념이 우리의 열악한 현실을 위로하려는 감상이 아니기를 바랍니다.

아름다운 패배

Beautiful Defeat • 180p

새해를 맞는 당신의 모습을 바라보며 나는 꼭 일 년 전에 벌였던 화려한 새 천년의 축제를 떠올립니다. 폭죽으로 밤 하늘을 수놓았던 밀레니엄 축제가 엊그제 같습니다. 다시 새해를 맞아 일터로 나서는 당신의 무거운 발걸음을 바라봅니다. 당신의 모습은 어쩌면 새해를 맞는 우리들 모두의 모습입니다.

돌이켜 보면 지난 한 해는 기업, 의료, 농촌, 교육, 금융 등 사회의 모든 영역이 자기의 권익을 지키려는 수많은 사람들의 몸부림으로 얼룩진 한 해였습니다. 일터를 떠나는 사람들이나 남은 사람들에게나 구조 조정은 희망이기보다는 불안이었습니다. 어떤 구조를 만들려고 하는지 어떤 방법으로 조정하려고 하는지에 대한 최소한의 대화나 신뢰도 사라지고 없습니다. 남에게 고통을 떠밀어야 하고, 고통뿐만 아니라 책임까지 떠밀어야 하는 싸움만 앞두고 있습니다. 이것이 우리가 마주하고 있는 새해의 현실입니다. 2000년이 새 천년인지, 2001년이 진짜 새 천년인지 알 수 없지만 어느 것 하나 새로울 수 없는 새해를 시작하면서 우리는 과연 무엇을 어떻게 해야 할지 망연할 뿐입니다.

당신은 이제 모든 것을 싸움의 승패에 걸 수밖에 없다고 했습니다. 그리고 싸움은 시작하면 이겨야 한다고 했습니다. 그러나 안타까운 것은 싸움이란 모두가 이길 수 없다는 것이 싸움의 비극입니다. 머리띠 두르고 싸움터로 나서는 당신의 모습을 보고 참담한 심정이 되는 까닭은 당신의 싸움이 외로운 싸움이기 때문이며, 외로운 싸움이기 때문에 결국 상처와 패배를 안고 돌아오리란 것을 알기 때문입니다. 당신의 상대는 매우 완강합니다. 자본과 권력과 여론과 보이지 않는 시장과 그리고 초국적 자본이라는 겹겹의 벽 속에 당신은 서 있습니다.

나는 당신에게 차라리 아름다운 패배를 부탁하고 싶습니다. 오늘은 비록 패배이지만 내일은 승리로 나타나는 아름다운 패배를 부탁하고 싶습니다. 아름다운 패배는 어쩌면 모든 사람들의 승리가 될 수도 있습니다. 그래서 나는 당신에게 패배하는 방법을 고민해야 한다고 했습니다. '누구'와 싸울 것인가보다는 '무엇'을 상대로 싸울 것인가를 물었습니다. 당신은 어차피 어느 한 사람을 골라서 싸울 수도 없습니다. 기업, 공공, 노동, 금융 등 4대 구조 조정의 모든 짐이 오로지 당신의 어깨에 짐 지워지게 되어 있고 겹겹의 포위 속에 놓여 있기 때문입니다. 그렇기 때문에 '무엇'을 상대로 싸우고 있는가를 밝혀야 합니다. 싸움의 이유를 널리 천명해야 합니다.

당신은 기업만 살아야 되는 이유를 모른다고 했습니다. 공기업과 금융 기관이 수익을 내야 한다는 이유를 알지 못한다고 했습니다. 20 : 80의 사회에서 20만이라도 살아야 언젠가 80이 살 수 있다는 논리를 믿을 수 없다고 했습니다. 결국은 공적 자금이라는 국민 부담으로 전가시키면서 그러한 이유, 그러한 논리를 펴는 것을 이해할 수 없기는 나도 당신과 마찬가지입니다. 비단 당신과 나뿐만이 아닙니다. 묵묵히 고통을 감내하고 있는 사람들도 알 수 없기는 마찬가지라고 생각됩니다.

당신은 계속해서 질문을 던져야 합니다. 경제 성장의 목적은 무엇인가? 사람이 사는 목적은 무엇인가? 우리들이 까맣게 잊고 있는 것들을 당신의 싸움은 드러내어야 합니다. 조정이 아니라 진정한 개혁이 아닌 한, 기업의 수익 구조가 아니라 국민 경제의 토대를 개혁하지 않는 한 어김없이 경제 위기는 또다시 닥쳐오게 되어 있다는 것을 이야기해야 합니다. 당신의 싸움은 바로 이러한 근본을 천명하는 싸움이어야 합니다. 공감과 감동을 이끌어 내는 외롭지 않은 패배여야 합니다. 그리하여 기어코 승리하는 아름다운 패배가 되어야 합니다.

새해의 벽두에 나누는 패배의 이야기가 다시 마음을 참담하게 합니다. 그러나 나는 당신이 패배의 이야기가 아닌 승리의 이야기로 읽어 주리라 믿습니다.

당신의 새해를 기원합니다. 새해도 모든 처음과 마찬가지로 그것이 새로운 것이 되기 위해서는 새로운 시작이 있어야 합니다. 바로 "오늘", "이곳"에 새로운 것을 심어야 합니다.

언젠가 당신에게 드린 글을 다시 씁니다.

"처음처럼—처음으로 하늘을 만나는 어린 새처럼, 처음으로 땅을 밟는 새싹처럼 우리는 하루가 저무는 저녁 무렵에도 마치 아침처럼, 새 봄처럼 그리고 처음처럼 언제나 새날을 시작하고 있다."

Shin, Young-Bok, a Great Mentor of Our Time

Life of a Conscientious Intellectual Representing Our Time

On August, 14, 1988, when the heat of Korean spurt towards democratization in the June Uprising, 1987 had not completely cooled off, Shin, Young-Bok came back to us. He had been arrested on account of the Reunification Revolution Party Incident in 1968 and was set free under special parole in celebration of Korean Liberation in 1988. It has been exactly 20 years and 20 days since his arrest. A 27-year-old young man has already become a 47-year-old middle-aged man.

Since his name was not known to us before because of his tight imprisonment and exclusion, his homecoming was an event which touched our hearts. There was a sensational response to the publication after his release of his prison letters, *Reflections from Prison* in 1988. Praise and compliments were heaped on this book. Rev. Chung, Yang-Mo considered it as a great blessing for our time; the novelist, Lee, Ho-Chul said that reading this book reminded him of Confusian *Analectic*, or Pascal's *Pensee* and Montaignue's essays. He ranked it among the best essays and meditations in Korean literature. Another passionate reader called him a Korean Ryushin. Since then, this book has continued to be a best seller, and has earned a secure place in the Korean classical literature of our time.

Since his release, Shin, Young-Bok had taught political-economics, the history of Korean thought and the philosophy of education at SungKongHoe University until his death in January, 2016. His classrooms were always filled with people—workers, teachers, among them—who, in their various fields, were struggling to make our society a better one. In a survey inquiring about "the best 5 intellectuals of our time,' people selected Shin, Young-Bok as the leading figure. A few years ago, he was chosen by the students of Seoul National University as their most respected graduate. As such, Shin, Young-Bok has continued to be respected as 'a great mentor of our time'. Indeed, his life provides a model of the conscientious intellectual of our time.

A Childhood, Born and Grew up as a School Master's Son

Shin, Young-Bok was born in 1941 in Milyang, KyungNam Province into a family with a profound knowledge of Chinese classics. Although his home town is MilYang, he was actually born in the official residence of a primary school principal in EuiRyung, KyungNam Province. His father graduated from DaeGu Teacher's College. While he was a college student, he joined a protest against a Japanese Dean and became a member of a secret circle studying Korean language, and because of these activities, he was once fired while teaching in the primary school.

Korea was liberated when Shin was 5 years old. An interesting episode tells us much about his character. It was on the day when Korea was liberated. The village young men gave the five-year-old boy an 'order' to keep watch on the residence of a then-runaway Japanese principal in the county of Milyang. It was a rainy night with strong wind. The little boy watched the official residence with its tatami-style rooms by himself the whole night long, with only a lamplight on a dish for comfort. In the middle of the night, the young men of the village came to check the security of the place and provided him with a couple of plums. It was such an emotional night for the boy, the son of a patriot who had fought against Japanese occupation. When young, he was jokingly encouraged by his father's friends, 'to become the Korean Viceroy in Japan when he grows up.'

The liberation period stretching from Korean emancipation from Japan to the outbreak of the Korean war in 1950 was a time of turmoil for a little boy with limited understanding of what was taking place. The sounds of talking and footsteps of the adult men who sneaked under cover of darkness, taking snacks for the night, and then suddenly disappearing to nowhere; the heads of the guerillas hung on the parapet of the Bridge NamChun in MilYang, all created terror for the boy as he made his way home from school... These scenes he had witnessed without any understanding. It was only when he learned Korean modern history after the April Revolution that he later came to grasp their true meaning, re-experiencing the period afterwards.

In the turmoil of the period of Japanese occupation and of liberation from Japan, people had to go through miserable times, but Shin, Young-Bok's childhood spent as 'the school master's son' was relatively smooth. After finishing his primary and middle school in his hometown, MilYang, he entered Busan Commercial Highschool. He had good grades in his school days and was popular with his friends.

His Activity as a Cheer Leader and His Excellent Literary Talent

When he was in his 3rd grade at the primary school, at the end of the semester when they got their transcripts, one of his classmates made a sharp remark that Shin, Young-Bok got the highest score only because the teacher favored him as the school master's son, and that the highest score really belonged to himself. He was older than Young-Bok by 2 or 3 years, having returned from Japan after Korean Liberation. Of course students knew that Shin, Young-Bok's father was the principal of another primary school and that the older boy's accusation was false, but to Young-Bok, a boy with a strong conscience, the episode came as a great shock. When he visited that friend's house afterwards, he was more shocked to find that the boy was so poor as to frequently skip meals.

After this, Shin deliberately became a naughty student who intentionally invite punishments by playing practical jokes at school. It was a quite normal scene that he was kneeling in the corridor; often he knelt down in the middle of the playground for all the students to see. But thanks to these pranks, he was chosen as a cheer leader in his 5th grade and continued to play this role until he graduated from his highschool. Following his sister and brother, he read a lot of books from his father's shelves and proved himself to be an avid reader possessed of literary talents of his own. He won prizes in several writing competitions. In one of these competitions held in Busan City, in celebration of Korean Language Day, and with 'map' as its subject, he mentioned the sadness of the division of his homeland and was complimented for that. He entered Busan Commercial High School because his family was not rich enough to send him, a second son, to a highschool in Seoul.

Shin, Young-Bok entered the Economics Department at the College of Commerce in Seoul National University on the strong recommendation of his highschool teacher who taught him Korean Literature. The teacher had a special affection for Shin, Young-Bok. When on 16 May the Military Coup took place, his teacher himself was arrested for his union activities after the April Revolution. He also dissuaded Shin, Young-Bok from taking an interview test at a bank which Shin, Young-Bok was supposed to take the next day after passing a written test.

Shin, Young-Bok attended university from 1959 to 1963, during which he witnessed the April Revolution and the 16 May Military Coup. A Korean poet, Shin, Dong-Yup described the April Revolution as a short moment of 'looking at the blue sky.' Before the April Revolution, in the Korean War, the country was swept by a raging wind of McCarthytic Anticommunism fervor after the heat of the Liberation Period was completely extinguished. In such a situation, hope of progress was thoroughly blocked. Nevertheless, the April Revolution revealed some potential for the future. Shin, Young-Bok, then a sophomore, was fully alive to the history unfolded around him. On the very day of April Revolution, he was at the forefront of the line of protesters in a protest march from his university at Jong-Arm Dong to the police commissioner's office at Hyo-Ja Dong. When the procession of demonstrators reached the streetcar stop at Hyo-Ja Dong in front of the police commissioner's office, the police started to fire and one after another, student suffered injuries. A senior student close to him was killed there.

The April Revolution started as a protest against the injustice and corruption of the ruling elite, but it soon developed into the general pursuit of democracy and reunification of the country. Living through series of these protests, Shin, Young-Bok confronted the bare face of the Korean ruling power and realized how it suppressed other classes. It was a turning point in his social consciousness; since then, he thought about, agonized over and recognized the overall meaning of liberation, division, and war in Korea.

Nevertheless, dark clouds were hanging again on 'the blue sky.' With a rush, the 16 May Military Coup trampled on what the April Revolution had achieved. The new administration formed by the military officers quickly has paved the way for dictatorship, while enforcing re-establishment of diplomatic relations with Japan and the dispatch of a Korean military expeditionary force to the Viet Nam War. They did all these under the banner of the 'modernization of fatherland,' with its pro-American and anti-Communist policies.

From his sophomore year, Shin, Young-Bok had almost lived in an office at the university. He was not only immersed in his studies, but also demonstrated his versatile talents working as an editor of the '*Review of the College of Commerce*,' as well as being a reporter for the '*Newspaper of the College of Commerce*,' contributing poems, academic articles, and cartoons. With his office equipped with calligraphy brushes and an ink stone, he developed his talent for calligraphy and often wrote letters to his friends in this style; he showed himself to be a man of affection, a kind-hearted romanticist. After the April Revolution, from his junior year, he showed enthusiasm in his academic society and student circle activities. He mainly took responsibility for leading academic seminars for junior members from the College of Commerce of Seoul National University, and students from other universities including Korea University, Yeon-Sei University and Ewha Women's University. He also involved himself, either directly or indirectly, into students' religious groups and evening classes for factory laborers.

After the Korean Liberation from Japan, the South Korean Administration failed to place itself on a legitimate footing and the colonial economic system has gone through only an extended process of reproducing itself. In such circumstances, the spread of injustice and corruption and the widening of the gap between the rich and the poor laid bare all the contradictions of capitalistic development.

Shin, Young-Bok's in-depth study of such problems in his graduate school drew him closer to Marxism as the most appropriate science for analyzing and overcoming capitalism.

Arrested, Being Involved in the Reunification Revolution Party
Incident

Upon finishing his graduate course in 1965, Shin, Young-Bok
started to give lectures at Sook-Myong Women's University,
and then, from 1966, at the Korean Military Academy. Well-
liked by several of his professors, Shin, Young-Bok was a
prospective scholar in economics. But an incident took place
and shook his whole life. On August 24, 1968, Korean CIA
announced 'Reunification Revolution Party's Anti-State Spy
Ring Incident.' With the objective of "carrying out the people's
democratic revolution, eradicating the semi-feudal social
system, establishing in its place democratic institutions, and
working for the reunification of the people," the Reunification
Revolution Party assumed the character of an avant guard
party aiming at a fundamental reform of society. It was led
by progressives whose presence was revitalized after the
April Revolution. Korean CIA, however, charged the party
with being a North Korean underground organization plotting
popular uprising and the overthrow of the country and finally
the communization of South Korea by military force. About
200 Democratic activists found themselves victims of this
accusation and ended up being interrogated or arrested.

Shin, Young-Bok, who was arrested while teaching at the
Korean Military Academy, was sentenced to death twice until
this was finally transmuted to a life sentence from the General
Court Martial of Korean Army. His reduced sentence, rare at that

time, was thanks to his professors including Professor Park, Hee-Bum and Lee, Hyun-Jae, who pleaded for his life to be spared, while testifying in his favor in court. At this time it obviously took a great deal of courage to stand in court as a defense witness, particularly for a member of the Reunification Revolution Party.

Getting Life Sentence & Entering into a Dark Tunnel with No exit in Sight

Prison became for him a dark tunnel. A blind alley and a kind of deep pit. At the same time, it became for him the center of the world in the middle of a challenging phase of history laying bare the naked structure of the contradictions of society. For Shin, Young-Bok, prison was a school in which he could reflect on the ideals of his life which up to that point he had pursued only as a pale intellectual. Now in prison, he could witness the life of those who consigned to the bottom of the society and learned how to live together with them.

Meeting numerous people in prison and being confronted with the heavy experiences they had gone through, Shin, Young-Bok came to realize how trivial and humble was the knowledge he has accumulated up to that point. As a result, he became able to read human beings, society, and history all over again from a new perspective. It was a process of filling his mind with the faces of real people and the problems overwhelming them, instead of abstract concepts and words.

It was also a way of personal rebuilding in which 'a callus made by a pen pressing on the middle-finger of his right hand' disappeared and a 'hard corn was formed at the tip of the thumb by the repeated use of shoe stumpers.'

Shin, Young-Bok's intense self-reflection was expressed in postcard after postcard he sent to his family. In them, we meet a respectable person forced to endure a life of pain. Through his own personal story we can also read the agony and conscience of our own time. As a lotus flower can bloom in the midst of mud, so Shin, Young-Bok strengthened his spirit enough to leap beyond the prison walls, ironically by putting himself at the lowest place. After 20 years and 20 days of such a life, he walked out of the iron gates of Jeon-Ju Correctional Institute into the dazzling sunlight. In a gathering commemorating the publication of his letters, entitled *Reflections from the Prison*, his university professor, Professor Byun, Hyung-Yoon remarked,

"We lost an excellent scholar in economics, but instead we gained a great mentor who would continue to teach us for ages to come."

At the Center of the 'Forest,' SungKongHoe University

When Shin was released on a special parole in August, 1988, the then-president of St. Michael's Seminary, Rev. Jae-Jung Lee met Shin, Young-Bok, at a restaurant in downtown Seoul.

As an admirer of Shin himself, he wanted to invite Shin to teach at this seminary, later to be renamed SungKongHoe University. To restore his position and the role he had taken before he was imprisoned, was "the best thing we could do for him," Lee later recalled. In his first semester of teaching, Shin's classrooms were filled with students, laborers, teachers and journalists from all over the country. Themselves already fervid readers of Shin's book, *Reflections from the Prison*, they were eager to meet him and listen to his lectures. In the ensuing years, Shin took many important posts in the university as professor and Dean of the Social Science Faculty, Director of the College of Labor and of Education in the Life-long Educational center, and the Schoolmaster of Humanities Learning Center of the university. He was at the center of the forest, called SungKongHoe University and helped lay down the foundations of the present university.

Shin used to say that his whole life was centered around schools and universities. He was born at an official school residence in a province where his father was the school master. When he was young, he and his family moved from one school residence to another, following his father. School playgrounds became his playgrounds, school residences were his homes. His life in schools continued until he graduated from the Graduate School of Seoul National University with a master's degree in economics. Then, he moved to Sook-Myung Women's University and the Korean Military Academy and taught as a lecturer until he was arrested, being accused of being involved in the *Reunification Revolution Party Spy Ring Incident* in 1967.

Shin referred to his prison life as his 'university days.' Stretching for 20 years and 20 days, this second phase of his school life brought a great change in him. In prison, he went through an eye-opening reformation of himself. Meeting various prison inmates from different walks and backgrounds of life and society, he took off his image of 'a pale intellectual' of theory and conceptualization and changed into a whole-hearted person with more practical comprehension of life and the world as well as a more solid and critical social consciousness. Getting to know the harsh realities of Korean society and the pain of the underprivileged class he met in prison, he learned to put himself at the center of social paradoxes, where the poor and the powerless people are exposed to the unfair social system and injustice. As was implied in his letters from prison, his strict self-scrutiny rapidly transformed him and he gained true insight into the reality of life and the world. While living together with socially unattended people, he learned the importance of taking the same footing with other people.

Although Shin's university major was economics, after his release, he began to teach many other subjects such as History of Korean Thoughts, Sociology of Education, Politico-Economics, and Reading of Chinese Classics. He was a person with all-encompassing knowledge in many areas and he established himself as an intellectual of consilience.

If intellectually and socially he became more realistic and more compassionate, artistically he became an excellent calligrapher while he was in prison. His writing style, called "EoGGeDoneMu Che," meaning the style of writing calligraphy letters as if they were in the shape of putting one's arms around each other's shoulders, is a metaphor of people's solidarity and equality. He held several calligraphy exhibitions and donated the profits to the university scholarship fund. He contributed his calligraphy writings to many democratic organizations and NGO or NPO organizations for free and supported them in their activities for social improvement and the country's democracy.

In 1997, with the support of Jung-Ang Daily Newspaper, Shin went around the country, visiting many historical sights of importance and interest and wrote reflective essays on Korean history and society. The end-product was another steady-selling book, *Trees, Dear, Trees*. Written in the same style as *Reflections from the Prison*, his writings touched many people's hearts by their profound reflections and critical evaluation of Korean history and society. If this book was focused on domestic travel, his 1999 book, entitled *Forest Together*, was a record of his trip around the world, highlighting many centers of world history up to the 20th century, including the earliest origins of world civilizations. The book poses many critical questions about the direction and achievements of world civilization up to that point and tries to suggest some new ways that will be fit for the new millennium. It is composed of reflections on the past and a search for new hope for the future.

As such, the last phase of Shin's life was spent at SungKongHoe University, where he practiced what he had learned in prison to his everyday meetings with students and colleagues. His role as the central figure in the university lasted until he passed away in 2016. For the 28 years of this stage of his life, he put his energy, time, and effort into SungKongHoe University. His commitment and dedication to the university was so great that the gist of his thoughts, 'Forest of Togetherness,' became the university's motto, along with the spirit of Opening, Sharing and Service. In 2005, he wrote a book on Oriental Philosophy and published it under the title of *Lecture: My Reading of Oriental Classics*. Just before he passed away in 2015, he published another book based on his lectures, entitled *Discourse*. In addition to these main publications, he wrote many essays and published them as *visits to the Peripheries, For the First Time (in English)*, *Memories of ChungGuHoe (In Korean-English Version)*, and *The Way For Many of Us to make the Forest Together*.

All in all, Shin was never diverted away from schools. His attitude was sincere, humble, serious, and exemplary. Once he put himself in the "chain of the link between a teacher and a pupil," he did his best to fulfill his role perfectly as a teacher. As a university professor, and a director of life-long social education and humanities learning, he endeavored to enlighten students, teachers, laborers, and CEOs of companies, emphasizing a relation-centered philosophy of life. He was not only a good listener, but also a practitioner of sharing and caring, who hoped to create a society where people can recover trust and be empowered in solidarity. In the field of education, he would offer wise advice and teaching to people about how to live together in hope and trust.

In 2008, Shin was awarded the Lim Chang-Sun Humanities Award for his contribution to Oriental Classics and, in August 2015, he received the Man-Hae Grand Prize in Literature for his great contribution to the improvement of Korean Humanities Learning. His books and teachings have left a great impression on the readers of all ages and generations. He was quite often invited to give lectures and seminars and provided inspiration and intellectual stimuli to people.

In 2016, the publisher, Dolbegae issued a posthumous book, entitled *For the First Time: Shin, Young-Bok's Promise*, a complimentary edition of the previously published book with the same title, and, on the first memorial of his death, it published a collection of interviews with him in magazines and journals under the title *Together, Hand in Hand*, and a collection of his representative essays and a few unpublished journal articles under the title *Where the Stream Runs To*.

Although Shin has passed away, his role as a great mentor/thinker continues and many readers and pupils still miss him for his genuine humanity and try to cherish his thoughts and attitudes towards life and society. As a Korean poet, Han, Yong-Un, wrote in his poem, "Although he left, we did not let him go.": —His spirit continues to influence many people's lives, now and for the time to come.

Translator's Epilogue

It was when I first heard of Prof. Shin's illness, near the end of 2014, that I decided to translate a selection of his letters and essays. It happened to be my sabbatical semester so I had some time to concentrate on this. For me, who greatly respected Prof. Shin and owed a lot to his family for their warm-hearted friendship and kindness on various occasions, it was intended to be a prayer for his recovery. Well, that was the only thing I could think of doing for him. I could not sit still without doing anything. I hoped this translation of his representative essays and letters could cheer him up and give him some consolation in his struggle against his illness.

Until Prof. Shin passed away in the middle of January 2016, he had borne his illness with extraordinary patience and perseverance. He was heroic: he did not show any sign of disappointment, frustration or pain. He looked like a person who transcended even the fear of death. He was peaceful and calm, meeting my university colleagues and me with a smile and good blessings when we visited him at the beginning of January, 2016, which sadly became the last time we met him in this world.

Now, a year and a half after his decease, my translation has finally taken its proper shape as a book. Through this memorial piece, we can recall happy moments when we were together with Prof. Shin, making a wonderful forest called SungKongHoe University. Indeed, he was at the center of this 'forest,' as the central figure, "standing firm and embracing others with his generous arms" (from Shelley's "Mask of Anarchy"). With him, we could always keep the festive spirit of happiness, the sense of belonging, and a strong solidarity as a big family. Wherever he was, there were touching moments of warm gatherings, hearty sharings and thoughtful considerations. As he mentioned in his calligraphy writing, he was "as warm as the spring wind when treating others, and as cold as the autumn frost when judging himself." We could realize the substantiality of this 'Forest of Togetherness,' each joining together to make a forest from the individual trees.

A famous Victorian poet, Alfred Lord Tennyson, wrote an elegy for the death of his closest school friend AHH (Arthur Hall Harlem), entitled *In Memoriam AHH* and, through this process of writing for 17 years (1832-1849), he was able to overcome his sorrow and come to terms with the void in his life. In the same way, now I hope that reading this work of translation provides consolation and encouragement for all those who went through a tremendous sadness and a great sense of loss with the death of Prof. Shin, as it did to me while I was translating it.

This selection of Prof. Shin's essays and letters was published in 2008 by Dolbegae Publishing Co., as a book of series under the title *Masterpiece Korean Essays Series, No.01: Shin, Young-Bok*. This book carries not only his representative letters and essays from his steady seller books, *Reflections from the Prison* (1988, 1998), *Trees, Oh, Trees!* (1997), but also other articles and essays in various academic journals, periodicals and newspapers. Among the selected letters and essays, "Memories of ChungGuHoe" is excluded here since it was already published in Korean-English version in 2008, by the same publishing co., and instead a letter entitled "A Prisoner's Teeth" is added. Presenting these writings in English is a way to share his ideas and perspectives, his thoughts and reflections, and his insights and inspirations with those who cannot understand Korean and those who want to spread his writings in the international context. I think that his writing has the scope and depth that would appeal to readers in other cultural areas and have a lasting influence on their lives and thoughts. In this global age, it also does not seem right to enjoy these wonderful writings by ourselves without sharing them.

Prof. Shin's writings carry the burden of the age he lived

through. Although his writings were drawn from his own experiences, reflections and thoughts, still they register the voice of the time that he lived in, participating in several important incidents as a child-witness, as an innocent victim, as a student-protestor and as a critical objector. As he mentioned in one of his writings, a person's fate reflects the fate of his country and its people, being closely linked to them. Through them, we can read the vicissitudes of Korean history going through various transitional events, including the Japanese occupation, the liberation from Japan, the Korean War, the April Revolution, the May Military Coup, and the fight for the democratization of the country. His writings, as a reflection of his time and his thoughts, indeed represent the conscience of the Korean people and society.

This book marks my third effort to translate Prof. Shin's writings into English, following *Memories of ChungGuHoe* (2008) and *For the First Time* (2008). Except for a few translations of childrens' verses, his books are about the only translations into which I would willingly put my time and energy. Several things struck me for the reasons. For one thing, his writings take special place in my reading experience. Most importantly, they raised me up intellectually and in my social consciousness. They touched the strings of my heart with a deeper and longer-lasting resonance than any others. Especially, his letters from the prison widened the horizons of my thoughts and my social consciousness: I began to understand the hardships of the prisoners in terms of the paradoxes and problems of life and the society.

Furthermore, the letters show what Prof. Shin was like in his character and his attitude towards life, and how his thoughts and his life were unified in his everyday life and his relationship with other people. As a living record of his prison life, his letters show the traces of the development of his thoughts that would be epitomized in his theory of relationship. Having been lucky enough to teach in the same university and to enjoy the privilege not only of having access to his works but also of being in his close circle of colleagues, I was able to witness what a wonderful person he was.

Prof. Shin was a great story-teller with a pleasant sense of humor and of calm reflection. In our after-luncheon meetings, his low, gentle voice used to tell various episodes of prison life and other topics of interest, and gave us fresh insights into the reality of the world and of life, for prison epitomizes society, as Prof. Shin pointed out, being located at the center of the problems and conflicts of its society. We had a truly enlightening time, sharing and having conversations on various other current issues as well as our life stories.

Prof. Shin's writings in prison have special literary value in both their prose style and the scope and profundity of their message. His letters from prison do not merely register the prison life as he went through. Filtered through his deep reflections and thoughts, everyday prison life is elevated to a state of art. Here we have to notice the objective conditions of letter writing in prison, which helped endow remarkable

d communication with every living being in a wide net.
ving the steps of his thoughts and reflections, we gain a
nsight into the solemnity of life and the importance of a
n-centered way of living and thinking. As the truly great
r that he is, his thoughts and reflections awaken us to a
truth about life and humans.

a translator, my deepest gratitude goes to Prof. Shin,
Bok. I was truly fortunate to have met him and enjoyed
ilege of being in a close circle of colleagues with him.
can imagine Prof. Shin's smiling face at the news of
islation completed. I feel relieved that I have finally
my duty and I hope that many readers will newly
wonderful thinker, teacher, and sage of our society.
e this to Prof. Shin with honour and respect.

sincere thanks go to a close friend, Prof. Roger
n, Professor Emeritus of the University of Winchester
. He made strenuous efforts to review my translation
ided some very helpful advice. I owe him a lot
lling acceptance of writing the preface, too. My
Min Young Tak, who teaches at the University of
re in the UK, and has known and respected Prof.
her childhood, has paid special attention to and
work. She was more than willing to help me with
draft and correcting some of the concepts of social
I would have mistakenly used otherwise. I would
ess my thanks to and love for her, who has now
grown enough to guide me.

uniqueness with his writings. First, by the prison regulation at that time, a prisoner was allowed to send only a postcard a month to his/her family. And because of such a limit, as he later interviewed, he had to repeatedly think and polish the contents of his letters until he had memorized the most complete version of his thoughts, thus, producing exceptionally neat, flawless letters in their final shape. Under such restraint, Prof. Shin combined condensed vocabulary and sentence-structure with copious thoughts, eventually touching the readers' hearts and elevating their thoughts with certain poetic effects. Writing a letter a month on a postcard was, however, never sufficient, especially for a young intellectual with full of creative thoughts and new ideas, Prof. Shin had to work on an extra job of writing, using two palm-sized recycled toilet papers provided to a prisoner a day, showing the catalyst of control and neat perfectionist's work of art.

The second condition of prison writing, that the contents of the letters went through a strict surveillance by the prison authority before being sent away, provides another momentum to keep the calm prose style of his letters. Needless to say, he had to be extremely careful of his choice of the words, images and tones, not to mention the contents of the message. In the country divided by ideology, and as for a prisoner who was accused of plotting Communist revolution, there should not be any clue of evoking the authority's suspicion. The reason why Prof. Shin's letters were directed to his father and his sisters-in-law instead of his brothers, consequently conveying an unprecedented message in a low and calm voice without inordinate sentimentality or exuberant figures of speech. As a result, his letters from the prison show a perfect balance and harmony between the strict restraint in their style and the highly condensed sentences that carry rich and profound contents. Furthermore, through his respectful tone represented in letters, we come to meet a warm person who appeals to our hearts with his sincere longing for communication and his attitude of modesty and politeness.

Yu, HongJun, a famous art critic, confesses his experience of reading Prof. Shin's letters, which all the other readers might agree to: the sentences on the postcard are "too intense and touching" that he had "hard time of moving on to the next postcard. He became numb on a page of the book, being immersed in deep thoughts. It took two months to finish (Shin's *Reflections from the Prison*)" (Requoted from Hong, YunKi, *Reading Shin, YoungBok Together*, p. 151). In the same way, many readers may have to wait for several days to completely get away from the moving wave his message renders. Lim, GyuChan, a literary critic and one of Prof. Shin's colleagues, refers to the "magic of Prof. Shin's prose writing" (*Reading Shin, YoungBok Together*, p. 91) He points out the harmony between warm-hearted affection and the logical development of his thoughts, which finally yields to a strong emotional appeal to the readers' sensibility. He mentions that "reason and feeling, the rational and the emotional are not divided, but dance together in the whole in his writings" (*Reading*

Shin, YoungBok Together*, p. 91).

Prof. Shin's thoughts and reflect the solid reality of everyday prison relationship with other people. For not display mere words of vaunt, conceptualization. With keen observa Prof. Shin drew precious wisdom himself on the same footing as h demolishes the walls of the re them and in no time, they expe and sympathy enfolding around understand the problems and confronted with in a wider contex they live in. Prof. Shin's warm clump of short field grass, a fled invites us to join his community living beings.

Reading his letters and es a change in which they are ne freedom, humanity and peace and between people and oth the world Prof. Shin hopes that is, a world full of sh humane world where huma life such as money, power, companionship in which are removed and where

Several colleagues encouraged my work and I would like to express my thanks to Prof. Kang, In-Sun and Prof. Chae, Ki-Hwa for their warm attention to each step of my translation, and to Prof. Kim. Chang-Nam for his advice on the possible media of publication at the earliest stage. My extended thanks go to my colleagues at the Department of English, Prof. Steve Solano and Prof. Assumpta Calano who, as the first non-Korean readers, have read parts or the whole of the draft and provided invaluable comments. Prof. Sabine Kim to whom I always turn for her near-native intuition revised and polished some English expressions with her insightful ideas. I want to express my thanks to her, too.

Last but not least, I would like to address my gratitude to the publisher, Mr. Han, Chul-Hee and the director of the publishing team Ms Lee, Kyung-A for their generous decision to publish this rather unplanned work and their substantial support for the publication of this book. Finally, I want to clarify that for any typographical or editorial mistakes and errors, I am fully responsible, I alone and nobody else.

August, 2017
Cho, Byung-Eun

uniqueness with his writings. First, by the prison regulation at that time, a prisoner was allowed to send only a postcard a month to his/her family. And because of such a limit, as he later interviewed, he had to repeatedly think and polish the contents of his letters until he had memorized the most complete version of his thoughts, thus, producing exceptionally neat, flawless letters in their final shape. Under such restraint, Prof. Shin combined condensed vocabulary and sentence-structure with copious thoughts, eventually touching the readers' hearts and elevating their thoughts with certain poetic effects. Writing a letter a month on a postcard was, however, never sufficient, especially for a young intellectual with full of creative thoughts and new ideas, Prof. Shin had to work on an extra job of writing, using two palm-sized recycled toilet papers provided to a prisoner a day, showing the catalyst of control and neat perfectionist's work of art.

The second condition of prison writing, that the contents of the letters went through a strict surveillance by the prison authority before being sent away, provides another momentum to keep the calm prose style of his letters. Needless to say, he had to be extremely careful of his choice of the words, images and tones, not to mention the contents of the message. In the country divided by ideology, and as for a prisoner who was accused of plotting Communist revolution, there should not be any clue of evoking the authority's suspicion. The reason why Prof. Shin's letters were directed to his father and his sisters-in-law instead of his brothers, consequently conveying

Translator's Epilogue

an unprecedented message in a low and calm voice without inordinate sentimentality or exuberant figures of speech. As a result, his letters from the prison show a perfect balance and harmony between the strict restraint in their style and the highly condensed sentences that carry rich and profound contents. Furthermore, through his respectful tone represented in letters, we come to meet a warm person who appeals to our hearts with his sincere longing for communication and his attitude of modesty and politeness.

Yu, HongJun, a famous art critic, confesses his experience of reading Prof. Shin's letters, which all the other readers might agree to: the sentences on the postcard are "too intense and touching" that he had "hard time of moving on to the next postcard. He became numb on a page of the book, being immersed in deep thoughts. It took two months to finish (Shin's *Reflections from the Prison*)" (Requoted from Hong, YunKi, *Reading Shin, YoungBok Together*, p. 151). In the same way, many readers may have to wait for several days to completely get away from the moving wave his message renders. Lim, GyuChan, a literary critic and one of Prof. Shin's colleagues, refers to the "magic of Prof. Shin's prose writing" (*Reading Shin, YoungBok Together*, p. 91) He points out the harmony between warm-hearted affection and the logical development of his thoughts, which finally yields to a strong emotional appeal to the readers' sensibility. He mentions that "reason and feeling, the rational and the emotional are not divided, but dance together in the whole in his writings" (*Reading*

Shin, YoungBok Together, p. 91).

Prof. Shin's thoughts and reflections are drawn from the solid reality of everyday prison life and from his own relationship with other people. For this reason, they do not display mere words of vaunt, nor just theorizing or conceptualization. With keen observation and loving affection, Prof. Shin drew precious wisdom of life. His efforts to put himself on the same footing as his fellow prison inmates demolishes the walls of the readers' prejudice against them and in no time, they experience warm compassion and sympathy enfolding around themselves. They try to understand the problems and conflicts the prisoners are confronted with in a wider context of the society and the time they live in. Prof. Shin's warm attention to a wild flower, a clump of short field grass, a fledgling, a strayed cat and a tree invites us to join his community of peaceful coexistence of all living beings.

Reading his letters and essays, all the readers experience a change in which they are newly illuminated by the values of freedom, humanity and peaceful coexistence between humans and between people and other living beings. We come to join the world Prof. Shin hopes to present through his writings, that is, a world full of sharing, caring, and loving. It is a humane world where humans come first, prior to any husks of life such as money, power, or capital. It is also a world of true companionship in which the walls of prejudice and barriers are removed and where we can reach a true understanding of and communication with every living being in a wide net. Following the steps of his thoughts and reflections, we gain a new insight into the solemnity of life and the importance of a relation-centered way of living and thinking. As the truly great thinker that he is, his thoughts and reflections awaken us to a deeper truth about life and humans.

As a translator, my deepest gratitude goes to Prof. Shin, Young-Bok. I was truly fortunate to have met him and enjoyed the privilege of being in a close circle of colleagues with him. Now, I can imagine Prof. Shin's smiling face at the news of this translation completed. I feel relieved that I have finally fulfilled my duty and I hope that many readers will newly meet this wonderful thinker, teacher, and sage of our society. I dedicate this to Prof. Shin with honour and respect.

My sincere thanks go to a close friend, Prof. Roger Richardson, Professor Emeritus of the University of Winchester in the UK. He made strenuous efforts to review my translation and provided some very helpful advice. I owe him a lot for his willing acceptance of writing the preface, too. My daughter, Min Young Tak, who teaches at the University of Bedfordshire in the UK, and has known and respected Prof. Shin since her childhood, has paid special attention to and love for this work. She was more than willing to help me with editing the draft and correcting some of the concepts of social science that I would have mistakenly used otherwise. I would like to express my thanks to and love for her, who has now intellectually grown enough to guide me.

Several colleagues encouraged my work and I would like to express my thanks to Prof. Kang, In-Sun and Prof. Chae, Ki-Hwa for their warm attention to each step of my translation, and to Prof. Kim. Chang-Nam for his advice on the possible media of publication at the earliest stage. My extended thanks go to my colleagues at the Department of English, Prof. Steve Solano and Prof. Assumpta Calano who, as the first non-Korean readers, have read parts or the whole of the draft and provided invaluable comments. Prof. Sabine Kim to whom I always turn for her near-native intuition revised and polished some English expressions with her insightful ideas. I want to express my thanks to her, too.

Last but not least, I would like to address my gratitude to the publisher, Mr. Han, Chul-Hee and the director of the publishing team Ms Lee, Kyung-A for their generous decision to publish this rather unplanned work and their substantial support for the publication of this book. Finally, I want to clarify that for any typographical or editorial mistakes and errors, I am fully responsible, I alone and nobody else.

August, 2017
Cho, Byung-Eun